Stefanie Keenan

About the Author

JODI WING lives in Los Angeles, California, with her husband. *The Art of Social War* is her first novel.

THE ART OF
Social
WAR

THE **ART** OF

Social

WAR

A NOVEL

JODI WING

HARPER

NEW YORK · LONDON · TORONTO · SYDNEY

HARPER

"Californication" / Red Hot Chili Peppers / Moebetoblame Music (BMI) © Moebetoblame Music 1998.

HarperCollins books may be purchased for educational, business, or sales promotional use. For information please write: Special Markets Department, HarperCollins Publishers, 10 East 53rd Street, New York, NY 10022.

FIRST EDITION

Designed by Jan Pisciotta

Library of Congress Cataloging-in-Publication Data is available upon request.

ISBN 978-0-06-156824-4

08 09 10 11 12   OV/RRD   10 9 8 7 6 5 4 3 2 1

*For my husband, Andy,
and my father, Richard,
for always having my back*

CONTENTS

I. LAYING PLANS

II. TACTICAL DISPOSITIONS

III. WAGING WAR

The Art of War is of vital importance to the State. It is a matter of life and death, a road to either safety or ruin. Hence it is a subject of inquiry which can on no count be neglected.

—Sun-Tzu, *The Art of War*

It's the edge of the world
And all of western civilization
The sun may rise in the East
At least it sets in the final location
It's understood that Hollywood
Sells Californication

—Red Hot Chili Peppers, "Californication"

PART I

Laying
Plans

CHAPTER 1

THE BEGINNING OF THE END

*I*t was the best of times, it was the worst of times . . ." I
played that familiar, bittersweet chestnut over in my mind
while anxiety outweighed my exhaustion: one defining area of my
life was to be settled shortly; another remained precariously up in
the air. In my deconstructed office, amid half-emptied filing cabinets and half-packed boxes of memorabilia, I signed off on my very
last media buy and contemplated the twinkling colored lights on the
cherry trees outside my window, damp with drizzle and descending
dusk. Holiday time here at Gracie Mansion. In ten days' time, the
iconic Waterford crystal ball would drop down upon Times Square,
signifying the official end of this crazy year. It would also signify the
official end of the Giuliani mayoral tenure. My tenure, too; we would
remain only to transition in the Bloomberg administration and tie up
loose ends.

I rubbed my tired eyes as they traveled along the wall of framed
photos and awards I still couldn't bring myself to take down these
last days—visual testimony to eight years, two full terms of touch-
stones and memories in public service to the City of New York. The
tickertape parades, Marathons, July 4 Fireworks, Mets and Yankees
Opening Day, and Thanksgiving balloons sparked such proud, joyful
emotions. Remembrances of Ground Zero, firehouse and police me-
morials sparked profound sadness. The best of times and the worst: I
had participated in both from a front row seat.

And it all came down to tonight. One last initiative, one last advertising campaign. My very last press event in this hallowed building. Ever? It hardly seemed real.

I forced my thoughts to the promise of the evening's festivities and pushed aside a stack of spreadsheets in favor of my makeup bag and a brand-new copy of *Emily Post's Wedding Planner*, delivered today as a parting "gag" gift from the Teamsters Union, along with a bottle of Lillet sherry and elegant crystal goblets. I suppressed a smile, squeezed the last drops from a super-sized Visine bottle and began to layer concealer under my eyes, reciting bits of old-fashioned etiquette aloud to revive my sagging spirits. A quick knock, and my assistant Cathy poked her head around the door. "Leslie just called, Stacey. There was another subway scare and they had to evacuate at 79th Street." I grimaced; it was three months post-September 11, and the city still suffered daily emotional aftershocks: bomb scares, anthrax alerts, tangible civilian fear. "The Mayor—*ex*-Mayor," she caught herself, "is doing a quickie phoner for Channel 7, and—" I shot up by rote to run to my boss' side. "No, he said not to bother you. You should concentrate on tonight. The ads look amazing, by the way; definitely worth the all-night editing session," she added shyly, acknowledging my obviously useless cover-up attempts. I smiled wanly in return; I would miss Cathy the most.

Spirited voices neared the door: emotional reinforcements had arrived at last. In swept Chanel-scented hugs bearing rain-spackled *Gloss* garment bags, the entire Revlon product line and endless support and energy: my oldest and best friends, my soon-to-be bridesmaids, Nancy and Leslie. Without pausing they made themselves useful, expertly preparing airline-bottle cocktails on the paper and makeup-strewn desk. "Stace, get Nance to tell you about last night's disaster date," Leslie prodded as she handed me a vodka tonic and a tube of something shiny she was promoting, miming how to apply it. "The chubby blond accountant from our house-share in Quogue, remember? Hung like a bunny, sadly. That has a flawless finish, by the way."

"He seemed so promising," sighed Nancy, eyeing my *Emily Post*, and then my ring. "Oh well. It's a numbers game. Stacey found her corporate raider in Quogue two summers ago; we'll see what this season's batch brings. Meanwhile, I'll just scrounge from the Superhero Squad—what few hockey players, Navy Seals and firemen you two haven't, ahem, *dated*. If your father only knew of your bad-boy-in-uniform past, Stace . . ."

My smile widened (the finish really was flawless!), and I unzipped the damp plastic excitedly, unveiling cocktail dresses more fabulous than any I'd ever drooled over in Bendel's window. "My father the police captain and his entire 19th Precinct are actually quite 'pro-Jamey.' Now that they've completed a thorough background check, of course. Jamey meets Dad's 'play clean, work hard' Boy Scout criteria." I held the coveted hangers under my chin, modeling one at a time for general consideration, then frowned. "Why are there giant holes in the back of each dress?"

Nancy waved a roll of duct tape at me. "They're numbered European samples. I snuck them out of the fashion closet—they have to go back. We're shooting Monday," she warned, "so no spillage, Cinderella, or else your father-approved Boy Scout will pay a king's ransom for your evening-wear instead of the wedding."

"Or the new apartment," Leslie added helpfully, chewing an olive.

I wrinkled my nose. "Ah yes: life on a lowly City salary. Thank God for outlet stores and the kindness of high-ranking best pals. I'll behave." I held up the hangers again. "So, which do we like? I wanna project 'sophisticated, polished, eminently hire-able'—you know, like Emma Peel from *The Avengers*." With my chin, I reverently indicated my most favorite engagement gift, courtesy of my brilliant staff: DVD boxed sets of the iconic sixties' British television series, Emma on the front of each, outstanding in her cheekbones and sleek catsuits.

The snorting chorus didn't hesitate. "The leather one."

Of course. I negotiated the packing mess and tried on the selection behind a tower of crates. Mental note: no solid food 'til the wedding. "Speaking of superheroes, Nance, Rudy was thrilled with your coverage in *Gloss.*" *Gloss* had the largest circulation in the country, and my maid of honor was the magazine's editor.

"He should be." She unspooled a loud and frighteningly large sheath of tape. "We put him on a par with Churchill and Kissinger."

"Did I tell you he's offered to preside?" All business, Nancy maneuvered around to strap me in as I sucked in and braced. "And he's getting us special dispensation from Bloomberg to hold the reception here, in the garden."

"Ha!" yelped Leslie, spraying vodka. "Did your mom have an apoplexy? She's had the Knights of Columbus Hall on hold since we were ten."

I tried valiantly not to laugh. Or breathe. "Ah, but she's got big-time beauty parlor bragging rights now. And everyone at Monsieur Giorgio's knows she's sewing all our dresses, the master seamstress—*not* that she's happy with the Vera Wang Butterick patterns I chose. Her words: simple and *baw*-ring. She pulled tear sheets from the salon's stack of 1980s bridal mags. Like Olivia Newton-John in *Xanadu,* I promise. You guys better schedule your fittings," I teased, "or I won't be held responsible for any 'tasteful design elements' she might add: epaulets, rosettes, ruffles. . . . Remember our prom dresses?" Indignant groans and protests flew as Leslie changed the subject.

"So Rudy *has* put in a good word for you with Mayor Mike . . ."

I hestitated. "About the wedding—yes. And I guess tonight's a kind-of 'live audition,' the screening of our last 'I Love New York' image spots: I really hope they go over—you know, in case my career ends tonight along with my job . . ." My anxiety trailed off as I twirled, all borrowed leather, lace, and duct tape for the girls.

"*Very Avenger-*y. Emma in the flesh!" sanctioned Leslie as I beamed. This was the utmost pinnacle of praise; it was widely known that Mrs. Peel, feminist heroine of untold wit, grace, and style, was my muse. I glanced again at the clock and felt better. Jamey's plane was due in from LA any moment. After ten days apart, the promise of seeing him made my pulse quicken. More mental notes: organize emergency bikini wax, hair glossing, field trip to La Perla sample sale, and . . .

Nancy cut through my reverie. "Seriously, Stace, you do *want* to stay on. Right?"

Averting my eyes, I picked imaginary lint off an array of duct-tape-hiding wraps: never let 'em see you sweat. "It's not up to me. A new mayor brings in his own team, and I haven't heard anything yet. I just have to wait." I took a breath. I *had* waited; no offer had come. "But, it has been a heavy duty run—triple time, when you consider the last few months. And, you know, I've been thinking . . ." It was as good a time as any to float a more controversial concept. "My personal life's been on hold for so long. I've hardly spent any quality time with Jamey since our engagement last summer. Unless a great offer comes before the wedding, I'm thinking more about closing on the new apartment and being, maybe . . . a *wife*, for a while. A wife with a life." There. I'd said it. Out loud. My eyes roamed over my vodka to gauge the reaction. They watched me closely, my best friends, my harshest critics, eyes narrowed. In unison, they burst out laughing.

"Yeah, right," Leslie snorted derisively. "This is lack of sleep or temporary insanity. You're saying that *you*—one step from textbook ADD—want to do a complete one-eighty, bake heart-shaped cinnamon cookies and be a lady who lunches? I so don't think so. My advice is this: take a week out in the Hamptons and join the private sector, with us. I'd give this desired 'wifestyle' a month, tops."

"Gee, thanks," I replied dryly. What did I expect? "How terribly feminist and supportive. Why can't there be a happy medium?"

Her blue eyes turned direct. "All I'm saying is, you've worked really hard to get where you are. We all have. We've come a long way since growing up off the Van Wyck Expressway, slaving away in the Ogilvy and Mather copy pool. Now here you are in the halls of Gracie Mansion; you're at the top of your game. It's like thinking of Nancy without the magazine or me without my PR agency. It's in our blood; it's our identity. You'd be lost without tenting Ellis Island, holding forth at Elaine's or mounting some *Norma Rae* moment against an evil Trade Union." She zeroed in. "*I* think you've been spending too much time with your fiancé's fancy movie pals and their Stepford Wives out in La La Land."

I winced at the mention of LA and reached into my desk for a piece of Nicorette gum, glaring at the NO SMOKING sign by the door. A painful poisoned arrow, aimed right at the heart of the matter. Oh, Jamey was enamored of his new Hollywood dealings; that was a fact. He'd been happily bunkered out there since Thanksgiving, negotiating to buy a movie studio to add to his collection of entertainment companies for Commerz General, the German conglomerate.

"La La Land? More like Valley of the Giant Barbie Dolls," Nancy winked sympathetically. "Those pod women don't 'work'—not with their minds, anyway." She drained her makeshift martini for emphasis. "They wake up camera-ready; a cult of personally trained, perfectly accessorized size twos with too much time on their hands. You wouldn't believe the hobbies and crazy causes I've had to cover so their husbands' publicists would let me near their projects du jour: bad Buddhist jewelry, overpriced crystal-studded handbags, 'Save the Dirt' fundraisers . . ."

Discomfited, I recalled the last few one-sided phone calls with Jamey. He simply adored LA and its nonstop opportunities for triumphs and victories, big and bigger. Part of me understood: business in New York was tough these days, stagnant at best. Commerz had an enormous pocketbook, and he wanted a new challenge, a new frontier. The film business was the Wild West, a dealmaker's paradise. Anything seemed possible. For my part, I could smell the stench of desire and half-truths three thousand miles away. I didn't like this conversation, nor Jamey's late-day conversion. Emergency mental notes: close on the overpriced apartment ASAP, find a new gig, and get Jamey excited again about our future together. In New York.

I mustered some enthusiasm and warmed to the theme. "I wouldn't know how to compete on that level. My brain would implode from Pilates-fatigue, ab-envy and too many blowouts. And by the way, I hate Barbie. That wench has everything."

Leslie examined me, then the Lillet, then unscrewed another tiny Ketel One. "What would you calculate the cost to be, Nance, to achieve and maintain that ageless look of success and well-being? More than an annual city income, I'd bet. You should do an exposé on *that*."

Nancy laughed bitterly. "Right. At an aspirational magazine. And alienate my readership, the industry and the talent I need to suck for exclusive content. My on-the-record position—at *Gloss*, anyway—is that these people are the one percent of the one percent: winners all in the genetic, social and economic lotteries of life. I exist to cover them, and they exist to be in my pages."

My head was spinning with vodka and doubt. I remembered I'd need to be in top form tonight, and shook away the heightened angst and insecurity. "Enough. Here's the deal: I need a tin of Altoids, one of those shawls, and then we really need to discuss your fittings, or I swear you'll end up reject extras from *Married to the Mob*." More indignant protests and memories flew as a knock came at the door.

Ex-Mayor Giuliani, in a good mood. "Stacey—I mean Norma Rae." He thought again. "*Mrs. Peel*: we're needed."

Exuberant images of mugging, fist-pumping baseball players on-screen dissolved first to the iconic logo, then to black. Their gruff, spirited voices belted out the familiar refrain: "*I love New York! I love New York!*" and faded to a hollow tone over color bars and running time code. One spot down, four to go. In the dark, I stood to the left of the almost-former mayor and twirled my engagement ring around my middle finger, attempting to console myself as I awaited my final grade.

I was marrying Jamey . . . and my heart fluttered a bit at that.

James Makepeace: heavy sigh. Who knew that, at thirty-five, after kissing a pond-full of disenchanting (and yes, mainly uniformed) frogs, I'd finally discover my very own Prince Charming? Well, I had to laugh: HRH's forty-two-year-old Long Island-bred brother, in any case! I made some lightweight, distracting mental notes: (A) Call the jeweler to get the damned ring sized already: bad bride-to-be! (B) Call the Knights of Columbus to confirm that Mom really did release her death-grip on the Pompeii Room. (C) Call Mom to re-reinforce my unilateral, zero-tolerance ban on glitzy ruffled rosettes. And then I counted all fifty stars on the enormous flag in the corner.

The lights came up, but the ovation didn't die away until Rudy demanded decorum. In back, my equally exhausted staff high-fived each other and celebrated; the all-hours shooting and editing schedule we'd been on had clearly paid off, in spades.

"Friends, colleagues, citizens. It's with a full heart I say we've turned a positive corner after a stretch of very dark days. And by your reaction I see you feel the same. This terrific advertising initiative will show the world that New York is *still* the best city on earth, to visit, to work in, to live in and enjoy. I want to give special recognition to the woman who, as always, is responsible for capturing this sentiment—and to congratulate her for getting you all to cooperate, I'm sure, with an 'iron fist in a silk glove' . . ." Knowing laughter and catcalls of "Sta-CEY!" erupted from the crowd. Through a sea of heads I spotted Leslie greeting a very tanned Jamey. LA certainly did agree with him: new auburn highlights appeared in his thick, dark hair. They waved and my heart surged.

The mayor turned to me and grinned. "Stacey, what can I say? When I was elected you agreed to leave a fast-track advertising agency to join me in the even more glamorous world of city government. And our city is better for it. Your enthusiasm, your rolodex, your ability to say 'no' and mean it, striking fear into the hearts of labor leaders and planning commissions alike . . . " More laughter, more catcalls. "Ladies and gentlemen, I give you Stacey Knight."

I fiddled with the mic, heart racing. "Thank you, Mr. Mayor, for your very kind words. I'd like to acknowledge my hardworking team—an amazing group of people, from whom I learn every day. I've enjoyed every minute of these past two terms. What more can *I* say? I honestly and truly *do* love New York!"

Dizzy with pride and relief, I started through the glad-handing crowd toward Jamey, accepting congratulatory embraces from the press corps and the usual assortment of business and media elite, glitterati and city officials. The city-supplied spread of pepper-jack cheese and jug wine was being cleared away, and wait-staff bearing trays of cheese puffs and champagne circulated among the crowd. Mayor Bloomberg stopped and smiled heartily. "Stacey. Give my office a call on Monday. I'd like to set up time to talk about our future together."

Next up was George Steinbrenner: "Stacey, let me take you away from all this. Why don't you come work your magic for me and the Yankees?" Wow. Over his head I could see Rudy winking at me. I winked back. A kick-ass job audition, indeed. Those heart-shaped cinnamon cookies might just have to wait after all.

I hugged my girlfriends, then threw my arms around Jamey's neck and covered his face with kisses. More than a week apart and a heart full to bursting will do that, you know? "I'm so glad you're back!" I exclaimed, elated he was here to share my shining moment.

"I wouldn't have missed it for the world." Jamey dropped his voice and spoke intently. "But listen, we need to talk. We have something else to celebrate. I tried to call before my flight, but—" Still buzzing, I returned an air-kiss to a *Sixty Minutes* producer, who'd mimed "Call me." I looked back to Jamey, eyebrows raised. "The acquisition—it came through! You're looking at the proud new owner of Pacificus Studios!" Nancy, Leslie, and I made appropriate cooing noises. I waved to editors from *Newsday* and *New York* magazine over Jamey's shoulder and double-cheek-kissed a *New York Post* photographer as she stopped by, promising a drinks date soon.

I smiled the biggest smile I could manage. "What great news! Now we can concentrate on moving on with our lives here at home!" I turned to the girls, beside myself. "Did you guys *see* Steinbrenner basically offer a position with the Yankees? Wouldn't that be a blast?" I whirled back to Jamey. "Hey—maybe you could buy a ball club for Commerz next."

"I'm crazy about Derek Jeter!" Nancy volunteered, her one-track mind racing. "Is he still twelve . . . and single?" She craned her neck, scanning the room for him.

Jamey cut in, impatiently. "Stace, don't you understand what this means, with Pacificus? A CEO title, a lot more money, two cars, a house—a pool, even. A whole new life. A *nicer* life!"

I waved across the room to Cathy, who waved back a huge bouquet of yellow roses and pointed to Donald Trump and his posse. I turned and mouthed an exaggerated "thank you" to the Donald's wingman, who patiently awaited acknowledgment. "Jamey," I started, distracted by all the attention, "what are you talking about? I like my life just fine. Even more so—*now*." I gazed around the friendly room; the world was my oyster! "The new building is prewar and doesn't have a pool, and we can't afford one of those fancy, swingly high-rises. And why would we need another car? I only drive yours, like, twice a summer on Long Island. And just to get milk!" I blew a kiss to the fire chief.

Jamey, frustrated, put both hands on my face and swiveled my head so I would focus only on him. "Stacey. Listen. We bought Pacificus. The deal went through."

I stared back, wide-eyed. "I know, honey. I'm so happy for you. What's next?"

"No, you still don't get it." He shook his head emphatically. "Remember all the craziness I was telling you about Pacificus' current management? It's always been part of the deal—the Germans want me out there to reengineer the business, top to bottom."

Swell. More flying, more LA talk. At least I'd have time to sift through the opportunities I'd uncovered this evening. "Well, I hope you're planning on hanging around long enough to get married," I replied sarcastically. The special, twinkly aura of my pretend tiara was fading quickly. "Let's talk about this later."

"What's to talk about? What could possibly be the problem?" Rudy appeared, gave me a quick half-hug and pumped Jamey's hand. "Your wife-to-be is Queen of New York tonight, James, and you're getting married in a few months. Life is good!"

"Hello, Mr. Mayor. I was just saying that to Stacey. Life *is* good—and getting even better. We have another reason to celebrate: I bought a film company in LA."

"I thought you owned one of those already."

"We had a small interest; I bought the outstanding shares. The deal closed today."

"Well, good for you! You can bring all your production to New York," he enthused, another one-track mind. "But that sounds like an awful lot of flying for a newlywed."

Jamey took an exasperated breath. "Well, sir, that's what I was trying to explain. The timing couldn't be better, actually, if you think about it—what with your last term ended, and all . . ." My girlfriends, sensing something interesting building, leaned closer. "We're going to need, soon . . . I mean, after the wedding, of course . . ." All eyes were on him; my heart beat faster. "Well, we're gonna have to . . . to move to Los Angeles, to be closer to the entertainment community and for me to run the company successfully." My friends gasped and exchanged anxious glances. A nearby cluster of colleagues from *Live at Five* and the *Daily News* stopped dead in their tracks. The mayor looked like Jamey had slapped him. I said nothing for a moment, stunned as I was at this casually delivered, mind-altering statement, but the room and its contents certainly did shimmer and buckle around me.

"He's kidding." I looked around wildly, helplessly, then back to Jamey, and mustered a confused laugh. Some staffers followed my lead, nervously, in support. "You're kidding, right?" Who was this man? And why would he do this to me—now, of all times? No one spoke. "Maybe, Jame, after our honeymoon I'll go out . . . *there*—you know, for a month or so, until you get everything up and running." I offered up this small acquiescence, willing the conversation to end.

"Now that's very funny, James," the mayor chuckled, trying to lighten the tension. "Stacey's the 'I Love New York' girl, and you want her to . . . *defect* to LA! Now there's a story for you, Nancy."

Nancy eyed me worriedly as I pulled Jamey away, hissing in his ear. "Listen to me! I know you're excited—it's been a big day for you. But it's also a giant day for me. Look around." I waved an arm expansively. "*This* is my life. This is my *future*. You can't actually expect me to leave everything—to abandon the city, to . . . to *live* in LA?"

Spike Lee overheard my last statement. "Who's going to live in LA?" He looked from Jamey to me, incredulous. "How could you even *consider* being a Laker fan after all those Knick games I've seen you at? That's sacrilege! Traitor!" he accused playfully. Colleagues from the Garden nodded in mock-disgust.

That did it. *Jamey* was the traitor. "He's joking," I reassured as I tugged Jamey's hand, "LA, right!" forcing him out the front doors of Gracie Mansion and into the chilly dark air of the driveway. Oh, I was furious, and gearing up to let loose on him further. I wheeled around, ready to go, but something in his face stopped me cold: he was clearly exhausted, drained. His eyes were shadowed in the lamplight, tired and lost underneath his suntan. And his shoulders sagged a little too much, even taking the long flight into account.

"Stacey," he started, quietly. "Listen to me. These negotiations have been brutal. The three Pacificus execs are like a Trio of Terror." He rubbed his eyes and took a new tack. "And anyway, I thought *I* was your future. I thought *we* were the priority." *Oh puhleeze!* My stomach leapt to my open mouth, heart still pounding angrily, but no words would come. "I've been trying to talk to you about this . . . *possibility* . . . for the last few weeks. Hell, the past few months! But you're always juggling so many people and things I can hardly get your attention." He ran a frustrated hand through his newly highlighted hair.

My left elbow began to tingle. I scratched at it absentmindedly, then caught myself. Oh shit. That's just great: those post–9/11 stress hives were back, needling the duct tape and threatening to creep up my shoulder. Shaking loose from the borrowed wrap, I squeezed my eyes tight to reverse their direction and channeled my inner Stevie Nicks, chanting my tried-and-true calming mantra: "White-winged dove, white-winged dove, white-winged . . ." Hallelujah! The tingling ceased momentarily.

I took an anguished breath and composed myself. On one level, I had to admit, Jamey was right—about the lack of attention part, anyway. I was aware I tended to glaze over and change the subject whenever he referenced the Pacificus negotiation: the crazy Hollywood players, epic power plays, insane deal points. I never could follow the illogic involved—the complete antithesis to my own traditional, ethical upbringing. His stories were hilarious, so extreme, so over-the-top, but I seemed to tune out the particulars, though I couldn't say why. I certainly had listened to and offered enough advice on all his other deals these past few years. What was it about this one?

I wanted a cigarette. And a drink. And a Benadryl. Badly. My bag was back in my office. I tried again. "Jamey, you know how I feel about leaving New York—or, obviously, you don't. I thought this film thing was just another in a series of acquisitions. I had no idea you were considering LA as a *destination* for us, for real. Or that you even wanted to run a movie studio, for that matter."

"Stacey, I don't want to fight, and I don't want to run the studio day to day. The current management will stay on—at least for a while. But the financials are a mess and it—the relocation, I mean—has become a condition of the purchase from my bosses. The studio's a great asset for Commerz, and anyway, I was hoping this would be a good thing, for both of us. Face it; you've been working nonstop since September, and crazy hours always, way before that. It's not like you haven't complained how overtired you are and that you can't even get a good night's sleep. *You* even said we should get the hell out of town." I glared at him; that was hitting below the belt. Everyone said that in fear and anger on September 12; no one meant it. "Rudy's out of office now, and we're getting married." He waited a beat and added quietly, almost as a throwaway, "It would only be for, like, two years, anyway . . ."

"Two years?!" I felt like I'd been hit by a truck. The tingly itching returned and crept determinedly up to my neck. A reversal of fortune, lifestyle and future, changed irrevocably in one evening with one little acquisition of a badly run movie studio.

He put his hands on both my arms, as if holding me up, and tried again. Soothing, earnest tones now. I let his voice wash over me and gazed longingly through the window back to the party, *my* party, as if masochistically reinforcing the hard truth of all I stood to lose. Where the hell did that peaceful white dove go? "Stace, you've done an amazing job here—everyone in that room thinks so. Isn't that enough? You're the Queen of Smoke and Mirrors, and we're heading to the epicenter of Smoke and Mirrors. You'll be fine. We're beginning a whole new life. *And,* I would like to think, as a team. How many people ever get a chance like this? Commerz will help with everything: packing, moving, a *house.* It's a perfect time for you to take a break and enjoy life, for a change. It really is nice out there . . . Honestly, it is."

"*Nice?*" I spat. "Nice ambush, Jamey!"

"You *like* movies . . ." he tried weakly.

"I like chocolate, too, but it doesn't mean I want to live in Hershey Park!"

He tried to look me in the eyes but I stood dumbly, staring at his collar, watching his jaw line move. "At least promise you'll think about it." He leaned forward and hugged me tight, even as my arms were folded stiffly across my chest. "Please?" Another beat. He pulled back slowly. "Let's talk in the morning—I've gotta get some rest. I love you, you know," he added for good measure. He kissed my forehead and turned away, heavy footfalls down the lonely drive. And all I could do was stand there, limp, tingling and cold, watching as my self-proclaimed future walked away, shoulders hunched against the damp chill.

I crumbled onto the front stoop, not caring about the soggy stone, the fraying, exposed tape, or the elegant couture loaner, cradling my head in my lap. I stared at the asphalt, listening numbly to the familiar city sounds around me: joyful, ambient strains from the party, an ambulance whirring up First Avenue, a car alarm honking steadily. My heartbeat slowed instinctively, rhythmically, in time.

After a considerable stretch, marinating in thoroughly heartwrenching self-pity, there appeared two pairs of (really pretty, actually) Prada boots in front of mine. My Canal Street Vuitton tote, a packaged antihistamine and the bottle of Lillet dangled into frame. I smelled the aroma of smoke and Chanel No. 5 and glanced up: the cavalry had arrived. My girls. As always. On cue. I took the proffered cigarette and squinted up at their faces, cutting the glare from the streetlights with my hand. "So?" I exhaled loudly, a semi-sob escaping my lips.

Nancy spoke gently. "Y'know . . . I hear that in LA you can valet park at, like, Bed, Bath & Beyond, Barneys, and all the dermatology offices in Beverly Hills."

I choked out a laugh in spite of myself, still dazed and unsure on the curb. With one last effort, the girls began warbling an entirely anti-feminist (but entirely heartfelt) rendition of "Stand by Your Man." I tentatively joined in the chorus and, with each friend grabbing an arm in support, allowed myself to be helped to my unsteady feet. "All right, Emma. Up we go."

CHAPTER 2

LET THE GAMES BEGIN!

Sun Tzu said: the art of war recognizes nine varieties of ground. . . . The different measures suited to
the nine varieties . . . the expediency of aggressive or
defensive tactics; and the fundamental laws of human
nature; these are things that must most certainly be
studied.

—Sun Tzu, *The Art of War*

ll right. So. It was an obvious, indisputable fact that Jamey
and I had each been a bit too caught up in our own personal
dramas and time zones to have thought through a workable, cohesive
vision of married life. "Pulling two lives into one is never easy, even in
the best of circumstances," my mother counseled, pinning my satin-
draped shoulder from the tomato-cushion at her wrist. And this last
year had been filled with anything but the best of circumstances.

At times like these I find it's important to remember the immortal
words of Cher (and I'm quoting here from her brilliant series of Jack
LaLanne ads a few years back): "Life is not a dress rehearsal." Oh no,
it most certainly is not. So: *Can this relationship be saved?* Hmm.
Compromise, that most revered concept bandied about by women's
magazines everywhere, was clearly our only option. After a weekend's
worth of intense girlfriend therapy (fueled by chilled Lillet and Advil)

and the ensuing lonely nights (made bearable by chilled Lillet and Advil) I arrived at this epiphany and set off, determined, for Jamey's East River apartment as dusk fell on a chilly Sunday evening. I wasn't about to let the best relationship I'd ever had vanish into thin air. And honestly, I couldn't bear the fact that he was actually physically here, in the city, and I wasn't with him. These last few days comprised the longest we'd gone without speaking since the night we'd met.

I decided I'd negotiate a deal, something right up our collective alleys. As the taxi jostled its way down the FDR, I re-rehearsed my monologue and strengthened my resolve: I could *do* this "lemons into lemonade," "one door closing, another door opening" kind of thinking—I'd made a career out of it, for godsakes! I would channel the indefatigable spirits of Emma Peel, Tammy Wynette, Eva Gabor (in *Green Acres*), Ann-Margret, Joan of Arc, even . . . *courage!* and wrap them all into one small (but fabulous) La Perla-clad and (newly glossy) brunette package. Oh yes: a seduction scene was most definitely in order.

I hesitated in the hallway, taking deep, even breaths. The door opened and there he stood—my future, rumpled in a denim shirt and khakis, the L.L. Bean poster-boy for the weekend exec look: totally, utterly, and completely adorable. My heart melted even further as I noted that he looked even more drawn in the entry hall light than he had off the plane. He looked how I felt. "Stacey," he said warily, and stood aside so I could walk past. "You haven't returned any of my calls. I'd just about given up on you."

I said nothing and laid my pea coat carefully on the one black leather and chrome chair not covered by files, stacks of contracts, and Pacificus-related spreadsheets. Cartons of half-eaten Chinese food and a bottle of Maker's Mark were open on the wet bar. *SportsCenter* played mutely on the telly. I smiled to myself: Ah, men—such perfect clichés. Another mental note: *when* my deal terms are accepted, insist on the immediate disposal of all black leather and chrome furniture. I mean, really . . .

"So," he began cautiously, "what have you decided we're doing with the rest of our lives?"

I gazed out the picture window and studied the traffic patterns on the 59th Street Bridge, headlights and taillights making their way on and off the island of Manhattan. I took a deep breath. "Come here," I said quietly, not turning around. He stood behind me, awaiting further instruction. "Put your arms around me." He did as he was told, and pulled me tight. My eyes closed instinctively, savoring the moment. "Now do that thing you do to my neck." He obliged, the scruff from his unshaven face stirring tingles, all right, but the good kind, this time. Yup. That intangible X factor—it was still there. God, I missed him. "Jamey," I started, "I want to make a deal with you."

"I'll make any deal you want . . . later." I missed the heat from his body. Slowly he unbuttoned my sweater, revealing the pearl-studded, scalloped edge of my new ivory lace teddy, and slid his hand down the front. Ah, La Perla! Always money well spent. "Did you by any chance have time to visit the Brazilians while I was away?" he whispered, warm breath in my ear.

"You wanna find out?" No sooner had I replied than he picked me up, he-man style. I shrieked with delight as he carried me to the (you got it—black lacquer bed with the pale gray sheets in the mirrored—Oy!) bedroom . . .

An hour later we nestled in amongst the tangled bedding, picking through remnants of sesame noodles and General Tso's chicken. It was time to negotiate; I figured I had a slight advantage, at least for the moment.

"Hit me," he said, folding his hands Godfather-style on his stomach. "Let's talk deliverables."

I laid out my concessions: after our honeymoon respite, I would indeed agree to leave my beloved city and its stellar career opportunities, my friends, family, my perfectly contented life of thirty-five years, and greenlight the move three thousand miles away to the loathsome, plastic land of Hollywood for the pursuit of domestic tranquility, my soon-to-be husband's professional elevation and, of course, the betterment of Commerz General, AG.

If: We'd close immediately on the prewar apartment (a great investment, after all, as well as a necessary escape hatch). We'd put our respective bachelor and bachelorette pads on the market, and get rid of any furniture and accoutrements whatsoever that *I* deemed necessary. We'd go to LA for a trial "development period." A "first look," if you will, with an "option to renew" after six months. In fact (and I'm sure you'll be impressed) I went one step further: in an immense show of good faith, I offered to fly to LA as soon as we returned from our honeymoon to get a jump on the house hunt.

Jamey was silent while I spoke, so astounded was he by this Herculean attitude adjustment. He moved the food cartons to the night table, left the room, and returned bearing *his* olive branch: a single sheet of paper from the sty of the contract-strewn living area, and laid it on the bed in front of me: his letter of resignation to Commerz, dated tomorrow, should his further employment be attached to the relocation. Tears welled on sight, so touched was I by *his* compromise. Oh, he was a keeper, all right. So: *can* this relationship be saved? You bet.

As he kissed my tears away, I pulled back and dangled the paper in front of him. "Jamey, there's one more deal point pending, and if you don't agree, everything we discussed is off." He opened his mouth to protest, but I put a finger to his lips and continued. "I will tear up this letter and do all the things I said I would, *if . . .*" I paused, "you willingly attend dance classes at Arthur Murray. Just enough so we can foxtrot semi-gracefully to our wedding song."

"'The Way You Look Tonight.' The Frank version, right?" He grinned, relieved. I rolled my eyes; as if there were any other. He held out his hand to shake as confirmation of a sealed treaty, and pulled me down on top of him. "This is gonna be great, Stace. A new year, a better life. You'll see," he murmured into my neck.

I turned my head slightly and sighed, staring at the bridge that led to Kennedy—my childhood, my past—until the colored lights ran together. It would now be the gateway to my future as well. "I know, sweetie. It's just the beginning of a wonderful adventure . . ."

After a blur of adrenaline-filled fittings, foxtrot classes, seating and catering challenges, and a requisite Weather Channel vigil, our big day arrived at last. About one hundred fifty guests; friends, colleagues, and family descended on Gracie Mansion to celebrate.

As my parents walked me down the petal-strewn aisle toward Jamey and Mayor Giuliani, I concentrated on my posture so my simple, unembellished shell pink almost-Vera Wang charmeuse gown would drape perfectly. I signaled to the girls (similarly swathed) to do the same. A thousand sentiments welled and crystallized: I felt profoundly humble. After all, here we were, months away from winter and fear, under bowers of lavender and deep-purple roses as the sun set on a glorious May afternoon. Over the sea of heads I could see the open tent set for supper: silver candlesticks gleamed and twinkled on lavender chiffon-swagged feasting tables, sparkly crystals dripping from the eaves. Scott, the wedding planner (my "something-borrowed," courtesy of *Gloss*), had done a spectacular job creating an ambience hearkening back to the swell elegance of the *Thin Man* era. A master special effect indeed, set amid the slowly illuminating purple-gray sky.

"I do." My voice didn't quaver a bit as I smiled into Jamey's deep brown eyes.

"Well done, Stacey," the mayor rejoined. "By the power vested in me by the State of New York, I now pronounce you husband and wife. James, you may kiss your bride." The applause, whistles and flashes came at us like a wall of sound. Snap, crackle, pop! We were being treated by my pals in the press corps to coverage from the *Times*, the *News*, and the *Post*, standing to the side with Scott in command.

The small orchestra struck up the first of many Cole Porter melodies; Bollinger Special Cuvée Brut (Emma Peel's favorite), salmon rosettes and cream-dolloped potatoes were served by white tie, gloved waiters. My quintessentially New York wedding was off to a wonderful start. Nancy and Leslie rushed over with Bellinis and kisses as our respective families congregated, congratulating each other.

Amid the hubbub I snuck away for a quick shawl redo with Scott as the photographers reloaded their cameras. Curiously, his attention was focused on a very blond, very curvy woman who was in the process of a very deep curtsy and even deeper into the process of falling out of a filmy red Roberto Cavalli cut down to there and up to here, dripping with feathers and beads. Although her back was to me, I still managed to overhear her strangely accented greeting to the press. "Hello, my darlings," she oozed, emulating Marlene Dietrich perfectly. She straightened and turned to Scott. "Listen to me," her pouty baby voice implored, "I do so *wish* not to upstage the little bride tonight, so please, *please,* do not let them photograph me anymore. I am feeling a bit tired and maybe I do not look my best . . ." she waited for him to protest. No protest came. She continued gamely, ". . . so, again, I beg you, if you wouldn't mind doing me the *teensiest* favor by keeping the paparazzi at bay, I would be *ever* so grateful."

To which Scott replied, "It's not a problem, madam—"

"Made*moiselle!*" she snapped indignantly.

Over her shoulder, Scott checked my raised eyebrows and held up a hand. "Again, made*moiselle,* it won't be a problem." A beat. "None of us have any idea who you are." What snarky flourish! The photographers snickered. My smile widened.

The Scarlet Woman blanched (even her spray-tanned back turned white), turned on a strappy red metallic heel, and stalked away. "Friend of yours?" I inquired, still bridal giddy, turning for him to wrap my shawl in a complicated manner only he seemed to understand.

"She's obviously no friend of yours," he snipped. "She's been flexing and vamping for the cameras since she arrived—seems to think your wedding is her very own fashion shoot-cum-press conference. *And* she tried to slip me a fifty! Tacky!"

Scott made a dismissive face as I suppressed a giggle: my mother would go bananas over that dress! "I'll have security check her out," he added, standing back to give me a final once-over. "*Gawjis*! Now go do your receiving line thang." I sashayed away in exaggerated fashion, all charmeuse-y and satiny as he serenaded, "*Sadie, Sadie, married lady . . .*" and took my place beside Jamey.

Midway through the procession of hugs and congratulations, I spotted some unfamiliar guests standing apart from the line: one slightly ridiculous, pinkish, porkish, blondish man, notable for his black-tie cowboy hat, bolo tie, and gangsta three-piece suit circa 1978, one frumpy woman dressed in a matchy Sally Jesse Raphael vein, and a tall, thin, nervous-looking man compelling only in that he was entirely colorless, gray from head to toe. I whispered sideways, "Jamey, who're those people?"

Jamey followed my jutting chin and frowned. "Oh. Them. That's Simon, Phil, and Barb, Simon's stepdaughter, from Pacificus." Ahh. My interest was piqued. So this was Pacificus' infamous Trio of Terror, the very reason we needed to uproot our lives and move clear across the continent. The scarlet woman joined them, fuming, security detail in tow . . . I was riveted. I immediately lost interest in my great-aunt Shirley and kicked myself I hadn't paid closer attention to Jamey's stories.

"And the blond woman? The scarlet disaster?"

"That's Simon's singer wife, Julia. She's some kind of former beauty queen, and I think she was once his nurse. She's Danish. No, she's American, from somewhere cold . . . but she lived in Denmark. Sometimes she speaks with an accent," he added unhelpfully, his reportage on non-business issues as always infuriatingly incomplete.

Right. Danish, eh? From what I'd seen I rather suspected she was filled to the brim with silicone and other advanced plastic derivatives. I caught Nancy and Leslie's attention and nodded in the motley crew's direction. I silently mouthed "LA," signaling them to get the skinny for later discussion and dissection. Leslie (so clever) mouthed back, "Slutty Bombshell Barbie!" The aging cowboy called Simon noticed our curious gazes and ushered the others to join the lineup, defaulting to standard social custom.

I racked my brain for snippets of useful information re the Trio, outtakes from Jamey's phone reports and Commerz-related dinners I'd attended. I could manage only a vague collection of colorful verbs and adjectives alluding to extremely bad behavior: ruthless blackmail plots, nefarious double-dealings, underhanded scams and schemes: patented film-noir scenarios. And then, like a movie, the images faded to black. Oh well. Fact or fiction, I knew they were widely held to be the ultimate bone of contention for many executives, past and present, of Commerz General. As it was, I could see that Jamey's colleagues were steering clear of them: furtively stealing amused glances, whispering and pointing, but definitely keeping their distance. I did know this: the Trio was known as much for their treacherous, cutthroat infighting as for their ability to close ranks and band together solidly, ring-of-fire style, to mobilize against any common enemy, real or perceived.

And now, apparently, responsibility for the day-to-day dealings with these mythic creatures would fall to Jamey, my brand new, unbribeable husband. Studying them all in person this first time, they looked so, well . . . normal. They hardly looked as sinister, as manipulative—nor frankly, as sociopathic—as I'd heard tell.

The receiving line dwindled; they were inching nearer. I took a deep breath and put my game face on, determined to be gracious and warm.

Barb Spurndoff was first to approach, smiling affably in a manner befitting a suburban bank president. She was a large-boned athletic brunette, tipping slightly over the line from attractive toward mannish-looking. I recalled some bodice-ripping, even liscentious intimations about her but, seeing her now, I couldn't imagine how they'd possibly be true. "Congratulations, Stacey. I've been so looking forward to meeting you."

"Me too," I replied, "I've heard so much about you all."

The pink, chubby cowboy flashed a practiced, dazzling smile and nodded. "Simon Mallis, ma'am." I detected a faint aroma of sweat and meatloaf. I remembered hearing he had a heart condition, but he looked pretty sturdy to me. Garlic pills, perhaps?

Phil (even up close he was entirely monochromatic) hunched over and talked to his shoes. "Phil Craven." Math guy. Got it.

And then. I heard her before I met her: the lovely Miss Julia, overly blond, overly statuesque and overly animated, loudly accosting Nancy, tugging at her dress and hurling aphorisms like spears: "*I'm Julia Mallis! That dress—it's Vera Wang! Vera's the new Blass! Do you know her? She knows me! You're with Gloss? I adore Gloss—it's the new Bazaar! That's shell pink! Pink is the new orange! So shell must be the new pumpkin!*"

"Isn't Bellevue the new Betty Ford?" Leslie quipped snidely in my ear.

Nancy looked to me, fascinated, and I attempted to step in (but not before something like ". . . your travel section: Ibiza is the new Sardinia!" escaped Julia's chemically plumped lips.

I held out a gloved hand. "Hi, Julia. I'm Stacey Makepeace."

Mid-aphorism, she narrowed her lids at my outstretched arm. "Stacey. Of course." I withdrew my hand. We stared blatantly, each sizing up the other. "Gloves!" she finally exclaimed. "Opera length. How . . . interesting. By the way, you have some very *useful* people here tonight. I hear that . . ." she started, then sniffed the air and Brite-smiled enormously: her eagle eye and nose for fresh meat had discerned new prey, better prey: Leslie, who visibly steeled herself. Mouth wide, Julia pointed accusingly at Leslie with a French-tipped fingernail, then seized her elbow and dragged her aside. "I know you! You handle Revlon! You know *me*, of course! Your last campaign was so . . . *quel est le mot? Outré!* Positively *outré*! I was just thinking:

Revlon is the new Chanel!" She dropped her voice to a stage-whisper, eyes darting to ensure secrecy. "You really *must* call me—I can help you. I am being chased by many beauty companies. Rivals! For multi-million-dollar deals, you understand, so you'll need to call soon. Halle knows me, Cindy too . . ." It was Leslie's turn to be blown away as Julia continued to purr, lick, and pour herself over *her* shell pink almost-Vera Wang.

I turned slowly to Nancy. "Oh. My. God," I mouthed. Nancy nodded solemnly and grabbed two glasses of wine from a passing tray. Here's what else I glimpsed: Simon pulling what looked like laminated swimsuit shots of Julia from his wallet, then presenting them proudly to the mayor and my dad.

Jamey, thankfully, broke the strange interlude by steering me toward the flower-draped reception area. Other guests milled about happily, and Jamey and I joined in the fun, sipping wine and decompressing—it really was a wonderful evening. As the requisite family portrait session began, photographers snapping away, I spied the Trio sniffing around the long tables. Julia was flirting outrageously with Nancy's date, Mark, who ran the Nederlander Broadway group, after she had done much the same to select other men, most of them married. All of them, I suspected, were "useful," in some way. Instinctively I was annoyed, and tried to keep one eye on her as well as that redoubtable cowboy hat, bobbing and weaving from afar. "Jeez, Jame, dinner doesn't start for another half-hour. Why aren't they at least pretending to mingle and enjoy themselves, with everyone else?"

His jaw tightened, but he continued smiling into the cameras. "Just try and forget them," he answered through his teeth, "and let's focus on celebrating tonight. There'll be plenty of time to worry about them, I promise."

Truer words have never been spoken.

Pausing inside for a final hair touchup, we readied to make our very first entrance as husband and wife. We waited for the drum roll cue from the bandleader to announce us. And waited. No drum roll came. How odd—where was Scott? The "run of show" had been planned to a tee. I forced myself to remain calm—it was only a minor glitch, after all. These things happen. "Let's go on ahead," I urged. "The band will start up once they see us, and everyone will wait to begin eating and toasting." Light as air, we approached the glittering tent hand in hand. No sooner had we turned the corner than our blissful smiles faded; we stood, gaping, in disbelief. Jamey squeezed my hand tighter, digging my new wedding band deep into my palm. I flinched and pulled away, shaking off the pain.

There was a dispirited air of confusion and disorder at my meticulously planned tables; Scott dashed about in a panic, hissing orders at the staff. No one seemed to know where to sit, and those that were seated were unhappy. Everyone, that is, save for Simon, Phil, Barb, and Julia. All four sat in a row, tucking in to the cracked crab, pouring champagne and chatting pleasantly among themselves. As I watched the uncomfortable scene unfold around them, it dawned on me that I hadn't, in fact, seated them all together. Not only had they changed *their* seating (an Emily Post etiquette breach of *immense* magnitude, by the way) but while they were at it I suspected they had shuffled other cards as well—apparently discarding some entirely, indiscriminately, along the way. Purses and shawls had been moved from where their owners had left them and were dispersed in random piles on chairs and (we later discovered) under cocktail tables. My blood boiled as Nancy hurried over, looking as distressed as I felt. "I *saw* them change the place cards around, Stace. They've ruined everything—on purpose!" Simon glanced up and smiled beatifically, unfazed by the discord. He'd noted the enraged look on my face and exulted at his team's well-timed sabotage and the resulting chaos. He raised a glass our way.

Jamey scowled but stepped in and took control. "If everyone could just take a seat—please! Any seat. We'll begin dinner and the rest of the program. Stacey and I will move between the tables. It'll be like the 'Mad Hatter's Tea Party!'" he enthused.

I plopped down next to my former boss and drained two nearby glasses of champagne in rapid succession. That all-too-familiar tingling sensation taunted, threatening, underneath the length of my left glove. Rudy tugged on my shawl. "So, Stace, Simon tells me he's looking forward to having Jamey work for him here in New York."

I reached for a third flute and stared at him. "Mr. Mayor—"

"Rudy," he smiled warmly.

"Rudy. *Barb* is CEO of Pacificus. Simon reports to her—he's her stepfather and some kind of financial advisor who helped sell off the remaining portion of Pacificus that Commerz didn't already own. He's helped her sell small interests in Pacificus to Commerz in the past. Jamey bought the remainder of the studio, so technically Simon *and* Barb will report to *him*."

"Well, just so you're aware, Simon said he'd guarantee that if you both *did* go to LA—which you really don't need to do, of course, as they have everything in hand—you'd be back home within a few months."

"Really!" My mind reeled. How helpful of him! "He's perfectly aware it's a done deal we're moving. It was the deal-breaker point upon closing in exchange for their payout. Simon, Barb, and Phil will remain on contract for continuity only until the end of this year, when Jamey decides whether to renew them. Or not." Regardless of how *I* felt about returning to New York as soon as possible (or never even wanting to leave), how dare that bloated, pompous cowboy make false representations and thinly veiled threats—and at my *wedding*, no less! Infuriated, I looked around to flag Jamey, finally locating him at the far end of the table with my father, who was readying index cards to make his toast. Barb and Julia, I noted, were chatting up my mother, Mom fussing over Julia's outfit. Now that just couldn't be good.

Seeing me glance her way, Mom rushed over, taking care not to trip on a ruffled flounce of her leopard-chiffon dress, clutching a folded note like a winning lottery ticket. "Honey, your friends gave me the name of the fanciest real estate lady in Beverly Hills. I wrote it down for you!" Barb winked knowingly down the long table.

Simon, by now, was deep in conversation with the bandleader, slipping him something from his gangsta lapel pocket. Well, I thought bitterly, I can kiss our well-practiced foxtrot goodbye. And sure enough, as the band played "our song," Frank's rhythm had unsurprisingly been changed to a waltz. Which Simon and Julia then performed, smashingly. As I reached for yet another glass of anything alcoholic, I caught Simon's eye. Oh, he was enjoying himself immensely, keenly observing the way the conflict had widened.

As my dad rose to begin his speech, Simon shot up quickly and dramatically cleared his throat, clipping the rim of his glass with a spoon. Dad, uncertain, sat down. Denied! My heart sank. Jamey hurried back over to me and squeezed my shoulder in support.

"If I could have everyone's attention . . . Please! Ladies and gentlemen!" Simon called over the commotion, a glint in his eye like a newly appointed South American dictator. "I'd like to say a few words, if I may. I'd like to offer up a bit of my favorite philosophy; words of wisdom from the most brilliant military strategist of all time, Master Sun Tzu." He pronounced the name reverently and with what I had to assume was the correct accent; it sounded like spitting.

I was immobilized, too stunned to move. Jamey's body tensed even as he bent to laugh softly in my ear, almost strangely pleased. "I just knew he wouldn't be able to resist, although I was hoping he would, this once."

". . . Sun Tzu's wise teachings have great application in business, as well as in life, I think you'll find," Simon continued. From his suit pocket, he pulled a well-worn copy of the *Art of War*—his bible and most prized possession, I'd soon learn, aside from his irrepressible wife.

He flipped to a paper-clipped passage and began. "To my new friend, James, and his *enchanting* bride, Stacey," he looked smugly at me, "on the eve of the formation of two portentous alliances: ours—

the front line, as it were, of Pacificus"—he nodded toward Phil and
Barb, then gravely to us—"and, uh, yours." The din and flurry had
subsided: Simon's conjuring of a 2500-year-old Chinese military
genius at Gracie Mansion had indeed commanded everyone's curiosity and attention. A forthcoming message, perhaps, in the harmonious spirit of love, understanding, and cooperation? Oh, I think not.

Simon took a deep breath, savoring his moment and milking
every second of stolen control as we waited, like sitting ducks, for
the inevitable assault of carefully crafted missives. "James. Stacey,"
he drawled, gearing up, "we are pleased to be invited here today, and
we are delighting in the opportunity to get to know you better. After
all (and I quote): *One who does not know the plans of the feudal
princes cannot prepare true alliances beforehand. One unfamiliar
with the terrain cannot advance his cause. And one who does not
employ local guides cannot gain advantages.*" The crowd stirred,
confounded anew. Simon raised his voice. "It is important to remember: *If you know your opponent and you know yourself, success will
not be imperiled. If you know Heaven and you know Earth, success can be complete.*" Simon stared (glared?) at Jamey, narrowing
his eyes. "*He who exercises no forethought but makes light of his op-
ponents is sure to be captured by them.*" Still, no one said a word, but
shifted uncomfortably in place. Ah, yes: clear, present, and imminent
danger. I got it, and swallowed, hard.

He paused, shrewdly assessing the effect of his performance. Satisfied, he smiled. It was not a kind smile. His voice boomed majesti-
cally, "To sum up, Stacey and James: may you cherish this moment in
time. May the immeasurably deep emotions you feel at this instant
never change. May they endure everlasting, always and forever!" Our
friends and families continued their silence, astonished, most likely,
at the seemingly innocent invocation so tauntingly delivered. I glared
back at Simon's cocksure, cherubic face, mustering all my energy to
beam disgust his way. "To the happy couple!" roared Simon, ignoring
my fury. Phil and Barb applauded him and raised their glasses. Where

had Julia gotten to? And more important, where were my friends? Still no one moved. Simon puffed out his chest, clearly delighted with the day's victorious strike. For a finishing touch, he crowed once more, "To the newlyweds!" and was duly rewarded with miserable groans of irritation from the ornery, hungry crowd.

Oh yeah. Here we go: let the games begin. The band struck up a tune, but it wasn't Cole Porter. Nor was it Frank . . . And what was this? I hadn't ordered a vocalist! I whirled around, confused, only to see Julia, the scarlet songbird, bumping and grinding seductively on the makeshift stage, belting out "Le Jazz Hot," then segueing smoothly into "Paris Makes Me Horny." I willed her to burst into flames; sadly, to no avail. True to form (and like a Mariah Carey parody) she used at least eight shrill notes where one would have done nicely. Nancy appeared magically at my side and took a sailor-like swig from a half-drunk bottle of Bollinger. Wiping her mouth with the back of her gloved hand, she threw said arm and bottle around my neck, giggling uncontrollably; I could tell she was extremely proud of herself. "What have you done?" I admonished, taking the bottle and swigging deeply myself.

"Why, I've done *this*"—she waved an unsteady arm toward the stage like a drunken game show hostess—"for you! You can thank me later," she said in all seriousness. I opened my mouth, but she cut me off. "Listen, that *Julia* has been draping herself across my date all night—that is, once she discovered what he did for a living. I overheard her blathering to him that Catherine Zeta-Beta 'stole' *her* part in *Chicago*, So for fun *I* told her he was staging a revival of *Victor/Victoria*—casting as we speak." She put a gloved finger to her lips: very hush-hush. "Anyway, I was thinking, things couldn't get much worse for you tonight, so I suggested she might 'audition' for him with a sexy number from the show." She grabbed the bottle back and swigged some more.

"Mark's doing *Victor/Victoria*? And you're helping her? Are you high?" I protested, incredulous. Heavily sedated with fermented grapes of all colors and sizes, but incredulous nonetheless.

"*No!*" she blurted. "He's doing *Agnes of God*, but I figured what the hell—I'll never date him again and you looked like you could do with a laugh."

Leslie stumbled up, concentrating intently on balancing three mostly full glasses of wine. Her gloves were soaked through. "What a great party!" she slurred. "Everyone's saying so. It's like participatory dinner theater!" She glowered in the direction of Julia, high-steppin'-a-plenty on the stage. "Well, *regional* theater, anyway . . ." She brightened. "Cheers!"

I took stock; amazingly, our guests were indeed enjoying themselves, drinking, dancing, and chatting up a storm. Even my parents seemed to have gotten back into the swing, slow-dancing along, somehow, to Julia's siren songs. Strangely enough, and certainly in spite of their best efforts, the Trio of Terror had managed to put on quite a unique and memorable floorshow.

"I *love* you New *York*!" Slutty Bombshell Barbie panted from the stage. "And for my *next* number . . ." I tuned her out, drained my glass and went to find my brand-new husband, now holding court in a cigar-filled powwow with his boss, Willem, and some other Commerz comrades. They were red-faced and roaring, slapping Jamey on the back. Angry mental note: forward all bills for this debacle to Commerz.

Actually, they were guffawing *and* exchanging money, apparently having taken advance bets on Simon's behavior. It looked as though Jamey won the jackpot. Big time. Although the aftereffects were still reverberating in my head, I counted calmly to ten (in French, for something different) and, for some comic relief, entered the circle of testosterone and asked the sixty-four-thousand-dollar question (to which I already knew the answer), "So, honey, you've made some nice new friends. They're obviously *very* much looking forward to working for you and welcoming us to LA. Since I'm not as fluent in . . . *ancient Chinese* as you apparently are: what do you think all this means?" I over-smiled over-sweetly, and raised my eyebrows inquisitively.

The guys burst out laughing. Jamey just grinned. "Well, Stace, I'd say . . . *that*, most definitely, is what's known as 'firing the first shot.'" More laughter, more bills exchanging hands. I reached in and grabbed a bunch, stuffing them into my built-in charmeuse-y bra, much to the delight of the equally tipsy Germans. "It seems, honey, our extremely subtle 'local guides' have put us on notice." Jamey kissed my forehead, clearly energized for the challenges ahead. "So, what can I say? Buckle up! This is gonna be one hell of a bumpy ride."

CHAPTER 3

A VILLA OF ONE'S OWN

Ground on which each side has liberty of movement is
open ground. On open ground, do not try to block the
enemy's way.

—Sun Tzu, *The Art of War*

Our honeymoon in Paradise (well . . . Paradise *Island*, anyway)
was wonderful, a much-needed break of tranquility and to-
getherness. Then . . . we landed back in New York. And the deal
I'd brokered back at Jamey's bachelor pad took on a life of its own:
the relocation process began in earnest. Jamey and his lawyers negotiated a special West Coast term with the company. Perky "relo
gals" phoned constantly, offering cheery advice and checklists.
Movers scheduled appointments for tonnage appraisals. Plans were
made to flatbed Jamey's old Mustang out west. Whatever I wanted,
they seemed happy enough to comply. Appointments, decisions, and
requests were magically, easily achieved. I was being "handled," I
knew, but I swam with the current, resigned to the fact that (A) I had
indeed made the commitment and was a woman of my word, and (B)
it was still my only possible course of action. Besides, these past few
weeks, I'd slept better than I had in months; I had nary one tingle I
wasn't supposed to and, finally, I was coming around to the idea that,

as Frank so often says, if I could make it in New York, I could, in fact, make it anywhere. Even in LA.

As promised, by mid-July I flew out to the Coast with Jamey. My mission: to unearth a suitable home. I warily checked out Julia and Barb's suggestion of a broker, who was indeed reported to be top of the line, an absolute rock star real estate maven. I'd forced myself to focus on the more appealing elements of the move, turning those lemons (as always) into lemonade. A *house*! With space! No city sounds! A garden! A pool! Sun! It was, after all, the American dream, *n'est-ce pas*?

Said broker's name was Sheila Yenta (all right: so it was Yetnikoff, but I promise you, you'll get the picture) and she meant business. After only a brief phone conversation, a very unpleasant picture congealed in my mind of Norma Desmond, black and white and crazy, direct from *Sunset Boulevard*. Within fifteen minutes of our eleven a.m. arrival at the swanky Pink Palace, the Beverly Hills Hotel, the phone rang: Sheila, a half-hour early and ready to rock. "Hel-lo-o," her gravelly, Brooklyn-tinged voice intoned. "I'm down in the lobby. Are you ready for me?"

I glanced at Jamey, ensconced at the desk, his attention divided between a heated German-lawyer speakerphone debate and a non-working computer modem. A nervous hotel technician was underfoot, rewiring, and the bed was covered with unpacking. "You're a bit early, Sheila. I'll be down in a few minutes, but I'm afraid my husband's tied up. You'll have to meet him another time."

"Oh no. That just won't do," she replied testily. "I *always* insist on meeting both my clients, *especially* the men. They pay the bills, after all!" she sing-songed, adding, "It's just the way I work, *hon*. I hate wasting time."

A flush of anger rose. I never could stand condescending bullies, and now I seemed to be meeting so many! "Sheila. Let me be clear. He's working. You and I have already spoken by phone. And how could you possibly be wasting time? We're a sure commission." Silence. I continued. "Here's how *I* want to work: you and I will screen properties over the next few days. If there's something I like, we'll revisit with Jamey."

More dead air. Then Sheila blurted nastily, "No. I *insist* on meeting him now. I'll be waiting. In the lobby." Click.

Jeez! I debated whether I should run with my initial impulse and have the concierge tell her to fuck off . . . and then I tuned in to Jamey's phone conversation: Pacificus' financials sounded pretty dire. Something about the niggling possibility of two sets of books . . . The honeymoon, as it were, was very definitely over. I motioned to him to wrap it up (by playing exasperated charades) and make a brief appearance to appease the overly aggressive bat. I was curious, in any event, to see if my mental image was close to reality. I'm usually pretty good at this stuff.

We rushed down the famed banana-leaved hallways to the lobby lounge (and almost smack into the Wu-Tang Clan, checking in). From behind a high-backed plum velvet couch, a sudden, savage, nasal voice pierced the ambient Muzak. "You're *rat*-fucking me, *Sammy*! Oh yes you *are*! Are *so*! Rat-*fucker*!"

Jamey and I exchanged amused glances as the wraithlike owner of this voice (you got it—our very own feral bulldog, Sheila Yenta) shot up from the couch, beady eyes glistening. She caught sight of us and melted instantly back into human form. "Gotta go, love. Yep. Clients from New York. See you at yoga. *Namaste*." She bowed. Pulling the implement of evil (her headset) from her ear, she marched past me to Jamey, hand extended. "I'm *very* spiritual," she offered by way of explanation, and melted even further, by maybe twenty, thirty years. "Why, George Clooney, as I live and breathe!" she gushed, channeling Scarlett O'Hara.

Gag. Sheila was a bone-thin dynamo from the old school with frosted lemon-icing hair, blood-red lipstick, and matching fingernails. An imposing, imperious vision in Chanel Couture for day, she would infuriate and frighten me near to tears on more than one occasion.

"Mr. Makepeace—*James*," she dripped, "do you have time to chat over lunch at the Polo? They're holding my usual table." She batted three spidery pairs of false eyelashes per lid at Jamey.

"No," he replied flatly. "I need to get back on the phone and head out to a meeting. What information can I help you with that Stacey can't supply?"

She didn't like that. "Let's sit a moment and get to know one another a tiny bit," she purred coyly. We sat. Jamey folded his arms. "So . . . the information I have from your *wife* contradicts the information I have from the Mallises." I opened my mouth to protest, vehemently, on so very many counts, but Jamey clamped his hand on mine. "Your *wife* had told me you were looking for a one-year-lease-plus-one. The Mallises say you're looking on a monthly basis. Which is it?"

Jamey spoke calmly and squeezed my hand tighter. "Whatever my *wife* tells you, obviously, is correct. Why would the Mallises know better? Who are the clients here, us or them?"

A sadistic smile played on her lips as she made extensive pretend notes in her Vuitton clipboard, held close to her concave chest. "Right. What is our budget, hmm?" she smiled encouragingly, as if to preschoolers. I studied her: varying expressions created no lines whatsoever on her taut, waxen face.

"Stacey's already discussed this with you, and I know the relocation group at Commerz has, too: whatever Stacey likes will be within our budget. Your job is to please her, and quickly."

Sheila tried again, dripping even more honey. "And what is our annual income? With your new position, and all. In case we decide to *buy* . . ."

Jamey cut her off. "Now *that* is none of your concern. We will lease, as you've been told. If this is a problem, we'll take our business elsewhere." She recoiled, like he had (finally) slapped her. Jamey stood, ending the conversation, and we two followed suit. "Let's try this, Sheila: why don't you look at Stacey as the client, not me—and certainly

not the Mallises. Now"—he leaned over and kissed me—"I have work
to do. Good luck, honey. I'll see you back at the end of the day."

We watched him head to the elevators in silence. Finally, I spoke.
Good cop, bad cop. "Sheila, would you like some lunch before we
go?"

"Lunch makes you fat!" she snapped, never taking her eyes from
the elevator doors. "Who could *possibly* take food at this hour?
Come!" she ordered. "Let's go."

I followed meekly out front where she slipped the valet a fifty
and climbed into her mobile office: an enormous metallic-gold Mercedes with tinted windows, drenched completely in Shalimar. She
tore out of the drive and motored through the Technicolor badlands
of Beverly Hills at warp speed, honking at slow-moving Star Tour
buses, nursing her bruised ego by pointing out her many conquests
and trophies as we toured along. "Mine! That one's mine! That was
mine too!" French Country next to Mediterranean next to Tudor next
to Adobe. In between, she managed to bark relentlessly at her assistant on her hands-free cell phone. "I've worked with all the big
ones, lemme tell you—Madonna, Warren, Arnold, Cher, Barbra!" she
chanted, world-weary. "They all know me."

She eyed me sideways. "Just so you know—and as I was *trying*
to tell your husband, I don't really *do* rentals. I'm just doing this as a
favor to my great friends, the Mallises." Another surreptitious glance
my way. "They're very prominent, you know. Real pillars of the community; opinion makers. Your husband's very lucky he's starting out
in this town working for such an important man." She wagged a perfectly manicured, bejeweled finger right under my nose.

Not that nonsense again. How tiresome. "Actually, Sheila, Simon
will report to Jamey, as it happens."

"That's not how I heard it."

"Well, that's how it is. Haven't you seen the articles on the Com-
merz/Pacificus buyout in the trades?" Even a novice like me knew it

would be highly unlikely for a shrewd cookie like Sheila not to follow such machinations minutely.

"I heard that was a misprint. They just received a cash infusion." Oh really—for what? A job well done? I dropped the subject. What would be the point?

She pushed her way brusquely through the first few properties, taking gleeful delight in bullying the other brokers as I followed weakly behind. Sheila was determined to find us a house suitable for "your husband's new position." Her personal translation, I immediately discovered, meant *big*. And not just Hamptons Big, clean and looking like a page out of a J.Crew catalog. California Big had something to do with the sheer scale of everything in LA: Big Sky, God's Country, Penis Size . . . and the fact that most homes are built to the curb with little or no land surrounding each.

"Sheila," I began carefully, "do you think it's possible to find a smaller house, maybe with more grass outside? I mean, we hardly know anyone here, and we're just two people . . ." My voice trailed off in direct correlation to her widening, horror-filled eyes; I thought her head might explode. She hustled me angrily back to the Mercedes tank, glaring all the while. I felt as small as my New York furniture would seem in one of those palaces.

"Here!" Sheila hurled some crumpled newsletters at me. "I brought these for you, just in case. I think you better read them!" she commanded. I unfurled the pages, smoothing them in my lap: issues of the *Beverly Hills Shinier Sheet*. "Get ready," she warned. "They're all gonna start calling."

"Who?"

"*Them!*" She stabbed at the photo collage from the Out and About section. "This is what will be expected of you in this town, and these will be your new friends."

"You've got to be kidding! I'm not part of this world."

"Oh yes you are. It's a fact. There are only ten studios, and your husband's now running one of them."

I stared at the pictures: beautiful women in beautiful clothing in beautiful homes. I had seen something just like it once, on vacation in Florida. "You know," I mused, "there's a *Shiny Sheet* in Palm Beach, full of social events, interior design and so on."

"Yeah, well. This one's Shinier." The irony sailed right past her head. Sure enough, this four-color weekly printed on heavy pink stock was of the same order, but in this version one thing was crystal clear: Julia Mallis was its unrivaled star. Every third photo, every third blurb, every third quote highlighted her comings and goings, aphorism of the week, and, most important, her costume changes. I made a note to check out its editor, Libbet something (the name was smudged with a blood-red lipstick blot, courtesy of Sheila), with Nancy. On the back of the latest issue, I particularly enjoyed a split bleed spread of Julia: a candid in her see-through film of red Cavalli, emoting heavily as, the caption explained, she was "begged to audition for *Victor/Victoria* before a live crowd in New York City." The other was taken more recently at an acid reflux benefit: Julia, chaste and enigmatic, swanning demurely in (wait for it . . .) *my* shell pink Vera Wang, sporting opera-length gloves! Underneath were two quips: "Opera gloves are back!" and "Shell is the new pumpkin!"

"Sheila, can I keep these?" I couldn't wait to show the girls.

"I think you should memorize them!" she snapped, with withering candor.

Four dispiriting hours and seven houses later, we arrived back at the hotel. I was hungry, discouraged, and in desperate need of a drink. Sheila put the car in park and sighed. "You know, Stacey, I'm gonna level with you. You're gonna have to break out of this 'small time, down home' thinking if we're gonna find you a house appropriate to your position. This is Hollywood—live a little!" She snapped her fingers and did a semi-enthusiastic little seat dance for me. "You're not in Kansas anymore."

"I'm from New York," I replied, very much taken aback.

"Oh yeah, that's right," she remembered, and glanced purposefully at my black slacks and boots. I bristled; they were Calvin Klein (outlet, but even so) and *very* fabulous. "I heard all about that from Julia. You . . . *worked*, or something. For the city. How very . . . *industrious*," she demeaned. "Tomorrow. Nine sharp." She sped away before I could think of an appropriately cutting retort. I went directly to the bar, to steady my nerves. Call New York. Lick my wounds. Cry.

Fresh the next morning, I suggested we case the Hollywood Hills. Sheila made a squinchy face, *not* at all happy, but by now, of course, I knew exactly what to do. I'd conducted extensive research in the Polo Lounge before Jamey collected me for dinner. "You know, Sheila, last night I was chatting with *Leo* . . . and *Justin*." (Her eyes bugged as the muscles in her forehead attempted to move in spite of themselves.) "And they're dead set on looking up there. So is half the cast of *Friends* . . ." I let my voice trail off, hinting I knew lots more. She relented instantly, deferring to the validity of the Beverly Hills Hotel bar for celebrity real-estate tip-offs, but agreed only to the "quickest of sniffs."

She bleated at her assistant for real-time information. The Benz zoomed east on Sunset and up a few blocks from a cluster of exceedingly well-patronized (during the day) liquor stores, tattoo parlors, the Whisky a Go-Go and the Viper Room. I soon discovered that her initial instincts had been correct: the hills were alive, all right . . . with the sounds of hip hop music. Clearly not an option; I hung my head. Onwards!

The beach (another adamant veto) was deemed too far away from town and not even up for discussion. The actual reason, I later learned, was that Sheila personally despised the sun; many thousands of dollars, a slew of off-label injections, and a staggering series of experimental cosmetic procedures attested to that. Brentwood and Hancock Park were also given the big thumbs-down. "Why pay extra for schools? You'll be outta here before you can even *have* a kid," she declared, knowingly.

By process of elimination (her process, naturally), our geographical search whittled down to the palatial Beverly Hills estates area. Sheila fixated particularly on a certain mansion in the Flats (her "exclusive") and insisted I return on three separate occasions to "make sure" I understood how truly fabulous an opportunity it was before I rejected it, as I had so many others. "*This* is who you'll need to be in order to compete!" she crowed triumphantly, pleased with herself. The house was owned by an older couple, once the toast of Hollywood's star-studded restaurant scene back in the Rat Pack days. Those must have been Sheila's salad days as well, as she fell over herself drooling flattery and fawning as if in front of royalty, practically kissing the hem of the woman's Pucci gown. Vintage chic? Yeah, sure. The woman (who resembled Cruella De Vil in the most horrifying ways) gave us a tour herself. Her head was wrapped tightly in a coordinating Pucci turban, and she clasped a tiny, quivering Yorkie against her impressive bosom. "Now *that's* style!" whistled Sheila. "Watch and learn."

The very *best* selling point, Cruella offered breezily (aside from her specially designed First Night Closet where I too could "store my furs and gowns" at a steady fifty-eight non-humid degrees), were the three distinct entrances for caterers and staff, as she was sure I'd be entertaining "lavishly and often." She and Sheila bonded deeply over that, naturally, being from the same grandiose era and socially ambitious frame of mind. Both looked at me expectantly, Botoxed eyebrows arched, collagened lips pursed and frozen. I crumpled off to the side, blinking back tears as they schmoozed it up.

I begged off to one of four downstairs powder rooms to repair my red-tinged face. As I turned off the faucet, I could hear Sheila complain, "You can always tell the wife of a relo, just like this one, shuffling her feet, lagging behind and sniffling. Just terrible." Yep, that was pretty much me: *Trouble child, breaking like the waves at Malibu . . .*

We reluctantly (but for different reasons) strapped back into the golden sedan and purred up yet another hill, Shirley Bassey on the speakers now for fortification. "Wanna get happy?" Sheila asked conspiratorially, pulling a vial from the glove compartment at a light. "Take this!" She handed me a small white pill. I blinked—an attempt at bonding?

"What is it?"

"Vi-cu-pro-fen," she overpronounced, as if to a slightly retarded child. "It's like Advil, but with the added 'kick' of Vicodin. You'll save on extra calories from the wine," she glanced meaningfully at my midriff, "and you can still drive. Baby stuff," she dismissed

"Sheila, isn't half of Hollywood in rehab for painkillers?"

"Nah, that's just code. They're all in rehab for coke. They use the pills to come down. This way they can blame bad dentistry or a failed stunt for the addiction. It's all crap. Everybody knows."

I didn't . . . Live and learn. "I'll keep it for later. But thanks," *Judy Garland*, I added silently, now fully aware I was trapped in an ongoing buddy movie from Hell.

"Suit yourself. Take a few more."

Hoping to speed (ha!) this insane process along non-narcotically, I had one last peace offering stashed in my bag: listings I'd marked that morning from the *LA Times*. Semi-impressed with my initiative, she pulled over and snatched greedily at the pad. Her amused smile turned quickly to a frown. "No, no, no, and *no*." She thrust the paper back.

"But . . . why? What could possibly be wrong with these, sight unseen?"

She oversmiled. "They're all Beverly Hills *adjacent,* hon. Post Office 90210. *Not* 90210 proper, an *essential* difference. Close, I'd say, but no cigar." She patted my knee indulgently. "Let's just work through *my* list, shall we? I am, you know, a licensed professional."

The furnished houses varied greatly between rococo elaborate (read: Saturday night Iranian Disco) and broken-down Ikea. "So you *rent* furniture! Think of these homes as stage sets!" Sheila's patience was eroding dangerously; she rapped her seventy-dollar acrylic-bonds against that ubiquitous Vuitton clipboard with increased aggression. "Enough with the melodrama, Sta-cey! Try some lighter fabrics, some actual *colors,* even! Highlight your hair, for godsakes! If you don't mind my saying, you really *should* start getting it together. And be a *help* to your studio chief husband! There are plenty of girls who'd be *thrilled* to be in your shoes! *Plenty!* You need to watch yourself," she warned darkly. "Believe me . . . I've seen it all. And yet, with just a little effort, you could go far."

Indeed I did want to go far, and soon—all the way back home to New York City. The enormity of this impending lifestyle change had hit me like a thunderbolt. Sudden mental flashes occurred: me in the not-so-distant future, a suburban-glam fifties-monster hostess. That vision projected, I was sure, direct from the Vicuprofen- and gin-soaked brain of Sheila Yenta. It made me shudder. My girlfriends would laugh uproariously; only a week ago, I would have, too. I wished it were possible to send telepathic video, to literally "*Be* John Malkovich"; so much easier than finding words to describe what the house-hunting process was really like: too expensive, too impractical, too glamorous, too tacky. Too too much in general. Who did we want to be, anyway—Jamey and me, on the cusp of a new chapter, the beginning of a brand new life? Yet another dimension of our future we hadn't really thought through. I tried my best to get with the program—mustering any semblance of enthusiasm, certainly while I was around Sheila. She absolutely scared the shit out of me. I wasn't sure if I could articulate what I wanted, but I knew I'd recognize it when I saw it. *If* I saw it. Sheila would only harrumph and narrow her surgically altered lids, endlessly frustrated and disappointed in me. The gold Mercedes would fire up, and off we'd roll. Back on her hands-free car phone, she'd berate her assistant, acting out her despair by punching the speed dial menacingly.

Somehow, on the third and final day slogging through the HGTV tour of greater Los Angeles, Sheila pulled it off. As if by magic, she produced a house I adored. I hadn't even seen the listing in the *Times*. "I've saved this *especially* for you," she teased slyly, as if allowing me a glimpse of stolen emeralds. "There are a *ton* of bids already, and the owners are *very* tricky, *very* particular . . . but I have my ways. *If* you want it, that is . . ." But I was already hypnotized, wandering entranced through the expansive Mission-style, Spanish-tiled décor. "The last Commerz guy lived here—for a while," she sniggered softly, cutting through my delight. Something struck me in her tone, and I made a mental note to find out what happened to this "last Commerz guy."

Nonetheless, my attitude changed on a dime. In a New York minute? Well . . . I did completely fall in love. With a house, in California. It's a fact. It was as different from city living—and my former City budget—as possible. Entirely the point, it seemed, and the best reason yet to move three thousand miles away. It screamed "effortless West Coast lifestyle," just like the photo spreads I'd compiled of Dream House Ideas that Jamey and I might one day consider. It certainly did reflect a Southern Californian ideal that had slowly taken shape in my mind: if I could emulate the urbane and sophisticated Emma Peel in New York City, then I would take inspiration from my other lifelong heroine, the equally fabulous Stevie Nicks, and transform into the mystical, shawl-draped white witch Rhiannon in the canyons of Los Angeles. Hurrah!

The object of my desire was a high-ceilinged hacienda dripping with rainbow-colored bougainvillea and passionflower vines. White oleander and tropical trees were set around rows of Moorish windows up high in the Canyon, yet only five minutes from Sunset Boulevard. The scent from surrounding eucalyptus trees was intoxicating, like living inside an Aveda bottle. It boasted high ceilings, four bedrooms (with existing beds!), and miles of white plushy carpeting upstairs. It came staffed with a maid three days a week, a gardener, and pool service. I took Jamey up the hill as the sun set that evening, taking care to light the wrought iron candelabra outside. From the terrace off the master bedroom, high above the Hills of Beverly, the lights of Los Angeles sparkled like a glittering velvet and crystal blanket. This house provided the answer to every question we could ever ask about our future, and I wanted it with all my heart. Stevie herself, I was sure, would have very much approved.

Back at the hotel, as Jamey drifted off to sleep, I stared at the ceiling and sifted through my fragile, uneasy emotions. The prospect of this instantly fabulous Hollywood Wifestyle served up on a silver platter (just add water!) in a magically prepared, funded home was at once dizzying, daunting, and terrifying. If Julia and her *Shinier Sheet* were the Snickers-bar gold standard in this nebulous new land, I knew all too well I'd spent the last thirty-five years honing completely the wrong skill sets. The Mayor's office, personal and professional accolades, and my independent, self-sufficient New York life seemed a universe away, fading like shaken Etch A Sketch lines. I was, after all, the "I Heart New York" girl, an outer-borough cop's daughter-made-good—and everything that entailed. It was the only reality I knew. Would anything I'd worked so hard to achieve and become translate at all? I buried my feverish face in the cool, billion-thread-count hotel pillow and resolved this: regardless of local customs, standards, and mores, I was determined to be a woman, a wife, *and* a thinking person in my own right. I just had to figure out how.

CHAPTER 4

THE LAST ROUND TRIP

When you leave your own country behind, and take your army across neighboring territory, you find yourself on critical ground.

—Sun Tzu, *The Art of War*

*W*e checked into the Admiral's Club early Sunday morning, heading back to New York for a Board meeting without any closure on the house. As Jamey droned on the line with Executive Platinum, waiting for our bump ups to clear and booking yet another LA excursion, I stared down at my once-fabulous/now travelworn slacks, investigating possible sources of a faint bluish stain on my once-crisp/now rumpled white linen shirt with a more permanent sense of dread.

If nothing else, the intense immersion therapy with Sheila Yenta Mentor had proved enlightening. Her *Shinier Sheet* stash was packed away in my suitcase—pictorial primers for my soon-to-be charmed life. I was almost afraid to show my friends, to relive out loud the depth of my insecurity and fear. "Why don't you go home and concentrate on your . . . wardrobe." Sheila's last battle cry. "Let me worry about real estate; if not this house, I'll find another. You like my taste." Terrorizing visions played in my mind of spending more time trapped in her aggressive, Shalimar-infused presence, searching for new ways to say no.

Blue Curacao—that was it! I shuddered at the suppressed memory, glared over at Jamey, and reached in my bag for yet more Advil . . . finding Sheila's happy pills instead. Oh what the hell, I thought, and popped one; I deserved a thrill after last night. In a horribly misguided (though well-intentioned) attempt to "find me a friend," Jamey had organized last evening at Trader Vic's, in the agonizing company of a quintessentially Hollywood high-life couple: his entertainment lawyer-crony John Sharp (who'd brokered the Pacificus deal) and *his* socially motivated, intensely rabid inhaler of all-things-Shiny wife, Mallory. Mallory: ugh! And that awful Blue Curacao. My stomach sizzled as a souvenir: multiple pineapply pu-pu platters followed by a rainforest's worth of very alcoholic, very blue liquids. In ceramic coconuts, naturally. Guzzled down in a determined effort to counteract the jarring audio-visual onslaught of streaked blond tresses, Acuvue-enhanced green cat-eyes, and metallic, expensively wrapped Italian cleavage (wrapped in the real deal, by the way, of one of Nancy's "European numbered samples"). And mean-spirited, slanderous gossip. About people I didn't even know. Ouch. I adjusted my sunglasses and attempted to gather energy to hunt for coffee.

Jamey snapped his cell shut. "Still nothing from Sheila."

Why wasn't I happy yet? I tipped up my sunglasses and studied him; his hangover was only one half-step behind mine. "Speaking of evil, menacing creatures, Jame, I was so marinated in tequila and Mallory I never asked how your staff meeting went."

He grimaced. "Let's see: Simon stormed out after hearing the new reporting structure, Barb screamed bloody murder in support, and Phil freaked completely when I explained how I plan to integrate elements from other Commerz companies. They used to report directly to Munich, and mostly electronically. As long as they hit their targets they were hardly ever interfered with. Now that's all going to change. Simon went nuts, veins throbbing, sweating, clutching at his chest. He always threatens a coronary when he doesn't get his way. I can only imagine what'll happen in front of the Board tomorrow.

Most of them are German. They're calm, reserved—they don't respond well to theatrics. I just wish I understood the film business well enough to get rid of them all."

He exhaled heavily—I'd never seen him so exasperated by a business issue. I leaned over and rubbed his neck. "I guess Simon's just trying to hold on. He gave up his consulting career to help Barb turn Pacificus around. Now he's king and doesn't want to let go. The change has to be tough, but he did sell the company for an awful lot of money. What could he possibly have expected to happen?"

The half-filled lounge was Sunday-morning quiet, signaling a relaxing, uneventful flight. My thoughts turned back to caffeine. I craned my neck to locate the coffee bar, standing halfway. Then I sat right back down, slumping low in my seat. Another buzzing sensation sizzled, but one not hangover-related this time: past the silent CNN broadcast, a curious couple had entered, noisily flanked by Special Service fanfare. All heads turned to suss out the commotion: the woman was Saran-wrapped into leopard-print Versace. The man wore a wide-lapeled, western-stitched tan suede jacket and bolo tie. Both sported oversized, tinted shades (hers were rimmed in rhinestone). Lots of bowing and scraping ensued. The source of the sizzle: a rakish, chocolate-colored cowboy hat and an armload of scripts. Yeeha! Instinctively, I slumped even further. This was the first I'd seen of the charming Mallises since the wedding drama which, thankfully, by now had diffused to become a wildly entertaining tale to tell over cocktails. You have to laugh at yourself, you know, or you'd just cry your eyes out. . . . This, I'd decided, would be my rational new approach in dealing with them all, going forward.

"Look who's here," I whispered as Jamey groaned unhappily, immediately matching me eye-level with the table. "We have to at least say hello. I'm sure they're on our flight."

More desultory grumbling, then Jamey grunted his assent. With a flurry of conspiratorial hand gestures, we agreed to do a "fly-by" on the pretense of stepping out for magazines and candy, never to return.

Unfortunately, as the overly animated air-kissing wound down, Julia announced she'd "a-*DORE*" accompanying us to get supplies, much to the dismay of both men: Simon looked like he might collapse, and Jamey poked me hard in the side.

The four of us made our way through security to the newsstand. Julia chattered away effusively (what *was* that accent? Danish? Not even. French? *Non.* Swahili, then?); the men trailed uncomfortably, silently, behind. Her chirpy, relentless monologue careened from the genius of Cavalli's fall line ("I am his *muse!*") to the evils of wheat gluten ("I *abhor* bloat!"), from her serious, intent study of Human Growth Hormone for ultimate weight loss ("I have a medical background, you know!"), to untold studio hours demanded of her by P. Diddy *and* Bono for duets ("They simply will *not* take 'no' for an answer!"). Finally, slyly, she asked about the house hunt.

"Well, we found something I'm crazy about, but it might be unavailable."

"I know the owners. I could put in a word . . ."

"Oh? You're familiar with . . . ?" I asked, confused, then just as instantly realized: duh. Sheila Yenta: double agent-slash-sieve.

She appraised me sideways. "Um, well, *yes.* Simon's last *associate* was there, for a time." Hmm. "It's a *very* good address, though. And if you really . . . *insist* on moving here, it would be perfect for you. In Los Angeles, you know, your home is very important. It is a showpiece when you entertain, your calling card; just like your cars, your jewels, and your . . . personal style." She snuck a dubious glance at my less than polished traveling attire, and I flinched slightly, as she continued smoothly, "But you should take all the time in the world. Simon has everything under control, as always. I absolutely worship him—*everyone* does, you'll find. Honestly, I don't see why you need to move at all!"

Indeed.

"I think of you often . . ." She stopped and affected a sad face, full of concern. The men stopped as well, swaying and gazing at anything but each other. "I saw a glimpse of your life at your wedding—I really did—and I know in your heart you don't want to leave New York. And why ever would you?" She gripped my shoulder. "It's simply *tragic*, I think—*tragic,* to be *ripped* from your life, from your dreams! I can't *believe* he would do such a thing to you!" She glowered at Jamey, then dropped her voice. "This causes problems, no?" I began to protest, but she forged ahead, dripping honey and painful subtext. "I imagine it will be so lonely and isolating—no reputation, no friends or family, your husband working all the time . . ." She paused for dramatic effect, then hooked her arm in mine, pulling me close. "It's very different," she warned darkly, "LA from New York. You'll find things don't . . . translate so easily."

Having quoted my worst fears back to me as a death sentence, she took a softer tack, now my savior. "Here's what *I* must do: *if* you come, I *must* take you under my wing! You'll need to meet all the right people, join all the right committees. I'll even arrange lunch with my great friend Libbet Fauning—the very *top* society planner in LA. Really, you *must* call!" She presented me with her card, complete with head shot, measurements, and contact numbers. "Do you promise?" She gazed sincerely, winningly, into my eyes.

"I promise, Julia." Oh, I had her number, all right, but at least I liked this last effort. How could I not? Vicuprofen or no, I quickly reminded myself that she was, after all, a performer, and attempted to temper the heady effects of her Shiny attention. I refocused on rooting out possible geographic sources of her changeable accents.

"After your wedding I fly to Milano, I sign a million-dollar deal to be the face of a luxury automotive company! Yes! At first they wanted Gwyneth Paltrow, that cow, but I won out. In New York now I visit the showrooms. It is very important to my position—and to my *public,* of course—that I am always pulled together. And it is very good for designers to align with *me*! Maybe," she dangled, "one day we see what exciting looks we find for you!" Ah, Julia. This knowledgeable, intensely Shiny creature, offering her well-honed Sherpa skills and select passage into her exclusive, glamorous world in exchange for . . . what, exactly?

We selected magazines; I chose a few, but Julia stripped the rows recklessly. I fumbled for loose bills in my bag, dropping my boarding pass on the counter in the fuss. Julia slapped down a Pacificus Corporate Card. I stared in disbelief at her name on the card; I couldn't wait to tell Jamey, the original corporate-governance Boy Scout. A sudden cloud of alarm appeared. "You fly coach," she murmured softly, and snatched the card away, backpedaling seamlessly. "I must tell you what a good corporate wife I am! I negotiated a *very* special rate with the Ritz-Carlton—down from $2500 to $1800 a night! I say to my friend GianCarlo, the manager: 'GianCarlo, you know I *always* reserve Presidential Suite, but now I am corporate, so I must watch the pennies!' It will be difficult, of course, but I will make do! GianCarlo would be sad if we did not stay with him! And yet, Simon tells me 'Darling, we must tighten our belts!' So I tighten the belt; I save our company money!" She smiled her most perfect Brite-smile (mental note: schedule dental cleaning), which sparkled perfectly in the white airport gleam.

Next stop: Starbucks. Julia traced the spine of the new issue of *Gloss*, nestled in the crook of my arm. "Those girlfriends of yours— neither has returned even one of my calls. I had my agents *and* my team of publicists follow up, too—especially on the beauty campaign your Leslie pitched me nonstop. I am repped by the *best*. Your friends would do well to speak to them. You will maybe let the girls know I'll be in town. At the Ritz," she added, like I could forget. So *that* was the quid pro quo: groove in LA for groove in New York. At a loss, I took a bite from a sample plate of cut blueberry muffin. Julia watched closely, as if fascinated, then blurted, "Oh, Stacey! When I get to be *your* age, I so *hope* I will be as secure as you!" Equally stunned—by her bluntness—I swallowed, hard. Assessing her here in the bright airport glare, even through her heavy makeup, I suspected she had quite a few years on me and undoubtedly many more miles. I held my tongue, mostly out of shock, but she followed up quickly. "Oh! Is maybe okay for *you* . . . but I could *never*!" Her hands passed over protruding, Versace-clad hipbones, and she puffed her cheeks especially to let me glimpse her fate should she indulge in one single excess.

In listening to the ensuing prattle (her monologue had cleanly segued onto the "mystical brilliance of Shih Tzus"), I realized that she truly had no idea what the future held in terms of Pacificus and her husband's business position. Simon hadn't told her anything but "tighten your belt," and I smiled a little sadly as I considered the shock and lifestyle change she was in for. The party, as it were, was very definitely over.

First Class was called to board, and Julia borrowed my coffee, popping two tiny purple pills into her mouth. Special Services ush-ered Simon forward (he had a death-grip on Julia's arm as if it were a child's favored stuffed animal), but she pulled back and winked to me, "I drink only hot water and lemon with this!" She held up a vial of cayenne pepper. "It has miraculous properties. I study for my up-coming movie! It's a small part, but the director, he loves me! I go for three days to Toronto! I play the funny neighbor, a nightclub singer with a heart of gold!"

Our names were called over the PA: our bump-ups came through, and we boarded in the second round. As the final preparation an-nouncement blared, Jamey's cell rang. "It's a *mitzvah*!" screamed Sheila, triumphant. Jamey and I yelped and high-fived; Simon and Julia glanced back to see what the commotion was about.

"We got the house!" I called up excitedly. They stared, stone-faced, then looked at each other. From what I could see as the cur-tains were pulled between cabins, they were smiling.

We touched down at Kennedy this last time, and the harsh reality of the real estate commitment began to sink in: moving day was just a few weeks away. There was no time to waste but there certainly was plenty of time to think. And, on my part, to dread.

My girlfriends, on the other hand, were holding up just fine, planning a bon voyage party at our favorite restaurant, Elaine's. The afternoon of this last hurrah, after bagging the last items destined for a Salvation Army pickup (I'd unearthed three pairs of acid-washed jeans and a jacket—who *was* I in 1987?), I dressed out of a suitcase in my bare, mostly silent studio. I selected a simple black silk tank dress and sling-backs, worthy of Mrs. Peel. So elegant. So flattering. So . . . funereal. And so appropriately suited to my tenuous mood.

I tried to shake away all weepy thoughts, envisioning spry hummingbirds zipping deftly around sunlit bowers of magenta bougainvillea, in place of the three hypertensive pigeons currently squatting on sooty barbed wire outside my window. That would, after all, be the glorious new view from my Mediterranean-tiled bedroom terrace, up high in the Canyon. "Onwards and upwards," I said aloud, oversmiling into a compact mirror, practicing being a gracious and composed Corporate Wife. I spritzed Opium into the air, stepped through the cloud of scent, and headed out into the navy blue evening.

The wine, champagne, and music were already flowing; warmth and familiarity hung like cigar smoke as I accepted embraces and well wishes. The mood was festive and upbeat and honestly, if it hadn't been for the fact that *I* was the one leaving on a jet plane, one-way, it would have been like any other convivial evening at clubby Elaine's. There was a large gift box on a center table, wrapped beautifully with red satin ribbon: videos including *The Player*, *Swimming With Sharks*, and *Day of the Locust*; books by Joan Didion, Raymond Chandler, and Budd Schulberg. "Reference guides for navigating the turbulent Pacific(us) waters," read the card, signed by all. Parting gifts, like on a game show.

Leslie pulled up with a glass of champagne. "How're you doing?"

"Kinda numb, actually." I gazed around the too-familiar room. "It's surreal, to purposely close out almost every trace of my life in New York."

"Well, tell me again about the dream house, and describe *exactly* how large *my* bathroom and walk-in closet will be." Oh yes: closets! A New York woman's wildest fantasy. That part truly wouldn't disappoint.

Words like enviable, glamorous, and once in-a-lifetime were being sprinkled about. What a wonderful decision I'd made! Oh, my friends were good, I had to admit. For a while, I almost did begin to relax and enjoy myself. Maybe LA wouldn't be so bad after all. And, once we were settled, I certainly could count on visitors. A Yankees game had just begun and played mutely on the TV. Every now and then a collective cheer or jeer rose from the gathering crowd—the standard end-of-summer soundtrack of New York life. Of my life.

Jamey ambled in, accompanied by an impressive brigade of pin-striped, blond creatures. Instinctively I stiffened, all good humor draining from my body. "The Germans are here," I whispered to Nancy. "I hate them."

She laughed and emulated Julia perfectly. "It's a little late for that. Get over it and greet them. *Nicely*, by the way. Be a lady and remember: no sulking tonight!" She pushed me forward with a sharp oomph in my lower back. I glared back at her, then warmly shook hands all around.

As waiters approached for drink orders, Willem, Jamey's boss and the chairman of Commerz, took my elbow and asked if we could speak in private. Uneasy, I tried to catch Jamey's eye, but he was already knee-deep in conversation with Willem's wife Ute (I liked to call her Uterus in private; it still makes me smile . . .) about their recent move from Munich to Scarsdale. Naturally.

Together, Willem and I braved the clusters of conversation and smoke and slipped through a doorway to the rarely used back room of the restaurant. We sat among the empty checkered tables, and I stared at his suit jacket, mesmerized by the prominent gold Commerz lapel-pin. Time for the pep talk, I braced. Placate the whining wife. Let's see: good corporate citizen, team player, probably something about the Gipper or, in this case, maybe a kipper?

He fumbled uncomfortably. "Stacey."

"Yes, Willem."

"It's good to see you." I nodded. "I know this has not been easy. I know you still are not . . . thrilled about moving to Los Angeles."

"No." Nope. I would not make this easy for him. So stubborn! But someone had to take the blame for this . . . life *disruption*, and I was long past blaming Jamey. I could tell Willem wasn't used to resistance—especially from an employee's wife, no matter how senior. Other Commerz spouses I'd met were supportive and amenable when it came to this sort of heavily compensated, work-related life shift which, if one really thought about it, on the surface wouldn't actually appear such a terrible hardship. It was only Beverly Hills, for godsakes; not Siberia or Timbuktu.

"Look," he continued, "I do want to thank you for being a trooper. We really appreciate you . . . pitching in for the team." Gag. He tried a new tack: "Maybe it will be fun. You may learn to love it there: movie premieres, new dresses, celebrities—Ute and I are crazy about Vin Diesel," he confessed excitedly. "You might even get to meet him!" Ah yes: life as an endless party. Double gag. What was I, a kitten? He checked my face and thought better of continuing in that vein.

He began again. "Stacey. We truly appreciate the . . . sacrifice you're making. We really do need James out there full-time to sit on Pacificus. You've met the senior management, of course." He grimaced; he and Uterus had witnessed the wedding blitzkrieg firsthand. "Anyway, we've got an awful lot riding on the success of that acquisition. It won't be easy, and James just cannot continue to run things from New York. They've been kicking up a storm in the industry and the trades, I'm sure you're aware—and we must protect ourselves. I mean, *your husband and I* need to protect ourselves.

The Board is *not* happy." He looked at me, steely now, for emphasis. "Can you understand?" I nodded again, fully aware that even now, with my brand new husband's career on the line, I was behaving like a contrary child. I tried, feebly, to make it better.

"It's just that, Willem . . . it's been such a crazy year, you know? I'm a hard-core New Yorker and I don't want to think of LA as home. And of course I've had the pleasure of . . . *them*. I promise you, there aren't enough parties or clothing or, frankly, anti-anxiety meds or dinners with Vin Diesel to counteract the emotional hurricane that is them."

He laughed. "Well," he said slowly, hopefully, "it's just for two years, you know; until things are settled. It'll go by like *this*." He snapped his fingers to show me. "I hear the house you found is beautiful. And the weather: Ach! Spectacular! I know what: think of it as your own private hotel in California. Just a hotel, that's all. The Hotel California! Now that's very funny!" He patted my knee. Good kitten.

Let's have some fun. "Speaking of the house, Willem," I emptied my eyes of guile, "I understand it was rented before, to the last watchdog from Commerz who 'sat on' Pacificus. Whatever happened to him?"

Willem winced and appraised me anew. He was debating with himself, I could see, and he chose his words carefully. "There have been a few, over the years, 'watchdogs,' as you say. But the one to whom you're referring, well . . . He was an accountant, and let's just say, there are many . . . *temptations* out in Hollywood, yes?" I waited. "It is difficult to resist, er . . . *temptations*, especially when Simon and Phil put them directly in one's path." I raised my eyebrows. "Yes. And then a private investigator is sent to 'capture the moments.' Crazy stuff, really . . ." He waved a casual, dismissive hand.

My mind played with the disclosure. Photos? Of what? Drugs, wanton underage nymphets . . . *animals*? A slew of senior finance watchdogs—adult *men*, neutered and rendered harmless as puppies?

So. The crazy stories were true? "They *blackmailed* him—and the company?" Jesus! This type of calculated entrapment was as far a cry from the silly wedding mischief as murder is from pickpocketing. What exactly were we getting into?

Willem shook his head very fast. "No, no. Blackmail's a very strong word, Stacey." Yeah, right. "It's more like they . . . *compromised* him. He was very weak." Willem hung his head, as if shamed by the character flaw. How, well, *German* of him, I couldn't help but think. "They can be a bit . . . predatory and cruel, that lot. Of course, the studio was privately held at the time; we had only a minority interest. And we could never really *prove* anything, outright . . ." Hmm. I was sure this unpleasant episode somehow related to the so-called "accounting discrepancies" I'd overheard Jamey discuss. "Anyway, his divorce is just about final, and let's just say he's resting comfortably now, back in Munich."

I smiled in spite of myself. "So, what you're saying is, 'LA proved too much for the man'?" I never could resist musical quotes.

"Gladys Knight!" he guessed correctly, relieved the worst was over, and added, "All irregularities are being, uh . . . cleaned up internally. You and James are seasoned, and just married. You won't be so easily led astray. Besides, now we own the studio outright; we'll have complete control over them and their activities. James has our absolute confidence and support." Willem beamed, hoping his seeming straightforwardness would end the conversation and allay any fears. I smiled wanly in return. He and Jamey simply refused to see the Trio as other than mischievous, colorful characters out of the *Little Rascals*, naughty troublemakers who could be kept in line with a firm hand.

Willem wanted a drink and a quick getaway. That much was clear, although he did wait for me to stand before he bolted to rejoin the party. I headed to the ladies' room for a few minutes of quiet, away from my over-cheerful friends. I opened a small window and lit a cigarette in the closed stall, joyful sounds muffling through the thin wooden doors. Let's see: just two years, eh? Yeah, sure. I exhaled loudly. Better make sure Jamey got that in writing and signed in blood.

At the sink I dabbed at my face, attempting to wash away my now certain foreboding that this glittering, corporately subsidized adventure in Hollywood would change our lives—my life, anyway— forever. I stared evenly at my reflection and took a snapshot, trying to picture what I might look like, who I might be, when I next gazed into this mirror. Oh well: it was a done deal. There was nothing left to debate, discuss, or negotiate. So, then:

Goodbye, New York. And hello to a whole new state of mind: Welcome to the Hotel California. You can check out any time you like, I hear. But you can never leave.

CHAPTER 5

THE HOTEL CALIFORNIA

> When he has penetrated into hostile territory, but to
> no great distance, it is facile ground. On facile ground,
> halt not.
>
> —Sun Tzu, *The Art of War*

*E*ight a.m. in the West!" proclaimed the Bose clock radio cheerily each and every weekday morning in my spacious yellow kitchen. And like clockwork here's what would happen: I sipped coffee in my CCNY sweatshirt and shorts, the sun shone brightly, birds chirped and screeched about, and the apoplectic German shepherd next door began his usual barking/yelping frenzy, heralding the arrival of that particular day's work crews, their assorted trucks and punishingly loud equipment. Adding to the din, the gate, phones, fax, and doors would begin to ring (eight a.m. decidedly the earliest New York or Germany would dare call the house) and a sartorially upgraded, Zegna-jacketed, Gucci-loafered Jamey would attempt to scooch past me, his assortment of PDAs having buzzed continually since six a.m. (never too early/late to call *them*). With the trades and his briefcase tucked under his arm, he'd attempt to escape to the office in his rental car to avoid what would or wouldn't happen within the next half-hour: the arrival of the purposefully disagreeable, always-surly Miss Isabel, our three-times-a-week housekeeper, who came with the house, came with an attitude, and would sashay in according to her very own schedule (with her very own key).

"Hey!" I managed to snag a passing belt loop as Jamey raced by. "Where do you think you're going? You need to stay and hear about how the tree roots have cut through the plumbing, gas, and electrical lines. I don't know what to authorize anymore or how to vet the pricing. You're 'the Man,' as Isabel would say."

The day we took possession of our Hollywood Dream House, we realized we were the proud new tenants of the prettiest house that didn't work, in even the most basic ways: one of the movers innocently flushed a toilet the first morning, sending an unending river of sludge down the driveway, narrowly missing a stack of prized boxes marked SHOES/FRAGILE! It had been downhill, literally, ever since; all key systems and utilities were in a similar state of disrepair.

Jamey (big soft eyes, voice beyond sincere) took my coffee and gulped. "Urgent meeting—sorry, hon. Gotta go."

"Oh I know. You're a massive big deal now and *everything* is urgent with you. But don't you 'hon' me. I thought we were in this together."

He handed me back an empty mug. "Stacey, I find it difficult to believe that someone capable of throwing together a New York City Marathon and coordinating seventeen city agencies for a World Series parade can't handle these work crews. This is not an apartment, this is a house, and this is what happens with a house: it falls apart. Let's get it fixed and move on."

"Yeah? Well, the thing is, *hon*, it's endless—these things that fall apart. And I signed on to be *your* wife, not the house's wife. I'm trapped here every day, let out only sometimes for lunch, lectured by plumbers, electricians, and utility workers. My brain's glazed over from atrophy and torpor. I actually *miss* the five guys who seemed to live in my basement in New York. I'd just leave the keys with the super and they'd take care of everything. When does the fun start for me?"

"Poor you, you sad, abused little housewife," he mocked, kissing my neck as I giggled in spite of myself. "You know I'd gladly trade places."

My heart sank a little: I knew he would. He'd been coming home at the end of each day more and more drained from the deepening battle of wills with Simon *et al.* I softened a bit; the Tom Cruise premiere had been a disaster. I could only imagine what his days were really like, trapped in that office with Them. I made a note to work harder on Jamey (who protested vehemently when I so much as mentioned the notion) to get in there (for lunch, maybe?) as soon as possible to check out the situation for myself. In any event, I supposed (and as Sheila had so eloquently warned), this *was* my end of the bargain. The least I could do was show my support and maintain the home fires, as it were . . . if only the gas lines worked properly! I turned and kissed him full on the mouth, squeezing him tight. This blissful domestic scene was apparently much to the dismay of the entering Isabel, who sighed dramatically and muttered mean-spiritedly under her breath like a demented Mexican Mrs. Danvers. "Ay! That stoopid *perro!*" She trilled her r's for added value. "I kill him one day! *Verdad!*" She glared at us.

"Hola, Isabel," we said in solemn unison, and watched her brush past (resplendent today in a ruched celadon Gucci shift and matching mules) to shut the radio and turn up the TV, changing the channel from a muted low speed/high speed car chase to Univision and her favored daily *telenovela, Un Día Grande.* God forbid there'd be a scheduling glitch—she'd never show up at all.

Ignoring me, she nodded respectfully toward Jamey, made a huge production of tying her "Kiss the Cook" apron and set about preparing *café con leche* for us all—the one thing she did kindly and without prodding. As soon as her program came back from commercial, she backtalked the screen intently in Spanglish, and I knew I'd lost her attention until the next break. Jamey took advantage of this lull to sneak out (not before pinching my butt, of course), but I did overhear him giving instructions to an array of handymen to snake the gutters, caulk the bathroom windows, and install a new water pump before gunning his rental motor and driving away.

The *café* was ready, and a shampoo jingle played on the TV. Isabel sang along lightly. "Isabel," I ventured, attempting to butter her up before asking her to polish the new wedding silver, "what a pretty dress you're wearing."

She smiled sadly. "*Si*—from Meeses Longon. I have a new photo. I show you." She perked up and ran to find her purse. Isabel rarely mentioned the brief tenure of the Commerz Guy (or the Idiot, as she so colorfully termed him), but she'd absolutely adored the couple who'd leased the house before him, the Longons, who were, in fact, long gone, having bought a tremendous mansion farther up the Canyon with a full-time, live-in staff of five. A tremendous mansion that, I assumed, worked just fine. Mr. Longon (or the *Good* Man, as she reverentially referred to him) was a music biz honcho and Meeses Longon was apparently quite beautiful and social. Isabel worshipped her and referenced her constantly. She displayed the prized photo right under my nose, carefully pincing the edges with cherry-red nail tips: the Longons, as featured in the *Shinier Sheet*, elegantly draped in evening dress.

She adored them mostly, I deduced, as they traveled much of the time and weren't around underfoot as I was now, constantly checking her progress. Also, Mrs. Longon periodically lavished Isabel with her castoff, "gently worn" designer clothes, and Isabel wore them proudly, to work even, as she had today. Another day might see her in a wispy lavender chiffon Scaasi cocktail dress and slingbacks, or perhaps a sea-green Bill Blass high-waisted luncheon suit with matching duster. She was heartbroken she wasn't chosen to go along to the newer, bigger, cleaner house and would often take this regrettable slight out on me. She'd respond to my most innocuous request by sighing heavily, hand on heart or shaking her head impatiently. "*Ay!* That is *not* how Meeses Longon would have done that. She was *very* smart." The implication being, of course, that I was not. "Meeses Longon always said the plumbing here would be the death of her. Poor woman! She was always so busy and social, always hostessing, going to parties. She had no time for all these workmen in the house." Unlike me: total loser. *I* think maybe, just maybe, if Meeses Longon had paid the slightest attention back then I wouldn't have been in this mess right now. . . . And let's not forget that Isabel had at least six months of extremely light work with no one living in at all (except, of course, the doomed Idiot), at full pay, while brokers were showing the property.

So there I was, trapped most days in the glorious but useless hilltop hacienda, phoning/waiting/supervising/unpacking and, of course, terrified of leaving so as not to miss any of these 8 a.m.–5 p.m. windowed appointments. On the days Isabel *did* show up—freedom! I would fire up our old Mustang and, armed with printed directions from MapQuest (I'd become Queen of MapQuest), practice driving, run errands, and test routes to markets, salons, cleaners, and shops I'd heard mentioned. This proved to be a frightening proposition for me (and for others as well), especially on Thursdays (Garbage Day!) when the narrow canyon corridors are crammed with large colored bins—a harrowing weekly experience, all three thus far.

I tried to amuse myself with my newfound domesticity and empty time, unaccustomed as I was to *not* having a mission, a goal, a pressing objective to occupy my mind every waking hour of every day. So . . . what did I do? I crafted detailed e-mail missives to my girlfriends back in New York—clever little anecdotes about my newly unglamorous homemaking travails as well as breathless reportage on A-, B-, and C-level star sightings at Costco, Ralph's, or Rite-Aid, ubiquitous as Ugg boots: "Kirstie Alley buys depilatory cream!" After seeing him three times in two days (Whole Foods, Home Depot, and Starbucks), I titled one essay, "On Nodding Terms with Scott Baio!" You get the picture.

I baked—you got it—heart-shaped cinnamon cookies and attempted other complicated recipes to the rousing approval of the

ensconced handymen, an adoring focus group, but much to the con-
sternation of a glowering Isabel. "These men—ugh! They are like
coyote: you feed them, they never leave!" she'd disapprove, then
swear like a sailor, bilingually.

For a brief period, I was so lonely I even attempted to befriend
Isabel, but was rebuked:

"I *would* teach you how to make empanadas, but I think you do
better to watch your figure!"

"I *could* tell you what's happening on *Un Día Grande* but is far
too complicated to explain."

"Tut, tut. Meeses Longon had beautiful fashion sense, and her
clothes were always light and airy, not dark and heavy like yours,"
she'd comment with yet another pained look, fingering my New York
Mrs. Peel wardrobe distastefully: a series of woolen jackets, sweaters,
and dresses. It was clear she would not be wanting my castoffs, nor a
photo, nor my friendship. At all.

Aside from tormenting me ingeniously (spices next to sponges, Mr.
Clean next to baking supplies, pasta next to soap), the one thing Isabel
did seem to enjoy was "neatening" (her phrase—mine was "going
through like candy") the expensive goodie bag swag I'd amassed in
my makeup and skin care drawers: the other half of the MAC, Clar-
ins, and Perricone product lines I *didn't* give her by rote. Every day
was spa day for Isabel! By the time her celebrity chat show *El Gordo
y la Flaca* began, she'd be contentedly installed at my dressing-room
mirror, Telemundo blasting, giving herself a facial peel and makeover.
And like clockwork, as soon as the broadcast ended she'd reappear,
beautifully turned out, and announce: "I going now. Meeses Longon
always let me leave early." At a certain point I was too demoralized
to argue.

But back to today. The phone rang and rang, though I could barely
hear it over the relentless banging of plumbing pipes combined with
stereophonic strains of *Bésame Tonto*, (1–2 p.m., Univision) blaring
upstairs and down. It was Leslie, calling from bed, nursing a flu. Or,

as she cleverly put it, "I'm eating salt, carbo-loading, and watching Julia Roberts die too young in something." I took the cordless and shut myself into the expansive, elegant guest bathroom, which was larger and better appointed than my entire studio on East 71st Street. Ah—so *that's* where the crystal candlesticks and pitcher had gotten to—Isabel! Workmen were in the kitchen checking the gas meters, Pacificus techs were in our office/gym, fixing DSL lines, and Isabel was somewhere, most likely squeezing the last bit of life from yet another sixty-dollar tube of Laura Mercier foundation. I sat on the closed toilet and sighed. Leslie spoke. "Stacey? Why are you whispering? What is that clicking? And which is it today, boredom or loneliness?"

"*Crippling* boredom and *stifling* loneliness, to be clear. And in massive quantities. I will perish here, I promise you. I'm hiding from the maid and the handymen as we speak. And the phone clicks all the time." I paused. "Welcome to my world . . ."

Leslie coughed. "Well I'm glad to see you're honing your excellent dramatic skills. Listen, I wanted to apologize for being out of touch—the office has been crazy."

"That's why I don't bother calling. I know you guys are busy moving and shaking . . ." I caught myself whining and stopped.

"No! I wanted to see if your e-mail was true—the silent treatment you received at that premiere."

I played with the toilet paper, rolling up, rolling down. "Yup." I made faces at myself in the mirror. In an effort to rescue his new bride (me) from the mountain of overwhelming suburban terrors, Jamey had planned our very first night of Hollywood dazzle: invites to the latest Tom Cruise spectacular and exclusive after-party at the home of the Paramount honcho who'd produced the film. Off I'd run, secretly thrilled at my first Hollywood Wife opportunity to overpay at Frederic Fekkai (after begging Leslie to get me in!). I'd starved and shimmied myself into a navy Prada cocktail dress I'd purchased (retail—ugh!) after successfully MapQuesting Neiman

Marcus. Jamey picked me up in a limo (!) and we headed in style to Grumman's Chinese Theater. The crowds parted as we walked the red carpet (thisclose to Angelina Jolie, I tell you!), cameras snapping all around as my heart pounded proudly, exultantly—it was, after all, every little American girl's dream, no? I felt so happy, so glamorous, so special. Maybe this move *was* a positive thing—maybe greatness awaited after all . . .

Jamey spotted some prominent agents and producers chatting in the lobby, and we went up to the group to introduce ourselves. We patiently awaited a break in their conversation, oversmiling; we waited some more. It was soon apparent that no acknowledgment would come. They continued on, ignoring us completely, like we didn't exist. Jamey gripped my hand, miserable, staple-gunning me to his side. Mortified, I willed the channel to change, for us to disappear while attempting to look nonplussed. During this humiliating, extended diss, I spied Simon and Barb in a corner, following our discomfort delightedly as they smirked, sniggered, and stage-whispered to yet another circle of familiar-looking people as well as some of the cast. It all clicked. I understood at once: widespread, massive damage had been done, and way before we arrived that evening. Another pointed message, delivered and received. Their first shot warning salvo at the wedding should not have been taken lightly, their intent crystal clear: this was *their* world, they'd marked *their* territory. Our most unwelcome presence would only barely be tolerated, and only momentarily. I knew all this in one single camera flash that glittering, A-list Hollywood evening as I looked on, heartbroken, watching my brand-new husband try—valiantly, gamely—to break through the premeditated, impenetrable wall of silence and dislike.

"Welcome to my world," I said again, dispassionately. "It's not all bad, though. As our psycho real-estate broker omnisciently predicted, they *have* started calling—girls from the *Shinier Sheet*, remember? Sheila said that wives of high-profile agents, executives, and film-makers would call with social invitations, by virtue of my being married to such an important man and so new on the scene. And you know what? She was right."

"Oh great. The Stepford Barbie Lunch Brigade. How perfectly fifties."

"You got it: the Hollywood welcome version of a Bundt cake. But I guess this is what goes on. I'll tell you, though, these girls can talk box office, test screenings, and media placements with the best of them. They're incredibly bright," I said, maybe a little too admiringly.

A pause. "Really," replied Leslie, dubiously. "I hope I recognize you when I see you next. Just don't . . . cross over. Don't let them infiltrate you."

"What are you talking about?" I sensed a not-so-muffled resentment.

"The pod people."

"Please, Les." What was I supposed to do, say no? And truth be told, the girls who had called seemed, so, well . . . nice. "I'm just trying to learn the ropes, here. Conventional, 'normal' rules and behavior don't seem to apply. It's like learning another language from scratch. I have to at least hunt for allies. There's a really nasty undercurrent of gossip and lies swirling about, and it's clear it all originates from the executive suite of Pacificus. I get a sense we're being warned about something. These marriages are really complicit; the women know everything that goes on. They're like . . . business partners, and therefore they're just as important. I've already managed to get Jamey two canceled meetings back on—Simon and Phil's dirty fingerprints were all over that. Jamey's calls to reschedule were never even returned. *And* I booked him a round of golf and got him into a charity poker night. All through the women. It seems to be a matter of dispelling the disinformation, one person at a time. Of me being a team player, helping Jamey." I was very pleased with myself on this end, actually. And after all, for the most part, it certainly did *seem* to be an intensely lovely if not an intensely seductive lifestyle on offer, sitting high in the rarefied air atop the rigorously enforced caste system in this one-industry town. Time to work out, to shop, and to not eat. Places to go to show off the whole package. It didn't really seem so very bad at all, now that I was privy to it from the inside. If only . . .

"Fascinating. Booking meetings and arranging play-dates for your husband as a matter of survival. What a great way to use your college degree. . . . It took you forever to pay off your student loans, Stace. I can't believe nothing's turned up work-wise, with your background."

I cringed even further at her tone; I agreed, and this was my ultimate sore point. The first few feelers I'd put out came back stone cold. The next batch, too. Never had I received such blanket rejection and stonewalling out of hand, and I wasn't at all sure how to handle it. Pointedly, probable opportunities vanished once these so-called prospects connected my new last name with Pacificus. More specifically, connected me with *Jamey*. . . . I didn't dare question anyone further, my confidence too shaken, too afraid of the answer to insist on clarification.

Leslie obviously took my silence as answer enough, as she carefully changed the subject. "Have you heard from the Silicone Bombshell?"

Another little pang. "Julia? Of course not. I lived up to my promise to call her, but I suppose ever since you X'ed her from her beauty campaign"—I waited while she finished laughing—"that *you* so feverishly pitched." More laughter, coughing. "Among so many other things, you know she holds that against me."

"Stace, no one's ever heard of her. And she's had so much . . . work done. *Bad* work. Listen, I have a favor to ask—it's more of a treat, actually. I have a prospective client, Dante, who runs a foofy salon out there. He wants New York representation to expand his product line. Will you check it out for me? They've promised a full makeover."

A catering van honked "La Cucaracha," and Isabel (inside) and the German shepherd (outside) both started howling again. "E-mail the info and I'll set it up. I gotta run, Les. The gardeners are here, and I need to talk to them about the vines."

I clicked off as she was saying, "G'bye, lady of the manor," and emerged from the safety of my cocoon. What I hadn't told Leslie was that not only had *they* been calling and taking me to lunch, but after Jamey and I were photographed by the trades at said horrifying premiere, so did boutique managers, stylists, and jewelers, offering their services and, in some cases, thirty-percent discounts. I liked those calls the best.

I went around back, mindful of the exposed electric wiring (we still had no overhead light in the kitchen) to meet Javier and his gardening crew. On one of my first frightful automotive excursions, I'd discovered a local garden center (via MapQuest) and set out to buy citrus trees, flowering bushes, clever-looking garden implements, and more. I felt exultant, very Smith & Hawken, very Martha. I eagerly envisioned creating the perfect outdoor living environment, now that I actually had an outdoors in which to live. If I had to be trapped at the house, I reasoned, at least I could put my time to good use.

As electricians and plumbers banged, drilled, and plumbed away, I would be outside potting, pruning, and Miracle-Gro-ing to the strains of old Fleetwood Mac. I was hoping to persuade Javier to oversee my efforts and get him to cut back some of the overgrown ivy and colorful vines that seemed particularly thick.

"*Cállate!* Shut up, you stoopid *perro!*" Isabel swore out the window as a handsome guy in jeans and flannel shirt offered his hand to me. "Javier," I began casually, "I had a thought we might cut back the bougainvillea. I think there might be some hummingbird nests in the overgrowth. What do you think?"

He stared blankly, sizing up my hysteria quotient. And rightly so. "Oh Mrs. Makepeace, those are not . . . hummingbirds. I'm pretty sure they're . . . well, I'm *sure* those are . . . *rats'* nests. No one's told you there's a rat epidemic in Beverly Hills? It's even worse out by Malibu. I saw one creeping around the roof a while ago, but you weren't here yet, and most people don't like to cut anything back, so . . ." He continued, but I heard nothing but ringing in my ears. You do *not* say to a New York City girl that she has rats in her overgrown but otherwise perfectly enchanting bougainvillea—that's a Health Code violation, for godsakes!

On and on he went (canyon rats . . . not like in the subway . . . natural habitat, nature preserve at the end of our road . . . blah blah blah) but all I heard was his final diagnosis: good-bye bougainvillea, at least until spring, and hello to an exciting new facet of my LA experience: Pest Control. From his truck he pulled a picture book, such as one might give to a child, and proceeded to teach me an entirely new vocabulary (*in color,* no less, so I could astutely identify local species: carpet beetles, scorpions, poisonous spiders, snakes of all kinds, carpenter ants, termites, killer bees) as well as keying me in to what other skulky creatures might be in residence (owls, mongoose, opossum, skunk). Javier gave the high sign to his crew, who enthusiastically set about hacking up the deeply upsetting vines, especially the once very charming ivy. "Rats *love* ivy!" Javier had mentioned. I now hated ivy. I sat off to the side, hyperventilating under my Smith & Hawken umbrella as he unearthed yet another too-large-for-a-hummingbird nest from the overgrowth. "You really shouldn't watch, Mrs. Makepeace . . ." I took him at his word and blared Stevie's *Wild Heart* CD to drown out the cacophony of hacking, scuttling traffic copters, and buzzing chainsaws.

Clutching the phone I escaped yet again to the safety of the powder room, awaiting any of three Pest Control companies recommended by Javier to return my desperate calls. I closed my eyes and concentrated, "White winged dove. White winged dove . . ." Calmer, I opened them. Ah, look! Joining the silver candlesticks were now three crystal ashtrays and a Delft ceramic pitcher. . . . Almost instantly there was a knock on the locked door: "I go now, Meeses. Is too loud, I can't hear my shows." Isabel, departing an hour early, heels receding on the tiled floor before I could even respond. I ventured out to the kitchen and poured some Lillet into a coffee mug (a little medicinal sherry, just to steady my frazzled-by-vermin nerves, of course). I sipped, then gulped, then poured a little more.

As dusk drew near the cleanup of branches and pipes was well underway. The handymen filtered out to their respective vans, and I went to receive Javier's report: nine nests of varying species uncovered; no one, happily, had been home. Relieved, I thanked him profusely, tipped him for the extra work, and walked him to his truck. "You'll get the hang of canyon living, Mrs. Makepeace, but you need to mellow out about the wildlife. Remember, it was their canyon first. I'm head of the local association, so feel free to call with any questions." I nodded, trying not to breathe on him. ("Mad Studio wife, pushed over the edge by rodent trauma . . .") "I'm gonna give you something that changed my life. It can change yours, too. Maybe you'll come to the Celebrity Centre one day." With that, he handed me a dog-eared paperback, penciled notes scribbled in the margins. I studied his gift as he drove away: a copy of *Dianetics*. I'd been recruited!

Emboldened by the Lillet and the "all clear" diagnosis, I trudged upstairs, determined to attack the last few remaining boxes. Shortly after seven, I heard Jamey's excited voice calling from the foyer, "Stace! You gotta see this!"

I scrambled down the steps, arms full of packing materials.

"You'll never believe it!" he cried. "We've got reindeer!" I flipped rapidly through Javier's flashcards in my mind's eye. "He ran out in front of the car—I almost hit him, but I stopped just in time! Isn't that cool?" Both hands splayed open on his head, the delighted New York City boy, making antlers, up and down. Dumping the bubble wrap, I dashed to the gate and sure enough, through the open bars I saw what he did: Rudolph—well, sort of. An enormous, healthy buck, anyway, trotting nonchalantly toward the low-fenced empty lot-cum-nature preserve at the end of our road. The German shepherd was going nuts, hurling himself repeatedly against his chain-link pen. I grinned back at Jamey in the doorway, intrigued. My eyes followed the huge creature's receding form as best I could in the deepening twilight, then settled curiously on some low shapes skulking slowly in the buck's wake. I squinted: skinny, hunching dogs paced nearer, completely unfazed by the shepherd's hysteria. A Ferrari purred expensively and slowed to turn two driveways down, its high-beams illuminating the street. And the skinny dogs as well; all four of them. Coyote. I'd never seen one up close, but I knew instinctively, anyway. An uneasy sensation flooded me: the largest one gazed back steadily, panting; its watchful eyes glinted, unafraid. I recognized that brazen stare: a challenge. I pushed back from the bars reflexively, my pulse picking up speed, and backed straight into Jamey. Coyote. I shuddered, oddly tense, as Jamey wrapped his arms around me, mistaking my fear for cold. Just as quickly the Ferrari turned and the street was dark again. But I could still feel their intimidating, lingering presence.

Jamey tried to break the mood. "Okay, *Discovery Live*'s over—let's go inside. I'm cooking tonight, remember?" he said brightly. I stood rigid, glaring defiantly into the darkness, wanting the intruders to go away. Jamey softened and spoke reluctantly into my hair. "They're usually around when I come home, and I see them sometimes early morning, too, from the treadmill. It's . . . unsettling, I know. We'll just have to remember to keep the gate closed."

I finally let my body go limp, and settled back into Jamey's body. Thoroughly exhausted, I allowed myself to be led back inside.

PART II

Tactical Dispositions

CHAPTER 6

WELCOME TO THE JUNGLE

> Mountain forests, rugged steeps, marshes and fens—
> all country that is hard to traverse, this is difficult
> ground. On difficult ground, I would keep pushing on
> along the road.
>
> —Sun Tzu, *The Art of War*

ante's *so* looking forward to meeting you! Are we considering . . . lightening up a bit, today?' chirped the perfect receptionist, Candy. Or was it Cookie? Either way, think Christie Brinkley, circa 1984.

"I'm staying brown, but thanks," I replied, filling out my NEW CLIENT card. So this was Dante's on Beverly, Tuesday at high noon. Pastel Venetian chandeliers multiplied in walls of etched mirror and chrome, as did Japanese-y bouquets of calla lilies and bamboo and dozens of gardenia-scented Slatkin candles, all underscored by Moby's techno strains. Stylist's chairs were filled with tin-foil-wrapped semi-blond heads, all talking and gesturing with red-stringed wrists between sips of branded bottled water. A living, breathing *Shinier Sheet*! I giggled to myself, formulating my next Letter from LA e-mail review: a sociological fieldwork experiment of epic proportions!

Six well-toned women, each resembling Goldie Hawn at varying life stages (*was* one of them actually Goldie? Hmm) in shimmery, gauzy butterfly tops and tight jeans waited impatiently on deck on Balinese benches, alternately glaring at their watches and at me, apparently for (a) poor outfit choice and (b) receiving ultra-timely VIP service courtesy of Leslie's PR pull. I made a note: buy gold/silvery/bronzey butterfly tops and shoes and somehow manage to wiggle into size 26 jeans. Pronto! My lunchtime makeover had begun, a testdrive of Dante's latest "Princess-in-an-Hour" offering. Translation: get beautiful, get distracted. Don't eat.

Midway to the treatment rooms in back, Candy/Cookie hurried after me, "Your robe, Mrs. Makepeace!" Dead silence broke out on the main floor. Sweeping soul-crushing judgment rang loud and clear in its place. Silver-wrapped heads turned and stared, gawking. Oh, yes. We certainly were curiosities these days, Jamey and me. Frontburner topics of conversation, in fact. You would think, wouldn't you, that after one whole month in town, the flame of novelty and fascination would have waned? You *would* actually think so, I do believe. But, as is so often the case with these sorts of oppressively provincial things, you'd be wrong.

Cringing, I ducked into the prescribed cubicle and unzipped my once-favored/now obviously uncool navy-and-khaki Ellen Tracy dress. It had looked so great this morning at the Peninsula, I'd thought, at "tea" with Libbet Fauning. Now I scolded myself that I hadn't gone home to change before descending into this Shiny vortex of fabulosity and groove. I sighed: at least Libbet had been sweet . . . but then again, Nancy had set up the tête-à-tête after researching the masthead. Libbet was thrilled at having been sought out by the editor of *Gloss*, and extended me every courtesy, including an "Arrivals" shot of Jamey and me at the ill-fated premiere, my navy Prada shimmering just the way it should. It was kind of a kick (if not a bit redemptive, I thought) to be included in the reportage.

And then. It began almost instantly: the disheartening (though not entirely unexpected) swell of the Greek Chorus. I could catch only every other morsel, but I got the gist of the prevailing narrative and filled in the blanks: "So *that's* what she looks like!" "Did you *see* that *dress?* Like a *tax* attorney!" "I hear she hates it here." "Do you blame her? I feel badly . . ." "Me too. I *was* gonna call, but Dan told me to stay away." "Simon'll crush them." "Tom says to keep out of it. She and her husband'll be back in New York by Christmas anyway, where they belong." Dot dot dot.

And so, there you go. Team Pacificus had been doing a bang-up job on *every* front: muckraking, disparaging, and defaming our characters well in advance of our having met much of anyone personally. We were outsiders, *arrivistes!* And from *New York,* for godsakes! *Civilians! Business* people. Insurgent interlopers from the *advertising* world! Ugh! Here to play power couple, destroy Pacificus, and meddle in Simon and Julia's affairs. Jamey didn't *respect* Simon's experience and abilities! We just didn't understand how things *worked!* Ignorant and in the hot seat, we were soon to be sent fleeing, by the masters, back to the safe, boring confines of the other, less interesting, less important coast . . .

My pathetic, masochistic eavesdropping was interrupted by a knock, and four intimidatingly hip stylists proceeded to consult, advise, suggest, and prepare me aggressively for every possible service item, all at once. Everything about me was wrong, apparently, and they most sincerely wanted to make me right. I was warned it might take two, even three visits, to get the job done properly. One called Luz produced a blond color wheel and all four cooed ecstatically, strongly urging me to strongly consider highlights . . . and maybe skip a meal or two. Oh, yeah. I was emotionally and physically trapped, now, in junior high school hell, no two ways about it. But I didn't dare leave; I was too terrified to move. I tried to relax, to tune out the drama and enjoy the attention, the tweezing, waxing, facial ablutions, hair color (I steadfastly insisted on renewing my Emma-mahogany), manicure and pedicure (I chose Jungle Red, by the way), but I was too existentially distracted, and my hardworking ears strained to grasp every emphatically negative syllable through the thin bamboo divider. Finally, the last technician pressed cucumbers on my eyelids and left the room to let the seaweed mask harden.

Alone and immobilized in my oppressive cocoon of algae, hair dye, humiliation, and anger, my heart pounded, my brain reeled, and my body perspired. This "princess treat" had been anything but. Oh . . . groan. No! But of course. How completely perfect. . . . Those all-too-familiar tingles threatened, then took hold, deep under layers of overheated, over-scented towels. "White winged dove . . . white winged dove!" I begged, desperately, in my silence. But this time they just would not be denied.

"And what is *this*?!" cried Dante, horrified, arriving for my cut and blow-out just as the facialist peeled the hypo-allergenic seaweed mask to reveal red, blotchy welts on my face and neck and . . . "Mrs. Makepeace! I cannot *imagine* what has happened! Luz! Jean-Pierre!" He flustered and swished wildly; his outcry enough to attract even some silver-wrapped choral members. I cringed even further, willing Dante to stop raving and end the theatrics. Paxil and Ativan were offered readily—Percodan, Ephedra, Adderall, and a formidable array of triplicate psychotropics, somehow, too. Wow. But alas, no Benadryl. Oh, I'd be the talk of tonight's idiot body-part fundraiser, you can bet . . . Restless Leg, was it? Julia'd have a field day—this was fodder for a week! "Please *please* do not tell Leslie—I beg you! I'll make this up to you—I will . . ." Dante wailed, but I could barely hear him. Nor did I care when I looked in the mirror and Sharon Osbourne stared back: patchy and crimson with wife-of-an-astronaut hair. It may not have been the blow-dry of a lifetime, but at least not one more word was said about going blond . . .

Spotty with Caladryl and wrapped in a borrowed neck scarf and Jackie-O-style blackout sunglasses, I peeked tentatively out to the larger salon, jonesing big-time for an antihistamine. Get thee to a Rite-Aid! By cleverly mimicking Mata Hari, I attracted the attention of a passing sweep-up girl, who very kindly (if very confusedly) snuck me out the rear service door, sending the valet around back with my car.

°   °   °

It was right there, staring at me as I entered the drugstore—pow! Just past Scott Baio. It practically radiated among Fabio-covered romances and Laker Girls calendars, next to the liquor section, right by checkout. The unabridged and complete *Art of War*. I sat in the garage and finished a cigarette (number two of a million), waiting for the Benadryl to kick in and thinking of the laugh I hoped Jamey and I would share. Alcohol, tobacco, *and* firearms: one-stop shopping at that super, super store! I hauled myself and my purchases out of the car and into the kitchen, thinking only of drowning the day's anxieties in Pinot Noir. And my residual anger too: how could those lemmings blindly believe the worst about me? Even worse—about Jamey?

The idea of dolling up for abusive display at yet another Industry event was too tiring for words. I kicked off my sandals, took a deep sip of wine, and checked the invite tacked to the cork board: Business Attire. I snorted: this particular idiom, I'd learned the hard way, meant full-on cocktail and every bit of jewelry one owned or could borrow. A box of precious Mallomars (rarer than snow in LA, FedExed by my mother) sat out on the counter. . . . I glanced at the Bose radio clock: just three o'clock.

"Jamey?" I called tentatively, not believing for an instant he'd be home in the middle of the day. No response. I padded into the living room. Jamey sat silently, hunched over handwritten notepapers, phone logs, and yellow stickies spread out on the heavy mission table. I leaned and kissed his bent head, slipping my news into his line of vision. "Look, sweetie: we made the Women's Sporting Pages." Jamey didn't look up but flinched uncomfortably when I reached to rub his neck. I exhaled slowly and sat down, scanning the papers in front of him. I tried again. "I didn't realize you'd be working from home. You'll never believe what just happened at the salon . . ." I started, intending to make a joke, but stopped immediately as the swimming scribbled fragments clicked into sentences. On letterhead, no less. "Holy shit!" I breathed. "'From the desk of Simon Mallis' . . ."

Evidence. Proof. Confirmation. Of the psychosis. Of the propaganda campaign. Of the jihad. Against us.

"Yup," Jamey sighed. "He's a ruthless, Machiavellian cowboy. I found these notes crammed into my briefcase after my breakfast staff meeting—probably by Guy, Simon's long-suffering assistant. Mine too, now. He must be taking pity on me. Three more meetings and a lunch canceled today, so I came home to try and connect the dots, think my way through it." He looked up, grim and dejected. "It isn't pretty."

I studied the legal pad in Jamey's lap. He'd assembled what looked like a plan, stickied with scrawled comments punctuated by exclamation points. Simon's plan. For dispatching us. Combined with what I'd gleaned by osmosis (and confirmed by today's salon debacle), there was little doubt, little amusement left: Simon was indeed flexing every muscle of his considerable influence, large and small; nearly everyone was under some sort of obligation to him, professionally and/or personally. The movie business was war for Simon, and winning was everything. He guarded his position ferociously, and would win at any cost. To win properly *and* realize true glory (in Simon's opinion) meant that his opponent should be neutralized, decimated, gasping for breath, eviscerated. Indeed, there were vanquished and bloodied bodies all over town (let alone Jamey's watchdog predecessor) that could attest to his skillful executions and Napoleonic campaigns of terror. He'd proudly seen to that, and that others would spread tales of his might.

"Simon's well aware that all their contracts are up at year's end. I can't be counted on to re-up them by rote and at huge increases in salary and perks, as other Commerz officials have in the past. If his first level of defense is offense, it looks like his weapon of choice is the relentless, no-holds-barred smear campaign." He handed me three pages of phone logs, from just yesterday and this morning alone.

"Right. Savage against you, nurturing and paternal to everyone else." I scanned the papers. Judging by the boldface names listed and volume of calls, Simon was wielding this tool like a scythe.

"As far as I can tell, the general theme is Public Ruination and Personal Damnation. Scenario One: 'Reach out to top creative leaders and distributors. Spread angst and uncertainty. Imply the worst about Pacificus' future in regard to Makepeace's capabilities'—*my* capabilities—'and their own financial futures if tied to me. Exhibitors and filmmakers'—stickie: those morons!—'will go crazy. Business will fail miserably.' He'll have *them* call *me*—stickie: the little prick!—'in fear and anger.' I'll have no choice but to re-up him, at any cost.

"Scenario Two: 'Reach out to the creative community: imply, hint, threaten, cajole. Business fails miserably.' The little prick, me, *doesn't* renegotiate his contract. Everyone calls *me*, hysterical, and *then* my German bosses in fear and anger. *They* re-up Simon, at any cost.

"Scenario Three: Everybody calls everybody. Hysteria and mayhem rule the day. Business fails miserably. The Germans fire me—stickie: as publicly as possible!—and reinstate Simon to right the studio at any cost. And oh, will he make them pay! Never will his authority or judgment be questioned again.

"And if all three scenarios fail there seems to be a Plan B: Burn down the building, destroy the business, and annihilate *me*." He paused for a breath. "In any event, Simon seems to figure he can't possibly lose."

"Charming. Nice heads-up by Guy, though. Shouldn't you call New York?"

"What's Willem going to do? He's been down this road before. Hell, he figures prominently on the phone log. And these are just calls Simon's made from the office." He sat back and looked at me for the first time. "Big hair, huh?" And then he added, "It's just a turf battle, Stace. I can handle it. By the way, you're pink. Did you know?" He leaned in and kissed my nose, then returned to mulling his compilation of doom.

Back in the kitchen, I poured another glass of wine and contemplated my not-so-very-funny-anymore gag purchase, Simon's crazy

Chinese war manual. I stared for a moment, hesitating, then opened the binding randomly: *"Ponder and deliberate before you make a move."* Hmm. *"If it is to your advantage, make a forward move; if not, stay where you are."* I wandered outside and considered our rapidly diminishing options. *"Only* a turf battle?" Please! If this truly was the Wild West, then Jamey and I—logical, rational, play-by-the-rules thinkers—were ill-equipped to deal with the lawlessness of it all. Aside from passively allowing the abuse to mount, I could discern only three possible courses of action, all equally unpleasant: Conform, compete, or die. I scrutinized the shorn trellis, ruminating. I mean . . . *could* all the purported wackiness be true? Were we *really* being set up to be run out of town? And: *did* this crap really happen? For real?

"Knowledge is power." I stared at the book in my hand, craving direction. Think, Stacey! We needed some sort of strategy, I knew that much. Some pragmatic advice, at the very least. Surely we weren't the only ones ever to find themselves in this predicament out here. I just wanted the antagonism to end. But where even to begin? Reluctantly, an answer did come to mind, but I hardly wanted to admit its validity even as I searched for the number and forced myself to dial. I had no choice, I repeated to myself; there was nowhere else to turn. There was, in fact, only one Wife I'd known for longer than one lunch . . .

"Hello, Mallory? It's Stacey Makepeace." Yup. Blue Curacao: Mallory Sharp. The social barometer girl in high school who made it her business to know everyone else's. I was sure she'd be right up to speed on our situation, and might just be thrilled to offer some guidance to a new studio chief's wife. If money talks, I figured, then retainers should blare, and on a very high volume: Jamey *was* her husband John's client, after all.

No sooner had a drinks invitation left my lips than Mallory gushingly whinnied her acceptance. "I've been champing at the bit to see your new digs! What's the square footage again?" (Everyone in LA is a real-estate expert, by the way.) "You *must* tell me the pedigree and provenance! But let's do lunch first. Let's see: tomorrow I have yogilates, pressotherapy, and a quickie committee meet in town. . . . How about La Scala at one?" I smiled: I'd been there four times in the past two weeks.

We listened (as I had the past four lunches) with rapt fascination and murmured appropriate yummy noises as our soap-star handsome waiter (Luca/Lorenzo/Tyler?) enthusiastically recited the day's specials (hunks of mèat and pastas smothered in cream sauce). As on every other visit, Luca/Lorenzo/Tyler acted crestfallen and shocked (shocked!) that we then murmured fat noises and declined all exquisite culinary delights in favor of chopped baby artichokes (no oil) and a plate of chopped greens (lemon on the side). Thus for the price of an Armani blouse (well okay, maybe *Emporio* Armani) two women can enable each other to not eat for an hour, leaving even lighter than when they arrived. Diuretic lunching—*bon appetit!* This scene (one of my favorites) was replayed at every table, every lunchtime, at a slew of similarly Shiny restaurants all over town.

Luca/Lorenzo/Tyler thus dispatched, Mallory presented me with a welcome gift: a series of phone consultations with an enlightened color expert, known simply as Magda. "She will absolutely change your life!"

"Does she not meet in person?" I was confused. "How will she know what colors I am?"

"That's the beauty of Magda. She's so incredibly clairvoyant, she can read you over the phone. She counsels Paris and Nicole, you know. And Lindsay Lohan." Ah yes: award-winning recipes for successful lives. Mallory shooed away a basket of freshly baked carbohydrates, pushed up the sleeves of her aqua cashmere twinset, took a notepad from her peach-studded Chloe bag, and got down to business, interviewing me as would a doctor: whom had I met, where did we go, what did they say?

"Well, let's see. I so liked Cara Fra—"

"Kleptomaniac."

"And I had a very nice time with Laurie Thom—"

"Just out of rehab."

"Then Jane and Annie joined me for coffee—"

"They're having an affair." She held my gaze. "With each other. No one knows yet."

"But you do."

"Of course! Listen, Stacey . . ." As she rambled (having written nothing) I realized that the net, apparently, amounted to a very troubling diagnosis for Dr. Mallory, and thus, for me: the friendly girls who had called, whom I liked, were—gasp!—B and C wives.

"Meaning?" I asked.

"Meaning their husbands have position, but maybe their last few projects haven't done so well and they're sliding." Oh. "Down the ladder. They'll be friendly because your husband's taken over Pacificus, but they'll wait to see who wins out, Jamey or Simon," she pronounced matter-of-factly. Hmm. As inevitably would she, I had no doubt. "By the way, when Julia hears you had tea with Libbet—*well*! That's her territory; she'll take it as a direct threat! She'll make your life and everyone in it miserable, in every way imaginable. You know," she lamented, "she barely even acknowledges *me* anymore, since John brought Jamey into Pacificus. I'm co-chairing a youth event with her, trying to get back in her good graces. We'll see if it works." Fingers crossed, her green eyes turned solemnly heavenwards.

An image appeared: Julia as a demented Evita. Ick. "Bottom-line it for me, Mal."

"My advice, Stacey, is this: figure out how to get along with Julia—and fast. *All* the A girls take their cues from her. And obviously, have your husband lay off Simon. Way off."

I almost choked on my iced tea. Like that would happen. "It's just business, Mallory! And by the way, there *is* no competition—Jamey bought Pacificus outright, and he'll do what he sees fit. It's not Simon's call." Why was this concept so difficult for everyone to grasp? How old were we? And where exactly was the source of the mysterious Kool-Aid everyone but me seemed to be drinking? I eyed her Arnold Palmer suspiciously and pushed some leaves around. "This is crazy."

"Oh, it's *effing* crazy," Mallory annotated cheerfully, highlighting the universally conformist Hollywood hypocrisy and its unquestioned acceptance. "But everything's interrelated out here: business stature equals social stature, especially in film. It's a clearly defined hierarchy, old as the Hollywood Hills. The law of the jungle rules, and Simon's the big cat. Who's got pole position. That's why you're getting the cold shoulder: they're running the court of public opinion; they have the upper hand. At least for now." She toyed with an armful of David Yurman bracelets, happily running scenarios and mixing her metaphors. She waved suddenly and oversmiled past my head: an ethereal blond lunched alone, loaded down with crystal amulets and gauze, surrounded by an impressive number of shopping bags. She didn't respond to Mallory's overtures but gazed dreamily at the clubby wood walls, fingering a red yarn bracelet.

"That's Inga Sturm," Mallory whispered, not quite sotto. "Better living through chemistry. Dabbles in Eastern philosophy, bulimia, and retail therapy. She'll buy *anything*—some deep-seated salesperson-acceptance thing. Her husband, Scott, is also a client of John's. *Big*-time box office—he's best in the biz at blowing things up. We're *very* close. Scott's a well-known Simon-and-Phil hater—they messed with his 'first-look' deal and slashed his budgets when he refused to cast Julia, then they came back after him when he walked out. He famously refuses to work for Pacificus, and it drives Simon nuts." She narrowed her lids and focused on my Canal Street Vuitton knockoff. I obscured it discreetly with my napkin. It hardly registered: Mallory was having a brainwave. I could see her agile mind working many angles at once.

"I got it!" she announced. "Scott might just be thrilled to meet Jamey and reconsider for the future, and vice versa. I'll set up a dinner at Morton's, Simon's favorite restaurant. We'll send a signal to the self-proclaimed King and Queen of Hollywood. It'll be fun to smoke 'em out, see how far they're willing to go. Leave it to me. Obviously, *you* have nothing to lose." *Obviously*, I agreed; although I had (as I always did with girls like Mallory) the sneaking suspicion that somehow there'd be something in it for her.

"Thanks for the invite," dribbled Scott, "we don't really get out much." Small wonder, I grimaced, swatting an errant paw off my thigh—and not for the first time, mind you. I glared at the unseeing Inga as the appetizers arrived and the third bottle of Opus One was drained. I'd just begun to like him, too, in a drunken fraternity prankster kind of way. Jamey certainly did. But his groping had recently ramped up in direct correlation to his alcohol intake. Which was a lot. I slapped at him and kicked Jamey hard under the table. Scott seemed to take my reactions as playful as he stepped his efforts up a notch with each parry. By the time after-dinner drinks were served (to him only) he was gassing it up big-time (or as Mallory might say, in direct correlation to his box-office). And what a contrast he was to poor Inga: downcast and translucent; as you waited for her to answer a question, the air seemed to leak from the room. I couldn't believe these two were a couple—of anything.

John turned to me and smiled. "So Stacey, Jamey told me about your reindeer adventure. Are you enjoying life in the Canyon?"

Good. A neutral opportunity to bypass my proselytizing Scientologist and get things straight on the local wildlife front. "Well, the gardeners had to cut back our bougainvillea. We had rats' nests."

"Rats are very good luck," Inga commented quietly.

"Rat *figurines* are lucky, in the Chinese Zodiac," Mallory corrected.

"Also," I continued, "we seem to have a whole posse of coyote living at the end of our street. What's that about?"

Scott blew a gutful of wine through his nose. "Coyotes love *pussy*! It's a delicacy!" His eyes twinkled with adolescent cleverness as he wiped his sweaty face with an Armani'd sleeve. "This town is infested. Keep your pussy inside or it'll get eaten . . ."

Inga ignored him and shuddered. "Coyote are very unlucky, in real life and in the zodiac. They are the tricksters of Native American lore and have only negative energy." She twirled the red yarn at her wrist. "Have you seen any snakes yet, Stacey? It's bad karma, you know, to kill them on your property. *Certain* financial ruin." After that grave pronouncement, everyone at the table would have crossed themselves if they could have done so without seeming silly.

I pushed past the karmic trivia. "Anyway, I heard them again last night—the coyotes, I mean—whooping it up and partying like rock stars."

Mallory's cat's eyes gleamed, excited. "That means they had a really good kill, like a Golden Retriever or something." Suddenly, Inga stood and headed yet again to the Ladies' Room, from which she'd return, I knew by now, with a slightly elevated (though barely evident) mood.

Mallory leaned close. "Inga's very . . . sensitive. But Scott's a *huge* client—*tons* of money," she reminded again by way of explanation.

"By the way," I swallowed a bite of swordfish carpaccio, "I received an invite to a charity leather-goods sale you're hosting. From my friend Nancy in New York."

"Really?" she hesitated, confused. "Are you thinking of coming?" I nodded, confused as well. Mallory composed herself. "One of the designers, Karen, is a very big deal—well, her producer-husband is—and Patsy's very . . . earthy. Not a lot of, y'know, money or position, but she knows, like, *everything* about fashion. She's from New York, too," she added, semi-deferentially. Ah, right. Hard-core, irrefutable New York street cred. At least I still had that, even in my current loser/pariah form.

As Inga reappeared, the men seized upon their main dish: a detailed history of dastardly deeds committed by Simon, the reigning

Sin-Eating Amorality Czar, latter-day Ovitzian Overlord, our self-declared foe. I listened a moment, then turned away in disgust. But my ears remained open. The town was polarized, it seemed, divided on the subject of Him, as it would be with anyone who'd survived twenty-plus years in such a volatile business. He wasn't loved, that was for sure. It was more a matter of respect, bordering heavily on fear. Simon was an information junkie, relentlessly hunting and hoarding others' personal information like a miser, using tidbits in sharply directed, well-planned strikes to control people and projects like puppets. At least *he* thought so. He hadn't been doing himself any favors these past few years by putting immense pressure on (some would say, and as Scott did say, blackmailing) various creative leaders to cast Julia in high-profile roles for which (as a former beauty queen/nurse/lounge singer with questionable skills and questionable accent) she had neither the calling nor the talent.

Simon always knew who was sleeping with whom, who was in debt and why, who was addicted to what. His "years in" and status ensured that he'd invested in long-term relationships; he'd been around as the current crop of established producers, actors, directors, and executives developed their own careers. He was a living Black Book, not unlike Heidi Fleiss. Or Anthony Pellicano. Oh, he knew where the bodies were buried, all right, but often because he'd helped bury them himself. And, as Jamey and John had learned during the due diligence phase on the acquisition, unproven allegations of bad judgment, "aggressive" bookkeeping, and security breaches had haunted him throughout his career. Those he'd made money with and for tolerated him and viewed him as a necessary evil. But there were equally as many who were secretly thrilled at Jamey's arrival. There was gossip in every corner of town about the possibility of Simon's ouster, and rabid speculation about who might replace him.

Distracted, the girls bantered about an upcoming spate of black-tie galas supporting local new-age gurus. I jumped in, fascinated. "Inga, tell me about your red string."

"This?" she touched the yarn gently. "It's my Kabbalah bracelet. Ancient Jewish mysticism. It wards off ambient negative forces and protects me against the Evil Eye. The color red absorbs bad energy." Cautiously I surveyed the room. Negative energy, here at Morton's? My eyes settled on a noisy table featuring Bob Evans, a crew of PDA'd, Gucci'd talent agents and a bevy of what looked like Russian hookers. Hmm. Maybe so.

Mallory jumped in too. "I stopped by the Kabbalah Center to buy more blessed water. Now that's big-time protection"—she looked at me—"from pure springs imbued with ancient meditations. The price just went up, by the way. It's more expensive than Evian!" That was a good thing, I assumed, judging by her expression. "Stacey, you should look into buying *all* the protective talismans—attending classes and circle, too." She arched her eyebrows pointedly.

"Maybe you should buy a *bagua* mirror for your husband's office, to deflect evil back on the evil doers," Inga commented darkly.

"Inga! You're mixing philosophies again!" sighed Mallory, exasperated, then brightened. "You know, I need to find a new discussion group. On the same social level, of course." She dropped her voice. "I'm trying to distance myself from Zandra—you know, John's partner's wife? I hear that Tom's leaving her for that exotic new actress on *General Hospital*. Zandra doesn't even know they're having an affair!"

"But I thought Zandra was your best friend! Why wouldn't you warn her?" Inga's eyes misted at Mallory's coldhearted disregard; she fingered the crystals at her neck anxiously.

"Oh don't get me wrong. I *adore* Zandra—we were practically raised together, but, you know, I don't want to make waves. Because of the *business*." She glanced nervously at John. "You understand—what can I do? It's gonna get nasty, and I don't want to, uh . . . interfere." Ah. So: by *rote* business alliances outweighed personal ones. And at the first whiff of any impending shit storm, everyone ran for cover from the impending fallout. I was learning a lot. Listening to

Mallory scheme, I was certain I was next on deck; it was only a matter of time.

"Of course," Inga agreed sadly. "Well, *I* study—very seriously, you understand—with Rabbi Schwartz at Lady Selena's home in Bel Air. She's right near Green's, which is useful." Mallory nodded solemnly. Green's, I'd learned, was the one dry cleaner in LA County who would handle high-end items, like evening dresses, without requiring a signed waiver. For this privilege, however, they arbitrarily assigned insane pricing, refusing to quote any final cost up front.

Inga continued: "We were off for the summer, naturally, but classes will start up again soon. He's unbelievably holy and enlightened, this Rav—he's tutored Madonna, you know." Mallory swooned at that, but Inga kept going. "When I meditate on his chanting, I can feel the vibrations. I can see about bringing you, if you'd like?" Her eyes drifted to the ceiling, a rapturous look on her face.

"The vibrations?" I asked.

Mallory answered offhandedly, "From the Zohar—the Kabbalah text. The classes are all in Aramaic; so are the texts you'll need to buy. You simply . . . absorb the energy and you're healed!" She whirled back to Inga. "Lady Selena Lawson? She's very private, practically a recluse. I would be too, I suppose, if I were, you know, *tainted* like her. I would move! But," she reconsidered, glancing my way, "she *is* staggeringly rich and *said* to be staggeringly spiritual. I wonder, though, if she and her friends aren't considered a bit . . . well, you know, *B-list*? Or even C?" Mallory wrinkled her nose, debating internally, and offered to me as explanation: "Her late husband owned the largest hamburger chain in Southern California, and then the world. Warren Beatty used to eat there, but then he stopped." She thought a moment, and looked back to Inga. "There *are* better circles, socially—but no one would ever need to know. And I *have* always wanted to see inside that house. . . . But you can't tell a soul, either of you."

"Lady Selena has a highly developed sixth chakra," Inga stated reverentially. "She even knits her own clothing—and yoga mats too, from yak hair. On a real loom. She spends a season each year meditating in a mud hut in Guatemala."

I piped up. "Why were your classes off for summer? Was she in Guatemala?"

They both stared. Finally, Mallory answered. "We were in Malibu and then in Capri, after the Venice Film Festival." Ah, so like Sheila, God and the Rav didn't like hanging at the beach, and followed a school-year calendar for a summer pass. Got it.

Inga smiled mysteriously. "Life is all about vibrations, Stacey." Deep. Still radiating, she pulled an envelope and wrapped packages from a giant Chanel sac. "These," she pronounced, "are welcome gifts, from me to you. It sounds like you can put these cleansing tools to good use."

"Inga, I don't know what to say." Truly, I didn't. I read the inscription aloud. "A gift of a *feng shui* consultation and blessing on your new home, with Contessa Madalena."

Mallory was wildly impressed. "She's *very* exclusive, the Contessa! Did you get her from Lady Selena?" she asked enviously of Inga, who just smiled serenely. I unwrapped the packages: a cow and a frog.

Inga recited, "That's a wish-fulfilling cow totem and a three-legged money toad. You put the cow on your desk for financial success, and the money frog on the ground. Be careful not to lose the coin I put in there—that would be a sure precursor of financial disaster!" Anxious glances were exchanged once again. Inga fingered her crystals, lips moving. My one wish for the cow was that it not be too bloody late in New York to call the girls! This chick had a dollar chip on every number on the instant karma roulette board—a sure winner, you can bet, in some transom, somewhere.

I thanked her and stashed the animals under the table. "So, Inga, what is it that you do?" I asked politely.

"Do?"

"Yes. With your time, I mean. Aside from your enlightenment classes."

She squinted at the ceiling, as if for help in answering. "Oh. Nothing."

"Nothing? That can't be."

We waited. Finally, Mallory offered, "Inga, I don't work in an office, but I'm the busiest person I know."

Inga stared blankly. "No. Honestly, I do nothing." A pause. "Well. I like animals. Very much. Scott makes an awful lot of money," she reassured us. A longer pause. "I caught him cheating last year with my best friend. So I decided to spend more time at home and now everything's fine. It's all just fine," she repeated singsong, twirling a loose strand of colorless hair. "Oh, and I have two Bichons, Missy and Sassy," she added, remembering.

Was it irony? I didn't think so. The guys stopped their conversation and looked over. Inga floated away again, eyes to the wall. I tried another tack. "Surely, then, these animals are a passion. Are you working on any committees?" Everyone was on a committee, I'd learned, for something or other.

"Well, yes. I'm raising funds to develop therapies for mentally defective animals. I handed in my list already."

"That's very admirable."

"Yes." A beat. "I have a very nice life."

Scott stood to introduce Jamey and John to some action-figure actor friends who held court at varying tables. As they left, Mallory, who'd been surreptitiously checking her watch, announced abruptly that she needed to call her sitter. I watched her head out the front doors, glancing back as she went. For no reason I could explain my heart beat a little faster.

Inga and I sat alone, staring at our plates. After a beat she leaned toward me. "I really need to confess something, Stacey. May I speak freely?"

"Sure, Inga. Is everything all right?"

She looked on the brink of tears. "Nothing is right at all! This morning I was in Sinfonia Folata's boutique. Sinfonia herself was there. I had pulled some gowns aside—you know, my Autistic Animals benefit? It's in a few weeks. Poor little dears, it really is so sad." I waited.

"Anyway, there were a few things I liked—you know she designs all animal prints." I shuddered slightly, but she didn't seem to notice.

"Three or four of the dresses looked really very nice on me, so I was thinking I'd pick one . . . but the salesgirls are *so* persuasive, and they always give me champagne, even in the morning. And then Sinfonia practically *forced* me to buy them all. *With* matching accessories. She said she'd give me a discount, not to tell anybody. It would be our secret. I mean, two of the dresses were around $2200 each—which isn't bad for daywear, right?" She didn't wait for a reply. "But the others, a beaded Dalmatian and a sequined tabby cat—the shawls have teeny-tiny cat and dog heads—they were $5200 each, plus shoes and bags." Tears welled behind glassy, dilated eyes. "Is it too much? What should I do?"

I was at a loss, I confess, confronting a one-day shopping bill equaling half of my education costs at CCNY—let alone of Sinfonia Folata junk. Inga obviously had serious issues, but I was in no position to turn away any friendship, no matter how insane. I was decisive. "Inga, we'll go tomorrow and return everything. You can't let them pressure you. I mean, salesgirls work on commission. It's their job to try and get you to exceed your limit. Scott will never know."

Inga's eyes cleared instantly. "I couldn't care less about the money, neither does Scott. He deludes himself that I don't know what he's doing with all those young girls on location. You'll see. You're newlyweds. Your husband still likes you. And the starlets haven't begun throwing themselves at him. *Yet* . . . You know," she gazed intently at me, "I can have him drug tested. Anytime I want." And with that, her eyes clouded over again. "So: do you think it's too much to wear Dalmatian beads or tabby sequins when there are so many damaged animals around? What about *that*?"

It was my turn to be aghast, unable to give her the absolution she so desperately craved. My eyes darted to search out Jamey, thankfully heading back from Colin Farrell's starlet-stuffed table, and not a moment too soon: the most unctuous of the chino-clad, knee-padded wait-staff led more of his ilk to our table. Barely touched plates and glasses were cleared (Scott snatched his back) and an enormous production was set in motion: a jeroboam of Dom Perignon, a decanter of iced vodka, and a kilo of Beluga caviar with accompaniments were laid out before us. Colorful china, shot glasses, crystal flutes, and mother-of-pearl caviar spoons were passed as we looked to each other to suss out the uber-generous party. By now, even neighboring tables were gaping openly, intrigued as well.

The waiter (Luca? Lorenzo? Tyler?) smugly recited (to the room): "'Scott, John, ladies—a simple oversight has prevented us from dining with you in person. We look forward to working with y'all again soon. Our compliments, Simon and Julia Mallis.'" LucaLorenzoTyler sighed, "What class! Mr. Mallis has *such* generosity of spirit! Enjoy!"

A camera emitted flashes on cue—a stringer for the *Shinier Sheet*, we were apprised by the card left in his wake. The surrounding tables applauded, impressed with such a bountiful and elaborate piece of theater. I couldn't quite read the expression on Mallory's face (since she wouldn't look at me). Was she weighing her own Julia-implied repercussions, or had she in fact sold us out in a bid to get back into Julia's good graces? Inga, in another rare moment of clarity, squeezed my arm in support; perhaps she wasn't as "out of it" as she appeared. Scott and John lunged at the bottles breathlessly, giggling like children on Christmas morning. I held Jamey's anguished gaze: aggravated, mortified, and ultimately undermined, again.

Jamey paid the bill (Simon had naturally charged his classy "generosity of spirit" to us), and as we all rose to leave, he alone slumped down in his seat again, jaw clenched, eyes dull. As I attempted to decipher the cause of yet more heartbreak, applause erupted once more and this time crescendoed to an ovation: Simon had entered the restaurant and was taking a deep bow, hat in hand. Behind him was Julia, vogue-ing energetically in the doorway. And then. Like an extended bad dream sequence, Willem and Uterus appeared and rushed past them both, and then past our table, making a breathless bee-line through the cheering crowd, heading toward . . . but of course! Vin Diesel, standing alone at an empty table set for six. Vin smiled, arms outstretched, expectantly awaiting *them* . . .

Without exchanging a word, I understood instantly that Jamey had no idea his boss was even in town. I grabbed his lifeless hand, pulling him through the unnerving conviviality outside to the valet. We picked up our dirty Mustang and headed up the hill in silence, narrowly missing a darting reindeer and a hunching, grinning coyote.

CHAPTER 7

DAMN THE TORPEDOES!

Ground the possession of which imports great advantage to either side is contentious ground. On contentious ground, attack not. On contentious ground, I would hurry up my rear.

—Sun Tzu, *The Art of War*

A few mornings later I stood underwhelmed, staring hopelessly at the racks in my closet. Thirty-five years of sensible work clothes and winter: what could I expect to find? I was attempting to determine what to wear based on the confounding directions set forth by the duplicitous Mallory's color guru, Magda the Annoying. After a worthless half hour (I am a green spirit, by the way: lush, full of life, etc., but only on the inside. Under no circumstance, in fact, am I to wear any semblance of green on my person), she asked what I had on tap for the day.

"I'm picking up my husband and taking him to lunch." After weeks of incessant hounding, Jamey had finally invited me to visit him at Pacificus Tower. Needless to say, I jumped at the chance to experience the office situation for myself.

"Ah! Stacey *Makepeace . . . right!* Pacificus!" Et tu, Magda? Did *everyone* in this town read *Variety*? "Now, this is all down to the

moon, which is very fickle by the way, so . . . today, I see that *protective* colors for you are *honeysuckle* and *primrose*. Call me tomorrow."
Click.

So now you understand my dressing-room dilemma, being that in point of fact honeysuckle and primrose are not actually colors at all. Jeez! I redialed for clarity. "Magda, it's Stacey again. I don't understand—"

"Of course you don't, darling; Mercury's retrograding through your twelfth house of ripe destiny. Try *iris* with a hint of *madder lake*, then. This combination will balance and calm you."

"But—" Click! So: blue or white iris? With or without yellow/purple stripes? And what exactly was madder lake? Oy!

I pulled on a charcoal Tahari suit over a white tee, stubbing my toe on the money frog (but not dislodging the coin) as I grabbed my MapQuested printouts and headed for the massive office tower in Century City (in the complex maze of massive office towers that is Century City) that housed the executive suite of Pacificus Studios. Jamey had started calling it the Tower of Doom. I couldn't begin to imagine why . . .

A hailstorm of invective and verbal assault rained pelting on the twenty-third floor as I buzzed through the security door: "Get *down*, you morons! *Down*, goddamnit!" Was that Simon? I crouched instinctively, eyes wild, as if for an air-raid drill. Combat-ready and crablike, I passed through the glass-and-chrome reception area of Pacificus Studios for the very first time. "Cover your desks, people! Cover *everything*! *Bastards*! I will *not* let those fuckers see what I'm developing! Jesus *H!*" Thus I was treated to a colorful interlude of flying paper and haphazardly scurrying infantry. Amid the chaos, a fey, blond man in his mid-thirties cowered, waiting to greet me, dressed like a throwback to a black and white Bing Crosby movie: Guy Nosey-Parker, ascot at the ready. Guy was the Trio's longtime executive assistant and had been appointed by Simon to work alongside Jamey as well, in the spirit of "cooperation" with his new boss until

Jamey hired his own West Coast support staff. This would, according to Simon, ensure a "smooth introduction and transition to the business." More likely, of course, the generous appointment was offered so that Simon could keep an eye on Jamey's every move.

"You must be Mrs. Makepeace. Welcome to Pacificus," Guy smiled thinly and winced as yet another high-spirited string of expletive-filled commands rang out. He took my arm and whispered confidentially, "This happens from time to time: Simon is famously paranoid. A helicopter's flying *thisclose* to the Tower. He hurls himself onto his desk to obscure scripts and budgets, then screams at everyone else to do the same. He's certain they're enemy competitor helicopters sent to spy and steal his ideas."

I laughed, uncertain. "But Guy, isn't it more likely that they're weather or police copters—even medivacs, flying over the gridlock of traffic? You *are* located next to two hospitals."

He raised his eyebrows and grinned. "But of course! Frankly, this is an appropriate initiation for you. Like I said, welcome to Pacificus."

I smiled; at least he had a game attitude. "Guy, where are you from? I was sure when we spoke by phone you had a British accent."

He seemed pleased I'd noticed. "Oh, that's my phone voice. Very professional, don't you think? I'm from Nebraska, but Mother was English and an old movie buff. She danced in the West End. She was a war bride, you know, and came to America to make her fortune. But Nebraska was as close as she ever got to Hollywood in her dancing days. After Father died, I moved us out here. She's gone now, I believe of a broken heart . . ." He sighed loudly, then stiffened. "My accent—it's not pretense, by any means. I am myself an *homage*—a tribute to her. That's why I went into show business." Guy brightened. "Mr. Makepeace is still in a meeting. How 'bout I give you a tour and then we'll end up at his temporary office—wait 'til you see," he sniggered. "We'll go the long way around, best first!" Guy pushed through heavy glass doors and led the way into a gleaming conference room with framed posters of recent Pacificus releases. A row of glass cases displayed awards and statuettes won over the years. He led me through a series of similar though smaller conference areas, each fully equipped with state of the art audio/visual gear. The last opened into a grand screening room, with plush burgundy stadium seating, rich brocade and tapestried hangings on the walls. It was quite a showpiece.

Guy winked knowingly. He pulled back a velvet curtain and motioned me to a small door. "That's the end of the public tour. Through here, well . . . here's where the action takes place, 24/7."

Hesitating, I took a deep breath and tried to reconcile the two worlds. Jamey had described the office to me, but he was right: I'd had to see for myself. "I know," said Guy. "Hardly what you'd expect from a film company. Still, low overhead and all that. The décor's actually worse on the other two floors, if you can believe it. This is where the higher-level executives work."

In direct opposition to the polished public spaces, the office interior had a labyrinthine, sweatshop feel: peeling movie posters were tacked or stapled directly onto utilitarian yellow-gray walls; faded, colorless carpeting was worn through in patches. Desks were crammed together, sometimes two or three to an office. VCRs and monitors were piled dangerously high with scripts, videotapes, and report files. The clutter continued down the obstacle course of narrow corridors. Piles and stacks had apparently accumulated over the years and were serving as dividers, separating the exterior offices from the jumbled maze of cubicles within. The air was musty and rife with servility. "Unbelievable," I murmured, wondering privately if this would ever pass health code inspection. I wheeled around to Guy. "Isn't there a cleaning staff to at least tidy up the overflow?"

Guy held my gaze. "I've been with Barb and Phil for about twelve years. We've had quite a few clean-up crews, but when Simon came along he was convinced they couldn't be trusted and were stealing information. These past few years he's brought in his personal housekeeping staff, from home. But I can't understand what they actually do." He reached to steady a particularly unstable tower of folders. "Recently there's been debris all over my desk in the mornings. I've had to spend the first hour of each day dustbusting." He paused. "You know, that's interesting. . . . Since your husband's arrival it's really been a mess, even by the low standards here—especially in his area. And no one's even used that room, well, as an *office*, anyway, in a long while." He watched me out of the corner of his eye. "I'll look into it. Anyway, they're packrats, convinced their most innocuous memo could have major value if it falls into the wrong hands. They shred *everything*." Now of that I was sure.

Guy continued conspiratorially, "This is very similar to Simon's home in Brentwood. The downstairs is decorated in grand style for entertaining—very *Gentleman's Smoking*." He affected a French accent. "But the upstairs rooms are quite basic. Not that I've been invited over *lately*, but I used to be. She hates me, you know," he added. "Miss Minnesota. Except when she wants something. Like petty cash, for instance, or to get her out of some traffic accident she's caused. Or to pick up clothing orders or refill her multiple prescriptions . . ." He broke off emotionally again. I looked away and waited for Guy to compose himself. I noticed for the first time that many eyes were upon us; heads poked out of offices and over cubicles. The ambient din of workaday chatter had subsided; everyone was silent, watching.

I followed Guy toward the corner suite where he, Barb, Phil, and Simon were housed. Although the rooms were larger, the décor was equally squalid, this time with hundreds of post-it stickies tacked on all available surfaces, including walls and windows. A giant, framed quotation measured the length of the wall: ALL WARFARE IS BASED ON DECEPTION—SUN TZU, THE ART OF WAR. I walked nearer, strangely compelled. "Simon's office," whispered Guy, with a trace of reverence. Or was it fear? Underneath were stacks of filing cabinets with computerized locks and keypads, like the ones on hotel safes.

"He changes the codes twice weekly," Guy added, eyes darting to the doorway so as not to get caught in the inner sanctum. On the opposite wall, over a Texas-sized desk loaded with scripts and video-tapes, were three provocative, autographed swimsuit posters—Julia, naturally, next to the Texas state flag and a hat stand displaying a Stetson assortment, day and evening. A low side table featured state-of-the-art medical equipment, all polished to a shine: hospital-issue scale, blood pressure equipment, a heart monitor, and a laminated, color-coded call sheet with emergency numbers of doctors and hos-pitals, ambulances and car services, acupuncturists and herbalists. Costco-sized bottles of multi-brand antacids were interspersed with prescription vials, jars labeled with Chinese characters as well as a "natural remedy" aisle's worth of homeopathic goodies: garlic pills (I knew it!), green tea capsules, and flaxseed oil.

Guy hurried me along nervously. Next up was Barb's office. Over Guy's shoulder I glimpsed princess-pink walls and brocade drapery, but I caught only a quick snippet of gilt-edged upholstery before Guy abruptly closed the door. "Barb's medium is casting a circle for an emergency session," he said anxiously. "We should move on. By the way, if you see her, be careful: I'm pretty sure she's off her meds again."

I burst out laughing.

He turned to face me. "I'm serious." Oh. He showed me through to a small alcove behind Barb's office with what resembled a mottled shower curtain serving as a door. Guy held the fabric so I'd have a full view of a dingy cubby with no windows. There was a wooden table stacked with papers, a telephone and laptop, a few folding chairs, and a *Sports Illustrated* wall calendar from 1997. A beaten up workout bench was shoved against a wall (covered with more papers and tapes); mismatched barbells were dumped atop a yoga mat that had seen better days. "What's this?" I asked in disbelief. And just as quickly, my heart sank: next to the laptop was our silver-framed wed-ding portrait. "Jesus," I breathed.

Just then a voice boomed and drawled from behind, causing Guy to jump. "Ah, Stacey! We've been expecting you!" I whirled around: Simon, baring rows of even, pointed teeth.

"Well, don't you just know every little thing," I replied dryly.

"It's my business to know, as you say, every little thing." We phony-smiled at each other evenly. "And what a lovely . . . dark suit. *So* New York. I see you've met Guy." He glared at Guy, who hung his head like a beaten dog and slunk away sideways. "Barb and I need just a few minutes with James, and then he's all yours. Oh, by the way, I have an invitation for you, from Julia."

I raised my eyebrows. "Really."

"Yes. She thought it might be nice for you to meet a few of her friends. You know, like a "girls' night." Casual; nothing fancy. *Intime*, she says. Next Wednesday at the house, around six-thirty? James and I will be down at the *Body Count* screening in Orange County, so I assume you'll be free." He waited a beat. I was well beyond respond-ing. "We seem to have gotten off on the wrong foot, Stacey. Maybe this will help right things a bit. What say we give peace a chance, hmm?" He smiled his most sincere smile and held it just a little too long.

I matched his lengthy smile and tried to foresee the catch. You know—the one where I ended up in tears, in hives, or possibly lynched. Of course, I assessed, regardless of outcome, what choice did I really have? "Well, thank you, Simon. That's very kind. Please tell Julia I'd love to come. By the way, where's the door?" I indicated Jamey's "office" with my chin.

"We, uh . . . had some problems with *that* a few years back, and we never got around to replacing it." Simon shuddered in spite of himself. "No one goes in there but Guy . . . and now James. It was the only space available—you moved so quickly after the, uh"—he low-ered his voice—"acquisition. And anyway, James had said he wished to be close to the three of us, to 'learn the business,' as I understood it." I said nothing. Simon smiled innocently, back in form. "In the past we used this room for storage as well as a makeshift gym—a write-off for insurance purposes. Barb and I had a pullout couch in here—before the desk, naturally, for when we were working late." He grimaced again and grabbed his left arm. Interesting. I caught sight of Guy, lurking down the hall a ways, fairly bursting at the seams. "Oh, and one more thing. You'll be happy to know we got all the temporary furniture from an Ikea tag sale. The pieces are only slightly damaged, and the savings were tremendous! See? You can tell James that Phil and I *have* been taking his cost-cutting memos seriously. It's so important to lead by example, don't you think? I sure hope he's pleased." Pink as cotton candy, he was satisfied to the gills.

I excused myself on the pretense of finding the ladies' room. Midway, I was accosted by Guy, hissing urgently from the shadows. "Stacey! Take tea with me next Thursday at the Bel Air Hotel! We should talk. There are things . . . you should know." He regarded me ominously, lest I think this a mere flight of fancy. "It's really in your best interest." Dot dot dot, I added silently, and suppressed a laugh.

When had my life turned into film-noir? I continued on my way, happier (and safer, I theorized) to wait out the next fifteen or so minutes in a tiled stall rather than chat with any more characters straight out of Balzac. Or *Underdog* . . .

As it was lunchtime, the maze was quiet, and I lingered over the old movie posters and signed scripts tacked to the walls. Somehow, I found myself wandering back by one of the conference rooms. Through a scrim shade I saw Phil huddled with two techs from the AV squad (Jamey called them Stupid Secret Squirrel Squad—I loved that) whom I recognized from their frequent trips to our home office. Stupid Squad was fiddling with a computer board attached to a larger video conferencing system. I called in to say hello. All three jumped like they'd burned themselves. Phil blanched and rushed forward as the AV goons fumbled gracelessly with the wires and monitors.

"Oh! Stacey," he stammered. "I thought you were having lunch out of the office."

How charming—everyone on staff was up to date on our schedule. "Jamey's running late and still needs time with Simon and Barb. What are you up to?" I tried to peek around him, but he blocked my view.

"Just prepping for a video conference with New York later today. The system's on the blink. We've had to postpone twice already and cancel Germany altogether. Your husband's *not* happy." He smiled unkindly. "Neither are the Commerz guys."

"I can imagine." Oh, I could imagine very well. But what could I prove? I readjusted and tried the benevolent, complimentary boss's wife tack. "By the way, Phil, I want to congratulate you on the tracking for *Body Count*. I saw Bruce Willis on *Oprah* the other day, for the full hour. It was amazing. You couldn't buy that publicity!" I smiled as genuinely as I could.

"Stacey. You don't *buy* publicity, you *buy* advertising. And you're supposed to be some big-shot New *Yawk* marketing whiz?" He sneered. "You'll have a very hard time finding work in *this* town with those confused ideas. I hear you've had no luck at all. But all the same, good for you that you keep up on such things." He patted my arm—a kitten once more.

A direct hit, finally. I chafed: Scott Sturm had even suggested (over a fact-finding Irish coffee or four at the Grill) that I have a baby rather than continue to look for work. "A baby would *complete* you, Stacey, it would *fulfill* you. Or, you could always get some dogs," he'd offered up, "like Inga."

Phil's impatient throat-clearing brought me back to the present. I was pissed, I remembered quickly, and had to take my frustration out on someone. I couldn't help myself and, anyway, I had time to kill. "Phil, are you married?" I inquired sweetly.

"*Should* I be?" he smirked. Oh please!

Unnerved by his provocative, snarky demeanor, my blood pressure finally shot to a thousand. "You know what? I couldn't care less—I was just trying to be polite. And by the way, knock yourself out with the computers; I'll be sure to let Jamey know you're on the case." I stalked back down the hall, fuming (and not terribly proud of myself), but halted midway, pressing myself flat against the wall as I heard the strains of intense verbal warfare from Jamey's shower curtain.

Simon clutched his arm again, blocking the doorway, but Barb must have been inside. I could hear vituperative, high-pitched screeching and whining. "But *why* are you doing this? You just don't fucking get it! *You* don't understand *anything* about this Industry! I *need* the charter to Maui! And I *need* the fully staffed ranch! It's right between the two big directors: Spielberg and Truehart! It's all about *presence*! We need fucking *presence*!"

This breathtakingly frothing harangue was interrupted by the appearance of Guy, who'd unfortunately selected this hypercharged moment to crawl up and tap Simon's shoulder. "Julia's on the line. She's upset. She says there's no food in the house."

Simon, completely shiny and Crayola brick-red (he obviously felt Barb's pain), whirled around and roared, "Not now, you simpering fucking dandy ferret! Can't you see I'm in a goddamn conference! Jesus *H*! Get her some fucking food then! She'll only throw it up." Very nice. And then (and I'm not making this up) he leaned forward to Jamey's desk, grabbed something solid and heavy (I think it was a stapler) and torpedoed it really *really* hard at Guy. The simultaneous body-thwacking, yelping, and mewling (poor Guy) could be heard round the floor. Heads popped out of offices, and just as quickly ducked back in; footsteps scrambled in any opposing direction. Ah yes, welcome to Pacificus Studios: the most dysfunctional office environment in the universe!

A brief respite (Jamey must have been talking) and then without another word, Barb and Simon stormed off to their respective offices, slamming their doors after them. Relieved, I ran past the angry offices (and past Guy who, abject and semi-fetal, was already on the line with Spago, ordering Julia a smorgasbord of gourmet pizza delights) and peeked around the shower curtain. Jamey had his head down on the desk, hands on hair execution-style. I poked him (not so very jokingly) to make sure he still responded to touch. "Jeez, Jamey, I can't believe . . ."

He very quickly put a finger to his lips and jutted his chin in the direction of a logo'd Vuitton sac (Barb's, I assumed) on a folding chair in front of his desk. With a pencil he flipped up the top of the bag revealing . . . a Dictaphone! And it was on! Of course! How positively . . . *Tom Clancy* of crazed, convulsing Barb! And . . . how freakin' clever was my brand-new husband! I almost squealed at his ingenuity. We locked gazes and burst out laughing. Well, really—what else was there to do? Jamey seemed reinvigorated by my presence (we need fucking *presence*!) which was, by the way, a very good thing, as Simon chose that moment to come storming back in (well, I really shouldn't say "in" as he stopped just short of the doorway, as if there was an invisible line of fire he dared not cross).

Jamey pressed his advantage (two on one in *his* favor, for a change). "Simon, this afternoon Phil, Barb, you, and I need to *calmly* go through the production budgets for next year's slate; some of these line items are either wildly padded or totally extraneous. For example, on the current *Body Count* production, my finance team uncovered what seems to be around fifty K of expenses . . . for *Julia*, of all people! Spa, clothing, and medical receipts from Aspen and Tucson, buried in a war movie shot in Laos with an all-male cast. Now, *I'm* sure it was just an oversight, sloppy bookkeeping on Phil's behalf. Not to worry, though, the New York math squad's on it—they love working on the movie stuff—and they'll forward the bills to you for reimbursement. I just hope they don't find any more such 'mistakes.' They're reviewing *all* invoices, FYI, going back at least a year . . ." He held up a thick pile of spreadsheets as the scurrilous, irascible cowboy struggled to remain in control; his pink scrubbed face darkened dangerously as Jamey went in for the kill. "I've done some advance reworking. We'll discuss before I submit the revised forecasts to the Board for approval."

I timed it: zero to sixty in two-point-eight seconds. "I've *never, ever 'submitted'* my plans to the Board! I've never had to *'ask permission'* or *'get approval'* in the past," Simon sputtered; making air quotations with furious snarled fingers. Purple veins stood out on his forehead and neck, throbbing with indignation.

"Well, that's how we'll be doing it from now on. I probably have a different management style than others you've worked with. You submit to me, I submit to the Board. We need to get these expenses under control—and quickly, if we're gonna meet our profit targets. It's a business, Simon. You don't have carte blanche." Jamey smiled angelically.

Simon stood frozen, staring daggers of hatred at Jamey. A cold film of sweat had erupted on his brow, his mouth was agape, his breathing shallow. He was palpitating so visibly, I had a thought he might implode if pushed any further and, remembering the professional-quality medical equipment, hoped Jamey wouldn't make any more incendiary pronouncements. For the moment, anyway.

Jamey opted for another tack. "On the upside, Simon, on behalf of Commerz, I'd also like to set up time, and soon, to talk about the renewal of your, Phil's, and Barb's contracts. I'd like to discuss you all staying on in your current positions . . . if we can come to mutually acceptable terms, that is."

Simon quickly reassumed his standard vulpine manner. "Oh, there's plenty of time for that, my boy. My lawyer's already drawing up our recommendations. I'll have him send 'em over so we can get negotiations underway. Only eight or so weeks 'til the end of the year, you know . . ." he goaded slyly.

"Exactly. I'd like to get the process started so in either case we'll have a smooth transition. I want everything to appear seamless internally as well as to the marketplace, so we can avoid any hiccups."

"Hiccups, yes . . . that would be bad, I understand." Simon's eyes gleamed, razor-gray irises catching a dusty ray of sunlight as he nodded slowly.

"So, then. We're on the same page?"

"Absolutely. You know me—always a team player, my boy." Simon gazed malevolently at Jamey, staring at him like lunch.

"Yes. Well." Jamey glanced at me, gathering strength. "You know, I took an executive training course not long ago, and I've been thinking about something I learned. It's an ancient Chinese tenet—and I think you'll like this one: *If your opponent is of choleric temper, seek to irritate him. Pretend to be weak, so that he may grow arrogant.*" Jamey grinned. "I just love that." He shoots, he scores!

Simon smiled unsettlingly, pupils dilating as they traveled from Jamey to me, appraising. "Nicely done, my boy. Nicely done," he murmured.

Jamey pulled on his jacket and held his hand out to me. "Stacey and I are off to lunch. I'll see you later for the video conference—that is, if Phil and Stupid Squad haven't sabotaged yet another hookup." God, I adored this man! "And I'll keep an eye out for your lawyer's document . . ."

CHAPTER 8

GIRLS' NIGHT

When a chieftain fights in his own territory, it is dispersive ground. On dispersive ground, fight not. On dispersive ground, I would inspire unity of purpose.

—Sun Tzu, *The Art of War*

I was extremely wary the day of Julia's "gathering." None of the women I had yet come in contact with seemed to be going—including a very offended Mallory, but then again, Simon had said it would be a small group. I couldn't begin to imagine why Julia would want to include me with her friends unless, of course, she wanted to vilify me further, as an extension of Jamey.

To that end, the groundswell of resentment and aggression toward us continued unabated. Oh, make no mistake: the SmackDown I'd witnessed during the Bring Your Wife to Work field trip had sealed the deal. I knew now, beyond any shadow of a doubt, that what we were dealing with was a very singular, very calculated, and very intense Social War. Whether Jamey agreed with me or not.

In the short time we'd been in town, I had a pretty clear understanding that while everything *looked* social and brimming with glamour, it was simply high-stakes ruthless roulette with only a thin overlay of varnish disguised as pleasure. So much was on the line at any given time: money, reputation, position, access—and the corresponding social accolades these things afford. And that is the major problem with living in a one-industry town: there is only one ladder, and everyone is on a different rung, trying to get higher.

Jamey and I entered the game late, from the outside and on a very high rung. This was bound to arouse jealousy, especially in Simon, Barb, Phil, and Julia, who obviously felt that one piece of the pie for us was one less for them. There being, of course, only one pie. It was a hopelessly perplexing dilemma to try to figure out how to coexist peacefully. The upshot? It was not possible to do so, and the battle lines were drawn. It was all just unfortunately designed that way.

Having to live our lives like this, as a competitive game fraught with warlike overtones, was exhausting. It certainly was far from what we had in mind when Jamey was offered the career-defining opportunity to oversee Pacificus. The relentless negativity and disinformation meted out by Simon and crew was triggering demoralizing feelings, fears and insecurities I hadn't felt for years. They were coming back to me now, all right—full-blown and triply enforced, and I could sense an oppressive, aggravating road continuing on up ahead.

During a barrage of cross-country conference calls I debated whether to go to Julia's at all. "But you *have* to!" cried Nancy. "You can't just roll over and let them win. You know, if it weren't for this insane power struggle, you and Julia might very possibly be friends." I waited; her statement didn't warrant a reply. "Well, probably not," she admitted, "but you'd certainly be able to get along with her. I know: call your colorist!" she teased. (I winced; I already had. Magda the Colorblind's daily clairvoyance pronounced "quartz and orange blossom with a smidge of propitious tartan . . .") "I mean—really, Stace, what's the worst that could happen?"

My mind raced with neurotic fantasy: a collage of angst-filled teenage scenes, in varying degrees of awfulness. Humiliation, flagellation, melodrama, tears . . . "Melinda DeMarco. Cafeteria. Eighth grade," I blurted darkly, and silence hung heavy in response.

"Yeah, well, you're all grown up now. Jeez, Stace. Relax. It's just a few women bitching and moaning over wine for a few hours, like we do all the time. Nothing you can't handle," said Leslie. "Same conversation, different town."

"Maybe . . ." I relented slowly. "It's just that anything that would normally seem simple ends up really complicated out here. It's like high school on crack, but with loads of money and power at the center and absolutely no rules. I *hope* I'm overreacting, believe me, but I just can't shake this weird feeling." I paced the kitchen floor and sighed. Why was I such a mess? Honestly, how bad could it really be? I mustered some enthusiasm. "So, what do we think? Jeans, butterfly top, Stevie shawl, silver Pradas?"

"Perfect!" they agreed. "We'll be at the Museum benefit until late, so call first thing in the morning," said Leslie.

I felt better after the phone therapy and set about getting ready. Maybe I'd meet some nice women after all. I MapQuested directions, grabbed the bottle of Danish aquavit I'd bought specially and headed over, turning into an impressively gated, landscaped drive, which led to an even more impressively landscaped Tudor mansion. Instantly, something didn't seem right: lights blazed, strains of lite jazz emanated from within. A team of tuxedoed valets waited atop the patterned-stone motor court, next to a high-end bar mitzvah's worth of cars: stacks of sparkling clean black Mercedes sedans, assorted Porsches, BMWs, Jags; even a few Bentleys. All with tinted windows—I thought immediately of Sheila and her sworn enemy, the sun. These were parked on one side of the fifteen-foot gothic front doors. The other side (the service area) was reserved for the limo-and-driver set. I considered the bevy of uniformed drivers, sipping coffee and joking, and gripped the wheel tightly, heart pounding. This can't be the right house for a few women sitting around drinking wine. . . . I glanced down at my California-chic ensemble, the style of which I'd only just begun to master, and . . . Oh, great:

A setup. I knew it. What a shock.

I double-checked the address with the valet, who nodded, confirming my fears. I assessed: Jamey was inside a movie theater with Simon; he'd have his cell turned off. And it was too early still for my girlfriends to be home from their evening event to start dialing for sympathy.

Clutching the aquavit like a weapon, I trudged slowly up to the house. How long had everyone been here? It was just six-thirty, the time I'd been told to arrive. Unlike New York, where the norm is to arrive fashionably late (thirty to sixty minutes after call time), LA is an early town. People tend to arrive on time, and nearly everyone leaves early.

I entered an octagonal foyer, twenty feet high and twice as wide, all hunter green marble and well-polished mahogany. Across the way were oversized French doors draped in aubergine velvet and gold braid, leading out to a lush, English-style garden. A flashbulb went off. I no sooner wheeled around (yup—the ubiquitous *Shinier Sheet* stringer strikes again!) than I caught sight of Libbet Fauning's Pepto-Bismol bouclé back, gold Manolos click-clacking as fast and as far away from me as possible. As Mallory had predicted, she'd evaded my follow-up calls magnificently after word "leaked" of our *Gloss*-induced tea. I'd bet all my Stevie CDs that I'd feature prominently in the next issue, my White Witch gear blaring "Glamour Don't" among the best of European Couture.

I took a deep breath and followed the trail of voices and music somewhere off to the right. The *intime* gathering was very much in full swing, a happening in a dark wood, red-and-gold-trimmed chamber with leopard carpeting. A Parisian bordello. Sorority rush in hell.

Thirty or so homogenously expensive women mingled in clusters, intently drinking some kind of punch, a Pantone palette of blond hair highlighted within an inch of their lives, like Julia. Also, like Julia, they appeared to be on a sliding scale in age from thirty-five to fifty-plus. So hard to tell but, I had to admit, they did look fabulous, if slightly underfed. I felt as though I'd stepped through the looking glass and into a tableau from W magazine: each was dressed to the nines in top-of-the-line Rodeo Drive, third-party-approved chic. Dior, Saint Laurent, and Gucci signature pieces abounded; the entire fall collections of Jimmy Choo and Manolo Blahnik were on display. Nothing unbranded; obviously no casual wear, no jeans in sight.

Except on me: Alice in Wonderland.

With a serene smile fixed wide, I meandered through the cliques, ostensibly seeking my hostess. As I cased the rooms, absorbing the Shiny floorshow, I managed to pick up some fascinating snatches of conversation:

"No, it was his pancreas. Our night nurse says it's only gonna get worse. I'll ship him off to Mayo when it does and have the bedroom redone at the same time!"

". . . his son is only three years younger than me. He finally dumped that snippy bitch of a wife from back east, and he's staying with us for a while. At least I'll have *someone* to escort me to the Blood Clot benefit next week. The Doobies don't start until ten and you *know* Marvin won't be able to stay awake . . ."

". . . you should *see* Lee's son's roommates at UCLA! I promise you, I was having a *Tadpole* moment! I have my eye on the tall blond one—Tim, Tom, Dan? like it matters—who's promised to give me 'tennis lessons' over Christmas break." Lurid sniggering ensued. Aha! So something else they had in common with Julia: these were all second and third wives, married to much older men. Shiny Trophies.

Smiling to myself, I accepted a glass of punch from the bartender (Purple Passion, I was told—the Kool-Aid at last! *"Drink me!"*) straight out of a Chippendale's floor show, and continued to circle the room. I noted that other such Chippendales strutted about as well and were being admired extensively. Party favors for later? I managed to avoid a few clusters, energetically debating the following:

"Rio Versus Mexico for Best Off-price Breast Augmentation, Lifting, and Liposuction."

"The Merits of Paxil Versus Klonopin re: Severity of Drug Hangover."

"Private Versus Group Kabbalah Lessons" and "Which of the Current Crop of Rabbinical Scholars Are Socially Acceptable for Dinner Party Inclusion."

Such lively talk! As I completed my first loop I landed, most unfortunately, in a very sorry bunch closest to the bar. It was the "When Bad Things Happen to Good People Who Wear Versace Couture" crew. The conversational theme went mostly like this:

"You know, I am *such* a giver. I give, and give, and give. No thoughts for me, not from anyone. I'm stretched past my breaking point, I promise. Even my psycho-pharmacologist says so. I'm on a new regimen: three visits a week, three new prescriptions. I made a vow in Group: I'm going to *make* time and focus on *me*! *I* have to be my own best friend. *I* have to take care of *me*!" I hung on every word, enthralled—and desperately wished I had had a tape recorder, to play back to my friends.

The others nodded fervently and drank up, as if in nervous competition. "*My* husband takes advantage of me, too," a honeyed blonde added, warming to the theme. "All he wants to do is play golf. Every day. And he expects *me* to go along and cheer him on. He tells me, 'I worked like a dog for years. Had all those kids. Now I just want to relax and spend time with you.' I'm supposed to entertain him, constantly. Just because he used to run that stupid network! I mean, I worked there, too. I know what he went through—I was his secretary, for godsakes! He thinks I should be more like his first wife, that moose. I have to fight to get him to go to events, even when I'm chairing. Can you imagine?" More fervent nodding, drinking.

I took a sip of my Purple Passion. It was sweet, but I could tell it would pack a wallop. I strolled out one of the French doors to escape the chatter. The garden was beautiful, even in this late fall season, and the clean chill felt refreshing after the haze of melodrama inside. I checked the clock on my cell phone and was surprised to learn I'd been there only twenty minutes. I'd already seen plenty. I debated: on a scale of one to ten, how rude would I be if I left right then? I hadn't even seen Julia yet. Very bad form, I knew. I sat on a bench, lit a cigarette, and pretended to be captivated by the keypad. I heard a rustling sound and braced myself, my eyes darting in the dusk: a provocative, golden blond in tiger-print Cavalli was approaching stealthily, a paperweight-sized heart-shaped diamond bulging at her neck. Grrr! I smelled a showdown. There was no one else around; I was her prey. "I'm Ritzy Snippington."

"Stacey Makepeace," I shook her hand.

"Ah, yes. *Stace*." She snapped imaginary gum. "I've heard *all* about you. You moved from . . . where?"

"New York," I replied.

She gave me a protracted once-over, taking painstaking mental notes. "Right. From somewhere between the two airports. I remember now. Well! You certainly look . . . *comfortable*. I suppose it does take a while to get into the right swing of things. But you'll learn, I suppose." She sighed, looking doubtful. "I'm originally from the South so I'm used to swanking up. I worked in client services for American Airlines, at a *very* high level, you know. That's how I met my husband, Max. He runs the Film Fund for the Bank of California—a huge big deal, 'specially 'round these parts. He's an old crony of Simon's, and that's how I know *Julia*." I smiled to myself and waited: here we go! Time for the intense devotional. On cue, she took a deep breath and began: "She's so . . . *continental*, don't you find? And from royal lineage, too—but, you know, she doesn't like to talk about it. It would be gauche, she says. Can you imagine?" I say nothing. "Anyway, I live right next door. I could even *walk* here, if I wanted to, through a path that connects the backyards. Not that I would, of course . . ." Ritzy grimaced as I stubbed out my cigarette, but didn't veer an inch from her reverent testimony. "Julia has *such* to-die-for taste! Only this morning she called and we rushed right over to Donaccia Scroccone's boutique for a private showing—she even had Donaccia close the store! For me! I bought the entire Spring line!" She preened and wiggled close on the bench. "Wanna hear something funny? Julia and I like to call these Girls' Nights the 'Third Wives' Club.' That's really *too* hilarious, don't you think?" She laughed hard, nearly spilling her punch as the taut tiger stripes jiggled dangerously.

"It's perfect," I agreed. "By the way, that's quite a necklace you've got there, Ritzy. It's so . . ." I scrunched my face, searching the appropriate word.

"Elegant?" offered Ritzy, hopefully.

Enormous, I was going to say, but I smiled instead, nodding my sincere confirmation.

"It's a locket. Do you really like it?" Glittering, manicured hands flew to undo the clasp. "Max says it's vulgar, but I don't care," she sniffed, then brightened immediately. "In here's my treasure: a picture of my baby boy, Luke. He's seventeen now and very perfect. Look!"

An angelic, teenage face stared vacantly back at me. "Very handsome!" I proclaimed, handing it back. That seemed to calm her, and, for a moment I think she forgot she was supposed to threaten, berate, and despise me by proxy. She sighed, remembering the task at hand, refastened the necklace, and reassumed her purposeful, haughty demeanor. I got the picture and lobbed her an easy one, just for fun.

"Ritzy, I haven't seen Julia anywhere." I held up my bottle.

"Oh, she's upstairs resting, I'm afraid. A small rear-ender on the 405 this afternoon. Poor thing. Third time in the last few weeks. Ever since she was *forced* so *unfairly* to give up her car and driver." Jamey, I presumed—killjoy! "It's *inhumane! And* she was on her way to meet with Quincy Jones. He's desperate to produce her." She glared and pouted at me, extra long for emphasis.

As if the fates had heard my silent pleas, another woman (think the unflappable Grace Kelly in *To Catch a Thief*) wedged in on the other side of me, bumping Ritzy off balance. "Sarah Truehart," she introduced warmly, ignoring Ritzy. "You must be Stacey. My husband had breakfast with yours this morning. Charlie said he and Jamey really hit it off, and he mentioned you'd be here tonight. I saw only the usual suspects inside, so I thought I'd come look for you out here. Gotta light?"

Ritzy, among other things, clearly hated to be ignored and bumped me back, hard. "Smoking is very bad for your skin, you know. Your injections will wear off like a whole month early!" she admonished. Sarah made a face at her. Lights flashed inside, and we heard the rapid *thwump* of a bass line. "Oh, goodie!" Ritzy squealed and shot up. "The dancing's started! Let's go back in! *Sarah*, are you coming?" She gazed meaningfully, narrowing her eyes.

"We'll catch up," Sarah replied, then looked to me. "I just need to adjust my crucifix." And though she glowered, Ritzy turned and raced excitedly toward the lights, as best she could in her stilettos over the dew-dampened lawn. Sarah and I looked at each other and burst out laughing. "Be gone, before someone drops a house on you, too!" she called mockingly, then turned to me. "Poor you. You have to try and not let them bully you. It will only set a precedent. Very brave stuff, by the way, walking into the lion's den all alone. I'm impressed."

Could I trust her? I sighed. "Don't be. What was my choice, really? Damned if I did; damned if I didn't. Simon said it would be just a few girls drinking wine. I had no idea it would be so . . ."

"Surreal?" she finished my sentence.

"Is Julia really hurt badly enough to stay upstairs the whole evening? Why wouldn't she just cancel the party?"

Sarah laughed. "I'm sure she's fine, just being dramatic. She wouldn't deign to be in the same room with you after the trash job they've done," she reported matter-of-factly. "She wants you to be uncomfortable, to feel out of your league. That's why she sent her most zealous minion to check you out," she jutted her chin toward Ritzy's divot path. "FYI, Ritzy serviced *all* the VIPs on the airline—Mileage *Plus,* if you get my drift. And Julia's got deals working everywhere; she's shameless. But not without *some* influence: when she coerces

Ritzy to spend, she gets graft—clothing, accessories, services. Ritzy has no idea." She laughed again at my confused face. "Simon's old school. Wants a trophy wife but doesn't want to pay. That's a major reason they're after you and your husband. You're the big, bad, bottom-line people, here to usurp their social positions and end all their fun. I heard the first thing Jamey did was take away her Corporate Card—what a scream!"

Oddly, my heart swelled with something resembling . . . pride? "But Simon made a fortune in product placement with his own company, and he hit the jackpot with the Pacificus sale. He engineered everything. Surely he can cover her expenses, within reason? And isn't she related to some fancy royal family?"

Sarah waved away my pointed questions. "Oh, who knows? Their grandiose stories are legion, planted to suit whatever purpose is at hand. They're 'selectively informative.' In the end the tall tales somehow contradict one another, and they only bother to deny something when it's true. It's too tiresome to unravel all their lies—they count on that. The net is he's a cheap bastard who's been writing off everything on his step-monster-daughter and Phil for as many years as they've allowed him to weasel in. He can't anymore, because of your husband—that's how they choose to see it. A piece of advice: watch your backs, of course . . . and your drinks." She nodded at my half-empty glass. "I've always wondered if they spike the punch, to loosen everyone up. Don't drink anymore, okay?" I spilled the liquid onto a hydrangea bush, and Sarah offered me her bottled water. Kabbalah water, I noted. Not her, too? My heart sank a little.

"Why are you telling me all this?" I wondered aloud. "I mean, no offense, but you're here in her house, too."

Sarah took a drag and exhaled. "The kids are out and Charlie's in edit. Honestly, once he explained your 'special situation,' I wanted to meet you and see if I could help, guessing you were most likely walking into a minefield tonight."

"Well!" I said, appreciatively, "then you have to be the kindest, most forthright person I've met since we moved." If Jamey trusted her husband, then maybe . . .

"*Nothing* is as it appears to be out here," she chopped the air, "and I've had the pleasure of being put through their Charm School myself, before Charlie and I got married. I was his contract lawyer. . . . Anyway, I'm sick of watching the maneuvering and doing nothing; I'm just trying to level the playing field a bit." She relaxed. "Besides, Charlie's a really big-deal director now, and those two can't touch us. God knows they've tried. Julia hits on him all the time, even in front of me, rubbing up against him like a cat in heat. Who can tell what she'd offer him in private, if she ever had the chance." Sarah paused, debating, then whispered conspiratorially, "FYI, Charlie used to be married to Barb." My mouth dropped open, floored. Two more different women I couldn't imagine. "It's true. They have a ten-year-old son together, Jules, who has a medical condition. Oh—and you should know, too, Phil used to date Julia."

"No kidding," I breathed, jaw dropping down to the grass. "What a tangled web!"

Sarah smiled ruefully, amused by my reaction. "Oh, you have no idea of the twisted history you've wandered into. This isn't necessarily the *best* time or place, but shall I give you the broad strokes?"

"Please. I'll take anything."

"Well, let's see . . . here's the condensed version: When they first married, Charlie was a struggling writer/director and Barb was just getting Pacificus off the ground with Phil. They'd done a decent job producing low-budget horror and action films, but they wanted commercial success. Barb initially believed in Charlie's then-offbeat 'art,' but, being a businesswoman, she began pushing him toward mainstream projects. He finally relented and agreed to direct *High Jinx* for her, a formulaic family-style script she'd found, but only if he was given total control. Barb and Phil were furious when they saw his reworked final cut, miles from their original vision and from the original budget. They were so concerned and desperate that

Barb reached out to her long-estranged, long-eschewed stepfather-cowboy-financier consultant, to get a handle on the overall business as well as to secure funding for future projects, should *High Jinx* have to be scrapped.

"Now Simon, the greedy bastard, saw this White Knight opening as his ticket in. Although he'd advised the Industry for years, with great success, he never could break into the studio system on his own. He preyed heavily on Phil and Barb's fears that all was lost, but privately he thought Charlie's edgy story and style might just resonate and put Pacificus on the map. He staged a three-city road show: premiere screenings in New York, for the investment and advertising communities, in Las Vegas, at the ShoWest convention for film exhibitors, and then finally a knockdown, drag-out event in LA—all under the guise of relaunching a new and improved Pacificus Studios. The movie was a wild success. money and attention were showered upon them (that's when Commerz first bought in), and everyone associated with the picture benefited. But no one more so than Simon: Barb was convinced he was a genius and openly revered him as her guru. She even gave him a percentage of Pacificus and declared him her partner, much to Phil's dismay."

"So far so good. But I've heard some pretty wild stuff about Barb. Did Simon cause their breakup?"

Sarah grinned. "I guess you could say that, but to be fair there was a lot of passive-aggressive behavior all around. Barb was furious with Charlie. She felt he'd betrayed her by not respecting her direction and budget. And Charlie couldn't stand that Barb didn't believe in him. Add to the mix Simon—and Barb's unabashed awe of him. They were running around the country, together all the time; the man who'd unceremoniously dumped her mother was now making all her dreams come true. Charlie saw it as Simon receiving accolades for *his* hard work and vision. Don't forget, Jules was a sickly child, and only one of them, Barb or Charlie, could go away at any one time. Charlie stayed in LA and didn't get to see the tremendous response to his own film. He only heard through the trades and Barb's gushing phone reports."

"Sounds messy—get to the good part!"

"Yeah, well . . ." Sarah grinned. "Suffice it to say that somewhere along the line Barb and Simon began *celebrating* . . ."

"What?!" I demanded.

"After the LA premiere, Charlie was looking for Barb and called her office repeatedly. No answer. Her assistant finally picked up and told him she was in a meeting with Simon and they weren't to be disturbed. Well, Charlie stormed over, followed the giggles to a small room off Barb's office. He busted down the door and caught the two of them, well, you know . . . *in flagrante delicto*."

"Ick!" I shuddered. "It's like a deranged Greek epic."

"No kidding. You can just imagine the scene: screaming, recriminations, total hysterics. So Simon had a heart attack—a gigantic massive coronary, right there on a couch in a filthy storage room." Jamey's "cubby," I presumed—no wonder Simon avoided it.

"Now, Phil had been 'loosely dating,' if you will"—Sarah made air quotes—"some low-end singer/actress/fill-in-the-blank at the time who'd gotten herself a gig working as a nurse/liaison/receptionist on the VIP floor of Cedars-Sinai . . ."

"Julia!" I interrupted, thrilled at making the connection.

"You got it. The lovely semi-Danish Yoolya—what a lucky night for her!—who had been 'dating' poor, sad Phil (in a sea of 'poor, sad Phils,' by the way) in the hopes of furthering her so-called career. Or at least her wardrobe. Or to meet someone through him that could help her—the next rung on the ladder. Anyway, Julia hooked them up and Simon mended, right as rain."

This was juicier than one of Isabel's *novelas*. "So . . . what? Simon saw Julia as the Angel of Life and Barb as the Angel of Death?"

Sarah laughed. "Something like that. After eight long days on the VIP floor, Julia dumped Phil and fixated on Simon. Apparently she'd sung backup for some French crooner and had bit parts in cabaret but, of course, she wanted superstardom. Badly. She got a whiff of Simon's money and his on-the-up equity position with Pacificus, and that was that. Barb sat by his bedside every day, completely attentive and doting, but Julia was on the 'night shift,' if you know what I mean . . . and in the end, she won out. Charlie left Barb, obviously, and word spread all over town—helped along by sad, devastated Phil and that sieve of an assistant, Guy. Barb bore the brunt of the public blame and was despondent over Simon, but Pacificus was firmly established as a Player. And Simon won out, on all fronts. Charlie received offers and funding for his own material: he was finally bankable. The only raw emotion left over is that he absolutely *detests* Simon. He and Barb are cordial, for Jules' sake. She remarried—some math teacher in the Valley—but they recently separated. I guess no one's been able to fill Simon's pointy boots."

"Eww!"

"Julia landed Simon *and* without a pre-nup—now in *this* town, that's saying something. Her 'training' on the continent, whatever it was, obviously came in handy. Of course, Simon promised to make Julia a society figure as well as a singing sensation—not so hard, you'd think, on Pacificus' dime and with their PR machine working overtime. A year or so after the scandal and fallout, Simon got sad, humiliated Barb to tell everyone—in a *letter*, no less, with head shot attached—that Julia was her cousin from Europe, ready to launch a career in the States. 'You *must* read her for stage and movie roles!' Charlie and I were together by then, and a package actually came to the house. Some PR boob forgot to take Charlie Truehart, famous writer/director/ex-husband, off the list. It's been followed up many times since by Simon himself, putting pressure on Charlie's staff, and not so nicely. Charlie had to use her in *High Jinx*, as a favor to Phil at the time. But she ended up on the cutting room floor. Not even her smallest walk-on has made it to final cut, for years now. And trust me, she's been 'seen' by everybody. At this stage she's actually 'best known,' if you could use that term, for attending other people's premieres and concerts. Simon has some faux-paparazzo he pays off to make sure she's photographed. Her one true celebrity moment."

"You realize, of course," I exhaled slowly, "that I'm living in an episode of *Dynasty*, circa 1982, and I'm at war with Alexis Carrington. I'm totally unprepared for this crap *and* my shoulder pads aren't working." We both laughed, again.

"Well, I feel for you, but I promise there are actually decent women in town who will see your situation for the shakedown it is. Almost everyone has a not-so-nice Simon and Julia Mallis tale to tell. They're just too drugged tonight." We giggled. She was right about the punch: I could feel its warming effects, but although I felt light-headed, I felt more relaxed, too.

I didn't want to go in just yet. The air was fresh, and talking to Sarah provided a perspective that talking only to Jamey couldn't. My girlfriends back home viewed each surreal incident as a comic vignette, cooked up for their amusement—like I used to react to Jamey's tales way back when. Finally, I'd met someone who could relate. "You know," I offered, "they changed all the place cards at my wedding. En masse."

Sarah choked on her water. "Well *that* certainly fits! I'm surprised they weren't more disruptive."

"I'll show you the video so you can see for yourself." I paused, shaking my head. "I can't believe this is my life."

"Welcome to Hollywood, my dear"—Sarah smiled with understanding—"and look where you've landed." Like a game-show hostess she gestured toward the flashing lights. "This is Ground Zero, an actual convention for the much younger trophy wives. Ritzy wasn't kidding." She stood and checked her watch again. "Listen, I'm co-chairing the Pediatric Hyperhidrosis benefit, unfortunately with Ritzy Idiot. We're raising funds for a new wing at St. Somebody's Hospital. Every year we do a huge Sports Night Gala, but we also have a pre-luncheon to find items for the silent auction. It's right after the holidays, and I'd love you to be my guest. It'll be nice for you to meet some 'real' women, as opposed to the apathetic Beverly Hills science projects here. I've gotta run now. The kids will be home from their acting seminar and I'll need to feed them." She handed me a card. "Call me. And let's put a dinner together with the boys, too. This weekend, okay?"

I watched her walk toward the house, and although my head was spinning, I did feel an unfamiliar little spark inside. Was it . . . happiness? Could it be that I'd just made an actual friend? My cell rang, interrupting this all-too-rare sensation. Jamey, heading home from the screening: "Stace, have you seen Simon? We had a blowout—it was pretty bad—and he stormed off an hour ago. Get out of there and I'll meet you at the house." He clicked off.

I sighed; Code Blue, yet again. Game face on (it was, after all, the last inning), I threw my shoulders back, sucked in my stomach, and headed toward the flashing lights, through which lay the motor court, and freedom. I opened the hallway door expectantly, and then froze, bowled over. The foyer had indeed been transformed into a disco, complete with colored strobe lights and intermittent, writhing bare-chested Chippendales. The techno dance beat was unbelievably loud, resounding off all the heavy marble. The miserable women from the cocktail hour, still in groups of three and four, were dancing intensely, suggestively even—with each other, biting their lower collagened lips, concentrating on their "moves." Overlooked, lonely, and bored at home, but not by each other. . . . They seemed intent on eking out every last bit of fun from the evening and, of course, aerobicizing away those troublesome calories from the punch.

Over their bobbing heads, I could see driveway lights through the windows atop the giant front doors. Bravely, I shimmied my way through the crowd, pouting my lips, furrowing my brow, nodding my head to the beat (when in Rome, after all), and pretending to be thoroughly into the music just to get through to the other side unnoticed. I was only a few yards from the door, the handle in my sights, when somewhere up to my left on the stairs I heard a menacing male voice threaten, ". . . that *fucking* kid! Thinks he's so *fucking* smart! Thinks he can undermine twenty *fucking* years of my reputation and work! Never!! He has no *idea* who he's fucking with! I'll fucking *destroy* him!"

Instinctively, I recoiled and tried to go stealth, moving faster, eyes down, boogying close behind a whirling strawberry blonde in a fiercely groovy Galliano jacket. But there were too many gyrating bodies and sloshing button-button drinks blocking my way. Suddenly, a hand grabbed at my shoulder. Hard. I spun around, almost swooning, too rattled and flustered to compose myself. Simon. Grinning slyly, hungrily, at me. "Ah, Stacey. Leaving us already? Julia will be so hurt." My heart pounded double-time; I thankfully realized I was still clutching my bottle of aquavit.

"I couldn't find Julia and didn't want to go upstairs uninvited. This is for you," I stammered, thrusting the bottle toward him. "I'm a little tired tonight. All the unpacking. Still, you know . . . Please tell Julia I hope she feels better soon."

As I glimpsed his wolfish, malevolent face through flashes of colored light, I could have sworn I saw something blink red and move on the wall behind him. No way! It couldn't be, could it? I could sense the floor sinking away under my feet and I grasped at the banister for balance. Oh yeah, but of course it was. A camera!

Sure enough, beyond the crafty smile I could just make out the eye of a lens dilating and focusing, opening and closing as it surveilled the room. The sinister son-of-a-bitch was taping all the action! But why? For what purpose? Who exactly were these people? I shivered involuntarily and a queasy feeling hit the pit of my stomach as the idea dawned that the garden was probably miked and monitored as well. Jesus!

My head began to throb. I lunged for the door and hurled myself outside to the valet, ticket already in hand. As I waited for the car, I made a plan. First, I would somehow manage to drive home, if I could only stop shaking. I'd find the rest of Sheila's pills and boil in a hot bath. Next, I'd Clinique my entire body and get rid of the layer of slime I felt covering my skin. And then I'd *force* Jamey to understand that we had to leave LA. *Immediately.* He'd simply *have* to get the company to move us back to New York, far from these mean-spirited, deadly vampires. I was resolved: I would repack everything myself, tonight, if we only could get the hell out and away from this living nightmare. Two years was *way* too long. It was an eternity.

CHAPTER 9

WHEN AGENDAS CROSS

Ground which forms the key to three contiguous
states, so that he who occupies it first has most of the
Empire under his command, is a ground of intersecting highways. On the ground of intersecting highways,
join hands with your allies.

—Sun Tzu, *The Art of War*

e just have to get through these first few months, best
we can," Jamey soothed as he stepped back from the
medicine cabinet, an uncorked bottle of Sancerre in one hand, an
industrial-sized jar of aspirin in the other. My private nurse, ready
to tend the wounded. Start the IV! He paced in front of the tub
where I soaked miserably, awaiting medication, sanctuary, and comfort after recounting the evening's sorry tale. Outside, the Santa Ana
winds howled and moaned. Tree branches beat mercilessly, smacking
against the house.

"This is so freakin' messed up, Jame." I was feeling hyperbolic.
"It's also exponentially worse than I expected: it's like an extended
death match. I don't want to compete with them, but I don't want us
continuing to be doormats, either. They're beyond ruthless and they
scare the shit out of me. Give them back the business! I mean it! I

want to go home." I dunked under the bubbles and stayed down a while, to emphasize my point.

When I resurfaced, Jamey sat on the edge of the tub, waiting for me to catch my breath. "Stacey," he started gently, "don't be so quick to concede anything. I have a few surprises in store for Simon. One of the reasons Willem wanted us here was to push his buttons, hard. Remember, Barb doesn't own Pacificus anymore. Everyone understands this but them. He's got to cooperate, or go. And his rumor-mongering works both ways. He's been wearing out his welcome all over town, believe me. People are coming out of the woodwork, rooting for his public comeuppance. Especially now that *we're* here, it's like they can see the blood in the water. You wouldn't believe the calls and e-mails I've been getting—people recommending themselves or others for their positions. Like it's a done deal they're out!"

Why didn't I seem to meet *those* people? And why then did they insist upon anonymity? Hmm: Hollywood Fear Factor. "And why *isn't* it a done deal they're out?

Jamey sighed. "The fact remains, I need them"—I splashed, angrily—"at least in the short term. People remember who made them money, and those alliances run deep. I *am* trying to get up to speed, but they're doing everything they can to create obstacles. *Giant* obstacles. You know that."

"I know. But in the meantime I don't like that they've decided to focus all their boundless negative energy on us."

"I can't afford to overreact, and unfortunately, they know it. Simon's stirring the pot, all right, but it's uncomfortable, not dire. He's petulant and arrogant, and it will be his downfall. He's got no restraint or self-control. Besides," he smiled, "what was this morning's meditation? *'Don't get carried away by emotion; it will destroy you.'*" I reluctantly returned his smile. I'd taken to highlighting useful tenets from Master Sun, pasting stickies on Jamey's briefcase each day. "I've hired a search firm who'll scout for replacement candidates. I intend to make a public announcement after Thanksgiving—the shit'll really hit the fan then!" He grinned widely, visibly thrilled at the prospect of provoking the master provocateurs. But then again, he wasn't at that haunted fembot disco tonight. . . .

I caught a glimpse of my soggy reflection in the darkened window and made a face: Woof! Like a wet dog. Such a pretty girl. On the upside, I considered, I *had* met a potential friend-slash-ally in Sarah, and that was promising, anyway. I looked back to Jamey and was struck anew by his face, so drawn and tired under the grin. My heart softened. "Listen, I'm sorry about freaking out. I was just so . . . sadistically blindsided, I guess." I rubbed his dry hand with my soapy one and stood carefully. He wrapped me in a towel and helped me from the tub.

"Here's something funny," Jamey lightened the mood as I pulled on a Knicks T-shirt and combed through my wet hair. "I've been trying to get Barb alone, to talk about her plans aside from Simon. She's been out sick a few days, and an urgent doctor's note arrived saying she's got a terrible throat infection. 'Almost fatal,' it says. She needs full bed rest—she's not even allowed to e-mail. Can you imagine a doctor looking down your throat and knowing you're gonna die?"

"Very progressive medicine." I gestured with my toothbrush, "Let's have Guy send flowers first thing—big, expensive arrangements, to the ailing Julia and the near-death Barb. We can't have them thinking we insurgent New *Yawk*ers have no manners, can we?"

We giggled, and then Jamey turned serious. "You're seeing Guy tomorrow, right? Remember, he has an agenda too. When agendas cross, all is well, but the winds around here tend to change direction constantly." As if to underscore the point, a loud crashing noise came from out back. I rushed to the window and saw my prized Smith & Hawken umbrella snapped in two, the heavy rod had smashed through a potted lime tree, and dirt, leaves, and pottery bits were scattered by the pool's edge.

I looked back to Jamey and held his gaze. Without another word, we climbed into bed and shut the lights. I still couldn't settle down; my mind kept flashing on the blinking camera light and Julia's overly swank, hyperreal-ly dosed coven. My nerve endings jangled with the images. Or were those pesky hives acting up again? Shit, it wouldn't surprise me in the least. I tried to concentrate on Jamey's rhythmic breathing and invoked my Stevie mantra. Both to no avail. Psychically drained, I padded to the window seat, wrapped my arms around my knees and gazed out at the lights of LA. The winds whooshed by unforgivingly around the house, but in the distance, everything looked still and calm.

"Stace? You okay?"

"I was just thinking. . . . It really is so pretty here, Jame, and it is a much nicer lifestyle than the city, everything being equal. But it isn't. Equal, I mean. I was so *effective* in New York. I accomplished things; I knew exactly what to do. Here, I just feel so lost. I have to be so careful all the time—what I say, what I wear, what I don't eat. I don't want to be as empty as Julia's Shiny social assassins, but . . . I *want* to be liked and make friends. And I want to help you. And us." I leaned my head against the cool windowpane and sighed. "Maybe the new year will bring answers. In the meantime, I guess I could *try* to rewire. When in Stepford, after all . . ."

A snort came through the darkness. "Listen to me, Stepford queen, and stop sulking before the winds blow you away." He bounded across the room and carried me back to bed, kissing me until our giggling subsided. Gently he recited into my ear, *"No ruler should put troops in the field merely to gratify his own spleen; no general should fight a battle out of pique.* Let's not do anything out of anger and emotion. At least not tonight."

I used my most breath-y Kathleen Turner-y voice. "So what *would* Master Sun suggest for a late-night activity?"

As his chin stubble brushed my neck, he murmured, "Ancient Chinese secret . . ."

*   *   *

The next afternoon, I waved goodbye to the evil Miss Isabel who of late had been muttering less noticeably than usual. Or maybe we were finally getting used to each other. I'd left her in charge of the gardeners (fishing what was left of our citrus crop from the pool) and the last of the electricians (three phone lines, only one working, those dastardly roots!). I knew she'd enjoy reigning supreme over what she considered her very own house. I lingered in the kitchen, entranced by a TiVo'd episode of *Un Día Grande*. My, that Paco sure was a randy one! I hurried to find my keys, grabbing the MapQuested printout as Isabel haughtily swished about, hurling Spanglish directives at the amassed workmen. She was a vision today in a stunning winter-white Anne Klein trouser suit. I was heading out to the Hotel Bel Air similarly suited (though in a Zara knockoff version) to meet Guy Nosey-Parker for tea. Things were looking up after the previous night's turbulence: the Santa Anas had swept the smog out to sea, and the sun shone brightly. Predictably, the New York girls had howled as I relayed the latest despairing lowlights from my newly dramatic life. Today's Letter from LA: "*Please Don't Eat the Daisies* meets *What Makes Sammy Run?*"

I fumbled to answer the cell, not taking my eyes off the road. Disappointingly, it was only the woeful Inga "Where're My Meds?" calling once again from the confessional of her closet, checking to see if I'd scheduled the Contessa (yes, by the way), updating me on clearance for Kabbalah class (still working on Lady Selena), then whispering the sordid details of her latest money-hemorrhaging meltdown, this time at the hands of Messrs. Dolce & Gabbana. Poor Inga. Call waiting beeped and I disengaged from her Xanax-dulled monotone.

Leslie, still snickering about the high dudgeon at Julia's. "Sorry if I'm choppy," I apologized. "I haven't mastered driving and talking at the same time. Remember when all my reports used to be about cute actors or rock stars I'd stalked at parties?"

"Oh Stacey," said Leslie, laughing still, "who're you kidding? This is *so* much better! I'm glad you're writing everything down so you can remember it. In a year you might not think it's so funny anymore."

"I don't think it's funny now," I said, feeling a whine coming on.

"Buck up," she admonished. "It's like Sarah said, 'Anyone worthwhile knows how psycho they are.' Jamey may have to deal with it at work, but just make sure you don't give them any more power over you personally than you have to."

Right. So very easy to do . . . But I was in a good mood today: Sarah had indeed followed through and invited Jamey and me to spend the weekend at her and Charlie's beach house in Malibu. A friend at last! I changed the subject.

"You know, our Jamey's become quite the mogul. He came home last week with a black convertible Corvette. It's fully loaded and he's crazy about it. 'It purrs,' he says. Made me think of your high-school boyfriend Ritchie and his Camaro. With the flames, remember?" We giggled and reminisced until I pulled into the secluded hotel drive.

I crossed the entry bridge over the elegant, swan-filled lake, and made my way toward the vine-trellised tearoom. Passing through greenery, I stopped suddenly at a sight at once foreign and familiar: a satiny, crystally, purpley-rose-bowered wedding was being assembled in a meadow. Emotions of every kind flooded my synapses. Could it really have been only a few months ago? It seemed like a lifetime . . . A handkerchief waving in the distance caught my attention and brought me back to the present, painted May colors of Gracie Mansion's garden dripping from my mind like wet pastels. I shook off the memories and headed toward the very dapper Guy Nosey-Parker, as always impersonating the Captain, awaiting Tennille.

He seated me in his corner booth, every inch the chivalrous gentleman. "I hope you don't mind I chose this table. I wanted to ensure our privacy—ears are everywhere, you know." Remembering the camera lens, my pulse grudgingly resumed its usual DEFCON 3, high alert status.

We ordered the full service of pastries, finger sandwiches, and scones. As the tea steeped we chatted lightly about the move and ongoing repair work. We were feeling each other out, as it were, although I could tell from his body language he was anxiously searching for a proper opening to begin confiding everything and anything he knew.

The waiters served the food and replenished our hot water supply. "So," Guy began slyly, stirring milk into his tea, "how did you enjoy your first Girls' Night?"

"You know about that?" I asked, shocked.

"Oh, those parties are legendary. Those women think it's better than going to bed with their geriatric husbands early, sober, and alone. *She* used to have me do her inviting and RSVP-ing. Now I'm persona non grata. And after all I've done for them!" He was in full sulk, and took an angry swallow of tea.

"Well, I wish someone had clued me in. I never even saw Julia."

"The succubus?" He shuddered. "The good news is she's leaving soon for a few weeks. Off to another 'undisclosed location.'" Guy made exaggerated air quotes. "Last time she pulled one of these 'gone missing' moments we had to pull her out of Mexico in the middle of the night, after yet another botched boob job! One can only imagine what body part's next. Not that *I'm* allowed to know anything, anymore." He sniffed, hurt again at the thought of being snubbed by the very people he'd invited me here to trash. Jamey was right: this one could go either way at any time. But, I reminded myself, he *did* sneak Simon's dossier of destruction to Jamey, so, I quickly concluded, Guy knew very well from which side his bread would continue to be buttered. "Would you mind if I switched to wine?" he perked up. "I'm feeling celebratory, being out of the office and here with present company." He smiled ingratiatingly.

"Not at all." I settled back on the banquette. I had a notion this "tea" would be yet another eye-opener. A full twenty-four hours of fun facts and trivia. "Let's get a bottle."

Order we did and Guy continued merrily. "It's all part of her plan to 'class up' her looks. To be 'Julia Mallis, First Lady of Pacificus'— well, maybe second," he tittered, "after Barb. But definitely not 'Yoolya Spraglet, Miss Small Town America.'"

"Guy, wasn't she some big-time beauty queen? I looked on the Internet but I couldn't find anything in the Miss America or States listings. Or even European titles."

"Ha!" he snorted. "Hardly—although she'd love that you think that. Hollywood is the land of reinvention, never forget. Anyone can go from shop girl or call girl to society maven with the right backing, a press agent, and a revisionist back-story. *She'd* have everyone think she arrived a fully formed diva married to Simon, when the truth is she hails from a little Scandinavian town in Minnesota called Jarlsberg. At sixteen she was elected Queen of the Julefest and rode on a makeshift float in the local Christmas parade. I found a picture of it online. Her prize was a trip to Denmark as an exchange student in some upper-class household and a little pocket money. She never returned, permanently deleting her less-than-glamorous origins—you know, she really *is* a farmer's daughter, although she hates to be associated with all that 'down-home' imagery. But the scent of livestock lingers." He sniggered at his own joke. "She used to talk of a royal European connection, but seems to have dropped that over the years. Anyway, she preferred to stay in Europe, doing God knows what. Singer, nurse, mistress, muse, pick a story. We may never know the truth," he sighed. "That's where her changeable accents come from—she thinks it's endearing, chameleon-like, and chic; *I* think it's just plain annoying." I smirked; this, from he who slipped in and out of a Brit accent with every other sentence.

"She came back to the States, to LA, on the arm of (or should I say 'in the bed of') some has-been French vocalist, traded up to a fatty fast-food mogul, then somehow took up with Phil. 'Eyes on the prize,' as they say. Oh, you should've seen her back then: before Simon, way before she was Miss Lusty Busty. She was always crazy

ambitious, doing almost anything to promote herself or snag an Industry hotshot—very Karen Black in *Day of the Locust*. But she was
almost sort-of sweet, then, if completely unremarkable—that was
her problem. Not a standout by any means. She auditioned constantly,
with little luck, singing at a Ramada lounge out by LAX for tips. Eventually she took a 'patient consultant' job at Cedars in the high-flyer
wing—very creative on her part. That way, while she was auditioning
during the day, she could simultaneously hunt for someone else to
pay her bills, by night, if you get my drift . . ." He leered at me. I recoiled slightly. "She used to confide in me, then. Now—well, now you
see what goes on." He made a dark face. I sensed additional lubrica-
tion was necessary; Guy lit up as I ordered another bottle. "I take it
you've heard some of the back-story, eh?"

I told him I'd met Sarah Truehart. "Oh yes," he nodded vigor-
ously. "They're very highly regarded. I've always liked Charlie. He
and Sarah were apparently seeing each other even before the whole
road show disaster. Simon found out about it at one of his—now
Julia's—infamous parties. He used it against them, of course; Sarah
had to resign from her law firm. And he went after Charlie for Barb's
custody and settlement, and also for Pacificus, for Simon's own future.
But now that Charlie's a three-time Oscar winner, Simon wouldn't
dare make waves. In fact, Charlie's one of the few people Simon can't
penetrate, if you know what I mean. Especially concerning Julia.
They would do just about anything to get in good with him; if he
would only do a picture for Pacificus—joy! And then Simon would
lean on him like he does everyone else to cast Julia and give her the
credibility she craves. Anyway, Charlie's office will barely return a
phone call, maybe one for every five. It makes Simon nuts!"

"So," I fast-forwarded, "the Simon/Barb thing . . ."

"The tawdry Greek tragi-comedy? Reverse Oedipus?"

"I can imagine it was pretty epic. But incest is incest, no?"

"Well, they're not *blood*! It's like Woody Allen. And Barb *was*
thirty-odd years old and hadn't seen him since he left her mother—

that was two, maybe three wives ago. But it was mad love, for both of them, just so you know. She still worships him. And she *hates* Julia, obviously, but gets along with her for Simon—and for the business's sake."

"Still, it must have been awful, being put through that kind of public ringer. All the innuendo, losing Charlie *and* Simon, and then Julia crashing onto the scene."

"Yoolya. Right." He took another long swallow from his glass. I reached to refill it before the waiter had a chance. "Oh, it was a complicated, messy scandal. In the end, though, Simon was a realist. He was crazy about Barb, all right, but he also knew the custody issues between Charlie and Barb had only just begun to hot up, and would likely turn vicious. Most important for him was to keep his working relationship intact with Barb and Pacificus—she was his meal ticket, after all. And Charlie was well on his way to becoming an influential opinion-maker. They couldn't afford to alienate him any more than necessary. Simon wanted to cut their losses and rectify the situation any way he could . . ." He held out his hand, prompting a one-word solution.

"Julia," I cried. "So: despite a completely Byzantine personal life, he somehow managed to finesse it all to his benefit, ultimately shifting the political and social winds in his favor." I was thinking aloud, and more than a little impressed. Frankly, this was no small PR feat. A "smoke and mirrors" Crisis Case Study, in fact, of the highest order. "But Guy, why did he marry her? I mean, I understand that now, in her bombshell state, she's every man in Simon's position's idea of a fitting companion . . ."

"In the end, I think it was mostly because she was there. *She*, of course, couldn't believe her extreme good fortune that such a powerful, rich, and semi-available man had landed in one of her VIP beds. Don't forget, she knew of him and his abilities from Phil—and Simon kept himself very well publicized in those days. While he recuperated, the Naughty Night Nurse 'performed a series of little miracles,' he once told me." Guy leaned close and winked. "She's very oral, I hear. Quite expert, too."

"Ugh! Please!" I made a face.

"Well, it was *her* wildest dream: to be the wealthy, respected wife of a studio head. To be a hipper, blonder Cher or Bette! Who can imagine the doors that would fly open with a snap of his powerful fingers—when on her own she'd had trouble keeping herself in bus fare. Simon had seen his own mortality, that sort of thing. It was a good idea to take a wife, distance himself from the creepiness with his stepdaughter. Plus, he probably did figure all he had to do was snap his fingers to get her work. For him to be married to an in-demand *chanteuse*, well . . . it certainly would jibe with his awesome vision of himself. Thing is, all his 'snapping' hasn't worked, and it's taken a toll. Directors and producers have shied away from doing Pacificus projects because of all the strings attached. Can you imagine, in this town? You have to be *really* pissed to walk away from a sure greenlight. And Simon can be terribly vengeful, too. You know"—he leaned toward me, extra confidentially—"I monitor *all* his phone calls. Especially now, with the current intrigue. It's amazing what you can learn. He doesn't even know!" He clapped his hands together, triumphant. Now here was a confession I was sure Jamey'd appreciate. And then . . .

Right on time; I smelled it coming: the requisite, obeisant pitch. The *true* point of this tea. He oozed masterfully, now, hand on mine, "I really *wish* your husband would take me into his confidence. I can be a *very* good ally. For you, too . . . Not that you'd know it, but there *is* actually a protocol out here, of sorts . . ." His voice trailed off.

I moved my hand. "I think we've learned that, Guy: personal agendas are pushed with corporate money, political skill is valued more than business acumen. Bad behavior, born of insecurity, desperation, or weakness, gets rewarded. *If* you can create a masterwork of offense to overcome your antagonists and a little bad press. And everyone trades on innuendo and gossip as fact. Simon's the ultimate example."

Guy turned direct. "Barb and Phil are in it all the way to their eyeballs, too, trust me, and they're still thick as thieves no matter what anyone might think. They have scores of hotel concierges, waiters, and shop girls on retainer as informants. They have so much dirt on so many people—or at least they maintain the mystique that they do, everyone figures it's easier to keep them close rather than piss them off and take a chance on the consequences. I've heard Simon dredge up all sorts of nasty secrets, people's weaknesses, and threaten oh so subtly should someone not do his bidding. It's quite something to hear."

I interrupted the data dump. "Guy, Sarah invited me to an auction after the holidays for St. Somebody's. For kids. Hyper-something?"

"Hyperhidrosis," Guy said, clipping the syllables. "A very 'A' event. The ladies' luncheon is one of the more social events on the calendar. It benefits children who sweat too much. Don't laugh, it's true."

"You've been out here too long. Sweaty children—now that's *very* sexy!"

"Honey, all it takes to successfully promote a cause is to latch onto a honcho who's afflicted or sympathetic. In this case both Ritzy Snippington and Sarah's husbands have kids with this problem. Jules, Barb and Charlie's son, suffers. You'll definitely see Julia there." Guy took birdlike sips of wine, then smiled naughtily. "You know, I saw her today . . . Miss Yoolya!" His eyes glinted.

"I thought she was laid up in bed. At least that's what I heard last night. Didn't we send flowers?"

"Of course. Very pretty ones. But she's always having an accident of some sort, always someone else's fault. It's just an excuse to get attention, or at least some more pain meds. She has an awful lot of prescriptions."

"Did she come by the office?"

"Simon won't let her. Too distracting—all her garment bags and high drama. What happened was this: Your husband asked me to go to that snappy place on La Cienega to plan the Board dinner—he said it was your idea, an excellent choice, by the way. So I did. And what did I see? I went to see the maitre d'-slash-catering person, Felipe (very cute, not my cup of tea, though), and there, big as day was Yoolya, dining with a very young, very blond, very handsome *boy*. He was nine, I promise. And she was *not* pleased to see *me*, I can tell you that! I forgot she eats there all the time—or at least she sits at table number one with egg whites and a bottle of Barolo. She used to have me make her reservations, once upon a time." More little sips. "Anyway, she got *very* nervous when she saw me—really a very *bad* actress! *And* she introduced loverboy as the new addition to her 'retinue' of agents! Can you stand it?"

I opened my mouth, but he forged ahead. "Anyhoo, I sit down with Felipe and plan the most fabulous menu. He tells me he'll call after pricing the meal and so forth. So I'm at the valet, I look inside and see Yoolya whispering heatedly to Felipe, waving her arms around. Back in the office there's a message waiting: 'Felipe has a price for me.' So I call: he wants $12,000! What a hoot!"

"For fifteen people?" I asked, incredulous.

"YES!" Guy screamed. "Isn't that something?"

Shot out of the water again. But one did have to admire her tenacity and attention to detail. "Well!" I started, but no other words would come. I sipped more wine. "So Guy, you think Julia's screwing around?"

"But of *course*! She's always in the middle of some pathetic tryst, usually with some random preschooler like today—one of her friend's chauffeurs or some kid from acting or voice class. I mean, look at Simon: he's always taking his blood pressure or weighing himself. And *she's* not getting any younger. Yoolya is nothing if not forward-thinking."

"By the way, how's Barb doing with her deadly bacterial throat?"

Guy almost choked on a crumpet. "She had liposuction on her stomach and thighs—this must be her third go-round. She used to work out all the time, but these past few years, well, I just don't think her heart's in it anymore. She's simply addicted to surgery, as if that'll help win Simon back." Hmm. Competing with Julia. No wonder Barb self-medicated. A losing battle, it would seem, on any front.

"So, what? She's home recuperating and can't talk or e-mail?"

"I heard her on the phone with Simon. They're pretty sure your husband's going to try to 'divide and conquer' them, maybe by offering Barb the chance to stay on and eighty-sixing Simon. Phil doesn't count, of course. He's just . . . inconvenient these days. They use him for leverage: three against one is always better than two. Barb, at least, will comply. She'll always do what Simon says, even to her own detriment. A driver's been running scripts back and forth to her house. She's holed up, reading away in a protective corset—ha! They're searching for a face-saving project because they can smell the coffee, now that your husband probably won't settle a new full-time deal. You'd know better than me what's in the fanciful new contract their lawyers are drawing up, but if I know them as well as I *think* I do, I'm sure their demands will be entirely unacceptable." He looked at me inquisitively. I said nothing.

He picked up his rhythm. "But I can tell you this: the office climate remains charged. No one knows *what* to believe, or whom to trust. Simon's constantly on the phone, whining about how destructive your husband is to the business, to its financial future. I feel for him, your husband. I really do." Hand on his heart, very earnest and sincere. "I listen to it all—for his protection, of course. Simon's pulling real manipulative martyr stuff: 'Call Makepeace and tell him you won't commit to the project without me.' 'He's gonna throw me out on the street, the moron.' 'Tell him you'll go to Sony or Warner's if I can't oversee the film.'"

He leaned close. "They're looking for a vehicle for Yoolya. I guess they figure *they* better create a job for her since no one else will hire her. They're hitting up Max Snippington for money. Also Lady Selena Lawson. They'd die to get close to her."

Lady Selena, Inga's friend the golden Seeker . . . I mulled this over, swirling my glass. Well, of course. What else *would* they do? Any smart businessperson in their situation would have developed an exit strategy—a plan B, C, or even D should Jamey decide to terminate. It was a fifty-fifty shot, at best. And what were their options? Their dubious reputations branded them un-hirable; they'd certainly proved untrustworthy partners to Commerz. Start another studio, another company, at this late date? Not without existing infrastructure and massive funding—and rule number one in Hollywood is: use other people's money or none at all. Even I knew that.

Guy must have taken my brooding for lack of interest, as he immediately offered up yet another morsel, eyes gleaming in the twilight. "Wanna know what *else* I know? At lunchtime today, Simon was stuck in traffic, inching along Little Santa Monica on the way to La Cachette, that adorable bistro. Do you know it? It's fabulous. Anyway, he was by CAA when he spied a black Corvette with the 'Beverly Hills Corvette' plates still on. I guess he'd tried to reach me, but couldn't get through. By the time he got to the office he was over-the-moon monkey nuts. 'That fucking Makepeace! Where the fuck was he at noon? If he was at CAA fucking around with Julia's fucking career, I'll fucking kill him!'" Guy trailed off, laughing.

Now I was really floored. "Who even *thinks* like that?" I demanded. "Even if Jamey *could*, after ten minutes in town, mess with Julia's so-called career, *why* would he do such a thing? That's insane!"

Guy smiled widely and sat back, satisfied. "*Now* you're getting it! *That's* who Simon is. He assumes every worthy foe thinks like him. And you know what it says to me? That for all his bluster and phone campaigning, *he's* actually afraid of *you*! You guys have his full attention, and that's saying something, good or bad. You're a more serious threat to them than anyone's been in years."

"Now there's a compliment," I replied dryly.

"Oh, but it is! You're younger, smarter, from *New York* . . . and with connections to the larger world he doesn't even know about. You have everything to gain. He's the one with roots here and everything to lose. He's protecting his turf the only way he knows how. It's kind of sad, really. This whole mess is essentially a personnel problem; *everybody* hates their boss at some point. That's what Simon forgets. He sold the studio for actual money, and does nothing but whine about it. You just need to give it time. It's only been a month, for heaven's sake. We all need to ride out the transition."

"Wise words, Guy," I said, considering his point. "I suppose there's nothing else we can do. But I don't like being ambushed, and my stomach turns when I think about them torturing Jamey when all *he* did was overpay for Pacificus, not launch and execute a hostile takeover." I sighed. Enough. "In the future, I'd appreciate if you'd keep your ears open and let me know if and when another two-ton truck is heading our way. Now. Let's order some coffee so we can see straight to drive home. And I want to run my holiday party idea by you. I'm hoping to combat some of our 'negative press,' so to speak, especially internally—and have some fun as well."

A few mornings later, the phone rang as I measured coffee grounds, bleary-eyed, into my French press: Nancy's office on the line. Why do my friends never realize those three little hours do actually matter, especially when it's six a.m. in my house? I sat back groggy but happy, expecting a nice long chat while the water boiled.

"Sorry for not getting back sooner. We just put our holiday issue to bed." I lit a cigarette and waited. "I have a proposition. A favor, really."

"Oh yeah?" Hmm. The last "favor" I performed landed me in beauty treatment-hell. "Tell me you want my brain. No one else out here does. I'm climbing the walls—that is, when I'm not fending off the evil Julia and her army of neglected trophy wives." I winced; we'd had yet another unpleasant run-in last night at the Anti-Fungal gala. On the upside, the Eagles had played . . .

"Well, that's exactly it. I need you *because* you're a 'Wife.' I mean, your stories are hilarious, and I'm sorry 'cause they're happening to you, and I know I shouldn't laugh—"

"So—what?" I perched on a stool, waiting.

"The charity shopping invite I sent you a while back: one of the girls is married to a producer—total hack but big-time nonetheless. His publicist won't give me access to the cast unless I cover his wife's 'hobby.' Anyway, their handbag sale is next Tuesday. At your friend's home."

Mallory, the Agenda Queen. Whom I'd just as soon avoid. "I don't know that I'd call her a friend . . . but yes. I know about it."

"Well you have to go," she commanded. "For me. *Gloss* will buy you anything you want. I'm gonna do a 'Ladies of the Canyon' story, like the old Joni Mitchell song, and I want your 'insider' take for veracity. And for fun. I'm betting there won't be any gypsy shawls or wampum beads in sight. I'm FedExing a few Jackie Collins miniseries to you for wardrobe inspiration—I'd die to see you in pastel!"

"Very funny. Truth is, I'm making yet another secret pilgrimage today to an outlet center I found by Palm Springs. The need for clothing here is insatiable. I've exhausted my New York wardrobe—which is all wrong, by the way. And I don't have our usual resources, sample sales or rooting through the magazine's closet. The girls out here buy strictly retail and wear the full-page ad all at once, as a badge of honor—or a badge of money. They'd implode with disgust if they knew I was paying off-price."

"Ugh," Nancy commented reflexively. In New York, outlet and sample sale shopping were practically competitive sports, saving (as opposed to spending) the true badge of New York Woman honor.

"But don't change the subject! Think of it as yet another sociological field experiment. I can't wait to hear what you think of these women. And the bags, of course."

"I can tell you right now what I'll think," I replied darkly.

"Hey, where's your sense of humor gone? You know, Stace," she chided, "Leslie might say you're getting soft out there. Maybe you should come home, for a tune-up . . ."

I'd been making faces in the oven door and frowned. She knew I'd promised Jamey I'd stay put for at least six months—deep-dish immersion therapy, through Awards Season. "Ha ha. But even I have my limits," I sighed. "All right. I'll see if Sarah will go with me."

CHAPTER 10

LADIES OF THE CANYON

Ground which can be abandoned but is hard to re-
occupy is called entangling. From a position of this
sort, if the enemy is unprepared, you may sally forth
and defeat him. But if the enemy is prepared for your
coming, and you fail to defeat him, then, return being
impossible, disaster will ensue.

—Sun Tzu, *The Art of War*

After only a small (and yet still unpleasant) scuffle with
Isabel (she blew into the house in pink moiré Valentino
and impossibly high heels and announced she would *not* be dust-
ing), she finally agreed to help me get the house in order for our
visit from Contessa Madalena. But only after *Un Día Grande* ended.
This was fine by me as—and I hate to admit this—I'd developed an
unexpected taste for the show (as well as for the spicy cinnamon can-
dies she brought with her), continually exposed to it as I was. We'd
sit, reasonably companionably with our fragrant cafés, entranced into
détente for an hour by the travails of the excessively macho Paco ("Ay,
that naughty Paco!" Isabel would wag her finger knowingly) as he
went about his gigolo business—and not without charm, mind you.
Not even the nuns were immune to his special brand of prowess.

The German shepherd let out a howl, and Isabel ran to the

window. "Hocus Pocus lady is here! She not even Chinese. But hey, maybe we get her to put a curse on bad doggie, eh?" she smirked malevolently.

"Be nice, Isabel," I warned, opening the gate for the Contessa. Into our midst swept a patchouli-scented redhead with kohl-rimmed, watery eyes, draped in layers of Hermès scarves. I noted her powder blue Bentley (complete with vanity plates that read MADI). I glanced at Isabel; she'd seen it too.

"Something is very *wrong!*" pronounced the ominous Contessa. She let out a tortured wail, reminiscent of the bad doggie, musky hands flying to musky bosom. "There's a *staggering* amount of *killing sha* energy. I'm *quite* overcome!"

Now that just couldn't be good. I glanced nervously to Isabel, standing by distrustfully with an expression of utter contempt. I knew that look well. "Isabel, please! Some water for the Contessa!" Isabel glared and pursed her lips but did as I asked.

The Contessa swallowed deeply, eyes squeezed tightly shut. Finally, she exhaled. "I don't even know where to begin . . ." I waited. She'd begin somewhere. Women like her always did. Isabel muttered and mock-crossed herself for my benefit. "First off," the Contessa accused, pointing, "you have coyote paw prints in your entryway." I looked at the afflicted tiles. So I did—funny, I hadn't noticed them before. Was this a problem? "This is a problem!" Oy. Surely she couldn't expect me to rip out the floor? In a rented house? Or worse, move? "Coyotes emanate a tremendous amount of negative energy. They are predators. Isn't it enough that they're roaming the hills? One shouldn't *invite* them in! There should be no sign of them in a harmonious household."

Isabel spoke up angrily. "In Mexico these tiles are laid out at night to dry. Coyotes are allowed to run over them, and the ones that have an odd number of paw prints are considered good luck. These are *positive* tiles! We are good people, and this is a *good* house, lady!" Take that, Contessa! I smiled. The flooring stayed.

"*I am a professional*! I know when my *ch'i* has been disturbed!" the Contessa huffed imperiously, matching Isabel's indignant glare. She tossed her shawls about and raised a finger to me. "One word, Stacey: dragons! Dragons are *glorious*! They symbolize new beginnings. But not for the bedroom—too *yang* and stimulating." She twirled expansively into the living area, chanting all the while, "*Clearing! Clear*ing!"

"Maybe some crane images *here*, for wealth and longevity; an eagle or hawk in flight *there*, to symbolize unlimited potential and possibility." Her face lit up. "Stacey, have you ever considered owning a bird? One word, darling: *prosperity*!"

"Birds are filthy," Isabel hissed to me. "I no clean them!" I shushed her impatiently.

"And you know what else? Candles!" the Contessa gracefully waved her arms and singsonged, "Let's *fill* this home with fame and fortune!" I looked uncertainly to Isabel, now mouthing "wax" and "bad" to me. Nonetheless, she remained glued to my side like a shadow.

The Contessa produced a Tingsha handbell from within her drapery and proceeded to tinkle and chant into the corners of the kitchen. Isabel rolled her eyes, mouthing "killing *sha*" derisively.

"*I know!*" The Contessa had a brainwave, and pirouetted for emphasis. "Stacey, take notes! We must have crystal clusters on window sills to disperse the negative *sha ch'i*. I will tell you where to procure them. There is a marvelous healer just off Laurel Canyon . . ." I dutifully jotted the address and necessary dimensions. "Some wind chimes, *here* and *here*—from a carpenter in Topanga. And of course, another wish-fulfilling cow from my Web store, *here*!" The list grew longer, naturally, as she continued room to room: an onyx ball for under the beds (protection), more chimes, a posse of froggies (three-*and* four-legged for varying purposes in varying locations), a fountain or running water (she handed me the card of a *feng shui*-approved landscape architect who could build one for me—her son, as it happened), dragons galore, and as many animal figurines as I could bear (but not bears: bad *ch'i*!). Enlightenment, I would later discover, does not come cheap, and the purveyors of its numerous related accoutrements (surprise, surprise) tend to prefer cash.

We entered the office, and once again, the Contessa was overcome, blanching considerably and collapsing on the desk chair. "More bad killing *sha*, right lady?" Isabel helpfully proposed; oddly, to no response. Isabel looked to me. "Maybe she sad because this is where the Idiot spent his time and she sense him?" The Contessa stared blankly, preoccupied, seeming not to have the strength either to glare at her or respond. This time, I wasn't so sure it was an act, half expecting papers to fly about the room and the TV to pop on, a la *Poltergeist*. Isabel crossed herself (seriously, this time) and, without prompting, hurriedly fetched our (now shared) bottle of Lillet. We looked on anxiously as the Contessa took deep "cleansing" breaths, sipping sherry in between.

"I am *weak* from something, but I cannot say what." She consulted her compass and a notebook of diagrams. "Honestly," she muttered, thinking aloud, "the layout is fine, the placements of furniture facings are correct, cow and frog positions are right, but still there's *something . . .* wrong. Something unwanted . . ." She looked up sharply and pronounced a grim diagnosis: "*Evil.* The evil eye is upon us. A black force is at work . . ." I took a breath. No kidding. Pacificus overload: constant torment, intense loneliness, and fear of public failure. Times two! Another few sips of Lillet and her voice regained its strength. "Stacey! Urgent notes! We need three convex *bagua* mirrors for this office. I will diagram *exactly* where to place them to deflect the negativity. But you must go at once."

"I have an appointment . . ." I started weakly, thinking of my *Gloss*-mandated presence at Mallory's.

"Then you go immediately afterward. This is not a game." Her resolve was strong, but she was visibly shaken and nervous—so much so that Isabel, in a heretofore unseen show of kindness, picked up the abandoned handbell and shook it sincerely at the Contessa, like a rattle at a baby, imitating her earlier energetic behavior.

The Contessa had a similarly fretful episode in the bedroom. More mirrors, it seemed, perhaps another few sessions would be needed. Isabel nodded gravely, solemn now in her agreement. As the ringing and chanting (and my hour-long consultation) wore down, the three of us ended up back in the entryway, staring down at those worrisome coyote prints that teetered on the yin-yang brink of half-glass-full philosophy. "Stacey," the Contessa said, "there is *one* more thing you need to do." She reached out and gently pinched my black silk tank and slacks. "I hope you aren't going to wear this to your meeting . . ." Here we go again. I'd already hung up on Magda the Confusing after today's inane direction. "Too much *yin*! Maybe berry colors or pastels. Black is the color of mourning and . . ."

Isabel cut in, truly excited, "I tell her all the time, Contessa, but she no listen! She should dress more like *me*!" I shot her a death look.

The Contessa said no more on the subject but rang her little bell for good measure. "We're finished here. You move those mirrors around, bury the dark colors, and get a start on that shopping list. This house—at least the *first* level"—she shot a fearful look up the stairs—"is now purified and blessed." She bowed deeply. I sighed deeply. Isabel preened deeply and crossed herself in the doorway.

Whoever said it's the little things in life that are the most special . . . was right. Sarah picked me up (after a bracing shot of Lillet and a costume change, naturally), and introduced me to an astounding, life-changing invention: a Global Positioning System! Making the need for MapQuesting (even *thinking* about MapQuesting) all but obsolete. I was beside myself, programming the coveted instrument until we arrived at Mallory's over-decorated castle up on Mulholland Drive. In fact, I'd been so enthralled that I'd barely paid attention to Sarah's running commentary on the presumed attendee list for today's accessory fiesta. I was informed that ("Turn Left," announced GPS) this would be another unique set to help with my social orientation of ("Turn Right") Wives' Lives, like a roadmap to the seating plan of lunchroom tables in high school.

Today I would likely meet the Mavens: women who knew everything about everything, and told you all about everything endlessly. In other words, women exactly like Mallory: status-conscious, gossipy, mean-spirited, and competitive. Excellent. We parked Sarah's black, tinted Jag in line with all its brothers and sisters (really, it was a late-model, black, tinted Jag convention) and Stairmastered our way up the steep drive. A uniformed girl-maid (sixteen at the oldest) opened the door, and we followed two more smiling teenage uniforms into what was quite possibly the loudest living room in America: gaudy, flamboyantly colored-rhinestoned merchandise screamed for attention amid a gaggle of ranting, gesturing, string-braceleted, hair-tossing, check-writing women holding forth breathlessly at once on every topic conceivable ranging from (best/worst) room rates on Maui, to (best/worst) Golf/Tennis Clubs, to which of their (best/worst)-dressed friends' husbands were on the (best/worst) box office/social "ropes" (and of course *why*—that all-important, heavily monitored 'A' to 'C' slide), as they gobbled wafer-thin organic cucumber slices and caffeine-free Diet Coke in their size 26 studded Blumarine jeans with fringe-y Chanel jackets over silky tanks and sparkly stiletto sandals with dangling charms. Whew! Trust me: no one in that room needed any more caffeine. I imagined hosting one of these overly aggressive shopping-slams at my house, and stifled a laugh as I envisioned the Extreme Fighting Championship I'd have to first survive with Isabel, let alone the meds I'd need to dose her with to make her behave.

Sarah and I stood stranded amid the high-decibel squawk fest ("*My* husband says . . ." "*My* surgeon says . . ." "*My* shaman says . . .") where what was said competed with the expensively overstuffed,

garishly colorful, excessively crammed rococo decor. I had a thought
that Mallory collected dolls. Hundreds of them.

"Stacey!" Mallory, at once respectful and malevolent, dashed to
embrace me, covering the air with kisses and Fracas without once
taking her eyes off Sarah. "I'm *so* glad you could come! You just
missed Inga—she bought everything! She wanted to know—have
you followed through yet with the *Contessa*?"

As she emphasized this last, covetous word, its invocation somehow cut through the astounding din, meriting envious oohs and aahs
and sparking another round of inside-track verbal jousting: "*My* chan-
neler knows a guy in the valley who, for two hundred dollars cash,
will balance your chakras, make you quit smoking, settle your aura,
and help you lose weight!" Oh great: Ritzy Snippington, smarming
about front and center. No one, apparently, could top that pronouncement although believe me, they tried.

Mallory whispered fiercely, "I didn't know you were friends with
Sarah *Truehart*! You should have told me you were bringing her," she
admonished. "I could have gotten coverage in the *Shinier Sheet*! Obviously Julia refused to come today"—she paused for effect, sulking—
"so Libbet canceled her photographer. This is Julia's pet cause, you
know. I was supposed to co-chair with her, and I was hoping . . ."
She pushed away from me, scowling, and focused all her bottomless,
drooling energy on Sarah.

"Mallory, do you collect dolls?" I blurted out.

That threw her off. "Why, yes—I have *hundreds*, actually, upstairs
in a special room." Of course she did. "I'll show you later. Have you
decided which bags you're going to buy? I've already bought three.
Oh—I need to introduce you to Karen and Patsy. Sarah, you might
know Karen. Her husband Marvin's new movie, *Midnight in Tahiti*,
just opened. John and I are *very* close to them." I myself had recently
met Marvin; I recalled a tyrannical, pudgy cretin, very much on the
order of Simon. Everyone (Nancy especially) not-so-secretly hoped
his picture would bomb . . . which it had, crashingly. I couldn't wait to

see his poor wife. "And then there's Patsy, the, uh, *earthy* one. From New York. They've been asking about you, Stacey." She hit my arm as her cat eyes chastised. "You never told me you were friends with the editor of *Gloss*! You're so *secretive* these days!" Luckily, her attention was momentarily diverted. "Estrella, no, no—not there! *Aqui! Aqui!*" she pointed impatiently at one of the uniformed girl-maids. "Excuse me, ladies. You have to watch help so carefully, you know, or they take *such* advantage."

We watched her descend on the teenager, then ventured cautiously ourselves into the vortex of noise to inspect what was on offer. Someone elbowed me in the ribs, hard. "They're really something, eh? The big bags, I mean, they're great, right? Great prices, too!" Patsy, I took it, of the eight thousand Jose Eber highlighted extensions, bad facelift, and calculating eyes. "So! Which colors you gonna get?" she hustled, tapping a Tiffany pen on her Vuitton-encased order pad. She took the opportunity to jab Sarah as well.

Sarah flinched but didn't look up, "We've just started looking— we'll let you know. Stace, what d'you think about this?" She held up a beaded necklace dangling a snappy six-hundred-dollar price tag.

"So *you're* Stacey! Nancy's friend? You're from New York! *I'm* from New York! A hundred years ago, but still! We should talk. I bet we have tons of people in common! Karen," she called to her partner, pointing rapidly at my head, "this is *Stacey*. *Nancy's* friend. *Gloss!*" Karen, I took it, was the slight, darting blonde with nervous eyes and manner hiding by the pristine dessert bar, attempting to cloak herself in the invisibility zone between heaping plates of petit-fours, iced cupcakes, and meringues—the one area she knew the narrative-spewing Mavens would avoid like the plague. She gave a small wave and continued blending into the wall. I glanced at the price of the tote bags Patsy was pushing: $2500. Got it. Poor Inga. I checked the room; many women had indeed purchased giant totes, in multiple—but for what reason? What would they possibly need to tote around? As it was, *my* prized, knockoff Birkin was packed away, somewhere on a very high shelf in its dust bag. "Listen," Patsy dripped in my ear like the devil, "you're a friend of Nancy's, and I know you're new in town. You can't possibly know how things work out here yet. Maybe that's why everyone's talking about your . . . simple style," she arched her eyebrows pointedly. "This bag is the one accessory you really need—to prove your social circumstance, I mean. A woman in your *position* really *should*, you know, have at least one, if not more, with matching accessories. Look at these girls," she continued her hissing, "they wouldn't know style if it bit them in the ass. Tons of money but no substance, no personal identity. And don't worry . . . I'll make it worth your while." Wink wink nudge nudge. She gave a sharp, direct look. No wonder poor Inga had bought anything she could carry. Oh, Patsy the piranha was the stylish, "earthy" one, all right, preying and feeding on the insecurities of her partner's peer group, whom she envied and despised.

A tap on my shoulder: Mallory again, this time with a flock of cackling, interchangeable blondes. "Stacey, these are some other Pacificus wives: Maryann, Irina, and Liz. They're on the committee," she introduced. They studied me with merciless eyes as I studied them: they were Julia derivatives all, as they would be. I could only imagine what they'd heard and from whom.

"Which are you getting?" the one called Liz inquired-slash-accused (her husband was head of distribution.)

"I bought the blue tote, a matching belt, and a makeup case," offered Maryann.

"I took three necklaces and a purse," sniffed Irina with a Russian accent (her husband was Milo, I knew, head of Stupid Squad). "It's for a great cause. We teach cooking and cleaning skills to inner-city youth, and provide jobs and bus service to our homes. If there's money left over, we support other worthy causes, like sending them to the beach—we have another facility there." She paused. "We at Pacificus *strongly* support this program; Julia's their main benefactor. She *would* have been here today, but . . ." Her voice trailed off as her eyes narrowed. Of course she would have been. So: this was the

Youth Education Movement, Beverly Hills chapter. And the heat was on to subsidize the Mavens' well-trained, underpaid teenaged laborers with overpriced, poorly made leather goods. Very nice. Mallory had practically killed herself to co-chair the event with the unassailably empowered Julia and gain social approval by association, or so she'd hoped. And all her efforts had very unfortunately yielded . . . me. *Quelle scandale!* I made a note to kill Nancy. Luckily, my cell rang: Jamey. I went outside and lit a cigarette. "Jamey, this is a total shakedown. They're gonna make me buy a bag I don't need!"

"Do you like it?" Jamey, as always, was more indulgent than understanding; he just wanted me to be happy.

"That's not the point. And there's a whole Pacificus-Wife-Gestapo—Julia-wannabes, leering, and it's, like, *pressure*! I want you to fire all their husbands. Today." I took a deep drag and exhaled, remembering. The last "charity" lunch I'd attended—Halitosis, was it?—was helmed by Julia at Sinfonia Folata's overpriced hooker boutique. Within an hour of arriving home, I'd heard from Guy that word was "Stacey showed up in a $2000 current season Narciso Rodriguez dress (yet another of my masterful eighty-percent-off finds!) and didn't even buy a shoelace." Oof.

"It's like they're threatening or daring me or something, especially since the Red Queen withheld her presence. I've got to hand it to her, though: if *she* can't actively humiliate me, she happily assigns the duty to her acolytes. But the point remains clear."

"Oh just buy it, honey. Really, don't worry about it."

Patsy slithered up. "Give me a check," she coaxed in a honeyed voice—she knew I was trapped. "I'll fill it in for you." Wink wink. "You can sign when you're done." I peeled one off (I hadn't carried a checkbook since college! So what *is* it about LA? Bad credit? Or does no one want their husband seeing itemized charges?), stubbed out my cigarette, and went back inside, conquered and resigned. Pay and leave. And find some place to *not* eat with Sarah on the way to Laurel Canyon and *bagua* heaven . . .

"Stacey, look! Magda's here!" crowed Mallory.

Instantly, I could tell that Magda (aging, raven-haired Maven, another bad facelift, beady hamster eyes) was displeased by my clothing choice of flared white Blumarine slacks (sans rhinestones or bric-a-brac, though), green palette Pucci-esque tank, and silver shoes. "I *told* you, Stacey," she tut-tutted, "*never* green for you! Lime and lemon *blossoms* today! You don't take direction well. You should heed my advice—I know all about you." Mallory looked away, but the Pacificus girls watched evenly, wriggling with delight. There was a brief, chilly silence.

I wanted to hit her. And them. I swallowed. "Magda, let me be clear, since you are not. As far as I know, lemon and lime blossoms are fragrances, not colors. It's also a point of fact that they are both white. My pants are white. I can't see your problem." I turned to the greedy Patsy monster and announced, "I'll take the grass green bag. It will reflect my lush and bountiful spirit."

Patsy handed me my "check" as Sarah handed Patsy a change purse she'd chosen. "I'll take this. Don't you think it'll be cute for my daughter?" Sarah asked me. The Pacificus girls had converged on Sarah, sucking up and admiring her extensively. I glanced down to sign: $2500, plus tax, made out to Patsy and Karen Inc.! Jeez! Where was my wink-wink discount? Where was my charitable contribution?

Just as she saw me gear up to question her, Patsy deflected my wrath with sarcasm. "Sarah *Truehart!*" The yapping and clucking halted instantly: the room was frozen. "*Surely*, Sarah *Truehart, you* can do better than this—seventy-five dollar *donation!*" she spat. "Really, it's hardly worth figuring out the sales tax! And it's for *charity* . . ." She made a hurt, pouty face, best her facial injections allowed.

The purse dangled limply from Sarah's hand as murmurs flooded the room. That was it: an old-school *Norma Rae* moment flooded my synapses. "Sarah, we'll be late if we don't leave right away. Oh, and Patsy, I'll make a special point of mentioning your . . . *kindness* to

Nancy. Which issue of *Gloss* were you hoping for again?" I smiled sweetly and handed over the blood money.

Score one (finally) for me. $2500 was a small price to pay for my reward: the silence of the lambs and the look on Patsy's face, although Mallory, I could tell, using two teenagers as supports, rued the very day she met me. Sarah tossed the purse back on the table, playfully linked her arm in mine, and we headed to the door. "Thanks for ending the pain. Sorry you got busted, though," she nodded at my bright green bag.

"I'll live. It was kind of fun, in an insanely sick way. I'll bill Nancy for the heartache plus a gallon of Maalox."

We'd just reached the entryway when Ritzy clacked up, an inch of orange Indian-print Lycra stretched across her impressive body, matching orange lipstick and heels. "Sarah," Ritzy panted (and pouted), ignoring me, "we need to talk about your auction prize for the Hyperhidrosis lunch. You haven't returned any of my calls! You're developing very bad habits." She glared at me. "And Stacey . . ." My turn. "I didn't see your name on the tables list. It's getting late in the day, you know. Of course, Julia and Simon have a prime table for Pacificus, but that was all planned up weeks ago. I bet there won't be any room left for you."

Sarah responded, very Glinda, Good Witch of Holmby Hills. "The Makepeaces will sit with me and Charlie. But thanks, Ritzy, for bringing the oversight to my attention. And don't worry. Charlie and I have something earth-shattering planned. We'll be sure to break all previous records."

We continued down the drive, Ritzy's eyes piercing our backs. "Sarah," I whispered, "what's the mysterious and brilliant auction prize?"

She giggled. "We haven't a clue! Let me know if you have any bright ideas."

CHAPTER 11

'TIS THE SEASON

When an army has penetrated into the heart of a hostile country, leaving a number of fortified cities in its rear, it is serious ground. On serious ground, gather in plunder.

—Sun Tzu, *The Art of War*

True to his word, right after Thanksgiving Jamey announced he'd retained an executive search firm, essentially putting Simon, Barb, and Phil's positions up for grabs. The compelling item ran as front-page news in both *Variety* and the *Hollywood Reporter.* We sat in the kitchen, letting the machine answer the incessant ringing, which had begun sometime after midnight.

"I don't envy you, Jame. Simon'll be apoplectic by the time he sees you; the bells and whistles on his medical machinery will ring like mad. Are you sure you don't want to work from home?"

Jamey grinned. "Are you kidding? I wouldn't miss this for the world. He and his lawyers have been dragging their feet on their supposed 'new deal' on purpose, to force me into giving them whatever they want at the eleventh hour. I expected a first draft weeks ago. I know this ploy is drastic but frankly, I'm hoping it will flush things out once and for all."

"Yeah, well, I'm pretty sure this'll get their attention." I held up the cover of *Variety*, which gleefully pondered, "IS TIME UP FOR MAKING PEACE WITH MALLIS?" The subhead read "BLOODLETTING AT PACIFICUS." The *Hollywood Reporter* ran with the inspired topline, "MAKE PEACE, NOT WAR: MALLIS TO BE REPLACED." These high-spirited bulletins topped the day's other big piece of news: famed writer/director Charlie Truehart was gearing up to mount a secretive, as-yet-untitled production. No studio attached—yet. Details and surprise opportunities to be announced at the Pediatric Hyperhidrosis luncheon after the holidays. Oh, quite a news day it was, though I could hardly be surprised: Charlie and Jamey had been planning this one-two punch for the past few weeks, probably hoping to give Simon another coronary.

The phone rang and the machine clicked over, again. I sighed, "Well, honey, it's a balls-out move, calling their bluff—and as publicly as possible. I know it's warranted after everything we've endured, but it *is* incredibly provocative and, you're aware, these are not the most stable of humans. They could be dangerous, even beyond the usual hurtful slander. . . . I think maybe we should batten down the hatches and get Commerz to hire us some bodyguards."

Jamey's good humor faded slightly. "I did factor in some backlash, Stace, before I went ahead. But really, what was my choice? I need to buy time. I ran it by the attorneys and Willem. I'm sick of being a walking target, and I want everything reconciled by Christmas. The situation's just too fluid. Simon continues to undermine me and has way too much control for someone whose contract is up in four weeks. Believe me, there are plenty of worthy candidates. But somehow he always seems to know who I'm talking to, and he's been scaring people off with his guard-dog tactics. Now the search firm can reach out and handle the screening rounds. When they have a short list I'll get back involved. By then I'll know what I'm going to do with team Mallis, and maybe we can actually relax for a change over the holidays."

We raised our mugs in a toast. Well, I'd certainly drink to that sentiment . . . not that I believed it for a minute. Jamey gathered up his keys, sunglasses, and briefcase and kissed me goodbye. The phone rang barely once and went immediately to voicemail. He shook his head. "Maybe you should let the tape fill up and use your cell."

"I will. I'm gone most of the day, thankfully. I've been invited to a working lunch at Donaccia Scroccone's boutique—a committee meeting to raise funds for Ovarian Research. Guy helped me put together a donor list yesterday." I actually was looking forward to today. Sarah had said I'd like this crew—the "Activists," she called them; bright women, stimulated by issues more weighty than the Saint Laurent boutique's upcoming trunk show. "And, of course, I have our party to organize. Liquor, decorations, heat lamps—I'm doing it myself to keep the costs down." He kissed me again, and we paused as the phone clicked over, yet again.

Turning up the volume on my *Belladonna* CD, I sang along with feeling. I'd left time to run a few errands locally before heading to Donaccia's; I'd tackle the party items out in Santa Monica afterward. At a light, I reached for my phone, thinking I might catch Leslie or Nancy before lunch in New York. I pressed the speed dial, expecting to hear ringing, but someone was already on the other end. Guy. In a panic and whispering breathlessly, standard operating mode.

"Thank *God*! I tried the house like a million times. It's an absolute *nightmare* here. How are you holding up?"

"I'm fine. Where are you?

"In the men's room. I've locked myself in so no one can overhear. Simon keeps bellowing, though, so I have to be quick. He's been holed up since God knows when, maybe all night, acting like he's commanding a war room. I got in around eight this morning and the strange thing was, he handed me an already-composed release to fax to the trades and the *LA Times*. *And* he'd cleared it all with his lawyers. By eight a.m.! He's called the papers to complain and is demanding front-page retractions, saying they jumped the gun: his new contract just isn't completed yet, a new one *is* forthcoming, they're still negotiating, blah, blah. I was trying to get through to give James a heads-up before he walked in. I wonder how Simon knew this was coming down? *I* didn't even know, for godsakes."

"I guess it's true he never sleeps. He probably smelled it coming, like the vampire he is."

"I bet in some small way Simon's impressed that your husband actually pulled this off. Everyone else is. You're right, though; he practically invented the press ambush. This is exactly the type of stuff he used to pull in his heyday."

"Charming. Maybe someone at the trades tipped him off?"

"I doubt it. The exultant overtones are more likely payback for years of abuse and lies. Anyway, he's made me hunt down half the Industry—putting him through to people's homes, in their cars, at breakfasts, at the gym. He's fielding incoming calls, spinning, ranting, and double-talking away. Barb's crying, Phil's consoling her, and Simon keeps screaming about his 'pound of flesh'! I've been listening in, of course, and I'll tell you: he's nervous. Really. Even if he was prepared for it, I don't think he can bear that everyone's almost *laughing* at him. And you know what? They are. Most of the conversations are one-sided; they just let Simon ramble. I think your husband just might have some leverage, now."

Like that wasn't the point. "You think so?" I swerved, trying to negotiate the phone and the Citibank parking lot simultaneously. "Well, Jamey *is* Simon's boss, last I checked. At some point he has leverage, no? Where's Jamey?"

"He's in with them right now. Simon was yelling like a banshee. About control, his reputation, being ambushed . . . then it got quiet. Anyway, I couldn't hear anything, so I thought I'd take a break and call you. See how you're doing."

I was annoyed; he really was so overcurious. Back in New York, I hardly so much as mentioned Jamey's assistant's name more than once or twice a week, let alone had extended personal or strategic conversations with her. I fidgeted on line, waiting for an open cash machine. "I'm fine, of course. But it's not my fight. I don't know what to tell you. I can't shed any further light."

"Do you think they're really 'out'?"

I sighed. "I don't think anything's been decided yet. I'd assume Jamey's looking to protect the company from exposure and to make sure there's a stable presence running the studio."

"I see." Snippy. An awkward silence. I finished my transaction and waited for the record to print. Finally, he added, "Oh. I almost forgot. Libbet Fauning, that greedy charity witch, called here and left a message with me, for you. I guess she'd tried to call the house but was sent to voicemail too. She said she left a message but wasn't sure you'd get it in time."

"Is there a problem? I'll see her at the planning lunch in an hour."

"Well. That's just it. There's been a change, it seems . . ." He paused, as always, for greatest effect. Out in the parking lot, I unlocked the car door and slid into the stuffy interior. Eighty degrees, early December. I started the motor and blasted air as vague anxiety rose to a flush of anger.

"What, Guy? Just tell me."

"She said they've changed the meeting location from Donaccia's boutique to—guess where?" He waited. No response from me. "*Julia's* house! They changed it just this morning, apparently. 'A last-minute decision,' she said. There'd be more room to spread out . . . or some such nonsense. Libbet wanted to let you know so A, you wouldn't show up at the shop and find no one there, and B, you wouldn't show up at Julia's and create a scene. 'Under the circumstances, dot dot dot,' was the phrase she used, I believe."

I sucked in my breath, blood pressure rising. I stared at the dashboard: only ten o'clock. What a day . . . already. "So, let me get this straight: I've effectively been thrown off the committee. Correct?"

"Correct."

"This has Julia written all over it."

"Correct."

"And I can't be involved at all, even though the cause is near to my heart, and I've had Jamey put aside Commerz money—"

"Well, now. That's why Libbet actually *did* try to get in touch with you. She'll wait it out and see which way the winds end up blowing. *You* can write the big corporate check—Julia can't anymore. That horrid woman will be happy to accept your money, and she'll say publicly it's a donation from Pacificus, to placate Julia in the meantime. So the origin will remain dubious to the world at large: is it you and your husband, the alien newcomers, supporting the cause, or is it Julia and Simon, her longtime allies in the Hollywood Axis of Evil? Julia's trumped you momentarily, my dear. She's arranged it so they won't let you join in their reindeer games. *And* she had that bitch Libbet call and let you know, in case you were wondering who had the upper hand du jour."

"Oh, for godsakes, Guy . . ." I didn't know whether to cry or scream. I pulled out of the lot onto Sunset. A bum stumbled in front of the Whisky a Go-Go with a placard: EVERYBODY LIES, NOBODY MINDS. On the speakers, Stevie warned, *No speed limit . . . this is the fast lane. It's just the way that it is here . . .*

"Well, then," I said to Guy. "It looks like I'll have plenty of time to concentrate on the holiday party. I need to go out to Santa Monica and run around anyway."

"Let me know what you need from me. You haven't told me how your RSVPs are going," he sniffed, "but I would presume that everyone will want to come *now*, even if they wouldn't before, just to see the fireworks."

"What do you mean?"

"Well, your husband finally fired back, didn't he? That takes balls, my dear. Especially against Sun Tzu's most ardent disciple."

*   *   *

With all the theatrics and information-trading going on at Pacificus, I had decided to (gasp!) handle the inviting and RSVPs myself. I thought it might be easier on everyone (except Guy, who was obviously miles beyond miffed) if going forward I kept as much personal intelligence away from that building as possible.

I hired a celebrity chef from a popular West Side restaurant to do something special—more personal and distinct to us than the traditional ham/turkey slice or the ubiquitous Tex-Mex fiesta, for one hundred fifty of our closest enemies. We decided on winter vegetable skewers and a shellfish raw bar for hors d'oeuvres; the house drink would be Long Island Iced Teas. Poolside, the chef would build a bonfire pit to steam a full-on East Coast-style lobster- and clambake, complete with corn and potatoes, and individual blueberry pies for dessert.

I unloaded my party hoard on the kitchen table and pressed the blinking message light on the machine—the number 27 pulsed rapidly as the tape rewound. I pulled up a stool and poured a glass of wine, pen poised.

Congratulatory responses, sniggers, and applause rained from the speaker. Libbet Fauning, that C-word: one, two, three messages. Guy clocked in with six. Nancy and Leslie. My mother. And Sarah, with Charlie roaring in the background. And then:

It happened near the end of the tape. Just hearing that strangely accented voice speak in my very own kitchen sent angry shivers up my spine: Julia. "Stacey. It is *me*. It seems we have yet another in a long list of problems. Simon and I are holding *our* annual holiday fete on the same date that *you've* scheduled for your little gathering. *Our* soiree is a celebrated Hollywood landmark. A *tradition*! You simply *must* change your date off that Saturday evening. And you should be *grateful* I'm giving you this heads-up, by the way. *No one* will think to choose your event over mine! Finally, I'm very upset that you've gone and swiped Marco de la Mierda, my favorite chef, out from under me. You should know I don't forget these things. I so hope that when I get to be *your* age I will have better manners than you!" Click.

I downed the entire glass of wine and sighed. Glad to know, I supposed, that I loomed as large in her world as she did in mine. Forlorn, I looked at the cheery decorations, candles, and lights I'd amassed; she was right. It wouldn't help Jamey's cause at all for me to compete head on, to be that confrontational, and . . . and *lose* on such a grand scale this early in this . . . game? I cringed at the word.

A quick mental flash: me, Jamey and Guy, Sarah and Charlie, too, sitting around an achingly fabulous raw bar, Iced Teas stacked in front of us. To knock back alone. A very festive holiday, indeed. One step up, two steps back. In every aspect of this newly overcomplicated life. I sighed, resigned, then picked up the phone and called methodically down my lists, changing appointments and call times all around. Sunday, then; a late-afternoon start.

The final preparations were going smoothly, although I'd spent much of the day orchestrating in jeans and hair rollers. (Dante had broken up with his boyfriend and no amount of pleading or money was getting him up the hill and away from his red wine, cats, and *Best of Bread* CD.) Heavy fir garlands tied with tiny white lights swagged the wrought-iron staircase, hippie-market candles glowed alongside farmer's market flowers. Latin and jazz-themed holiday music played indoors and out. The house looked spectacular, warm and inviting.

With little more than an hour until guests were due, I was satisfied. Time to change into my swingy new "Santa Barbara hostess" outfit. Jamey emerged from the office just as the bartender poured my first Iced Tea. "I hate to do this, Stace, but I need another half hour on the phone with New York. I just received Simon and Barb's so-called new deal. Suffice it to say I'd laugh—if it weren't so entirely fucked up. He's crazy, you know."

"The understatement of the century."

"No, I mean it this time. There's shooting the moon and all, to see what you can push through, but this is off the charts. It's so out there, it's almost on the order of blackmail. It's like he's intimating he's got a switch he can throw to destroy everything—and me, unless I sign this into law."

"Well, that's how he operates. A little truth goes a long way. Do what you have to, but hurry."

Ten minutes (and multiple futile attempts with a daunting ACE-bandage corset) later, the doorbell rang. Guests, so early?

In despair, I grabbed the nearest presentable jacket, threw it on over my jeans and Keds and scrambled downstairs. At least I'd had time to peel off my Crest Whitestrip and comb through my hair! Jamey's door was closed; he'd just begun his call. I peeked my head in, "People are here!" I mouthed urgently. He waved me off distractedly and continued droning into the phone, red-markered papers fanned before him.

I descended the stairs, hoping to see a friendly face that had arrived early "just to help," so I could finish dressing . . . and all too quickly, my heart sank to my stomach: Simon and Barb stood in the entryway, chatting up a cater-waiter. But of course. Just another little ambush, and a Merry Christmas to you too.

Hugs and air kisses abounded, smothering in their phoniness like a thick mask of Crème de la Mer in a sauna. Achingly sweet, our Simon: "Phil sends his regrets, Stacey; he's been hit with the flu. And Julia, sadly, is indisposed as well."

A likely story. "I've heard there's something going around." I glared toward the closed office door. Their "soiree" had been the night before; somehow, I figured, the ailing absentees had found a way to attend.

"No, nothing like that. A small traffic incident this morning on her way to meet with Mick Jagger."

On a Sunday morning? "Of course," I commented icily.

". . . and her back and neck are bothering her. I thought it best she rest, poor baby. You know, I don't think we'll even make it to her family's castle in Copenhagen. They always put on such a spectacle. But I just don't think she'll be comfortable enough to sit through such a long flight."

Hmm. Surely there was a drug cocktail somewhere in her overstuffed medicine cabinet to knock even her out . . . all the way to Minnesota. "That's too bad. She does seem to be very accident prone, especially with the car. Still, it's the holidays, and I'm sure her family's important to her. Please tell her I hope she feels better," I say. Gag, gag, gag. I out-smarmed even myself.

Barb pushed past the niceties. "Yes. Well. I hope you don't mind that we stopped by on the early side. We have three more events to attend tonight. Very exclusive parties, *very* high-level business contacts. It's exhausting, of course, but you understand, everyone's . . . *concerned*. There are all *sorts* of rumors and innuendo in the marketplace." Barb rolled her eyes and shrugged helplessly. Simon nodded, brow furrowed. Barb continued, "We need to reassure everyone personally that the future of Pacificus is safe and still under control."

I was seething, but I didn't flinch. "Pacificus *is* safe and under control. And its best interests are being looked after. By its owner."

Barb ignored me and made an elaborate display of undoing her fur wrap, dictating extensive instructions to a catering girl how best to handle it.

"What *is* that, Barb?" The fur had the same coloring as her newly lightened hair.

"Wild coyote." I smiled to myself: of course! My *ch'i* had been disturbed by the negative predatory energy in the house.

Simon tapped my elbow. "Stacey," he drawled nonchalantly, "I assume the Trueharts are expected? I want to chat with Charlie about his new project. We've been trying to arrange some time, but can't quite seem to get it together. I know Barb'll see him in Maui over the holidays, but I'd love to get a look now—for Pacificus, of course." He attempted an ingratiating smile, but somehow it still came off feral. So that's why he actually showed tonight: to continue the prowl. "We didn't see them at our party last evening, but then again, it was so heavily attended . . .".

I replied as evenly as I could, considering that (a) *we* hadn't been invited to their (Pacificus-funded) party, and (b) we'd dined at the Trueharts' instead, rerouting our group Christmas trip to Mexico after warning Charlie and Sarah off Barb-infested Maui, and (c) Jamey and Charlie were naturally well into discussions. "I'm sure Jamey will have a word with Charlie on Pacificus' behalf."

The catering girl stood ready to steer them toward the bar. Barb bypassed her overtures and took me firmly by the arm, cooing as she pulled me through the living area, ostensibly to have a private chat. I could tell she was appraising every square inch with her voracious, observant eyes. "You know, Stacey," she patted, feigning mentorship, "the next time you want to host a little group, you really *should* call me first." She fixed her gaze pointedly on my jeans and Keds. "Really. You should, and don't be shy. I am, you know, a *hostess*, very highly regarded and sought after. My parties and style are legendary," she boasted primly. My mouth fell open as anger percolated from my kneecaps. "There's a definite art to socializing and entertaining, make no mistake. *I* understand that you're out of your element, especially here." (Cluck, cluck, pat, pat.) "You can't be *expected* to know the correct way to entertain society, right out of thin air."

Steam began to emanate from my ears. I wanted to scream, "You trout! I'm from New York City, for godsakes, not Appalachia! You have the balls to show up an hour early to throw me off, and then imply . . . !" Just as I opened my mouth, Jamey (thank God) arrived to relieve me of his pet pathological step-disasters. I glared at him savagely but took advantage of the diversion to run upstairs and put on some real shoes, at least. Jeez!

From my closet, I could hear the muffled sounds of more guests arriving. I stared sadly, longingly, at the elegant holiday outfit, crumpled now by the side of the tub. Too complicated a mission to attempt now, with shaking hands and about thirty seconds to go. . . . Defeated, yet again. I pulled on a vintage Emma Peel chocolate blazer (from my stable of vintage Emma leather items), painted on more makeup and assessed myself in the mirror. I forced my mouth into a smile of comedic proportions, spritzed a huge cloud of Opium, and hurled my body back down the stairs.

The house had filled up nicely. By anyone's estimation, the turnout was terrific, and everyone relaxed and chatted amicably. Even happily. Among the crowd were big names, small names, clients who'd been kind, some who just wanted to see the house (real estate is *endlessly* fascinating!), all melted into a general ambience of warmth and good cheer. Considering I was the hostess and the only person timecrunched into wearing jeans, I felt vindicated when Sammy Generosa, West Coast style editor for *Gloss* (sent by Nancy), pronounced me the epitome of California hostess chic: a woman secure enough to wear jeans to her own evening event, putting everyone at ease. Absolution! His professional (national, even!) proclamation was loud enough for Barb to overhear. She whispered rabidly to Simon as they glowered in a corner. And just as quickly I turned to another guest and forgot all about them.

A while later, I ran into Guy at the front door—by this time he'd taken over Jamey's "greeter" duties, wobbly drink in wobbly hand. Although more than a bit tipsy and his holiday ascot askew, his bloodhound senses remained razor sharp. He was keen to report that Simon and Barb had left their apologies and slithered off into the night. "They were just *dying*, those two. They thought with just a quick word, most people would shun you. Well, they all showed up, didn't they, *and* they're having a good time. Ha! I have to say, this was a great idea every way around. Here's to you!" Wobbly hand lifted a wobbly drink in a wobbly toast.

I shrugged off the standard reportage of bad manners and worse behavior and reached out to try to steady Guy, who was swagging dangerously near the swagged fir on the banister. They'd never let up. And this one night, I didn't even care.

Sarah and Charlie had indeed come, as did the Sharps, the Sturms, and assorted other Mavens and Shinier couples. Even the nasty gaggle of Pacificus wives and their husbands. In fact, everyone on our list showed up, save for Julia and Phil. Now *that* should show Simon, I thought. Let him bring *that* home to Julia in her sickbed. I felt almost . . . exonerated, strangely, here in my own house. Trays were passed, glasses were clinked, hands were shaken, cheeks air-kissed. One by one I met Jamey's senior staff in person, putting names with faces. It truly was like reassuring the world that we didn't have horns or the plague, just as Jamey and I had hoped. I could sense an odd sort of curiosity being satisfied, and felt just as huge a sense of relief.

When there was a lull I decided to slip upstairs and refresh my makeup, maybe grab a cigarette for a quiet minute. I headed up the darkened staircase and was surprised to see a faint bluish light underneath the slit of the office doorway. Could Jamey have really snuck up to work while the party was in full swing?

Curious, I poked my head slowly around the backlit door and— Time stood excruciatingly still. My heart pounded double-time, and blood rushed furiously in my ears. My mind reeled. I felt disembodied, anesthetized, as if I were watching the scene from above. Lo and behold, in the pale-gray monitor tinge of the darkened room was none other than Simon, hungrily crouched over our computer, typing frantically on the keyboard. And of course, his steadfast step-accomplice Barb was bent at his side, prowling an inbox full of Jamey's folders with her greedy claws. I must have cried out in shock, as they looked up and froze as well, mouths agape, eyes gogging wide. Deadly silence. Utter silence. Painful silence. We stood paralyzed, gawking, not daring to breathe; only the walls undulated and rippled around us. The scene was right out of a really bad movie, to be sure, even by Pacificus' standards.

After what seemed a slow-motion eternity, awakening from my own stunned mortification, I finally spoke. "You've *got* to be kidding!" We continued on motionless, riveted in position. "I heard you'd left. What the hell do you think you're doing, scavenging around up here?"

After a few more painful beats, Simon rearranged his body, very calmly indeed. Spin, spin, spin, you slimy bastard. And quickly. "For Chrissake, Stacey, you startled us. Testy, testy! We were just checking the weekend's box office before we go to our next event. It's at Tom Pablum's home and his movie just opened. We simply wanted to get a sense of how it's doing, to know whether to congratulate him or offer condolences. He's got a new script we're trying to secure—for Pacificus, of course—so we wanted to be prepared. Barb was just moving things out of the way to get a better view. Jeez, you New York gals, you're very suspicious! *I* suggest you look into your trust levels."

He flashed what I'm sure he thought was an award-winning smile. Maybe twenty years and thirty pounds ago, you Cheshire Cat prick! But I could see Barb's Adam's apple (oh yes, she has one) pulsing rapidly. I knew *she* knew *I* knew I'd nailed them both and wasn't buying any of it.

I held the door open, still dazed and furious as they filed out. I grabbed the files from Barb's hand, which trembled slightly. They scurried down the stairs and out the door without another word. I followed, shaking still and livid beyond belief. I forced myself to smile, air-kissing and hugging my way through the crowd of smiling, air-kissing, hugging revelers to hunt down Jamey. I found him outside with some of his staff, smoking cigars and laughing, listening to and telling tall tales. He looked so genuinely happy and relaxed, maybe for the first time since we left New York, that I honestly didn't have the heart to tell him what I'd discovered. There'd be plenty of time for more misery, I reasoned. As Jamey had once told me, there always was. I'd let him get through the next few hours, and then we'd sit down and decide what to do.

The caterers finished cleaning up and pulled out around eleven o'clock; by midnight the last guests had left. Like children on extended best behavior at a grown-up's party, we said goodbye to the stragglers (having managed to discover and eject a B-level starlet and her boy du jour from the guest bathroom), kicked off our shoes, and ran to raid the fridge to see what goodies were left over.

Over forkfuls of blueberry pie and a bottle of pink champagne, we rehashed the evening's events. I wrestled with disclosing the illicit sleuthing, but I couldn't bear to kill such a rare, joyful moment. I waited until we went upstairs to undress.

Jamey sat quietly, troubled, as I ran down the incident. After a beat, he spoke slowly, thinking aloud. "They were obviously looking for anything related to the contract negotiations, or their possible consulting agreements. And of course any financial or personal papers they could use against us. The search firm stories in the trades still have them up in arms. They're running for their lives." He sighed heavily.

"I want you to show me exactly where they were. I need to make sure they didn't make copies or remove anything important. I just pray he didn't plant a virus to mess with the Commerz system or delete any files, just for fun."

We entered the office and switched on the lights. I showed Jamey the stack of papers I'd taken from Barb, blocking the scene to show him where they were positioned. The computer screen was still open to the box-office results, the Pablum film highlighted. Taking a key from his pocket, Jamey unlocked a filing cabinet and pulled out a thick red folder, motioning me out of the room. He then locked the office door, warding off entry to Isabel, who (we hoped) would be arriving in only a few hours to help clean up.

"Here's what they were after, I'm sure." Back in the bedroom, he dumped the heavy file marked "Mallis/Spurndoff/Craven Employment" on the bed and flipped open the cover. There were multiple bound documents, Jamey's chicken-scratched notes all over the margins in red ink. "I'll read you a few lines of their fiction—their 'additional benefits' requests." He laughed bitterly as he paged through. "Remember, their objective is to be kept on full-time in their current positions. There's language about being 'company people,' wanting to 'cooperate' and 'do what's best' for Commerz. Verbiage like 'integration, synergy, growth, and compliance with corporate governance'— business and legal concepts that are totally foreign to them. Now keep in mind these perks apply to all *four*: Simon, Barb, Phil—and Julia." He took a breath and began reciting. I (naturally) interjected my own comments afterward:

"One: Unlimited first-class travel and accommodations, minimum 'suite' level, domestically and abroad."

"But of course, *dahling*."

"Two: Right to charter a jet if necessary, re inconvenient scheduling conflicts and commercial timetables, domestically and abroad."

"*So* tiresome, flying commercial. And those baggage restrictions— so *medieval* when one is jetting back from the Couture!"

"Three: Twenty-four-hour car and driver."

"At least that'll save you insurance dollars on her accidents and pain meds. I actually agree with that one."

"Four: Unlimited at-home client entertainment subsidy (to include: food/beverage service, live music, fitness trainers/personal chef/related staff)."

"Ah! Endless Girls' Nights—Ritzy Snippington will be thrilled! I trust this broad line item covers the cost of the extra-special ingredients for their house drinks. Or maybe Julia economizes (now that she's 'corporate') and uses her own meds—kind of an OxyContin/ecstasy cocktail. *And* there are bound to be heavy film-and-processing costs for their 'security' cameras: the high price of blackmail! Such fun to be had taping your houseguests doing coke and/or each other in the bathrooms." Jamey smiled and continued:

"Five: Unlimited medical benefits, to include *any* elective surgery." We both laughed hard at that.

"Finally—and you'll love *this*, Stace; it's my personal favorite: Corporate Card and petty cash rights reinstated immediately for Julia Mallis, as well as annual clothing/styling budget, amount TBD. Also: immediate reinstatement of Julia Mallis' 'Special Agent' status for Pacificus, at premieres and other Hollywood events, Film Festivals, and Award Presentations. Domestically and abroad.'"

He put down the document and looked at me for my reaction.

"Wow!" I said. "Big, fat, arrogant balls! This can't possibly be standard stuff, even out here. Is it? If it is, then I want a clothing allowance and a driver, too."

"Well, you know Simon *knows*, in actual fact, right from wrong. He's just been allowed to go unchallenged for such a long time. In this case, I'm sure he's throwing it out as a crapshoot, to see if I'll pick up any percentage at all of the gigantic cost of her maintenance, to keep him happy and engaged. You know he keeps threatening to leave me high and dry if he doesn't get his way, even as he poisons everyone against me.

"The most telling part, though, has to do with the obscenely inflated salary and bonus structure he's created for them. Simon adamantly refuses to acknowledge that the future path of Pacificus is *not* his decision, that it's not their company anymore."

He sighed, frustrated, and I glanced at the clock: one a.m., now, on a Sunday night. The sum total of these relentless emotional attacks had worn Jamey down, just as team Mallis had hoped; office time with them tomorrow (today) could be the final straw.

"They're such little spooks, Jamey. Master manipulators. I wouldn't put anything past them after catching them tonight." I laughed, "Hey, let's get the tool kit and figure out how to unscrew the phone receivers. We can check and see if they've left us a little 'present.' You never know, maybe they're listening to us right now."

Jamey's mood darkened visibly. "That's not funny." He grabbed the bedroom phone and examined the receiver intently. "You know," he mused, dropping his voice to a hiss, "it is like they know exactly what I'm thinking. They seem to know what New York and Munich are thinking, too: that the business is vulnerable and we're too anxious to terminate them, once and for all. We're afraid with all his machinations the business *might* actually fail without them. Somehow, they're working this whole situation from every side." He continued staring purposefully at the phone, a strange expression on his face.

"What are you saying?" My voice dropped instinctively to match his. I was fully alert now, my pulse picking up speed.

Jamey turned the TV volume high and motioned to me to follow him out onto the balcony off our bedroom. Softly, he closed the glass door. "Let's just say that they have—or at least pretend to have—information not meant for their ears. Unrelated people I've spoken with confidentially have told me Simon's called afterward, screaming bloody murder for even talking to me, telling them 'how dare they!'—they were absolutely not qualified for top spots at Pacificus. How could he have known? I've always called from here and met outside the office. *And* he was too well prepared for that story I planted in the trades. His attorneys vetted their legal responses the day before the articles even ran. There's no way they could know half of what they seem to. No amount of experience or dumb luck would allow for it. Information's been leaking every which way since we moved. There are still clicking noises on the phones. You've had Verizon and SBC here a few times, aside from Stupid Squad's ongoing maintenance, right?"

"Yeah, but they've all said it's because we're up in the Canyon. Sometimes clicking and other interference can happen because the wiring is old or shaky . . ."

Jamey shook his head quickly, picking up steam. "There've been e-mail mishaps, too: interceptions and deletions. I know for a fact it's not Guy. He doesn't have the private address or passwords I use for Germany and New York. There'd be no trace through my computer at work. Whole files have been misplaced or have simply vanished into thin air."

He paused, his mind working overtime. "You know, maybe it's been in my subconscious, but these past few weeks I've stayed away from Pacificus. It drives Guy crazy, but the information's too sensitive: strategic plans, financial projections, and budgeting for next year. I'm trying to get everything organized so I can run an actual business, as opposed to dealing with all this personnel nonsense. At the very least, Simon knows my plans are due to the Board this week. I'm sure that's why he was skunking around tonight, to see what I'd written about his future."

I was well aware that late-night and early-morning calls with New York and Munich had been taking place. Jamey was a walking zombie and was hardly sleeping, or at least he wasn't sleeping well. Millions of dollars had been sunk into Pacificus on Jamey's advice to buy the business wholly: the would-be jewel in the Commerz crown. And one desperate, seditious, megalomaniacal cowboy was doing his darnedest to destroy everything, from Pacificus to other Commerz holdings to my overworked, overtired husband. Jamey brooded, his body tense, staring back through the door at the phone as though it would eventually tell him something.

"I wonder . . ." I began, and stopped as a coyote howled, not far away. I shivered involuntarily at the sound.

"What?"

"Well, I was thinking—and this may be totally crazy—but . . . remember when we moved in, Guy sent the head of Stupid Squad, that guy Milo, to work in our office for a few days, to make sure our computer was compatible with the Pacificus system? He was here—in the office anyway, alone. I had workmen in every corner of the house. How do we know what he was doing? He could've installed something or tapped anything and everything. He had total access, not only indoors but out back by the telephone closet, too. He came and went freely. He said he'd needed more wires and coding." I was afraid, now, for real. "He's been with Simon a long time. He's absolutely loyal to him. And I've met his wife; she worships at the altar of Julia. I'm sure, like everyone else at Pacificus, Milo would do whatever Simon told him. We know Simon's not above monitoring his wife's social functions, so this would hardly be a reach. If anything, your movements are critical to his future, and we know he's expensed security firms and PIs in the past . . ."

We stared at each other, letting the awful possibilities sink in.

"I need to think about this," Jamey said gravely, resigned. "But I know what I need to do tomorrow."

We lay side by side in the dark, any residual party afterglow dissipated, and I felt him toss and turn all night. I think we both saw every hour on the clock. I must have finally fallen asleep, because when I awoke the next morning, the house was silent, and Jamey was gone.

CHAPTER 12

SECURITY!

Ground that is reached through narrow gorges, and
from which we can only retire by tortuous paths, so
that a small number of the enemy would suffice to
crush a large number of our men: this is hemmed-in
ground. On hemmed-in ground, resort to stratagem.
On hemmed-in ground, block any way of retreat.

—Sun Tzu, *The Art of War*

*N*eedless to say, quite an issue had presented itself. The
queasy feeling that first hit as I left Julia's Girls' Night
had ossified into a permanent knot. I just couldn't shake the sicken-
ing feeling we were being watched, monitored, spied on at all times.
I avoided the telephone, even to call Guy after he'd left a message
regarding Simon's latest phone campaign, his summation to the wider
universe about our party: "Those fucking Makepeaces—like fucking new oil bastards, throwing money around all over the fucking
place!"

The situation was vexing, to be sure but, in retrospect, hardly
unexpected. These were true masters, after all. The sad part was re-
alizing how naïve we'd been, Jamey and I, even after years of working with *Fortune* 100 companies. We weren't protecting research and
development patents for cancer-curing drugs, for godsakes, or even

the formula for Viagra. It would never have occurred to either of us that such a thing could really happen; certainly not in our own home. And over information about *movies*, no less—what a disconnect it was! The night of our party, however, we realized we'd only begun to grasp the gravity and depravity of fear, insecurity, and desperation in this town.

Now, I have always subscribed to the belief that when one spends time around paranoid people, it's easy to become paranoid oneself. And then, there's the simple truth of yet another familiar adage: just because you're paranoid, it doesn't mean they're not really out to get you.

Jamey refused to make any further calls, fax, or e-mail communications from the house, getting up even earlier, coming home even later, if that were possible, slipping out instead to payphones in nearby hotels. Too much was on the line, now, for the business and for us personally, and that line had been crossed. He wouldn't take any more chances.

And that was truly the crux of things: even though other Commerz businesses were separate and distinct from Pacificus, Simon's reach and contact base extended far and wide. With the verticalization trend among entertainment companies—each with their own music, film, television, merchandising, and home entertainment divisions—client bases eventually crossed over, especially at top decision-making levels. A cleverly placed monkey wrench here or a hint of misleading information there had very real consequences, and might just put the larger picture at risk. All on my husband's watch.

So, taking a page out of Simon's psyche (we *are* all living there now, aren't we?), Jamey quietly made inquiries and hired a government-level counter-espionage service to conduct thorough searches for evidence of compromise. I like to think of them as the Men in Black, since their business cards had no company name, titles, or contact numbers. I canceled an appointment with Dante (and suffered Candy/Cookie's snooty wrath) to wait for them late one afternoon, the day of the *High Jinx Part Four* premiere: a particularly horrible Pacificus release Simon had endorsed as an outstanding favor to someone, one can only imagine why.

The *High Jinx* concept had majorly deteriorated since Charlie's original, brilliant take, but Simon and Barb insisted upon milking the franchise, releasing almost anything at all (with I'm sure the added bonus of pissing Charlie off) under the banner of his breakthrough hit. Let's just say that from the trailer alone (if not the title) it was destined for really *really* late-night cable placement, after something starring Shannon Tweed. Or Carrot Top.

The drill: the spooks would search the house thoroughly and then, after business hours, they'd go through Pacificus' executive floor. We'd meet up at Pacificus while Simon, Phil, and Barb were occupied at the film's after-party, to hear the report.

One did have to hand it to Simon: any Pacificus film—including a *High Jinx Part Four* disaster—was reason enough to put on a full-blast, gala-level event with budget to match. Julia adored all premieres, to be sure, but Pacificus events were her own personal coming out party. Of course, if they could have figured a way to exclude us, you know they would have done so. As it was, for next year's release slate (of widely varied but ultimately worthless films) Jamey had already slashed event budgets by many zeroes, with a mandate to cut nonessential spending on lesser titles, such as this.

But back to the matter at hand. The team of four security experts comprised ex-Naval Intelligence, ex-MI5, ex-CIA, ex-LAPD. Dark suits, white shirts, pocket protectors, *Cool Hand Luke* shades. Very *Dragnet*, resolute and impressive. "We're here to conduct the Technical Surveillance Countermeasure Survey, ma'am," the lead spook announced. The others unloaded shiny black briefcases of expensively high tech equipment, which they hauled upstairs to the office.

"This should take about ninety minutes. We'll need access to the garage, car keys, your PDAs, and the telephone and electrical closets out back. Your husband should be arriving soon with his PDAs, and we'll search his car at that time."

I remained in the doorway, transfixed by the serious equipment and the even more serious professionals who'd probably swept embassies and safe houses in the Eastern Bloc for a living. And here they were now, sweeping an office-slash-gym in a rented Beverly Hills hacienda, knees on the floor next to our treadmill, Stairmaster, and free weights. Suddenly, I felt like an idiot.

"Does this actually happen in real life to actual people? I mean, it's just the movie business! I can't conceive of what my husband or I know that would be of such value to warrant . . . *espionage*, or this level of search. Now that you're here, I feel a bit silly."

The agents chuckled. "Your husband said the same thing when we first spoke. But then we went through a detailed threat assessment. From his description of what's occurred, who may be involved, and what's at risk, we felt it essential to go forward." He smiled reassuringly. "We're mostly here to check for the obvious and to make recommendations for the future. You wouldn't believe the number of entertainment clients we service. There's no telling what bits of information are important, or to whom. It's easy for systems to be compromised, and it's essential to learn how to protect yourself. After tonight, we'll compile a report outlining safety measures to prevent future incidents."

"Well, we certainly appreciate it. I'll be down the hall if you need me."

"You may want to close your door; you'll hear some very loud noises when we run the radio frequency, carrier current spectrum, and nonlinear junction detection analyses. They can be frightening if you're not expecting them." The other three agents had already pulled on headsets and were readying boom mics and recording equipment. I lagged in the doorway yet another minute, transfixed as they dismantled the computer, fax, and phone with swift, decisive motions.

By the time our limo arrived at the theater in Westwood, the festivities were well underway, an earsplitting, Technicolor *Tiger Beat* convention of adolescent hysteria. I thought back to my own all-encompassing Shaun Cassidy obsession and smiled. Teenaged girls screamed and convulsed to either side of the velvet ropes, brandishing posters and swearing undying love for the all-heartthrob cast. Industry bigwigs glad-handed, flashes strobed, and press was everywhere. Through the circus-like thicket of TV cameras, hormonally charged girls, bobbing signs and police, I could see that every inch of the red carpet unoccupied by hobbit-sized male teenagers was being worked to death by none other than our pal Julia, dressed to kill in a form-fitting Sinfonia Folata cheetah-sequined gown.

Starring in this scatological stalk 'n' slash-fest (the sequel of the sequel) was Tommy Duncey, an elfin twenty-two-year-old (playing an elfin fourteen-year-old) who had his own very popular television series. He also had, I'd heard, a major coke habit. In his blacked-out Ray-Bans and purple Versace suit, all five-foot-two, red-eyes and rabbity nose of him emoted intently to reporters from *Extra*, *Access Hollywood*, and *Entertainment Tonight*, who emoted back just as intently at him. Julia strutted desperately back and forth, back and forth, as close as possible to Tommy, his rabid press following and his equally emaciated, adolescent cast. Curiously, one lone photographer followed Julia's every move, snapping away. I elbowed Jamey. "Hey! What's the deal with that guy shooting only Julia?"

I had my answer soon enough: a half-moment later I spied Simon quietly stuffing an envelope in the photographer's camera bag. "Priceless, no?" snarked a voice in my ear. Guy N-P had arrived, sporting satin paisley accessories for evening. Simon hurried over with Barb and Phil, all fawning mock love and excitement. The trade guys went crazy, jockeying for photos. Oh, it was quite a show we put on: one big happy family at Pacificus. Guy stepped back, Julia stepped in, and we embraced deliriously, mugging for the cameras and, of course, our Commerz stock portfolios.

We took a collective breath, smiles fading fast, and broke from each other as if from a huddle. I felt a pinch, hard, on my bare upper arm and swung around: Simon, smiling smugly. Julia (after all her hanging around, batting of eyes and, oh yes, *cleavage*) had been granted a quickie interview with *ET*, and he wanted me to see, I suppose.

I overheard this tidbit, in an even more curious accent than usual (Russian, perhaps? *Nyet*. Israeli?) ". . . Oh yes. I usually play leading lady-type, but here I hone my chops as character actress. I have small but critical role; I am pivotal character. Only because I respect the young director did I even consider to take this role. You watch, you will see. I dispense much advice to the boy and he listens very much. The whole movie turns on *me*."

Guy practically lunged at me, bursting to comment, but there was no time. We grabbed Cokes and popcorn and took our seats just as the houselights dissolved. I had Jamey to one side; Guy scurried in on the other. Simon and Julia were seated on the other side of Jamey. Well prepared as always, Guy had snuck in a flask of rum and set about dosing our sodas while frantically making "scissors" gestures at me with his fingers. Connecting the dots (and trying in vain to translate his desperate pantomime). I assumed this was to be Julia's "singing neighbor" moment, the one she'd told me about way back at LAX.

The movie was simply awful. I'd expected that. But at least I'd have my first chance to watch Julia on the big screen (not that the impromptu wedding burlesque hadn't been enough). I waited, and waited some more: the only inclusion of Julia was a quick background shot in a smoky bar, and then from behind, yelling indecipherably from a doorway at boys who ran away after throwing rocks. I sat back, deeply satisfied, and scissored "cut" back at Guy. Sometimes life really *is* good, isn't it?

Julia, naturally, was getting crazier by the minute. I could hear the hissing three seats down, way past Simon's ears, "How could you not fucking *tell* me I was cut? *Nothing* ever works out. You *promised*! Now they'll *never* include me in the *ET* package!" Oh, sometimes life is good indeed. I rubbed Jamey's leg with warmth and affection.

The credits ran, and we made our way to the after-party. I was feeling a bit tipsy but pretty refreshed, considering. As I chased down a server bearing shrimp skewers, I spied Julia behind a potted palm, continuing to berate Simon ferociously. You go, girl! She'd make him sorry, you can bet.

Jamey hurried toward me and snapped his cell shut. "One lap around and we're outta here. The guys are ready for us. Surprise surprise, they found something big. In my and Guy's stuff . . ." A sobering statement if ever there was one. We found our limo waiting on a side street and headed to the Tower of Doom.

Now, Century City is daunting by night. It's bad enough during the day; all those identical, high-rise dominoes soaring stark and high in the otherwise flat landscape of strip malls and the traffic parade that is Santa Monica Boulevard. To my mind it serves mostly as a visual reminder that LA is, in fact, an actual city in the midst of wildly expensive suburban real estate. At night, desolate and deathly quiet, it's a barren, otherworldly wasteland. An eerie location, to be sure, straight out of an *End of Days* Kurt Russell epic.

We rode in nervous silence up to the twenty-third floor. Sandy, a sweet-natured legal assistant, met us at the elevator bank literally shaking with excitement. He was part of a highly trusted contingent that had moved from New York to help Jamey transition into Pacificus. "I'm so glad you guys are here. This place is even creepier at night. I think they've found whatever you were looking for, Mr. Makepeace."

Jamey strode past him; I tried to keep up in my heels. Sandy was right: the office ambience was downright apocalyptic, an image accentuated by the ear-piercing electronic womps, whirrs, and whistles that heralded our arrival at the now-disemboweled executive suite. Pre-search "positioning" photos were tacked to the walls for continuity; debris-covered ceiling tiles were marked and numbered, stacked on the floor. Office furniture was marked and pushed to the edges of each room. Files, papers, and videotapes had been pulled out of cabinets and were deposited on any free surface. Overhead and desktop lighting fixtures were dismantled. Computers, fax machines, printers, and telephones sat dismembered in heaps. Wires were everywhere. Dust and debris covered it all, the desks, chairs, and floor.

We stood three abreast, taking in the scene. The lead agent poked his head through a displaced ceiling square. "We hit pay dirt, folks!" Clearly satisfied, he jumped down and landed on Guy's desk, knocking over a well-polished silver frame of Guy (in short pants) clinging to someone straight out of a Monty Python drag sketch.

"What we got here"—the agent pulled on an overhead wire, dislodging a small, furry microphone and a whirring black box—"is similar to the multiple transmitting devices we discovered at your home, in the office and bedroom vents." Jamey and I exchanged horrified glances.

"Pretty standard stuff, really, as this sort of thing goes. These office models are updated versions of the gear in the house. Those, unfortunately, have been there for a while . . ." Jamey and I locked eyes, understanding at once: they'd uncovered the subterfuge behind the disgraced German's downfall. The house had *always* been wired for sound; it was a trap, a contrivance, a cage . . . and a direct link to Simon. *That's* why Julia had pushed us toward Sheila and that particular address! My mind raced with the intrigue, fitting together seemingly unrelated puzzle pieces as the agent continued speaking. ". . . also tracking devices under the hood of the Corvette and in the glove compartment of your Mustang, ma'am . . ." That snapped me to attention. "This mechanism is a highly sensitive interception device"—he held up the black box—"capable of receiving and transmitting intelligible conversation. It's set and wired with a mic up here"—he pointed above Guy's desk—"and there are two more mics with attached wires. One runs into that small space there"— he pointed to Jamey's cubby—"and another into that room there." He pointed to Phil's office.

"The cords all tie into a receiver that's stationed . . . here." He led us into Simon's office and took the framed quote off its hooks on the wall. Of course! ALL WARFARE IS BASED ON DECEPTION. Duh! Words to fucking live by! I stared at the tenet until the letters blurred. So: Simon had majorly amped up his eons-old war game, taking full advantage of the current technological age. An oddity sprang to mind: I understood Simon watching Jamey, naturally. Even Guy. But why Phil? He practically *ran* Stupid Squad, for godsakes! He was the Crypt Keeper!

Jamey remained impassive, shoulders slumped as he too stared at the quote. The agent glanced at Sandy and me and then to Jamey, as if to check how much more he should reveal. Jamey waved his concern away.

"As for your computer systems, we found some evidence of tampering, but it'll be much harder to prove out. I can recommend an excellent team . . ." He watched Jamey for any sign or response. Nothing. He continued, his tone softer. "Sir, to sum up: you have indeed been compromised. Your enemy's here, internally, right within your space. We can take your wife home and continue this conversation tonight. Or else we can start first thing in the a.m. Your choice. But I'd sincerely like to sit down as soon as possible, take you through our findings, and put a game plan together to secure the gaps quickly."

Without moving a muscle, Jamey spoke at last. "Sandy, we have a car waiting. Would you please walk Stacey down? And then go on home and get some rest. I'll see you tomorrow."

Sandy nodded to me and set off to gather his belongings.

"One more thing," the agent spoke grimly. "We left the devices in your home intact so as not to alert the culprit you're aware of being monitored. We find it's best, at least until you figure out with your attorneys how you want to proceed. In the meantime, we'll continue our investigation and try to prove out who the perpetrator is, beyond a reasonable doubt."

A surge of fury rose through me, and I looked from the agent to Jamey in disbelief. "You're kidding, right? We're supposed to *stay* in that house and go about our business as though nothing is wrong?"

I turned to Jamey. "We *know* who the culprit is. *And* you know we'll never be able to prove it—I'm sure he's covered his tracks well. He always does. But, can't we do *something*? Can we get a search warrant for *his* home? This is all so . . . *violating* . . ." I broke off, trembling. Jamey put an arm around my shoulders and led me numbly to the elevator bank.

"I'm gonna stay, Stace. I'd never be able to sleep. And I need to have a recommendation ready by the time New York wakes up."

"A *recommendation*?" I pushed him away, blood slamming in my head. "Are you high? They've been listening to us for months! Jesus! I can't believe we had Stupid Squad in the house. We *invited* them, for godsakes. For what? To allow them to update their spying software?" I shuddered. "Can we get a restraining order? I mean, they're unbalanced, right? They're certainly dangerous, and these activities are by definition illegal. At the very least we have proof of *that* now. I wonder what *else* has been 'compromised'?" Another bolt of fear struck, and my voice dropped to a whisper. "Do you think they planted cameras? Jamey, do you think Simon has pictures of us?" My stomach churned, queasy again. "I'm calling my father."

Jamey exhaled. "I've already spoken to him. At length. That's how I found the security team. Let me go through the full rundown now, then I'll deal with legal counsel in the morning. At least we know we're not crazy, right?" He smiled sadly, working hard to calm me down. "I don't know what else to say; it's gonna be a long night."

Through the glass doors I saw Sandy, waylaid by an agent holding an electric drill. Keeping an eye on them, I whispered fiercely, "I don't like you keeping them on as free-floating, overpaid consultants after the New Year. It's extortion—total blood money! Cut the cord already; cut the access. We'll deal with the fallout. Let's just get them out of our lives!" Jamey said nothing and stared at the floor, calibrating calm, inflaming me even further. "Why does bad behavior continually get rewarded out here? I'm telling you, this pathological, no-accountability shit would *never* fly in New York! No one would put up with it." How could he still be this maddeningly naïve?

Jamey shook his head tiredly. "Look around, Stace. We're not in New York, and this shit works here, really well. Simon has relationships that go back years, and those relationships matter in this town. *I'm* the one, unfortunately, who has to play by the rules. I'm a senior officer of a public company. Simon's been calling everyone—especially Willem—saying I'm not in control, I'm a nice guy but in over my head. We're losing credibility and projects, all because of me. He's still undermining my authority internally, and he's bullying candidates off talking to the search firm. Meetings still cancel—less frequently, but still. I'm just trying to 'keep my enemies closer,' right?" He forced a laugh and looked pleadingly to me for support. I shook my head and looked away, still furious and uncertain. I didn't like the conclusions I was leapfrogging to, about Jamey. . . . He waited, clearly stung, as if reading my ugly thoughts. He ran a frustrated hand through his hair and lowered his voice. "Listen. There is one angle I'm working through. . . . I know Simon has a 'slush fund' somewhere. I just can't find it or prove it. Yet. I've been through the books a hundred times, but so far they're a dead end."

"A *slush* fund?" I whispered, interested now, eyes widening. "You mean he's . . . embezzling? Stealing?"

"Not really. A 'slush fund' is a reserve, an unrecorded account where he's probably stashed a few mil to use as padding, to pay people off or secure a script or something he wants as an investment, without having to go through Commerz red tape, or through me for permission. Now, once he's not an 'employee' anymore, that money becomes fair game. . . . Do you see? Until then, even though I desperately want to, I just can't afford to cut them off completely. They'll blow up the business or die trying. I need to give them time to come up with a face-saving plan, or this . . . this *war* will just escalate and they'll disrupt our lives forever." And there it was again, I thought bitterly, as always: *their* faces, *their* reputations, and *their* time took priority. Over us. And Commerz would write yet another check for the privilege.

Tiny, niggling worries and doubts that had been bubbling up inside me now formed a single, solid question in my mind: *did* Jamey actually know what he was doing? Maybe Simon *was* right, after everything. . . . Jamey's stoicism at this stage seemed infuriatingly passive; it was like sending Gandhi off to fight Al-Qaeda. Mistrustful, disappointed, and wavering, I looked away from his pleading face again. I didn't like thinking this way about my husband, whose business acumen I'd always revered by rote. But now . . . I wasn't sure what to think. About anything. At least Jamey had finally acknowledged, out loud, that it was an actual War in which we were embroiled; that was something . . . or was it? And was he still up for the challenge? I reflected on the sad fate of the last ridiculed, defeated watchdog and nameless, faceless others before him. They had tried, just as valiantly, and had failed, miserably. Maybe we were doomed. Maybe we really *were* next. Maybe Simon just couldn't be beaten. . . . I was thankful Sandy pushed through the doors and hit the elevator call button.

Jamey hugged me and whispered, "Please don't give up on me . . ." He pulled back and searched my eyes imploringly. Remembering Sandy, his voice resumed a normal tone. "Don't use the hard lines, obviously, or any of our e-mail accounts until we have them checked further. Stick to your cell. Although you could call your mother in the morning. I'm sure Simon would enjoy getting caught up on the doings at Monsieur Giorgio's." I smiled weakly and dutifully pecked Jamey's cheek.

Sandy and I headed down in the elevator and walked to the waiting car. I was quiet, treading water in waves of anguish. "Pretty wild, huh?" he broke in. "I guess all those crazy stories we heard back in New York really are true."

"I never would've believed any of it until we moved here. Now I'll

believe anything. How nuts is all of this going to sound when Jamey
gets on the phone with the lawyers?"

"Probably not so much. They're used to dealing with these kinds
of issues with the utility holdings in Europe. This may be a different
industry but at the end of the day, corporate espionage is still corporate espionage."

"If they can prove anything, that is, and it's actionable," I said, forlorn anew. What a night. I just wanted to go home. Really home, all
the way back to New York City and our silent, waiting apartment on
Lexington Avenue. We could make a fresh start, maybe, far from this
enervating, hopeless place. Or maybe, a darker thought occurred, *I*
could go home. Alone. . . . The driver pulled away from the curb, and
I turned in my seat, staring skyward as the Tower of Doom receded
in the moonlight. Overwhelmed with guilt, heartache, and confusion, I strained to count the floors to where Jamey would be pacing,
awake and alone, all night long.

Overwrought barking and high-pitched whooping sounds assaulted
my ears as soon as the driver opened the car door. "Coyotes on the
prowl tonight," he remarked, listening. "Sounds like a big kill. Your
neighbors shouldn't leave that poor dog outside. He's an open target."
I nodded sadly in agreement. That wretched, tormented creature,
barking endlessly, uselessly, alone: my kindred spirit.

Entering *my* cage, alone, was unsettling as well. I turned on every
light and poured a glass of wine. I thought again and took the bottle
upstairs, padding over the paw prints quietly, as though I might disturb someone. The thought made me laugh aloud, impulsively. Hello,
Simon? You awake?

I hesitated outside the darkened office, afraid to look in. Taking
a deep breath, I switched on the light and forced my body to enter:
the security team had restored everything to its rightful place and had
even vacuumed and opened the windows, but still the room felt stifling,

uncomfortable even to breathe—"compromised," the agent had said; the word rang over in my mind. I stared at the vent in question, just next to the ceiling-high screened windows above the desk. A stream of chilly air wafted in, bringing strains of more baying and whooping; it sounded like babies crying. Team Mallis: shapeshifting into their nocturnal familiars. As if on cue, hivey tingles crept up my left shoulder blade. I scratched automatically and shut the window tight.

How could we not have known? At least we should have sensed . . . something. Ah, but the Contessa had, I recalled. Killing *sha* energy. And she was right: the Evil Eye really was upon us. A camera hadn't been mentioned, but I felt as if there was one right then, trained directly on me. I shuddered involuntarily and wondered how I'd ever feel comfortable in this room again. In any room.

Predators in the hills, predators in the walls. Enemies howling, taunting, threatening; morning, noon, and night. We were led like children, by the hand; manipulated to this scary place through well-planned deviation and deception. Deceptions in the town, in the business, in the house, and now . . . in our marriage and in my mind. Deception, duplicity, and deceit. And that's when it hit me: POW! Like a lightning bolt; I had to grab the edge of the desk to steady myself. The minor tingling gave way to a spasm of rage so fluid I had to crouch as tears of guilt and anger welled hot behind my eyes. "All warfare is based on deception." Of course! They *were* words to live by! Simon's multilayered, relentless disinformation campaign had worked on me, too. Of all people! I'd been acting like one of the herd, passively standing by trying to ignore the ugly reality of being cast out. I had bought into our own negative PR and the Trio's mythic social might. I'd been lulled into second-class high school complacency by Julia's junta of social assassins and my own fanciful free-form Rhiannon muse—ugh! Wiping away the rage, I realized at once: if there was one lesson learned, it was that running away from a pack of wolves only triggers their instincts, their radar, for pursuit. I needed to toughen up, straightaway, and grow some leather shoulder pads!

I backed out of the office, incensed, and headed to the bedroom. Again, I turned on every light, and as I leaned in to press the TV volume high, my eyes snagged the pristine, long-neglected *Avengers* boxed set stored below. I met Emma's direct, concentrated stare, transmitting boundless courage and fortitude. Rarely was the fearless Mrs. Peel bested in a fight, and—it's a fact—she gamely rescued her partner, John Steed, as often as he rescued her. I ripped off the plastic wrap and popped the first black-and-white episode into the DVD player; I needed all the support I could get. The series would continue through the night, as would I. Take that, Simon!

I knew now exactly what to do, exactly how to help Jamey. And myself. I needed to act instead of react. I'd have to adapt and fight fire with fire. Enough one-off tactics; we needed a well-thought-out, well-executed strategy of deception of our own. Jamey might well be a senior officer of a public company, but I surely wasn't.

So, first things first: to catch a raging narcissistic sociopath, one has to learn to think like one. Right? I'd need to edit all pre-existing rules of conscience and behavior and somehow limit my endless capacity for guilt and self-torment. I'd take a page—literally—out of Simon's well-worn and well-used playbook of choice, and beat him at his own diabolical game. If it was trench warfare he wanted, then a shit storm of offense is what he'd get. I rummaged madly, radically inspired, until I located my prize (under the bathroom sink supporting an excess cache of Kiehl's goodie bag swag . . . Isabel!) *The Art of War*, in all its soap-spattered glory. On my quivering lap, the binding fell open to the following passage:

> If you know the enemy and you know yourself, you
> need not fear the result of a hundred battles. If you
> know yourself but not the enemy, for every victory
> gained you will suffer a defeat. If you know neither the
> enemy nor yourself, you will succumb in every battle.

Oh, we knew our enemy, I'd say, only too well. But maybe now we could finally concentrate on knowing ourselves. The security sweep had uncovered the root of our enemy's deception and manipulation. But deception and manipulation, in Simon's case, would only be effective if he were able to conceal his own plans and weaknesses.

> Rouse him and learn the principle of his activity or
> inactivity. Force him to reveal himself, so as to find out
> his vulnerable spots.

Luckily for us, these people were hardly opaque; they were in the habit of screaming their desires from the rooftops, betraying their every intention and revealing their methods. Hardly subtle, hardly secretive, and in no way disciplined. They could be taken down! Heaven knew they illustrated every weakness and character flaw Sun Tzu despised: arrogance, greed, social motivation, frivolity, brutality, selfishness, irascibility—and, as Master Sun confirmed, these toxic vulnerabilities could be exploited to cause their downfall. Simon didn't follow the *spirit* of Sun Tzu's strategy; rather, he employed the tenets randomly, slapdash, to justify any and all whimsical acts of terror. That was a big no-no, I understood at once.

> The general that hearkens to my counsel and acts
> upon it, will conquer: let such a one be retained in
> command! The general that hearkens not to my coun-
> sel nor acts upon it will suffer defeat: let such a one be
> dismissed!

Another bolt of clarity struck: the single (but very critical) advantage we had as of this very night was that *they* weren't aware that we knew of their surveillance. They had a false sense of security, assuming they'd forever be one step ahead. They'd exhausted their resources, but we hadn't even begun to fight!

> He who exercises no forethought but makes light of his
> opponents is sure to be captured by them.

Just as Simon warned in his wedding toast; I would use their ill-gained strengths and ill-gotten ammo against them. The direct and open link could work both ways.

> To secure ourselves against defeat lies in our own
> hands, but the opportunity of defeating the enemy is
> provided by the enemy himself . . .

Inspired, I turned the pages quickly and made a list: I needed massive intelligence, trustworthy local guides, clever spies, and some irresistible bait to plan a winning offensive strategy and help Jamey unearth Simon's secret slush fund, and fast. This one-sided War of Attrition would end tonight. My heart pounded with excitement; I felt on fire, engaged, alive. Finally! Something I was well-trained for and uniquely well-equipped to do: create and execute a strategic campaign, combining the Art of Smoke and Mirrors with the Art of War!

I awoke, disoriented, to the sound of my cell phone ringing. I was face down in the open text, torn pages from a legal pad strewn all over the bed. The last DVD had ended, and *Bewitched* played mutely on the TV—yet another woman with husband-related work issues! I glanced at the clock: seven a.m.

Jamey. "Everything's finally cleaned up, if you can believe it. I just got off with the lawyers, and . . ."

Lawyers—how boring. As he droned $600-an-hour legalese, I grabbed my how-to war manual (of which they'd mightily disapprove, I was sure), made a face at the phone, and hurried outside to the balcony, notes in hand. What a difference a day makes! Oh, I had big plans: with the help of a highly ingenious ruse, Sun Tzu's brilliant mentorship, and a really good day spa, I'd more than make up for the momentary emotional abandonment of my husband *and* dispose of our enemies, once and for all. Starting now.

I surveyed the incomparable view from one of our café chairs, my bare feet propped on a small mosaic table, bathed in golden tangerine light. "Jamey, meet me at the Polo around 6:30, okay? I have something I want to run by you." We would not make any more mistakes. Sun Tzu, I knew, would be proud.

CHAPTER 13

THE ART OF WAR/ CALCULATIONS

The general who wins a battle makes many calculations in his temple ere the battle is fought. The general who loses a battle makes but few calculations beforehand. Thus do many calculations lead to victory, and few calculations to defeat . . .

—Sun Tzu, *The Art of War*

On the patio of the Polo Lounge, Jack Nicholson's table, 6:35 p.m. The waiter turned the heat lamp up high, added another two votives to the table, and deposited the iced Bollinger, strawberries, and cream before taking his leave. I slipped him a fifty for his trouble.

An exhausted Jamey slid onto the banquette next to me. "I almost couldn't find you, hidden behind ze potted plants, my chic and seductive super-sleuth!" he approved in a bad French accent. Indeed. Painted in poison-red lipstick, I'd channeled Mrs. Peel for wardrobe, naturally, and Mata Hari, and Rene Russo in that Pierce Brosnan movie and . . . oh shit: a disturbing cartoon image of Natasha Fatale flashed in my head. I faltered slightly, then adjusted my sunglasses and pulled my leather trench tighter (with matching wedding-dyed opera-length gloves: no fingerprints!). "But why are we outside? It's freezing! And it's nighttime, by the way." He tweaked my shades.

"We're gonna play a little game, Jamey." He poured the champagne and looked at me indulgently. "And the name of the game is War. You named it yourself." I placed my cleverly disguised file folder on the table between us.

"*Variety*?" he remarked, confused.

"Hardly." Feeding off of last night's frenetic brainwave, I'd read through my notes, jotted haphazardly in that furious college-lecture hall way. I was delighted that, in the clear light of day—even in a crude state—what I'd scribbled was most definitely the groundwork for a Highly Ingenious Plan. I then slipcovered the pages (along with downloaded scholarly commentary) with today's *Variety* for safe transport to the Polo Lounge. *Subtlety! Secrecy!* Master Sun had counseled. "If 'all warfare is based on deception,' Jame, then we need a clever deception of our own. You and I . . . are gonna create a Sting." I pulled off my glasses, fanned out the papers, and gazed evenly at him.

Jamey's amused smile faded. "I don't know what to say."

"Just hear me out, then say yes. The nut is this: *Hold out baits to entice the enemy. Feign disorder, and crush him.* We know our enemy, we know what they have, and we know what they want—aside from our heads on a platter or on a plane to New York: money, reputation, power, and glory. With me so far?" Jamey nodded, hands on table.

"The one thing we have that they don't is access to Charlie Truehart"—Jamey watched me carefully—"and access to his unnamed, highly anticipated film project. They want in. Desperately. Do you see?" He sat silently. "*Attack him where he is unprepared, appear where you are not expected.*" I pressed on. "*Success in warfare is gained by carefully accommodating ourselves to the enemy's purpose.* We have a perfect battle site: Charlie and Sarah's luncheon. *Whoever is first in the field and awaits the coming of the enemy will be fresh for the fight; whoever is second in the field and has to hasten to battle will arrive exhausted.* As of dinner three nights ago they still hadn't come up with any groundbreaking, surprise auction ideas. Well I've thought of a few—to especially engage and ensnare Simon and Julia. *He sacrifices something, that the enemy may snatch at it. By holding out baits, he keeps him on the march; then with a body of picked men he lies in wait for him.*" Still nothing from Jamey. "I've got a ton of planning and persuading to do, but still. Hyperhidrosis is important to Charlie. As a Big Idea marketing person, I'll 'donate' my time to the organization and provide beguiling concepts that will raise as much money as possible. Anything Charlie does or says is big news—the whole town will want in, anyway. He'll raise a fortune.

"*By holding out advantages to him, he can cause the enemy to approach of his own accord; or, by inflicting damage, he can make it impossible for the enemy to draw near.*"

Jamey smiled. "Charlie *is* pretty subversive, for a stand-up guy."

"All I need is his buy in. Remember out at the beach? I had him howling at my collected Letters from LA. He'll love *this* even more: grand themes on a grand scale, epic characters, flawed beyond redemption; the opportunity to restore the balance of good and evil, and so on. I'll work on him in Mexico, but I'm pretty sure he'll be intrigued."

"Okay," Jamey said thoughtfully, slowly, "I'll give you that Charlie'll probably go along with you—you two think alike. But how exactly do you plan to 'crush' Simon?"

"Easy. *Begin by seizing something which your opponent holds dear; then he will be amenable to your will.* With his pocketbook and corresponding ego. We'll expose Simon for the nefarious predator he is by catching him with his greedy paws in the cookie jar. We'll make him bid at auction out of his hidden slush fund. He'll lead us right to it; he'd never use his *own* money, willingly, for anything. We just need irresistible cookies as bait; freshly baked and designed to tantalize. He'll have to bite.

"Then, we run the numbers up to where you and Phil figure we'll deplete Simon's fund. Once Simon activates a wire transfer from the not-so-secret account, you'll have him dead to rights."

"Wait, Phil? Are you on drugs? Have you forgotten he's Commander of the Dark Side? And tomorrow's the deadline to negotiate their 'consulting' contracts. In a week, they'll no longer be employees. I'll have no control over them . . ." He winced, having caught the silliest statement of all time escaping his lips. Even he, the original Dudley Do-Right, no longer believed that this legal dismemberment would lighten the emotional toll of the past few months (in fact, we were both pretty clear it would only serve to amp up the bile exponentially), having lost any and all illusions of justice and fair play.

I grinned. "Play their game, use their rules. All you need is the right leverage. And here's a fun nugget for Phil to chew: covertly wiretapping your head henchman is no way to inspire and maintain loyalty, nor to achieve undying devotion in your soldiers. You have solid proof of that, now. *The enemy's spies who have come to spy on us must be sought out, tempted with bribes, led away, and comfortably housed. Thus they will become converted spies and available for our service.* If I know Simon, he'll leave Phil swinging in the wind, and Phil's future with the studio will be wholly up to your discretion. So! *Your* deliverable will be a well-timed disclosure to 'convert' Phil and secure his participation. He's critical—he's the only one who can help us find that money. We have two days before we leave for Mexico and six weeks until the auction. We'll keep the wiretaps in 'til then and use them to leak scripted information. I'll 'run lines' with Guy, Sarah, and Charlie; whatever we want Simon to 'know.' You get Phil on board, I'll handle everything else." I paused, secretly wondering where I'd find an army to Master Sun's specifications on such short notice. I swept that niggling thought away; details! I smiled my most angelic smile. "So: whaddya think?"

"Well," Jamey started slowly, wheels turning, "it's certainly compelling, but . . ." He drained his glass and laughed, rubbing his tired eyes. "This scheme is insane, Stace. You know that."

"Oh, it's *fucking* insane, sweetie," I amended, smiling. "That's why it's gonna work." I flipped open the file and pulled out our plane tickets to Mexico: a "tactical withdrawal" to rest and plan for the future. The Trueharts and Sturms would vacation at the same resort. I had plans for them, oh yes, big gigantic plans. They were my resources, my reinforcements, my local guides, my bait! They just didn't know it yet.

Jamey looked at me pointedly. "Doesn't this technically make us as bad as them?"

I thought of the emotionally ravaged German shepherd and ran a finger slowly around the rim of my flute. How much more could we honestly take? It was only a matter of time before we, too, were truly crazy. Or divorced. . . . I shrugged. "I've had an awful lot of help getting to this scary, scary place, Jame. We have to do *something*, and Master Sun says, *Standing on the defensive indicates insufficient strength; attacking, a superabundance of strength. Ground on which we can only be saved from destruction by fighting without delay, is desperate ground. . . . In desperate position, you must fight.* The hunted will become the hunters. So be it. It's the law of the jungle. They won't change and this town won't change; *we're* the ones who need to change and adapt to our surroundings and circumstances. We need to rise to the occasion. And I am, after all, an 'Avenging' spirit . . . with a wicked sense of humor and a *mad* sense of style."

On cue, the waiter reappeared and laid a domed silver tray in front of Jamey, winking as he departed. "We will avenge our honor and decimate our enemy, but first we need to seal our covenant. Open it," I urged, excited. He lifted the lid and grinned: a sampling of naughty La Perla underthings, gourmet body paints, and brushes.

I feigned surprise. "So *that's* where my outfit's got to! I've been looking everywhere. I thought I might've lost it at the Brazilians' earlier today. All this time I've been wearing *nothing*, but"—I scanned the deserted patio—"*this*. . . . " I unbelted my leather trench to reveal . . .

"A room key on a chain!" Jamey crowed. He kissed me tenderly, and I shivered. But not from the cold.

"You know, we *are* still newlyweds. I've ordered dinner for us upstairs and . . ." He kissed me just south of the dangling key, halting the need for any further words.

CHAPTER 14

THE ART OF WAR/
RECONNAISSANCE

> The Art of War teaches us not to rely on the enemy's
> not coming, but on our own readiness to receive him;
> not on the chance of his not attacking, but rather on
> the fact that we have made our position unassailable.
> —Sun Tzu, *The Art of War*

*O*of! Where *was* Isabel? I checked the clock, exasperated; only fifteen minutes until *Un Día Grande* and I'd raced back from the hotel to meet her, to tidy my multi-papered war room and pack for vacation. My cell phone beeped with a message from Inga: the long-awaited invite to Lady Selena's much vaunted, highly inspirational Kabbalah Circle had come through. Today was the last meeting of the year. I checked the TV: no Paco. In his place was wall-to-wall coverage of yet another low-speed/high-speed car chase. No Paco, no Isabel. I clicked off the remote and called Inga to accept.

"Please don't tell Mallory," she added. "Lady Selena turned her down flat. But she seemed very eager to meet *you*, when I mentioned your name." Not telling Mallory would not, of course, be a problem.

I packed some toiletries, showered, and dressed, fighting the impulse to call/argue with Magda re appropriate Kabbalah attire (Inga informed me I'd be meeting the Seekers, a very A list of spiritually prominent wives) and selected a brand-new dusty rose Dana Buchman suit. My first pastel anything! This heroic fashion conversion would meet with howls from the New York girls, of course, but I knew I'd receive ecstatic approval from Isabel, that self-obsessed arbiter of ladylike style, and thus hopefully please the regal Lady Selena.

The front door opened. *"Feliz Navidad!"* Ah, so the lovely Señora Isabel would be gracing me with her presence after all. And only an hour late; things were definitely looking up. I peered over the stairway: strikingly festive she was in red and green raw silk Oscar de la Renta and elaborately knotted hair. Well, such extensive beauty takes time, I reasoned. A smile of utter pleasure spread across her face as she assessed my outfit. "Now you look like *me!*" she proclaimed proudly. We exchanged gifts and (gasp!) pleasantries. I handed her an envelope containing her Christmas bonus; she gave me a tin of holiday cookies her daughter had helped bake.

Hoarse barking outside (and Isabel's Spanglish invective inside) alerted me to the arrival of the UPS truck, and I went to check the mail. Back in the kitchen, my attention flickered between bills and holiday cards, a detailed critique of Sun Tzu's "Military Methods" and TV-directed slams from Isabel of "Slut!" or *"Idiota!"*

During a commercial break, Isabel bustled back through with an armful of laundry, humming the theme from the next-up *Bésame Tonto.* Spotting my sorted piles, she dropped the washing at my feet and hurried to fetch the Longons' holiday card for me to admire. I made an appropriate fuss, not wanting to wreck our tenuous ceasefire. I praised the paper stock and their Warholian portraits on the front. She was delighted.

In her own attempt at largesse, she picked up my cards and just as slowly commented through. At one in particular she paused, held it as to a light, squinting with a quizzical expression. Her eyes widened and she giggled, quietly at first, then louder until it became a full-on roar. I leaned over to learn what sparked this strange reaction.

But of course: Simon and Julia, dripping in grand portrait finery. Did *everyone* know them? They were inescapable. The card was a numbered edition photograph, shot through Vaseline and professionally retouched. Interesting that they had overlooked deleting us from their Christmas list; it was unlike them not to be thorough. I laughed along with Isabel, but apparently not for the same reason.

"You know this lady? Or do you know the man?"

"I know them both. The man works with Jamey. Why?"

"The lady, I know her. I mean I've seen pictures. She looks different; it's the hair, and also the . . ." She cupped her hands out in front of her chest. "This pink man, he is *married* . . . to *her*?" She looked disgusted.

"Yes, why?"

"Because I know it's her, and I tell you, she *no lady*." Harrumph!

"Well," I explained, intrigued (and wanting to laugh out loud again) by Isabel's definitive tone, "Her name is Julia Mallis, but her maiden name was Spraglet. She's from Minnesota. She's a truly bad actress now. Before that, she was a truly bad singer. Maybe she's been on one of your shows?"

Isabel snorted with contempt. "I *knew* it! I remember from my magazines. She not a *real* actress! She could *never* be on one of *my* shows!"

I smiled. It was fun to see Isabel riled up about someone else besides me. "I think you may have her mixed up with someone else, really." I tried to dismiss the conversation.

But Isabel was having none of it; she shook her head very fast and stabbed at Julia's photo. "I telling you: I *know* her! She's the naked girl who comes out of the bottle of tequila. She changes from the worm to a woman. She's the 'Big Stud' condom girl!"

I was awestruck; a priceless visual played in my head, engraving itself. Our Julia: mercenary, covetous, imperious, narcissistic—*and* a trashy beer babe, to boot! If it were true, that is. "You're joking, Isabel, right?" Isabel shook her head firmly. She knew what she knew. "How can you be sure?" My hunt for intelligence had begun.

"Well. It was on the TV and in all my magazines. Before the white hair and big boobs. She did the condom commercial *after* she ruined the reputation of Pedro Cojones—he was the older priest on *Una Vida de Amor*, Padre Victor. He and his wife and family—grandchildren, too—they were always on the cover of *¡Hola!*. Ay! They were so happy!" she sighed, very personally involved.

"And then *she* came along . . . the *bad* lady." She glared with contempt at the card. "It was a big scandal, oh yes. You know, I love him, since I was a young girl. My sister too. He was disgraced, in front of God and everyone, and they took him off the show. I mean—a priest! The woman has no shame!" She tapped furiously with a candy-red fingernail. "They killed him. *Verdad*. They even showed the body, so you *know* it's real." She crossed herself dramatically, eyes to heaven.

"Wait a minute, he died?"

"On the *show* he died. Same thing," she shrugged. "He was helping get gang children off the streets. He was so kind! And then he was shot dead."

"So, what you're saying is, he repented for his sins in the end," I said, not mistaking the irony.

She sighed again. "*Sí*. He tried. It was very sad. But his wife left him anyway. And *then*, *she* did that ad—that *tramp*!"

"Yes, well . . ." She'd moved on to the last two cards. One was a "Save the Date" for the Hyperhidrosis lunch; the second was an invite to yet another Shopping-at-Gunpoint fiesta for the so-called Youth Education Movement. Isabel now recognized Julia's name and glowered darkly.

"The tramp runs this group? They come to my daughter's school, these . . . *ladies*, to convince the young girls they can make money and clean for important Hollywood people." She thought a minute. "You no like her, right?"

"That's putting it mildly." Maybe I could add Isabel to my list of available resources. One could only imagine how deep *her* network really ran.

Her eyes danced. "I take this card home, okay? I bring it back after holiday." She walked past me to the fridge, took out the Lillet, and brought two shot glasses to the table, settling in for *Bésame Tonto*. I declined her offer of a nip. "I no clean *killing sha* room today," she announced, making an excellent show of shuddering with fear even as her eyes twinkled. "Next time . . . I *try*, okay?" She raised her glass to me and crossed herself playfully as I opened the garage door.

After a quick stop at Citibank (to spring three dresses out of hock at Green's Soup Nazi Cleaners) I headed to the Bel Air Hills and the consciousness-expanding aerie of the reclusive, iconic Hamburger Queen. Now (Inga had informed me), the compelling back-story went that the Queen's late husband, Lord Lawson (the very dead Hamburger King) had been an obese womanizer who tormented his doting Queen with his many sordid infidelities. He died a spectacularly scandalous Old Hollywood death: after an evening of heavy drink and heavy cream at Le Dome, he had a fatal stroke in the arms of his underage hooker mistress (who interestingly enough turned out to be a mister). In said mister's distress, he'd left his leather zippered thong along with matching mask, whip, and Hollywood High ID amongst the Hamburger King's disheveled sheets in a bungalow at the Beverly Hills Hotel, having called *Variety before* calling the police but only *after* leaving the scene. . . . But, as Inga hastened to suggest, "I wouldn't necessarily bring this up." In any event, Lady Selena duly inherited his weighty empire, survived the wagging tongues and, having had ten billion head of cattle slaughtered to give thanks for her good fortune, was by all accounts repenting ardently through vegetables and good works in this lifetime in enthusiastic preparation for the next—a mulligan, if you will; a do-over shot. Hence her devotion to all things eastern and mystical, especially the study of Kabbalah and its happy promise of reincarnation.

Golden "om" symbols welded to a wrought-iron gate heralded my arrival. I added my newly pristine Mustang to a lineup of ten pristine Mercedes and Jags and Bentleys and hiked up the drive to an enormous, strikingly modern edifice, all glass and white brick and circular arcs—a hard angle could not be found. The front door was ajar and I wandered tentatively into a Zen-like, minimalist sandstone/limestone gardenia-infused atmosphere. My eyes watered immediately, the scent was so concentrated.

I could hear the Contessa in my head—"*Clear*ing! *Clear*ing!"—then remembered that Lady Selena kept her on retainer. Inga appeared out of nowhere, with unkempt hair and red-rimmed eyes. "Inga!" I was shocked by her appearance. "Are you okay?"

She wrung her hands. "I had a very . . . *unsettling* experience at Gucci earlier. I was buying swimsuits for Mexico, and those salesgirls . . ." She shuddered. "Where've you been?"

I checked my watch. Exactly on time. "Am I late? I had to stop at Citibank."

She looked at me blankly. "Why?"

I looked at her blankly. "To get money."

"But . . . doesn't money come home to you in a little pouch?" she inquired, confused.

I answered, confused, "What?"

"Our business manager sends money to the house. In a pouch. Doesn't yours?"

Oy. "Inga, what's wrong? Has the group started?" I couldn't hear a sound except wind chimes on a breeze.

"I called to see if you'd have lunch with me. Scott came home and was going to make me eat but I said I was meeting you."

"So . . . you didn't have to eat. That's . . . good, right?"

"Yeah," she perked up a bit. "And no, nothing's started yet. Lady Selena's hatha yoga session's running long. I'm very upset, but I'm sure the vibrations will heal me." She twirled a loose strand of colorless hair, eyes wafting to the indoor waterfall.

Just then a door opened in the seamless limestone wall. I peeked inside: a mirrored studio contained a nut brown swami, turbaned and sweating in white linen, bowing toward quite possibly the thinnest (and most flexible) older woman I'd ever seen: Gumby in a flesh-colored Danskin thong. *Namaste!* The woman (Lady Selena, I took it) stretched expansively, flipped her pale bobbed hair, and turned toward us.

"I'm sorry to have kept you waiting, girls, but that was *very* invigorating! *Completely* life affirming!" A tuxedoed, white-gloved butler buttled in, handed her a towel and a white silk robe, and buttled away again. She dabbed at her glistening, unlined brow. "Inga darling, is the Rav here yet? I can't quite . . . *feel* him." Wow.

"He's in the loo, I believe. Something about the salmon pizza at Spago not agreeing with him."

Lady Selena snorted, then looked to me and brightened. "You must be Stacey."

"Yes, Lady Selena. Thank you for including me. I'm interested in learning about Kabbalah, and Inga was kind enough . . ." Now my nose was running, too; I fumbled in my bag for a tissue.

Lady Selena proffered one quickly from her robe pocket. "The gardenia scent helps free one from all selfishness, envy, anger, and self-pity. I have it piped in—but it does take some getting used to," she added helpfully. "We must let the *light* take over!" She thrust her hands heavenwards, then dropped her voice. "We're very traditional here, Stacey," she warned. "Today is not discussion day; rather, the Rav will recite in Aramaic. It should be interesting for you to observe and absorb." A smile played on her lips. "I've been looking forward to meeting you, you know. She cocked her head. "You remind me of Diana Rigg, from *The Avengers*? You should dress more like her, instead of in pastels. It would suit you. I hope you'll stay afterward." Was she kidding? I worshipped her instantly.

We followed as she padded down a long hallway and into her violet-tinged, gardenia-saturated study, where eight red-stringed, pastel-colored women chatted quietly on a semicircular violet suede couch. Zohar texts, pads and pens sat ready on their laps. Inga whispered excitedly, "The couch is the same color as Lady Selena's aura! An exact match, don't you think?"

I didn't even understand her question. I recognized some of the women from *Shinier Sheet* photo blurbs, publicizing their many good works. Most (if not all) had entire wings or funds or cures at local hospitals named for them and their spouses. From my daily *Variety* perusals, I knew that more than a few had husbands recently ousted from power positions: series cancellations, mergers-and-acquisition-related eliminations. In most cases these public "demotions" were more circumstantial than deserved, at least according to *fact*, and yet I was aware, as they were, that many (like Mallory) would (and did) consider them "tainted," sliding. Just like me. So we all had that in common: birds of a feather.

A colorful array of Kabbalah-related accessories were displayed on a glass table: red string packages, cube necklaces for healing and protection, stones and crystal charms empowered with the seventy-two names of God, key chains, baby gear, and more candles and incense than you'd find at a Venice Beach head shop—all to ignite the energy of love, healing, wealth, and safety, or so the little signs said.

An untouched buffet featured mounds of multicolored leaves, raw veggies, and crystal bowls overflowing with the most beautiful fruit: peaches and cherries and grapes of all colors. In among everything, white candles burned, tied with the ubiquitous red string. The effect was heady and solemn, like a sorority ritual room on initiation night.

Lady Selena sidled up and whispered in a naughty tone, "I call these meetings 'Herbage and Verbiage.'" She smiled conspiratorially, then announced to the group, "Girls, come meet Stacey." She reeled off their first names quickly, too quickly for me to retain. One woman in sea foam kept winking at me; it was a bit discomfiting. Well, Mallory had warned it might be a wonky circle. "To properly welcome you, Stacey, I will tie your first string." She tapped my left wrist as the women gathered to observe Lady Selena's perfect protocol, knotting the string seven times and reciting a special meditative prayer, the *Ana Be'Ko'ach*, I was told. I was as entranced by her chanting as by the gardenia immersion.

A male voice draped in Giorgio Armani robes cleared his throat, and the women quickly resumed their seats. I sat next to Inga to share her Zohar. Giorgio offered a quick prayer in Hebrew, instructed everyone in English to open their texts to the *"Pekudei"* section and, in an energetic, rhythmic singsong, immediately launched the room into hypnotic Aramaic overload. The walls fairly hummed with transcendence. French-tipped nails scanned pages, highlighted heads rocked in time to Giorgio's raga beat. Rapturous, transported expressions abounded. I whispered to Inga, odd man out, "Do you understand what he's talking about?"

"Clothing!" she breathed back dreamily, and without missing a beat (literally), she handed me an English-version Zohar from her bag. "I scanned the English briefly. Forget the Gucci girls. The Rav's talking about what to wear to be seen by God!"

Clothing? Well, sort of. In translation, the section spoke of Sacred Robes. The soul has special garments appropriate to each place visited: man's raiment is a uniform of the secular world, there are special robes for temple, and celestial robes made from supernal light for above. Our clothing in the next world will be made from our good deeds in this one. Oh—and they all have corresponding colorations and meanings that the radiant light reflects upon them. My mind reeled with irony: a chance to crack the infuriating Beverly Hills Dress Code *and* take Magda the Ridiculous down a notch or two. Could there be a more perfect use of my time? Giddy with a hundred one-liners for Jamey, Sarah, and Charlie, I noticed Lady Selena's gaze upon me, head tilted to one side. I sobered up immediately, a child caught passing notes in class. Curiously, she smiled and pointed to her watch, and then to the doorway.

The assignment was explained for the next meeting (the *"Lech Lecha,"* the portion about earning the appearance of one's soul mate, or strengthening the bond with one's current partner). The group murmured appreciatively, and as I followed Lady Selena from the room, I could hear Inga arranging a private tutorial. An incensed statement (well, for Inga) ". . . and the second-floor girls at Neiman's are even worse!" followed me down the hallway.

I perched contritely on a stool in an immaculate white kitchen, awaiting what I supposed would be a well-deserved lecture on respect and self-containment. Lady Selena returned from the back pantry with two glasses, opened a refrigerated drawer, and produced a chilled bottle of pink Billecart-Salmon champagne, which she popped and poured with practiced flourish. She pulled another drawer and sighed happily. I leaned over: the otherworldly Lady Selena was a junk food junkie! Yodels, Ring Dings, Twinkies, and fluffy pink Sno Balls abounded. Her eyes rolled back as she bit delicately into a Hostess Apple Pie. "Don't tell anyone," she murmured. "This'll be our little secret." I selected some Mallomars and sat back, nibbling slowly.

"Stacey," Lady Selena began, "I know a little about you. And your husband, too. Certainly I know about your . . . *situation.*" I stopped nibbling. "I do hear things, you know, in spite of my so-called monastic legend." She leaned close, examining me. "Tell me—how are you holding up?"

I held her gaze, appraising her back: friend or foe? "Living under siege is . . . annoying but, then again, I suppose one can get used to just about anything." Nothing. Then I added, *"It is better that my enemy speak ill of me, than not at all . . ."* She waited still, unmoved by my flippancy. I sighed, letting go. "I'm sorry to be glib, Lady Selena. It's been a really tough road. I don't think today's gardenias and Aramaic vibrations have helped release my . . . my desire to . . . retaliate. Against certain people." My eyes roamed tentatively over my Mallomar, and I braced again for a deluge of expected white-light-ish rhetoric.

She wrinkled her pretty nose and smiled thoughtfully. "This can be a very cruel town, a very heady place. And how could it not, with everyone running around begging for validation all the time? Wealth is consistently mistaken for brainpower, one recent success or failure overrides years of work. Careers, reputations, and bank accounts can be made or broken in a day. Feelings of isolation and emptiness are rampant, especially among the women. They're all searching for relevance, significance, *gravitas*, and to be heard. Just like the girls inside. They're used to being judged only as extensions of their powerful husbands. It's very limiting and ultimately unrewarding. I don't want you to become like that, Stacey. A word of caution: temperance. Don't lose the good in you to revenge." I looked down at my hands; if she only knew what I was planning.

Her smile turned conspiratorial. "I'm not sure if you know this, but your nemesis—the biologically very . . . *unusual* Julia Mallis— was the favorite of a stable—what my late husband once called"—she grimaced—"his 'air hostesses.'" My eyes widened in disbelief: *could this day get any better?* "It's true," she continued. "At the time she was on maybe her fifth au pair job somewhere in Europe, singing backup or . . . something with a fading crooner in a lounge act. Suffice it to say she met my husband at a nightclub and he . . . hired her to '*service*' his flights as he expanded his empire of . . . *meat* on the Continent. He paid for her very first set of boobs!" She checked my captivated expression and, probably sensing my insatiable hunger for any bits of biography re the air hostess, changed direction carefully, matter-of-factly. "The thing you have to remember about Julia is that she was and is unremarkable. That's why she behaves the way she does. There's nothing worse than mediocrity and self-loathing. It's a huge burden to carry. Not all the women around here are so voracious. *She* just happens to be 'caught up in your underpants,' as my mother used to say." She thought a minute. "A targeted strike is what's needed."

I grinned, blown away. "So, you agree I need to *do* something."

She opened a packet of Yodels and laid them lovingly on a Lalique dish. "I agree that . . . sometimes it's appropriate to hasten karma, if the person—or persons—are truly a threat." Her eyes turned merry and direct, my newfound local guide, my untold resource and ally, as though it was preordained, this meeting, and unfolding right on schedule. "You quoted something interesting, before; I think you're on the right track. Come back to Circle after the New Year and let me know how I can help."

A voice of reason in a sea of insanity. . . . I sipped contemplatively and changed direction myself. "Lady Selena," I ventured, "do you really spend six months a year in a Guatemalan yurt, knitting yoga mats out of yak hair?"

She roared with laughter. "How delicious! Those are the best rumors yet! See what happens when you don't ever bother to set the record straight? But let me see, what can I tell you? I do support a few villages in Guatemala, and I *adore* yoga, but I've never met a yak in all my born days, and I have no idea how to knit. All my clothing—yoga-wear included—is Givenchy. Couture. I am a true sensualist, my dear; I spend three months a year at my vineyard in Tuscany, and another three at my villa in Cap Ferrat. I intend to live the best life I can, and, strangely enough, I do like it here—even if the local demi-monde has fangs and tails and leaves an awful lot to be desired. What can I say? I like the weather."

"Me too," I laughed and toasted the sentiment. And, as the sugar and champagne took effect, it dawned that maybe, just maybe, I'd found myself a recruitable army! Oh, I'd be back, you can bet.

CHAPTER 15

—

THE ART OF WAR/STRATAGEM

Thus we may know that there are five essentials for victory: (1) He will win who knows when to fight and when not to fight. (2) He will win who knows how to handle both superior and inferior forces. (3) He will win whose army is animated by the same spirit throughout its ranks. (4) He will win who, prepared himself, waits to take the enemy unprepared. (5) He will win who has military capacity and is not interfered with by the sovereign.

—Sun Tzu, *The Art of War*

*Y*ou made it!" Sarah greeted me outside the poolside casita she'd reserved, supervising the kids splashing about in the water. "Where's everyone else?"

"Inga's melting down at the gift shop and Jamey and Scott are playing tennis." I indicated the files and books piled in my arms. "I wanted to find you. There's something I want to run by you and Charlie." At the sound of his name, melodramatic moaning groaned loudly from within the canvas cabana. I smiled. From the moment we'd met he'd been my best audience and sounding board; he seemed to appreciate my social dissection of Hollywood and outsider point of view. He'd question me endlessly, roaring at my mimicry and commentary. Needless to say, I adored him.

Sarah's face clouded. "The creative genius"—she jerked her chin toward the tented flap—"is inside searching for inspiration on which, if any, of his 'secret, half-finished, untitled projects' he'll declare, finish, and entitle. And then there's the auction problem." She smiled wryly and shrugged. "I'm glad you and Jamey are here; he's been a bear."

"I've got just the thing. Charlie?" I called from outside the cabana. "If you're up for company, I've got a puzzle for you—well, it's more of a game, actually, but if you play your cards right, you could be a general . . ." Nothing. I dangled a glossy, black-and-gold Chinese-charactered book through the flap. Singsong, I teased, "Jamey's already playing . . ."

"What's on offer?" replied a half-comic, half-petulant voice.

"A unique and ingenious revenge fantasy, designed to decimate a few fiendishly diabolical villains. All of whom you know." I grinned at Sarah, who grinned right back. "Besides, I got your auction prize sussed."

I heard masses of paper crumpling, and then, "En-*ter!*" came the command, Walter Matthau-perfect from *The Sunshine Boys.*

Sarah flagged the poolboy for margaritas and chips (brain food), and I set about outlining my plans, disclosing our recently discovered security breach and my intentions toward Phil, the hidden slush fund, and the Kabbalah Circle. Naturally, I quoted Sun Tzu as often as possible to bolster my case. It was plain I had Sarah from word one, but Charlie listened intently, all the way through, rubbing his beard. When I finished, he said nothing at all but scrutinized me carefully. At last he spoke. "Balls o' steel, kid. And *very* enterprising. Are you really up for this?"

I nodded gravely.

"Well, then"—he broke into a wide grin, pushed aside stacks of scripts, and picked up a blank legal pad—"we've got work to do."

Side by side, we brainstormed and scribbled away, Charlie's own projects long forgotten. Preparation is everything, Master Sun always counsels, and we took him at his word: *"When able to attack, we must seem unable; when using our forces, we must seem inactive; when we are near, we must make the enemy believe we are far away; when far away, we must make him believe we are near."* We debated and strategized, exploring character motivation, action, and reaction; scripting detailed conversational plotlines for me and Sarah, Guy, Jamey, and Charlie to enact. The process was that of real-life storyboarding, just like an intricately crafted movie plot. It was quite a heady learning experience, being privately tutored by a creative genius.

Each evening the bigger group would convene at the thatched outdoor lounge, debriefing, rehearsing, and laughing ourselves silly. We'd agreed at the outset to go democratically down the menu of all seven cleverly named umbrella drinks—a new themed cocktail for each evening. Cactus coladas, in multiple! Which proved very helpful, especially as Jamey and I accepted input devising a "pantomime language" for use in our bugged living quarters. Scott had just wrapped a spy caper and had excellent dialogue suggestions—but the more savory ones turned out to be from a talky bondage-porn script he'd found, to be read in the bedroom, naturally, to satisfy any over-eager, inquiring minds.

Alone in our ocean view suite, things were even better. "I can't remember the last time we did this," mused Jamey, his head in my lap, both of us tangled in sheets. "It's like a tonic: an expanse of time just to relax and be among actual friends, instead of reacting to crises all the time." LA and its perilous social issues melted away, at least in the evenings and those sexy, tequila-tinged nights.

I kissed his forehead and stroked his bare chest. "I know. Life without eavesdroppers or Pacificus-related distractions. *Now* I remember why I married you!" My eyes filled with tears—happy ones, no pills necessary. Jamey just laughed and pulled me on top of him. Again.

PART III

Waging War

CHAPTER 16

MAY THE FORCE BE WITH YOU

> Thus, what enables the wise sovereign and the good general to strike and conquer, and achieve things beyond the reach of ordinary men, is foreknowledge. Hence the use of spies . . .
>
> —Sun Tzu, *The Art of War*

We landed back at LAX, gathered our bags, and stopped at Whole Foods for milk and other necessities. As Jamey paid the driver and unloaded our luggage, I set about making coffee, opening windows, and dismantling the plastic-wrap-covered bathtub greenhouse I'd rigged for my orchids. "Stace, there's an envelope here for you."

"Who's it from?" I called, reaching to drain the murky water.

"Doesn't say. No postmark, either. It must've been hand-delivered."

Curious, I dried my hands and examined the brown paper envelope, which contained a single sheet of paper. I stared at the unfamiliar, boxy lettering: "Stacey. Check out www.mujeresexotics.es." It was signed, simply, "A Friend."

Jamey and I raced to the office and, mindful of the taping devices still snug in their vents, turned the TV loud, booted the computer, and typed in the Spanish Web address. The site flashed on the screen. *¡Dios mío!* There, big and hairy as day (and at least three or four cosmetic surgeries ago), was my favorite Big Stud condom girl, our very own small-town pastry from Minnesota, the lovely and talented Señorita Yoolya.

Upon closer inspection, it really was more of a photo timeline for surgical enhancements, once you got past the in-your-face full-frontal nudity and clever props. Her hair went from dark mousy to almost white (all over, I might add—no detail too small, as always); relatively flat chest to hubba hubba; nose, chin, teeth, lips—all changed. In fact, if it weren't for the chronologic progression, you might have thought it was an entirely different woman.

Neither of us could speak for a good few minutes, gawping open-mouthed as we were. Finally, I whispered, "So *this* is how she subsidizes her extreme clothing habit—a $9.99 membership fee. I suppose it could add up to a Sinfonia Folata frock. Or ten."

Jamey whistled through his teeth. "Wild stuff. At least we know all those vague medical bills Commerz paid were put to good use. How often do you suppose she updates the site?"

The photos didn't look all that recent to me, but what did I know? With professional hair and makeup, proper lighting, computer retouching . . . anything was possible. I shrugged. "Do you think Simon knows about this?" I answered his question with one of my own.

Jamey snorted. "If she's making money, then rest assured he knows about it. Any annuity is a good annuity to Simon."

"That may be, as a rule. But I have to say, as shrewd as he is in business, he's amazingly unaware when it comes to his wife's activities." We gazed at the screen, pondering this disconnect in Simon's character.

I moved on to a more vexing issue: from where did this note come, and why? I mean, why me? "Why does Deep Throat want me to know this exists, and what do you suppose he wants me to do about it? Do you think someone's blackmailing Julia?"

"Can't be. Too many shots from too many years, and they're not candids. She's aware of what she's doing."

I zoomed in and out distractedly. "A Friend." Who could it be? We'd been with Sarah, Charlie, Scott, and Inga for an entire week: it wasn't them. Isabel? Maybe. But why wouldn't she just tell me in person? "It could be Guy, but he'd never be able to restrain himself from divulging something like this. Besides, he's already said worse about her, and only ten minutes after meeting me."

Jamey's cell rang, and our mutual contemplation was broken. Vacation was officially over. Jamey mouthed the name Phil, and as he listened, a huge smile spread across his face. He put the phone to his chest, and smiled. "I'll take this outside." Happy New Year! "The next phase of our master plan has officially begun."

About a week later, fate stepped in, and another phone call provided a well-timed opportunity to reach out to Lady Selena to convene an emergency session of the Kabbalah Circle. I psyched myself up, rehearsing and refining my pitch in the car as I raced to pick up Inga (who was in no condition to drive, poor thing). Today's meeting would be a huge gain for me, I hoped—but a Circle of Pain, I was afraid, for poor Inga.

Lady Selena greeted me and the heavily medicated Inga at the door. "The Rav's jet isn't back yet from Miraval, but his son's agreed to fill in. So no Aramaic today . . ." She eyed me over Inga's slouched head. "Ready?" she whispered. I nodded back.

The calm of the violet couch was interrupted by the entrance of an energetic, handsome, Ralph Lauren-clad preppy who offered prayers in Hebrew and then in English. "I'm aware, ladies, that you've been off for the holidays. Before we begin, I understand there are some pressing issues you'd like to discuss."

I nudged Inga, but she just slumped listlessly into my shoulder. The Winking Wife raised her hand. "Rabbi, your father's coming for dinner next week. I wanted to ask, which fish are kosher?" The others reached for their pads and pens.

The rabbi grinned. "Kosher fish have gills, fins, and scales." I smiled. "Dad likes salmon, though." He winked back at the Winking Wife.

A strawberry blonde named Christine, fretting in buttercup yellow, raised a timid hand, "Rabbi, I've been divorced three years now, and I just broke up with yet another jerk. I still haven't met my soul mate. Is it possible he didn't make it down here this go round?"

The others looked worriedly to the rabbi. "Oh, he's here." Everyone exhaled; God is good. "You just need to keep attending classes and let more white light into your system in order to see him." Hmm. A male model dispensing redemption, eternal life, menu *and* dating advice? Oh, I'd have Sarah, Jamey, and Charlie rolling on the ground at dinner tonight with this.

Focus, Stacey! I nudged Inga again, a bit harder. A muffled sob escaped and I put my arm around her for support. "It's okay, Inga. Tell everyone what's on your mind."

She struggled to get it together. "Well, we got back from vacation. I was in such a good mood." She nodded to me, then broke down again. "Oh, it's just too horrible to say!" We waited as she regained her composure. Finally, she managed to blurt, "Last night I discovered . . . my Missy, my Bichon, my baby . . . was *eaten* . . . by *coyotes!*" Horrified gasps flew from everyone's perfectly painted lips. "There's a pack of them, right now, in my backyard. They're using a drainage pipe for their den. Scott's just started a film in Vancouver and I went looking for her and"—she lowered her voice, angry—"I *saw* them! I'm so afraid for my Sassy, Missy's sister!"

Lavender-shifted Amy's hand shot up, "My two tabby cats were eaten right before Christmas! I found their collars on the lawn, along with bits of fur . . ."

A honey-blonde in mauve added, "My Rottweiler was in a terrible fight with one last year. She hasn't been the same since. They come around and torment her in her wire pen!" I thought immediately of my pathetically unhinged neighbor and sighed. I'd have to get Isabel to lay off the poor creature, somehow.

Bettina in a sky-blue A-line chimed in darkly, "My Boxer's in heat. I had her outside with me, and these coyotes started baying from behind our bushes, almost . . . *wooing* her. I think they wanted to . . . *mate* with her. My poor Ginger!" More shudders and cries of horror ensued.

By now the entire violet couch was in tears, gesturing madly and sharing pictures of adored pets pulled from Chanel croc wallets. Ralph Lauren ran from one to the next, comforting as best he could, but the ladies would have none of it. "The Kabbalistic prescription for letting go," he called over the din, "comes from the Seventy-two Names of God. It's the Ayin-Lamed-Nin, the fourth name from the right in the top row. It helps ward off negative thoughts and keeps us on the right path." The tears and sniffles only increased. A most unhelpful prescription, it certainly did seem. Ralph tried valiantly again. "If your souls are truly connected then you will be together forever, in this lifetime and the next." The women looked up. "The more we go outside of ourselves, the more light comes inside us. Anxiety and sadness are manifestations of darkness. Light floods the darkness. Let's concentrate on the light." A bit better. But not nearly enough.

"I say we kill them," Inga glowered menacingly, dabbing at her eyes. "With knives and guns and poison. Bastards! Who do they think they are, taking what they want, whenever they want? My Missy never did anything bad to anybody!" she wailed anew. Rabbi Ralph looked on in alarm as the others murmured full approval of Inga's drastic call to arms; the cupcake-colored ladies were turning nasty.

I finally had my opening. The intense flash of innovation that struck when Inga first called had crystallized: this was all too perfect an allegory for the even more frightening two-legged predators in this town. For Simon, Julia, and others of their narcissistic, sociopathic breed. I knew at this critical time I could invoke the Moral Law: *The Moral Law causes the people to be in complete accord with their ruler, so that they will follow him regardless of their lives, undismayed by any danger.* Yes! I caught Lady Selena's eye; she'd been watching me carefully. It was confirmed: I had discovered the perfect way to engage them, my soon-to-be loyal recruits, my army, my useful local spies! *He will win whose army is animated by the same spirit throughout its ranks. My* very own Circle of Pain! But first I'd need to help them with their four-legged foes. My mind raced: *Now in order to kill the enemy, our men must be roused to anger; that there may be an advantage from defeating the enemy, they must have their rewards.*

I stood, confident; empowered by truth, justice, and my brilliant 2500-year-old compatriot. Yup: it was finally time for my *Norma Rae* moment. "Ladies! Listen to me: I have an idea." I waited until the couch quieted some, the sniffling and dabbing subsided. "Sadly, we can't kill them, these . . . *coyotes*; they're just an unfortunate fact of life around here. Besides, it would be cruel and very probably illegal. They do have a right to exist. But still, we do need to protect ourselves and those we love. Let's think for a moment: what is it about these . . . coyotes, these tricksters, these *predators*"—I paused for emphasis, making individual, Dale Carnegie-approved eye contact—"circling our town, our homes and backyards from above, roaming freely about the Hills of Hollywood, tearing up, beating up, and, frankly, *screwing over* (sorry, Rabbi) anything or anyone that might innocently stand in their treacherous path?" The women were listening now, rapt; I had struck a nerve. I had their full attention. Even better, I had the Big Idea! I continued, "There's simply too much greedy, ravenous, blood-thirsty behavior going on here, in *all* our backyards. It's evident in every facet of our lives. Who *hasn't* been affected by troublemaking, covetous vultures who threaten our peaceful ways with their own agendas? Only if we band together can we do something about it. We must take control, ladies; we must remove the darkness and the physical danger, not only to our pets, but also to our families. I say we go down the line, case by case, based on peril. Our first project will be securing Inga's home, dealing with the den that's taken up unwelcome residence there. We'll learn more about them. For instance, I've heard from my gardener that coyotes are very good ratters, useful for rodent control . . . maybe there's somewhere they'd be helpful. We'll work through our grief and our pain, and heal by creating something positive, something nonviolent, something *unifying* . . . and we will bring *light* inside." (I glanced at Ralph.) "We'll start a . . . a Coyote Relocation Program!"

Gasps of joy flew from the couch. Ralph nodded his overwhelming approval, Inga's teary eyes sparkled, Lady Selena clasped her hands together, and the Winking Wife winked incessantly. Bettina immediately offered, "I know an animal psychic! She can ask the coyotes where they'd like to go—like a . . . a coyote whisperer!"

Christine the Buttercup cried, "My ex owns like a billion trillion acres in the desert, by Joshua Tree. He has a production facility there and the soundstages have major rodent issues. We've just started speaking again. I'll ask him for ideas!"

Amy piped in, "My husband owns a movie merchandising company. I can have T-shirts printed up."

Exhilarated, I grabbed my notepad and hastily drew a circle. The girls huddled close as I sketched a likeness of a smarmy agent inside, Ray-banned and PDA'd in both ears. Then I drew a slash right through it. "Here's our logo!" I cried. This won a blazing smile from Amy and belly laughs from the others, followed quickly by a chorus of "Aww!" as I reluctantly crossed out the agent and sketched another circle with a cunning coyote face inside. *Be subtle!* Master Sun whispered in my ear. . . . Was he kidding?

And so it went. Schedules were set; ideas, phone numbers, and e-mail addresses enthusiastically exchanged. *Concentrate your energy and hoard your strength. Keep your army continually on the move, and devise unfathomable plans.* I was debating the pros and cons of enlisting Javier the Scientologist to help when Lady Selena tapped my elbow and motioned me to follow her to the kitchen.

"Stacey," Lady Selena began, excitedly arranging Ding Dongs on a Christofle tray, "that was quite possibly the most inspirational meeting we've ever had. I haven't seen such enthusiasm since, well . . . since the Heidi Fleiss scandal and the ensuing Divorce of the Week Club!" We both giggled. "And what an empowering speech! The girls are riled up and ready for action. They'll follow you just about any-where, but somehow I think you knew that." She raised her eyebrows. "But I must caution again: temperance. Avoid the karmic ripple. Deal with your own personal predators, then get on with your life. You've used your vacation time well. I will be your first sponsor and offer you everything in my power to help. As you know, my late husband was one of the biggest predators of all." She grimaced briefly, then brightened. "Now!" she bit into a Ding Dong, "tell me how the girls and I fit into your plans."

CHAPTER 17

MEANWHILE, BACK AT THE RANCH

Having inward spies (means) making use of officials
of the enemy. Having converted spies (means) getting
hold of the enemy's spies and using them for our own
purposes.

—Sun Tzu, *The Art of War*

I pulled into the Pacificus garage around six-thirty and parked
in Barb's vacant spot, next to Simon's and Jamey's, close to
the elevator. Guy had mentioned that Barb had booked yet another
post-holiday-pre-Awards Season "renovation retreat"—in Aspen,
maybe? Or was it Arizona? Something with an A, anyway. Would it
be belly or thighs this go-round?

I'd just managed to clean up after the third Coyote Club outing
of the week (this time the site was Bettina's French-country estate off
Coldwater Canyon). I was now picking up Jamey to meet Sarah and
Charlie at the Polo Lounge, our final strategy session to prepare for
next week's Alien vs. Predator Auction SmackDown.

My Coyote Club innovation provided great companionship; the
girls were warm and kind. Way more than a mere army, I had friends
at last—a whole pack of 'em! Much of our fun centered on the wacky

coyote whisperer and her translated storylines that rivaled the best of Isabel's *novelas*. For example, after heated debate amongst themselves, Inga's coyotes (domineering mothers, abandonment issues) wanted to relocate to Santa Fe. Second choice: Tahoe. The Rottweiler's visitors (den wetting/nocturnal emissions) wanted to summer in Sun Valley, and Bettina's Boxer's boyfriend, when pressed, just wanted to stay put and moon over Ginger. . . . He'd professed his undying love. Too bad. They were all going, via specially rigged Hummer (donated by Lady Selena) and accompanied by Javier and his wildlife Scientologists, to Joshua Tree to clean up Christine's ex's many soundstages. Never forget, these were Hollywood animals, after all.

I rode the elevator to the twenty-third floor and peered out tentatively: no incoming mortar fire this evening. A passing secretary let me through the security door. I waved away her offer of guidance and made my own way back to the executive suite. Jamey was huddled with Phil over spreadsheets in one of the small conference rooms—even through the scrim shade I could make out the faint purple stripes of his favorite shirt. Phil was merely a paler mass of monotonous gray. They'd had their heads together an awful lot; Phil had indeed completed his conversion as undercover Secret Squirrel double agent, disclosing both the existence and location of Simon's clandestine fund: three to five million dollars in an unrecorded corporate account, kept for his private use away from Commerz's (and Jamey's) prying eyes. Jamey would eventually reward Phil by naming him his number two and reorganizing Stupid Squad, casting out Simon's nefarious techie junta. I hummed happily; with one week to go, all necessary elements were falling into place.

As I approached the corner suite I heard Simon's voice through his closed door; he was on the phone, apparently, and speaking loudly. I caught my number-one spy's eye (listening in, naturally, on his headset and flipping through a recent issue of *Gloss*), put my finger to my lips, and snuck into Jamey's cubby to wait.

Although he'd been famously terminated (the Shot Heard 'Round the Trades) and relegated to consultant status, Simon continued to come in to the office every day, avoiding the hostile home front and Julia's increasingly emotional tirades (Guy had delightedly reported). Now that Simon's once-unassailable position was in peril of evaporating, she behaved even more erratically, spent even more wildly, and was demanding actual results from his original promise to make her a Star. Simon, in turn, was driving Jamey and Guy nuts, tormenting them as best and constantly as he could: glaring daggers of hatred and blame their way, sotto mutterings of "ingrate," "Judas," "traitor," and "turncoat," any time he passed either in the hallways. He'd often slam his door for emphasis, to fully express his displeasure (and, of course, to covertly brood and scheme in private) and spitefully disallowed Guy to place or answer any of his calls. Withholding access— like *that* would show him! As Simon would most definitely say: "Sissy dandy ferret! Fucking fuckhead fucker!!"

He was on with Barb, I took it, discussing the many aspects of their new "production gig." Job one, it seemed, was refurbishing the pool bungalow on Simon's property to serve as their base of operations. Guy had gleefully informed me this would require quite a bit of décor and lifestyle change, as the pool house had been serving Julia as her own cozy retreat in which to entertain a steady stream of willing swordsmen. And so: out with the ermine comforter, plushy carpeting, and wall-to-wall Dux bed; in with desks, cork boards, swivel chairs, and filing cabinets. Naturally, I heard Simon snigger, Julia was miffed at first, hearing she'd have to forgo her nest, "but she calmed down once I explained our 'priority one' objective was to find a breakout script to display her many charms, for her to receive recognition as the blindingly shining talent she was destined to be. . . . Oh, and I promised she could oversee the redesign. That should keep her off my back! God but she's high strung! Not at all like you, Barb," he said in a softer tone, sighing loudly. A touching moment—I exchanged raised eyebrows with Guy, who shook his head slowly, rolled his eyes, and put a hand dramatically to his forehead.

Poor codependent, unfulfilled, tragic Barb; the only one who'd ever truly understood and adored him unconditionally. She'd stood by him always, suffering silently, and yet nobly. . . . I made a Camille-like gesture back at Guy and adjusted my shell satin Prada top ("shell *is* the new pumpkin!") that had hiked up with the effort, and settled back in Jamey's chair to continue listening.

"When're you coming back, anyway? You know you look great to me just as you are . . ." Simon whined. Then, as an afterthought, he wondered aloud, truly mystified, "Hey, why do you think she had a ten-K Dux bed in there in the first place? It's a pool house, for Chrissake!" He waited for an answer I would have loved to hear myself. Guy guffawed silently, hands over mouth; he had the head-set, after all.

"Yeah, yeah, I'm keeping an eye on her through phone reports with American Express Platinum. A nightmare, I know; like a god-damn open vein. Jesus!" Heavy exhale. "Anyway, I'll send you my meeting schedule. I'll use that newfangled wireless piece-a-crap that prick Makepeace forces us to use. It keeps buzzing and I can't even see the goddamn screen it's so small! Goddamn Blackberry! Jesus! It's doing it again!" With that came a huge smack on the desk, presumably Simon's attempt to silence the gadget. I could hear him breathing heavily.

Guy poked his head in and placed a folded piece of notepaper in front of me, then disappeared. I opened it and suppressed a guffaw: Guy had written the words "Xeroxed and Pilfered" next to "From the Desk of Simon Mallis," the words "TO DO" scrawled underneath in the aging cowboy's hand:

1. Inventory Pacificus office; commence hoarding supplies, furniture, and electronic equipment.
2. Redo "bungalow." Get rid of giant bed and fur blanket. Confront J about stash of papaya enzymes, laxatives, cayenne pepper, and

Human Growth Hormone—must she be into every goddamn trend? Her goddamn colon will explode one day!

3. Question: what the hell is "feng shui" and why are there huge invoices for it? And who's this freak "the Contessa"? Note: Six hundred dollars for chimes and frogs? Jesus!

4. J needs to work. Make use of her idiot compatriots and their equally stupid husbands to raise capital. Producer titles for everyone!

5. Flag the more important social invitations addressed solely to Makepeace. Write letters taking credit for imminent donations/subscriptions. Push through expenses for benefit tables for next six to twelve months, minimum.

6. Organize fittingly opulent industry tribute to self. Get Makepeace/Commerz to pay.

Simon's muffled voice cut in to my reading, "Don't worry. I'm all over the other studios looking for financing and distribution. I've got Julia on the Snippington twinkie as we speak, working the money side—her half-dead husband Max's film fund. Also, I wanna hit up that wacked-out Hamburger Queen; she's rolling in it. According to Julia, her dead husband doted on Julia like a granddaughter. We'll have Makepeace (that prick!) treading water, if that, trying just to stay afloat and break even. Ha! I know what we have to do. We have to strike quickly, and often, or while the iron is hot. Or something's still burning, or on fire, or aflame. . . . What the hell is that expression again?" Another *thwump*—I was sure he was thumbing through his Sun Tzu, looking for an appropriate passage to support his manic reasoning.

There was a commotion in the hallway: Jamey and Phil headed toward the suite, slipping papers and hand signal orders to Guy. Phil covertly swiped his nose at me and kept walking. Guy grabbed his jacket and the papers and rushed away like his pants were on fire. Without looking my way, Jamey went straight to Simon's door and knocked.

"Simon, do you have a minute?" Jamey entered the office, leaving the door ajar. I peeked around from inside the cubby and saw Simon take a Costco-sized bottle of Tums from a desk drawer. He was tossing back a handful of berry-flavored tablets as Jamey sat down on the other side of his desk. The phone rang.

"Guy!" bellowed Simon.

"I sent him on an errand. Sorry," Jamey smiled, relaxed. Simon glowered, annoyed, and exhaled sputters of berry powder onto the desk. He turned and answered his own phone.

"Mallis here!" He listened quietly, then held the phone away from his ear, wincing. Even I could hear the high-pitched, excitable rush of narrative spewing tinnily into the room. Simon rolled his eyes, which then came to rest on the gleaming blood pressure machine standing ready on his desk.

"Julia! For Chrissake! Calm down. How can anyone possibly *need* a hundred-thousand-dollar necklace?" More tinny words, even faster.

"Well then *don't* shop with Ritzy. You're not in competition. Jesus!" More tinny words, faster still.

He sighed, rubbing his eyes. "You know I can't do that anymore . . ." He glanced quickly at Jamey, who responded by raising his eyebrows. "I know, I know. Well. Try this, tell 'em the usual: you're a famous European singer, much photographed and in demand, blah blah, and you want it for free. . . . Listen, I gotta go. Yeah, sure. Call me back." Click.

Jamey seized the moment of distraction to begin. "Listen, Simon, we need to talk about you and Barb vacating the offices. I feel it's disruptive to the business and unfair to the staff that you continue to stay here physically. I'd like to settle on an exit date, and soon. Preferably over a weekend. What d'you think?"

The phone rang again. Simon stared straight ahead at the wall, eyes narrowed. He picked up the receiver without averting his gaze. "Mallis here!" More high-pitched, excitable noises.

"Well, then *negotiate*, Julia. You know how. Move on to plan B. Say you'd like to borrow the necklace, for your new movie or for credit. Or if you have to, go to plan C. You want it at a big-ass discount, blah blah blah. Tell them you'll do an ad campaign for them in Europe, for Chrissakes. They should love that, the bastards! They should count themselves *lucky* a classy woman like you would even want to wear their crappy baubles! Whatever it takes . . . Yeah, yeah . . . I gotta go."

"So . . . what d'you think, Simon?" Jamey began again.

"What do I think about what?" he snapped.

"Moving out of the office soon."

"Oh, that. Well . . . we never agreed in the consulting contract to any hard date. I'll get my lawyers on the phone right now, if you like. It's only been a few weeks. We need time to set up our offices. Besides, you don't want to be seen by everybody as champing at the bit to, uh, 'throw us out in the street,' now do you? It's very, uh, *disrespectful* to a man of my, uh, *stature*." A sly smile spread over his face. "By the way, you should know we have some *really* big deals in the works; *tremendous* films are planned." His smile turned smug and he reddened a bit, the steam never far from the surface.

"Right. Well . . ." The phone rang again. Simon lunged for it.

"Jesus, Julia! I canNOT meet you for lunch! I'm *working*! *No!* I don't *know* when—maybe tonight. No lunch tomorrow, either. I'll talk to you later." Click.

"Jeez!" He ran his hand across his head, smoothing the wispy, silvery-yellow strands. "She always used to be so busy. Now she's got nothing but time on her hands . . ." he mused, bewildered. He readjusted and flashed his practiced smile. "I'll talk to Barb when she calls in next and get back to you with a possible date. Okay?"

"Fine. Let's try to do this amicably. And by the way, Simon, if I find that any of your *tremendous* scripts come from the properties group of Pacificus, be prepared for a *tremendous* lawsuit." Jamey stood to leave. He turned back at the door and faced Simon. "Remember, Simon: *To fight and conquer in all your battles is not supreme excellence; supreme excellence consists in breaking the enemy's resistance* without *fighting*. Truth and justice, Simon. Truth and justice." With that, Jamey shut the office door lightly behind him. He turned toward me and smiled, pumping his fist in triumph. We heard something smash, hard, against the door from inside the office—the Blackberry, perhaps? Or was it the Tums? Jamey and I grinned at each other, silently high-fived and hugged each other tightly.

CHAPTER 18

SMOKE ON THE WATER, A FIRE IN THE SKY

Reduce the hostile chiefs by inflicting damage on them; and make trouble for them and keep them constantly engaged; hold out specious allurements, and make them rush to any given point. O divine art of subtlety and secrecy! Through you we learn to be invisible, through you inaudible; and hence we can hold the enemy's fate in our hands!

—Sun Tzu, *The Art of War*

The Day of Reckoning had come at last. Friday D-day. I finished my last-minute scripted phone calls from the hard lines to Sarah, Jamey, and Guy, and realized I was running late. My stomach fluttered with each conversation, little clicking phone noises indicating our pointed messages were being received. Dante flitted about to bad disco in my dressing room and I fought distractedly with a hovering, Lillet-toting Isabel over outfit and lipstick selection. I examined the mirror: even after fresh coats of paint and spray from Dante's magic wands, I was discouraged. Nope, I never would be as cool, calm, and collected as Mrs. Peel, regardless of Lady Selena's estimable praise. I might look like her in one of my better moments, but today I'd simply have to settle for dressing like her.

On my behalf, though, I will say that all the scheming and subterfuge these past six weeks takes a lot out of a girl! From our prearranged code, I understood that Simon had indeed blocked off the time of the auction; he'd given Guy strict orders not to disturb him on pain of death. Jamey and Phil were standing by at the Tower of Doom, and I would be the mole "on the ground," sending and receiving real-time info on my brand-new, untapped PDA. I stashed some emergency Benadryl in my bag, just in case.

Variety's ebullient pre-luncheon write-up, spread underneath Dante's wares, trumpeted all manner of speculation about Charlie's imminent announcements—everything from his auctioning script rights and actors' roles (true) to his launching a line of hair-care products (false) to his early retirement to run a llama farm in Montana (huh?). The best part of the story, however, was that it ran across from an interestingly informative blurb: over the holidays, Simon Mallis had been "chosen to be honored" (read: he'd lobbied for the honor *before* he was publicly axed from Pacificus) by the WHY (Wayward Hebrew Youth) organization. *Variety* had never heard of them, but nonetheless fervently urged "Save the date! Buy your tables now!" and offered as incentive that Julia would host an "informal barbeque" for larger supporters. I had to smile: oh, those Mallises! Hearts and wallets bursting with kindness for all of today's young people! I wondered how much he'd paid WHY for the honor to be honored and if, when he'd "accepted," he'd informed them he'd be out of power, unable to have Pacificus underwrite the "tribute." It seems our targeted slush fund was earmarked for very many uses indeed.

I checked my list, then my face: in both cases, not too bad. I bid adios to Dante (still shakin' his groove thang), took a bracing, front-loading draught of Lillet, and glared witheringly at Isabel (who was immune in any case, fingers snapping in time to Dante's swaying hips and receiving a two-hundred-dollar trim). It was time, thankfully, to drive down the hill to the Beverly Hills Hotel for the cocktail portion of the Pediatric Hyperhidrosis luncheon and live auction.

On the elaborately printed insert (included with the elaborately designed invitation), it stated that the "price of admission," as it were, was to bring a desirable item or unique experience valued at $500 or more, for inclusion in the silent auction for the evening benefit. Most of Sarah's friends attending today, I'd been apprised, were wives of current or former athletes: the "Glamazons." All these women had to do was have their husbands sign a bat, a ball, a hockey stick, or glove and *voila!* Instant perfect auction item. Sure enough, in the vestibule outside the ballroom, the line at the check-in table looked like Christmas rush at Niketown.

My former assistant, Cathy, now working for the Peninsula Hotel chain, had assembled a stunning New York Weekend package, complete with hotel stay, airline and show tickets. It was in certificate form, however, and I was glad I'd also had Guy put together a giant Pacificus DVD basket, extravagantly wrapped in satin ribbons and bows.

As I awaited admittance, I gazed through yet another Darwinian sea of expensive hair, privately trained bodies, and fabulous clothing, amusing myself by naming the spectrum of blond on offer (having by now memorized Dante's color wheel): caramel, honey, sunshine, Donatella . . . and those were just the solids.

A siren went off in my head: Shit! Ritzy Snippington, twelve o'clock. Anchorwoman red Moschino and giant diamonds were heading at me, as if on a mission. I glanced about furtively: there was nowhere to run, straining as I was under the oversized basket of home entertainment product. I stood helpless, a deer caught in headlights, waiting for the inevitable . . .

Phew! That was a close call. She was snared, luckily, only a few yards away, detained by an extraordinarily similar-looking woman. Much air-kissing and animated grasping transpired, allowing me a moment to stabilize and dispense with my donation on the table.

Done. But not before I noted the dismissive expression on the committeewoman's face as she looked disdainfully from the basket to me. And then it dawned: Julia must have arrived already. This was her turf, after all—and probably a smaller version of her usual gift. I dashed through a Birkin-saturated grouping of St. John Knits and ran smack into a frazzled, peach-suited woman, knocking a heavy folder of papers from her arms.

"I am *so* sorry! Please, let me help." I knelt to gather stray sheets, very much in spiking peril by the Spring line of Sergio Rossi. From my knee-high position it was easy to keep an eye on Ritzy's red kitten-heeled Jimmy Choos. Happily, they clicked off in another direction. A wave of relief swept over me.

"Thanks! By the way, I'm Francie." Still crouched, we shook hands. "You hiding from the red shoes too?"

"I'm Stacey, and truthfully, yes. How pathetic am I?" I offered her my share of the paper chase.

She laughed. "It took her three weeks to decide on a color scheme for the invitation. She changed her mind every day, really upset. Finally her husband called and said she just couldn't handle the decision, she'd been 'overwrought.' He told me to 'run with my gut.' So I did, you know? Now she's hunting me down, probably to rip out my heart. How long d'you reckon we can stay down here?" Aha, a like soul. We giggled sheepishly and helped one another to our feet.

Just then, that voice: "Stacey?" Oy! Big red everything, bearing down like a locomotive.

"It *is* you! Kiss *kiss*. I *thought* I saw you, but then you were gone. I'm surprised you showed up at all today, after yesterday's *Shinier Sheet*." Newly giant collagened lips (*someone*'s had a busy holiday!) pecked aggressively, stopping just short of each cheek. She raced on, tone and movements amplified as she scanned me head to toe. "Well bless your heart! So *much* better! After seeing those giant color shots of you in that STOP THE PREDATORS! T-shirt all dirty and smudged— and with that woo-woo C-list psychic-healing crowd Mallory tells me you're running with now." She tut-tutted distastefully. "You really do need to consider your husband's position a bit more, if you don't mind my saying. It's so—*careless*! However could you've let them photograph you like that?"

I hadn't, in fact, allowed anyone to do anything. Inga must have innocently told Mallory, who must have (not so innocently) tattled to Julia, who must have *ordered* Libbet to send a photographer, who must have hidden in the bushes, *tout de suite*! I sighed. It would all be worth it, in the end, I knew: eyes on the prize! The coyotes were working their trickster magic all around the desert soundstages, Christine and her ex had gotten back together. Bettina's Boxer was weaning off her doggie Prozac, and my fellow Kabbalists had a new cause and lease on life. Many more outings were planned.

My devoted Coyote Club had readily taken a prime table, helmed by an ecstatic Lady Selena; after meeting Jamey (over pink champagne and Mallomars), she adored him almost as much as I did. She'd insisted on attending—her first public appearance in many moons—to help "relocate *Jamey's* trickster coyotes." The pastel girls' wallets and paddles would happily dead-bid the pricing into the stratosphere. Out of the corner of my eye I saw Bettina and the Winking Wife checking in; the other Seekers wouldn't be far behind. I'd helped them with their problems; they were now ready to help me with mine.

"Stacey!" Ritzy snapped me back to the present. "You were very wrong to alienate Magda the way you did. She has 'the gift,' you know. But I did enjoy the way you dispatched that awful Patsy." She wrinkled her perfect nose. "And, I suppose, I do have to commend you: you're more 'on' today than 'off,' for a change. That's Carolina Herrera . . . am I right? I know I'm right."

"You got it, Ritzy." Yup. Remedial child, that's me; a would-be *heaven-born captain* in bargain-priced cashmere and silk, my latest outlet-center score after copiloting Christine's batch of varmints to a Palm Desert soundstage. "Ritzy, have you met Francie?" I'd almost forgotten she was still by my side.

I could feel Francie stiffen. Without taking her eyes off me, Ritzy replied coldly, "Hi, Franny."

"Fran-cie. But you know that." Francie was empowered. She gripped my arm in solidarity and headed off toward the bar.

"Yes, well. Anyway . . ."

"Ritzy, why did you ignore that woman?" I cut in. "She's very sweet."

She waved her manicure close to my face. "Her? Oh. She's just a *working* girl. She's not like *us*."

"*That* woman's a *hooker*? She can't be. She looks like an advertising executive!" On my former planet, most women at equivalent luncheons (including me!) resembled Francie; Ritzy would have been odd-man-out.

"No, *no*. She *works*, I mean—like in an *office*, is all. With the foundation maybe, or St. Somebody's. I, y'know, call, and tell her what to do, and she does it." Her voice trailed off, bored. She studied her nail polish more closely.

Oh Ritzy . . . I spied Barb off in a corner, sporting oversized wrap-around shades and a turtleneck (hmm: eyelift? neck lift? both? I wondered). Oh what the hell, I thought, I had time. I hadn't even seen Sarah yet.

"So, Ritzy. Francie, an adult working *woman*, by the way, most likely earns a smallish, not-for-profit–type salary to run these events, attract sponsor dollars, and deal with whimsical, self-involved people like yourself. *Working*, mind you, for the very cause that is so important that you're chairing the event. Right?" I took a well-deserved breath.

Ritzy, entirely missing the point, focused still on her hands: shiny shiny rings. "Right. It's a very 'A' event, Stacey." She glanced up. "She's basically just a secretary. I don't know why you'd care."

Truly dumb as a post. I opened my mouth to go back at her, but Sarah arrived to my rescue, elbowing Ritzy to get her attention. "Sinfonia Folata's here with Julia, and they look like they're up to something. Why don't you go find them?" Compelling, but useless. Ritzy refused to budge.

Sarah turned to me. "Stacey, come to the bar. I want to introduce you to a few friends while we wait for Charlie. He has some last minute details he wants to discuss." Ritzy's jaw dropped, indignant, as Sarah continued to work her. "Charlie's so excited about emceeing the live auction. He thinks we can get maybe twenty, twenty-five thousand for the first item alone! Just think of the money and publicity we'll get for the research program!"

"I know!" Her enthusiasm was catching, and the trap we'd set was rich, even though I thought the cause inane. "I've never heard of such a thing before! The foundation is lucky that you and Charlie have the ability to offer such one-of-a-kind experiences!" Well-rehearsed, gushing lines to cover our tracks.

Ritzy seethed, smelling subplot. "Sarah, I need to talk to you."

"Later."

"No, now! I mean, y'know, we *are* co-chairing and everything; the emphasis on '*co*'! If your items are what Julia *thinks*"—she paused, petulant—"well then that's not fair."

Sarah softened. "Charlie's items are secret. You know how creative people are. I don't know how Julia, of all people, could possibly know anything. We're in this together, okay? I saw the Cartier necklace you're donating. It's beautiful, and Max will pick the winner from the podium. There'll be a ton of photographers."

Ritzy brightened slowly. "Then I look forward to seeing what happens. And about your *items*: I don't usually like surprises, but I guess I have no choice." She threw back her shoulders, glared at me, fluffed her hair, and fixed her smile. She was good to go, and go she did.

Sarah and I followed her lead, plunging forward through the sea of pastel air kisses toward the bar. On an interesting note, as we muddled through, more than one woman slipped a card to me, whispering that they'd like to "learn more" about the Coyote Club, and wanted to know how to join . . .

Sipping a Bloody Mary, I met two very different sets of women. Sarah had taken two tables as chairwoman, one for the Glamazons: wives of prominent athletes, music, and film stars; the other for her Mommy friends from the exclusive day school her children attended in Beverly Hills.

Both groups were beautifully dressed and coiffed—there was little physical difference, actually. The contrast was more apparent in their behavior. For example, the Mommies literally hummed with excitement just to be present and included. They seemed elated even to know Sarah and hung on her every word, fighting with each other for her attention. As Sarah rattled off names, Maggie, Cindy, Lizzie, etc., by way of introduction, each responded overenthusiastically, like airline stewardesses of yore. They couldn't place me from their *Angeleno* or *Elle*, but they sensed that if Sarah singled me out specially, so should they.

As Sarah greeted more arrivals, I was cornered by the rabidly deferential Mommy set, who attempted to decipher who I might be and why I was destined for the alpha table and not the secondary table, with them.

In the inescapable cross-questioning, I learned that Maggie's husband was a top veterinarian. Apparently so special was he that Oprah *and* Martha Stewart flew him bi-monthly to Chicago/Connecticut to attend their respective pets. Sandy's husband was a prominent teen psychiatrist. In LA, mind you. One need obviously say no more, but she certainly did: "I shouldn't say this—and my husband would *kill* me, doctor/client privilege and all that"—she waved her hand dismissively, pooh-poohing the law (*so* dull)—"but my husband has *personally* handled the Osbourne kids, all the old *Saved by the Bell* cast, *and* Pamela Anderson and Tommy Lee's kids!"

Lizzie waited out the ham-fisted name-checking and finally cut to the chase: "So, Stacey. How do you know Sarah and Charlie? Where have I seen you before? Or would I know your . . . *work*, maybe?"

The other girls turned instantly, quizzically, expectantly to me. The moment for which they'd been waiting had come: my unmasking.

"Well . . ." I couldn't figure out exactly how to respond. "My husband and I moved from New York a few months ago, and I used to be in marketing." Still, they waited.

"And your husband, what does he do again?" prompted Cindy.

"Actually, I don't believe I said. Jamey's company bought Pacificus."

"Ahh!" they chorused, somehow relieved; another exciting game of *What's My Line?* satisfactorily resolved. A perfect example of yet another LA social divide: the Mommies had gobs of money, that much was clear. Probably even more than the Glamazons, as fame and access are project based, and these athlete-husbands were veteran players, having completed their tenure before the big-money contracts came of age. But the Mommies—*civilians*—assumed second-class citizenry because to them money meant nothing without the access it could afford in Hollywood—the concept, not the town. I, then, was the only woman at Sarah's table whose husband had *not* been on the cover of *Vanity Fair*. To sum up: money *plus* access equals power; money on its own buys dinner but doesn't necessarily guarantee a prime table at Mr. Chow.

It was during this epiphany that I saw Maggie's eyes widen. An arm came from behind, grabbing me in a backwards bear hug as a cheerful voice boomed, "Ready for some fireworks?" My partner in crime, Charlie Truehart. He grinned and led the way into the elegant pink ballroom; crowds parted as we searched out our perfectly positioned/satellite-friendly table, checking our PDAs one last time for good measure. As we nibbled salads, Sarah and I to either side of Charlie, I caught a glimpse of Julia and Barb at Ritzy's table, contemplating us in silence. Ah, yes: high school. How well I remember. I shook them off and joined in conversation with the Sports Wives.

No sooner had the entrees been served than a bejeweled hand landed on my shoulder. Julia. The table fell silent, and I braced for an imminent onslaught of clipped diction, pretend air kisses, and indirect, grovelly obeisance to Charlie, the one person in town whose approval she intensely desired and who (as always) ignored her presence expertly, concentrating instead on his poached salmon.

"Stacey! I've been meaning to call about missing your holiday party. I'm all healed up now and ready to work again." Hmm, that accent, how it comes and goes—today's was "Madonna as English rose." "Charlie, Sarah. How are you?" Such a lady! She scanned the table, awaiting acknowledgment. None came. "That's a wonderful Carolina Herrera, Stacey, though it's not exactly current season, now is it?" She tsked out the compli-sult; I really should know better, her pursed lips implied. "Charlie, as you know, Simon and I are longstanding advocates of your excellent work for Hyperhidrosis." She glanced again at me. "I'm sure I speak for everyone when I say Pacificus will strongly support the upcoming gala. Stacey, you and James never RSVP'd. I'm sure Guy forgot to forward your invitation. He's really very lazy, you know." Yeah, that must be it. She's not such a bad actress after all.

I smiled sweetly. "Julia, I must thank you for sending Libbet's photographer my way. The grass roots coverage will be so helpful to our cause." Denied, Julia sauntered back to her table, fists clenched. The three of us burst out laughing.

As the dessert service began, Ritzy sashayed to the podium with her color-coordinated index cards, hauling a barely lucid Max up alongside her. Sarah and I applauded her loudly. Charlie added an ear-piercing whistle and a few catcalls. Ritzy loved it—it brought out the southern belle in her—and she preened, blushed, and drawled, milking every second before she pulled the raffle winner's name from an enormous Baccarat crystal tureen that (as she informed the crowd) she had brought from her very own extensive collection of enormous Baccarat crystal tureens.

Her flush disappeared as she pulled the winning raffle ticket. After a disconcerting minute, Max had the good sense to take the paper away. "The winner of the Cartier necklace is . . . Francie Connor! Congratulations, Francie!"

Sarah and I cheered as a timid but ecstatic Francie approached the stage, zigzagging the tables to approach from Max's, not Ritzy's, side. Not that it mattered. Ritzy had already stalked offstage, refusing to appear in the photo op and leaving poor old Max to find his way back to his seat himself. Score one for the good guys!

Now it was Charlie's turn. A hush fell over the room as the great director cleared his throat and tapped the mic. As he began his preamble, the phalanx of press swelled to three deep, jostling and jockeying each other for position as they awaited his words.

Sarah grabbed my arm excitedly. "Wait 'til Julia discovers she's been seated in a 'dead' zone with no cell coverage—not that Guy would put her through to Simon anyway. I can't wait to see her bid for herself." I glanced over: Julia was indeed frantically trying to position the phone for better coverage, to no avail. She split her time throwing hateful daggers at Sarah and me and making adoring moo-eyes up at Charlie onstage. Ritzy was back next to her, in full sulk beside a slumbering Max. Oddly, Barb was nowhere to be found, her seat now occupied by the horrid Sinfonia Folata, Spice-Girl-on-Crack in a beaded zebra-print halter-top with matching head wrap. My pastel army of Coyote Kabbalists sat gamely at attention, paddles ready for action. I caught Lady Selena's eye and she swiped her nose; I swiped mine back in response: the Sting was on! *God* I adored her!

Charlie addressed the audience. "My wife Sarah and I are thrilled to co-chair this wonderful event, and we are even happier to be in the position to offer the Pediatric Hyperhidrosis Research Program two unique items for auction. I know there's been lots of speculation, but I'll set the record straight in good time. For our first item, I propose to auction off a secondary female role in my as-yet-untitled film, which I am currently in the process of writing. The role will be specifically written for and tailored *especially to* the winner of this chance-of-a-lifetime item—abilities, personality, looks. All of it."

The room buzzed as reporters scribbled away and camera shutters clicked rapidly. "Now, some might say I'm crazy to take such a risk with my art—and maybe I am—but I truly believe this will help break Pediatric Hyperhidrosis through the clutter of ancillary diseases and into the forefront of medical attention, where it belongs."

The crowd thundered its applause, nodding fervently and cheering. I noted that the "usual suspects" were on red-alert; Julia continued to stab at her cell phone feverishly.

"Let's see . . . shall we start the bidding at say, five thousand dollars?" Ritzy's hand shot up. She blew an air kiss at Julia. Then she stuck her tongue out at Sarah and me. Charlie smiled, pleased it had started well. "Excellent, Ritzy. Do I hear seventy-five hundred?" This time it was Sinfonia Folata, zebra spangles aglitter. And so it went. Two or three others jumped into the fray, and the bid on the floor multiplied up to thirty thousand in no time. Charlie was thrilled. Julia sat ramrod straight, an anesthetized smile pasted on her anxious face as it volleyed back and forth with the bids. An opportunity to star in (well, sort of) a Charlie Truehart picture! I could almost see into the rapturous cartoon bubble floating above her head: gliding down the red carpet in a specially designed Oscar creation, world press focused only on her, at last!

At the fifty thousand mark, two Foundation women, cordless phones in hand, hurried onstage to Charlie. "Wonderful!" declared Charlie into the mic. "It seems we have some anonymous phone bidders who wish to participate. Let's move the bid increments up to ten thousand, eh? That should make things more interesting! Do I hear sixty thousand dollars?" Ritzy and Julia exchanged nervous glances as Max snorted himself awake. He pressed his hand over Ritzy's and shook his head firmly "no." Julia, frustrated, mangled her phone yet again. Lady Selena (who looked stunning, by the way, in a sleek white Givenchy column and diamonds as big as the Ritz) raised her paddle. Then Bettina. Then the Winking Wife. Lady Selena again. Hurrah! I thought Sarah might cut off the circulation in my arm. The bid-

ding war hit a hundred thousand dollars and showed no sign of slow-
ing. I could see even Charlie was having a hard time believing this
great luck—we'd only estimated the role would go for fifty grand on
the outside. At the two hundred fifty thousand mark, the live auction ceased in the ballroom, and all attention focused on the dueling
phone bidders. The crowd was silent, enrapt in the action.

Charlie increased the bid increments to twenty-five thousand, and
you could have cut the air with a knife. Julia didn't seem to be breathing, clutching her cell like a rosary, moving only to press the redial
button. The phone bidders took longer and longer between responses,
prodded along now and again by Lady Selena. At four hundred fifty
thousand to one of the phones, I signaled nervously for her to "hold"
with a covert blackjack gesture. Charlie glanced at me and began the
count, "Going once, going twice . . ." The tension mounted exponentially.

Just then a high-pitched female scream erupted from the center
of the ballroom. "Five hundred thousand dollars!" Every head rico-
cheted around. Sarah dug her nails into my arm: it was done.

"Sold! For five hundred thousand dollars to paddle number 253!
Congratulations . . . *Julia!* You've bought yourself a movie role!" Charlie crowed and swiped his nose at us, pink with delight from behind
his beard.

Julia had shot up from her seat, bewildered by the sound of her
own primal scream, so self-absorbed and palpitating she looked
almost demented as she goggled around the room. Loud murmurs
and more than a few sniggers and jeers bubbled from the crowd,
which gave way to thunderous applause, for Charlie.

It was more than had ever before been raised for this strange
little charity for sweaty children—and quite a coup. Done done done.
Charlie's gavel sounded to hoots, hollers, and a standing ovation.
Crack! Charlie bowed deeply as a dazed Julia was led away by Francie to vet her financial information. Mission One: accomplished!

I checked my Blackberry; a message from Guy flashed: Simon was crazed, desperately trying to find out who had beat him out for the role. I smiled to myself—the action was unfolding even better than we'd written it. From my prearranged "live" zone, I e-mailed back "JM--500K! Shh!"

The room was electrified once again—the "grand prize surprise" was next up. In this brief interlude, the crowd had filled to SRO proportions. Oh, word sure had leaked (what a town!), nudged along by Charlie's agent to ensure a huge payday. Studio execs, financiers, and producers galore had crammed the pink ballroom, wrangling for pole position to bid on the sure-fire burning hot commodity from the three-time Oscar-winning writer/director. Julia reappeared with her herd of adoring disciples (who dutifully trotted after her) as she paraded the ballroom in a victory lap, throwing air kisses to Charlie onstage and relishing her star turn as Queen of the Pediatric Hyperhidrosis luncheon.

The Kabbalah table was partying in high style. Lady Selena had ordered up a case of Cristal and sent a few bottles our way for Sarah and the Glamazons. Some of the Coyote Club were joined now by their husbands, readying for the next task at hand. They may have been out of power momentarily, but by God they were rich! And on our side! Sarah and I raised our glasses; they waved their paddles back cheerfully. *When there is much running about and the soldiers fall into rank, it means that the critical moment has come.*

"And now for our grand prize item," Charlie began as the crowd hushed, "I'll be auctioning off the script rights to my next film— writer/director attached, of course. My agent's having an apoplexy backstage . . ." Chuckles peppered the jostling onlookers. "We're on a roll, so how 'bout starting with an opening bid of five hundred thousand?"

I tried to remain calm as Charlie riffed and teased the producers who were bidding up the script in $50,000 increments. Early days. At one point five million I began paying closer attention. Sure enough, our anonymous phone bidder was back in the game. That was Lady Selena's signal. At three mil most of the room dropped out. Scott Sturm (with Inga on his knee) was HackySack-ing back and forth with Lady Selena (who doffed her paddle and was having a ball dreaming up clever Ashtanga-enhanced ways of signaling Charlie); a guy from Universal, a woman from Sony, and two New York producers jumped in.

"Do I hear three point three million?" Charlie asked the room. The lady holding the phone bidder signaled yes. Three four, three five.

"Three point six million!" an enraptured Lady Selena cried aloud. Universal quickly stepped in, then the phone. Sony; then Lady Selena again. Sarah and I were about to achieve liftoff in our seats. I tried to catch Lady Selena's eye to make her hold, but she was quite caught up in the moment.

After a very pregnant pause, the phone lady signaled four million even with a thumbs-up sign. Charlie grazed the room, checking with each of the previous bidders. All held, but I could see it was all Lady Selena could do not to raise some incredibly flexible part of her body one more time. "Going once, going twice, then . . . sold! To our anonymous phone bidder, for four million dollars!" Crack went the gavel. The crowd went berserk; a veritable stampede of applause, whistles, and cheers. I was frantically Blackberrying Jamey and Phil when Charlie grabbed the mic again. "You know, folks, I'm so excited and thrilled, not only that someone had the blind faith in me to buy an untitled, unseen script—but that we raised this unprecedented sum for Hyperhidrosis. Where is that masked phone?" The woman vetting the winner's information handed it to him. "I don't know about you all, but I'd certainly like to thank my benefactor on behalf of all the doctors, researchers, parents, and patients touched by this affliction. Hello high bidder? Are you there?" He spoke into the phone. "Ah, yes, what a happy surprise!" Charlie swiped his nose again, exhilarated. "If I may, sir, I'd like to connect the line to speakerphone so I can thank you publicly." After a small commotion, the line was indeed connected to the PA system. "To whom am I speaking? Name and affiliation, please," requested Charlie.

"Simon Mallis," drawled the voice, slow and proud. "Crossfire Features. Very happy to be working with you, Charlie. Your movie will be our second production—after one starring my lovely wife, the very talented Julia Mallis." The initial oohs and ahhs that arose from the crowd turned quickly to sniggers, then outright laughter.

Charlie laughed too. "Well now, Mr. Mallis—Simon—you are aware, of course, your lovely Julia bought our first item, a lead in my—now your—script. You two are truly a most philanthropic couple!" He looked out among the crowd, eyes landing pointedly on the press tables. "To buy a role *and* a script, even though some might say that the right to cast the role comes *with* script rights. Now *that's* support, above and beyond the call!"

Dead air hissed a moment too long, then heavy breathing and wheezing were heard over the PA. A croaky voice crackled, "Yes, well, we try to do our part . . ."

"Simon, do you know what time it is?" inquired Charlie, buoyant, like a wacky game show host.

"Yes, Charlie. It's two o'clock."

"And the banks close at three!" he goaded, fired up. "I know you're good for it, of course—everyone knows your reputation . . . but why don't you start the paperwork on your wire transfer right now! Your total is four point five million dollars, and I'll put the head of the foundation on the line to give you the account numbers. Ladies and . . ."

"Pardon, Charlie . . . four point . . . *five*, you say?"

"The fifty cents is for Julia. Stay on the line, now," Charlie directed coolly. Increased uneven wheezing and coughing were heard until the speakerphone detached. Julia, idiot, preened at the sound of her name and threw her hair around for a bit. Gag. I drained my champagne. Charlie thrust his arms up in victory and crowed from the stage, "Ladies and gentlemen: I give you . . . Simon Mallis!" He handed the phone back to the foundation woman and headed toward me and Sarah through the cheering, glad-handing crowd.

"Well done, honey!" Sarah cried, throwing her arms around Charlie's neck.

"I don't even know how to begin to thank you," I managed to say.

Charlie winked. "Don't worry. I have an idea on that front—but all in good time. And the jury's still out on whether, after Simon's trapped by Jamey, he'll reach into his own pocket to cover his debt. That's a big personal sum, for anyone, even to save face."

"Well," I sighed, eyeing an exultant Julia undulating Janet Jackson-style in front of the press table, "it still kinda kills me that after everything, she's gonna get what she's wanted all along . . . but"—an idea occurred that made me smile—"at least, Charlie, now you get to write her the role of a lifetime. And what's her choice, really, but to play anything you say?"

"Yeah, Charlie," Sarah laughed, "you can make her gain twenty pounds. That'll destroy her. Maybe she can be a Satan-worshiping trailer-park wife, fat and toothless with five kids by five different men. Gritty, totally non-glam stuff. *And* she should go into a coma in Act I."

"Make her gain thirty!" I managed to choke out. "Let her suffer for her art! And *then* have her go through hours of makeup. Hey, what about a prosthesis?"

"Well, I *did* say," Charlie smiled slyly, "that I'd write to the winner's personality and attributes, now, didn't I? She's rife with pathos! It won't be a loss, don't you worry."

Lady Selena had made her way over to us, a bottle of half-drunk Cristal in hand. "What fun! Kudos, Charlie. And Stacey, of course, thank you for including me. I sent Inga and Scott ahead to hold a table by the pool. I take it we'll be hearing from your darling husband very soon with some big news?" Her mischievous eyes danced.

Just then, my cell rang. Jamey. "It's done."

CHAPTER 19

THANKS FOR THE MEMORIES

> The onrush of a conquering force is like the bursting of pent-up waters into a chasm a thousand fathoms deep. If asked how to cope with a great host of the enemy in orderly array and on the point of marching to the attack, I should say: "Begin by seizing something which your opponent holds dear; then he will be amenable to your will."
>
> —Sun Tzu, *The Art of War*

*O*h, what a wild aftermath it was, replete with all the compelling elements befitting any worthwhile Hollywood scandal: dastardly behind-the-scenes machinations, grand gestures and wild turnabouts. I wish I could say it was the calm after the well-planned lightning strike but truly, the storm had only begun to brew. The town was abuzz—alight, aflutter, agog; gossiping endlessly about the gothic drama and the ensuing passion plays unleashed by the heady auction fireworks. Our "army" stayed mum (*Subtlety! Secrecy!*), but even without the "whole truth" leaking per se, there was plenty of tantalizing fallout to keep the town fed for days.

First thing Monday, the security team arrived to remove (at long last!) those hateful/helpful monitoring devices and to swap out new phone and computer systems. Jamey and I hunkered down in the kitchen, fielding congratulatory phone calls and reading aloud to each other from the trades. *Variety* crowed: MALLIS UNPLUGGED: WIRE TRANSFER GOES SOUTH! The subhead: RECLUSIVE HAMBURGER QUEEN SAVES DAY! MAKEPEACE, TRUEHART BIG WINNERS!

Not to be outdone over such tempting material, the *Reporter* cleverly punned NO MALLIS FOR TRUEHART, HYPERHIDROSIS. COYOTE CLUB WHITE KNIGHT MAKES PEACE WITH DEBT! Both papers had breathlessly e-mailed their reports as "breaking news bulletins" to their info-hungry subscriber lists around midnight Sunday, should morning come too late for the ravenous industry grapevine.

At 2:17 p.m. on Friday, Simon, no longer a Pacificus employee, had indeed followed through and activated, for his own personal use, the four-point-two-million-dollar corporate account he'd kept hidden, which of course belonged to Pacificus. Jamey and Phil had eliminated Simon as signatory and liquidated the account, outfoxing the fox and catching him red-handed. Jamey and Phil then confronted Simon, tarring and feathering away happily as was their due. Guy had rigged Simon's office phone in advance, and conferenced in both my and Charlie's cells to listen fly-on-the-wall-style to the War of the Worlds, a master class in self-deflection and distortion. Which we did, leisurely sipping the last of Lady Selena's excellent champagne, poolside at the Beverly Hills Hotel: "Phil, you maggot, surely *you* understand? It's all a goddamn write-off! A charitable contribution, for Chrissake! How *dare* you question me! Goddamn Germans! And fuck you, you prick Makepeace! You fucking motherfucker! Stop fucking grinning!"

The trades, who'd witnessed the auction live (and who were called immediately afterward by a gloating Simon), lay in wait that Friday afternoon, hunting Jamey's corporate spin as well as comments from all involved. Simon tried one last time: "Wouldn't you boys consider taking a write off for at least the five hundred K?" Hmm. No mercy! The "boys" took great pleasure in that one last denial. But, we were all aware, Simon would eventually cover *that* debt: "fifty cents," as

Charlie so charmingly put it, was a far less bitter pill to swallow than half his net worth should Julia leave him. No pre-nup, remember?

Lady Selena, as the second highest bidder (and in an astonishingly stylish act of benevolence and grace) made good on the unclaimed debt, producing instant funds for a cash donation to Hyperhidrosis. In an even more spectacular, jaw-dropping twist, she then gifted her prize— Charlie's script—to Jamey, free and clear, the film to be produced and distributed by Pacificus. Well! Slow news days these were not.

Another choice factoid (from the vault of choice factoids) that *wasn't* written up: the "anonymous" bidding war for Julia's hard-won prize (unmasked by Guy, naturally) comprised none other than Simon . . . and Barb! Unbeknown to each another (and to Julia as well), they had both tried to gift her the role she'd claimed for herself. Now *there* was a three-way operatic death-match I'd have loved to witness—but Guy did gamely act it out for me, complete with tears, accusations, and recriminations, trooper that he is.

On the defensive front, a special edition *Shinier Sheet* was crashed in response to the exuberant trade stories and high-decibel chatter. In direct opposition to truth and reality, it featured a glamorous double-truc photo feature on Julia, "setting the record straight" about her husband's "victimization" and the "lies being bandied about by those horrid tabloid trades." After settling the security agents in upstairs, I found the newsletter waiting for me in the kitchen, taped to the Sub-Zero like a child's arts-and-crafts project. Julia's photos had been magnificently "retouched and enhanced" courtesy of Miss Isabel's sharp-witted imagination and an array of colored markers: Julia now sported horns, fangs, and demonic eyes.

Her narrative spin was even more colorful, although, of course, the Hollywood grapevine chatter works both ways. As you can imagine, Guy (let alone Mallory and my supportive "army") called in constantly with the latest breaking rumors and tall tales. Guy was in rare form, thrashing about in the muck and mire, gossiping madly and reporting back in a frenzy of italics and exclamation points. Everyone had loads to say about Julia's "To Do" list (which Libbet faithfully printed, even matching the page color to Julia's now-signature shade of shell pink), which Sarah and I had great fun decoding. According to Julia, she was "Charlie Truehart's hand-picked selection for a starring role" in his upcoming blockbuster: "It's very hush-hush; no one else has even been cast!" Her schedule, on the other hand, was very public:

1. Exclusive Spa week in the Santa Barbara mountains. "I need to 'recharge' and focus on me for a change. I must 'detox' from my fast-paced Hollywood life and its overwhelming social and professional obligations."

   Read: She'd high-tail it out of town and let Simon suffer the brunt of the humiliation alone.

2. Finish redecorating chic bungalow headquarters for rainmaker/ adoring husband Simon Mallis' exciting new film venture, Crossfire Features. "He worships my taste! And, you know, he simply had to stay independent, in order not to hurt our friends' feelings by choosing one studio over another."

   Read: Simon pulled her decorator budget; no studio production deal had been offered.

3. Begin preproduction and voice training for starring role in *Lolly Popps' Adventures*, rainmaker/adoring husband Simon Mallis' highly anticipated musical extravaganza for his exciting new film venture, Crossfire Features.

   Read: A kiddie movie for Bombshell Barbie! Kinda like The Sound of Music, *but (naturally) without all those downer Nazis.*

4. Oversee as chairwoman (and proud founder!) highly regarded Youth Education Movement's exclusive A-list shopping/luncheon/fashion show at close personal friend (from European society!) Donnacia Scroccone's outré Beverly Hills boutique, raising funds to send inner-city teens to Laguna. "It feels so good to give back!"

   Read: Raise funds for three-day seminar on non-fat cooking and master stain-removal for underage household staff.

5. Design menu, control burgeoning guest list for hot-ticket barbeque
   at resplendent estate, Casa de Mallis (in the chicest part of Brentwood!) feting rainmaker/adoring husband Simon Mallis as he ac-
   cepts "Man of the Year" Honors from WHAT (misprint) WHY.
   *Read: Hire excessive staff for superfluous event benefiting un-
   known semi-religious organization. Or, suck up to Guy, big time,
   and make him—NO!—allow him to do it. Invite Hollywood heavy-
   weights; screen three-minute overview. Somehow bill everything to
   Pacificus.*

You just had to laugh. *We* sure did, for days and days. And then:

About a week later, it happened. It had to. It was inevitable, after all.
Guy was completely deflated, his energy and ebullience all but vanished. No spring in his step, no wind in his sails. He would wear black
only, as if in pious mourning, accessorized discreetly by coordinating
black-on-black patterned ascots:

Simon and Barb moved out of the Pacificus offices. Without warning. Without a word. Without a note. And basically without a trace.
They did, however, manage to take with them the entire contents of
both their offices and much, much more, leaving only threadbare carpeting and thumbtacks in their stead. Like thieves in the night, they
hired a truck and a team of movers, and methodically looted, pil-
laged, and stripped to the bare bones the executive suite and most of
the tangible assets of Pacificus Studios. Guy was the first to discover
their evacuation, alone and very early on a foggy Monday morning.
When he called the house, nearly hysterical, to inform a just-out-of-
the-shower Jamey, he was instructed to make a comprehensive inventory of the items that had been removed. "But, it's a total disaster—I
wouldn't even know where to begin!" he lamented, overwhelmed.

"They're fucking psychotic!" Jamey fumed as he slammed down
the phone, angrily pulling on jeans and a sweater.

"No, honey. They're 'psychotic-*adjacent*'! There is an essential difference. I'm coming with." He grabbed the car keys and dialed Phil to meet us at Pacificus.

We entered the twenty-third floor of the Tower of Doom and found Guy rocking slowly on the floor of Simon's ransacked office. Jamey stared down at him and shook his head. "Those two are going to be the death of me," murmured my poor husband.

"Two? You mean three!" I murmured back, glimpsing some laminated lingeried tear sheets of Julia strewn about the floor. Interesting . . . "They are the Bermuda Triangle of humanity and good sense." I coaxed Guy to his unsteady feet and planted his mute, slack body on the workout bench in Jamey's cubby, where he stared blankly at the wall, muttering inaudibly.

Aside from the standard plundering of office supplies—entire storage cabinets-full, I might add (hell, they took the cabinets!)—they took the phones, computers, fax machines, printers, even the damaged corkboards and stickies off the walls. Monitors, VCRs, film projectors, all gone. The shredder (Simon's most-prized appliance aside from his medical gadgets) had vanished. They'd ravaged the film library and archives.

Phil arrived with a sleepover date in one hand and his Secret Squirrel key ring in the other. He pulled the security tapes from Stupid Squad's locked and hidden internal monitoring system, and the four of us (plus the semi-lucid Guy) watched as—my, but Barb *did* look trim in her black catsuit!—a team of overalled, faceless men wrapped and heaved furniture, artwork, lighting fixtures, and files about under her expert supervision, stripping the pink princess office down in no time flat. Meanwhile, Simon (on camera two) in his special occasion desperado hat, depleted the Duty Free-type stash of perfumes, cigars, Tiffany trinkets, expensive chocolates, and cases of Dom Perignon that were used as congratulatory gifts, sent on behalf of Pacificus upon the premiere of a film or the signing of a deal. These luxury goodies had been stored in a triple-locked industrial case in Jamey's cubby—he'd taken the keys from Simon and Barb when he first arrived. Fittingly—and it was clear Simon delighted in this: he sawed all three locks cleanly in two, then carefully arranged the pieces, heart-shaped, on Jamey's desk. "Just another rogue socio-path, taking pride in his work," Jamey commented wryly.

Trophies, awards, and statuettes were stolen out of the heavy glass cases in the reception area; framed and signed film posters were gone from the walls. As a prankish finishing touch (and as if to polish off the massive despoiling), they also snatched up every roll of toilet paper from the restrooms as well as the tattered yoga mat and weights from Jamey's office.

It wasn't until much later that we learned they'd actually rerouted or cancelled all Pacificus subscriptions to the trades, the *Times*, the *Wall Street Journal*, and so on, and had instead ordered "replace-ments" for all to *Hustler*, *Guns & Ammo*, and *Seventeen* magazine.

Oh. And for their grand finale, they managed to hack into the mainframe of Pacificus' e-mail system and plant a virus, basically ensuring that all internal and external e-mail communications and activities would grind immediately to a screeching halt.

A perfectly detailed strategic plan, perfectly tactically executed. Simon looked in rare form that night, I thought distastefully—some lazy, Bizarro-world interpretation of Sun Tzu's teachings—his zeal-ousness made clear by the exasperating havoc he'd unleashed. I was sure he'd been up all night in his refurbished bungalow, deliriously anticipating Jamey's imminent discovery. It was just too bad he'd never get to view the ensuing free-for-all.

The upshot? A free-for-all indeed it was. Jamey, furious, was up a tree and shaking with rage. Back in New York, Willem sputtered in rapid, splenetic German through the speakerphone. Commerz lawyers around the globe were on alert, busily conferring with each other as well as with outside counsel while waiting to hear the extent of the damage to the computerized systems and general ledger. Phil, on the other hand, was reborn, reinvigorated; blood flowed through his usual waxen pallor and he seemed to have grown three inches overnight. He and Jamey taped off the twenty-third floor like a crime scene and the best of Stupid Squad was summoned to work their IT magic. Guy somehow managed to break through his Valium torpor long enough to activate an emergency phone chain, rerouting the more senior execs as well as Phil's accounting group to our house instead.

Staff was already pacing outside the gate as we arrived back up the hill. Within a half hour, administrators assembled makeshift workspaces in the guest bedrooms and living areas. Accounting teams worked desperately to reconstruct their reports, budgets, and P&Ls from paper files. Every phone rang at once; fax machines spewed paper continually. E-mail accounts were instruments of unending information, incoming and outgoing across the time zones. Fury and hysteria ruled the day, except for one very fascinating thing—and Simon never could have envisioned this: their renegade nocturnal activities had in truth succeeded only in creating a newfound sense of unity among the employees. They were finally working as a team, united toward a common goal. And Jamey and Phil were firmly in control.

Nonetheless, I couldn't wait to get out of the house, which had taken on a heady War Room ambience. Only Guy remained inconsolable, unable to perform even the simplest task. To try and cheer him, I took him to tea at the Bel Air Hotel, and ordered just about anything they offered that was fabulous and crazy expensive on the menu. Just to see a smile. Or to hear a bit of gossip. Maybe a coherent sentence? No words came forth, on any count: he lapped at his Bellini despondently, between heavy, lung-emptying sighs.

By the time Guy and I arrived back at dusk, the frenzy had settled and most of the employees had gone home. Only the finance group remained, helmed by the newly dynamic Phil, who knew only too well to concentrate on the one area that mattered most to Simon: the expense submissions. Amazingly, they'd managed to uncover previously hidden carrying costs for our house-slash-trap, post-Idiot/pre-us, as well as that pesky "fifty-cent charitable contribution," which had somehow miraculously appeared as well. Hours of dull mathematics had taken their toll, and exhaustion replaced the intensity of the morning.

Jamey kissed me wearily. "I just got off the phone with the IT guys. Thankfully, the damage is more mischievous than permanent. Still, it'll take about a week before they can get everything back up and running smoothly. I'm wrecked," he yawned. "How's Guy?"

"Passed out on top of some beach towels. I don't think we'll see him until morning. How much longer will everyone else be here?"

"At least a few hours. We still need to prepare for the offsite meeting in Scottsdale. Simon's made a real mess, Stace—let alone having committed grand theft and larceny, with a few misdemeanors thrown in. Willem wants me to call in the Feds and have him arrested. The lawyers want to sue the shit out of him, except that he hasn't touched the general ledger—it's only the e-mail system, really. But it's still a major nuisance. I just want a gun."

I just wanted some of Guy's Valiums.

As Jamey left to check on his team, I phoned in for pizza delivery and made yet another giant urn of coffee. I also made a mental note to call St. Somebody's and investigate emergency shock-therapy camp for Guy, to treat his deep-seated abandonment issues and obvious case of (belated) Stockholm Syndrome.

Twenty minutes later the doorbell rang. "Got it!" called Jamey. He came back into the kitchen holding a brown paper package, a strange expression on his face.

I looked to him expectantly. "What is it? Not pizza, I take it."

He unwrapped the package: the silver-framed wedding portrait he'd kept on his office desk. He passed it to me distractedly, examining the included note. "Simon, you cockroach!" whistled Jamey. He looked up. "He's like an elf on crack. This is like a . . . a *ransom* note for everything they took. Listen to this:

James:
Hence a wise general makes a point of foraging on the enemy.
One cartload of the enemy's provisions is equivalent to twenty
of one's own, and likewise a single picul of his provender is
equivalent to twenty from one's own store.

Ah yes. From the "Waging War" section. Bravo! I recited along, by rote, in my head. I had to smile. "Jesus, Jamey. He needs a very long rest. You do understand this would actually be hilarious—if it weren't so tiring."

"Yeah, well, ha ha. Wait 'til you hear what he wants. Actually, it's sort of more '*how*' he wants what he wants. You were right this morning: he is psycho-adjacent."

He closed the door so as not to be overheard, and began:

James:
By now you know I have your stuff. Actually, of course, it's my
stuff, and it represents my history, but that's neither here nor
there at the moment. You've paid a dear fee, so in the end I will
have no problem relinquishing the property back into your
care. Material items and worldly goods, James, are trophies
that are earned or won over the course of time, but are none-
theless replaceable. What is not replaceable, my boy, is a career
of memories and accomplishments. A career of respect and
honor and achievement on the very highest level.

Jamey rolled his eyes and looked like he might gag. He massaged his neck and continued reading:

You have been a worthy and courageous adversary. And I
cannot say our interaction has not been intriguing to me—
amusing, even, in certain ways. But even I must admit, or I'd
like to think, that we have both exhausted our supplies of emo-

*tional endurance and intellectual forbearance in this matter. It
is a young man's town, our Hollywood—I recognize that, even
as you cast me aside—but I would like to believe that although
you are younger than me, you and your German compatriots would understand the value of this sickly gentleman and
the dynasty he has built. I would like to believe you would
do the right thing, in the eyes of an industry of which I am a
prominent leader. I would like to believe that you are noble
and appreciative of my earned position, since that dynasty is
now your own, won fair and square. I would like to believe you
would want to honor me graciously and sincerely—*

"For godsakes, Jamey," I interrupted, amazed. "He's stumping for
a party! A 'last hurrah'!" Had it *always* been this transparent? Jeez!
If we'd only known then what we knew now . . .

"No kidding—I like the part where he says I '*won*' the business.
That's a nice touch. Now hang on—it gets better in the closing."

"Thank God. The string section was driving me crazy."

*Should you agree to these simple terms, I will be happy to have
my men deliver back to you the items that have gone missing . . .*

"Blah blah blah." Jamey looked up and smirked. "He adds: 'PS:
Barb and I are keeping the lumbar chairs. Julia ordered these goddamn wooden benches from Finland and they're killing my back.'"

I smiled sadly. "You know, Jame, Sun Tzu would warn, *Peace pro-
posals unaccompanied by a sworn covenant indicate a plot . . .*" I had
a flash of clarity. "I know what he's up to! He wants you to underwrite
that barbeque Julia's throwing before Awards Weekend. It's like killing eighteen birds with one check—brilliant, as always." I ticked off
Simon's probable list of objectives: "One party paid for by you covers
a shmancy send-off for Simon and Barb from Pacificus, the launch
of their new company, Man of the Year honors, the fundraising pilot

for Julia's latest star turn, and, most essentially, a public apology from Commerz. And from you."

Jamey yawned again and then chuckled, tiredly, appreciating the irony as well as Simon's thoroughness. "That cowboy's a pro. I'll bring this to the offsite and have the attorneys take a look; they're on their way out west as we speak. I need to report on everything in person anyway—total corporate governance overhaul. When I get back I'll call Simon and force him to sign some sort of 'covenant.' Anything, finally, for detente."

With Jamey gone, the house was quiet, and I finally had time to concentrate on subjects other than Simon, Julia, and Sun Tzu. Three whole days on my own! There was so much I'd neglected that I didn't even have time to "not eat" with Sarah. Phone calls and urgent requests piled in concerning my initially tongue-in-cheek, means-to-an-end lark Coyote Club. Word had spread like wildfire after the initial *Shinier* coverage, but it really took on a life of its own after *Variety*, the *Reporter*, and the *LA Times* enthusiastically picked up the heroic tale of Lady Selena's karmic auction actions. I forwarded the online stories to Nancy and Leslie, for a laugh. Events had transpired so quickly (and so intensely and so strangely) these past few months, I hadn't the time or the wherewithal to explain either myself, our increasingly dire situation, nor my close, personal relationship with a long-dead military genius to my New York girlfriends. They hadn't been in the loop on much since before our holiday party.

Mallory, predictably, sent flowers and called nonstop, glossing over her considerable tome of wicked transgressions in favor of sucking up hugely ("bygones, Stacey!") and begging admittance to the Club. Oh yes, me and my once ragtag band of tainted, unfulfilled C-list wives were definitively on the upswing. We were "cool," now, very much in fashion. We were the "It" set—and, more important, we were gatekeepers of the "It" accessory and logo. Everyone wanted in. I couldn't help but laugh: as Julia herself might decree, our STOP THE PREDA-TORS! T-shirts were becoming the new red-string bracelets! I privately wondered (and worried a bit, too) if anyone had even the slightest in-kling that there was an actual higher purpose to this club, aside from a mere wildlife preservation craze, or if they just wanted to be part of a new trend, an anti-chic buzz clique backlash. Mallory's rabid inter-est spoke very obviously to the latter. I promised I'd put her name up to a vote (and run her application by my Very Reverend Grand High Priestess and Consigliore, Lady Selena) at the next meeting, but warned her that there was a long waiting list. And in truth there *was* a long list; women from across all social sets had been calling with questions: "What's the protocol to join? I belong to Riviera—is your membership process like that?" "Does the cute T-shirt come in tank *and* belly-cut?" And, "Do you sell at Kitson or Fred Segal?"

Even more surprisingly, checks and donations were arriving daily with some very big names attached; Lady Selena and I had important decisions to make, and quickly.

Jamey arrived home earlier than expected and found me in the kitchen, sautéing the filling for an empanadas recipe Isabel finally deigned to teach me. The dough was chilling in the fridge and the chopping boards were loaded with onions, tomatillos, and garlic. Flour and eggshells were everywhere. Naturally enough, Isabel had dusted herself off, made a face at the mess, and retired upstairs to fix her face. Jamey handed me a thick manila envelope, smiling mysteri-ously as he hugged me. "I found this outside, stuck in the gate. Same block caps as the New Year's package."

I groaned—not Deep Throat again. Just when it had gotten so nice and quiet. I shook it, hesitating. "Jamey, what do you think is happening? And why now? I can't decide if it's interesting or too weird for words."

"One way to find out . . ."

I slit the seal and dumped the contents on the counter. Tear sheets and newspaper clippings tumbled down; translations for the text were attached with paper clips. I spread them out with my palm. Sure enough, there was Isabel's condom ad with a nude Julia climbing out of a tequila bottle, as well as the *¡Hola!* cover story about her part in the dissolution of Pedro Cojones' marriage. An ad for low-end Spanish *cerveza* featured a sexed-up, topless Julia as a cocktail waitress, seductively enticing a bull—who, unnervingly, was *very* responsive! Pages of Julia from naughty Dutch and German lingerie catalogs, fabrics cut away in all the usual, revealing places. Skin magazine layouts and profiles abounded, listing her as a "top Broadway performer and high-end couture model." She was even named "Mademoiselle Avril." Her likes were attention, wealth, movies, and fashion. Dislikes: children, parents, boredom, and anonymity. Hmm.

A series of what looked like surveillance photos were clipped together, black and white and blurry of Julia engaged in clinches with much older men on yachts, in cars, and on apartment terraces in various European locations. A photo of the Hamburger King's jet, Julia out front in a skimpy "stewie" uniform . . . an exceedingly busy and well-traveled young lady, our Julia! There were European tabloid clippings, blurbs about misadventures in other people's marriages, as well as some notices about minor nightclub appearances, some of which I'd vaguely heard about before.

Most interesting by far, however, were photocopied documents accompanied by translations of lawsuits and legal notices, going back a number of years. Let's see . . . at nineteen, she was arrested for pandering on a beach on Marbella. Well, she was young, I theorized. I'd give her that one. She probably had no idea, and it *was* possible she might have been entrapped, especially if the officer was cute . . . Or maybe not. I read on. It happened again a few years later at a nightclub in Juan-les-Pins. And after that, she was picked up for solicitation at a hotel bar in Cannes during the Film Festival. Her parents flew over from Minnesota to help her out of her legal woes. *Ha!* Julia was eight years older than I.

I glanced at a bemused Jamey and continued reading, captivated.

The next batch of legal-looking papers revealed that Julia was named as a correspondent in no less than three upper-crust European divorce proceedings, all within a few years of each other. Spain, England, and France: she'd graced the courts of them all. All three men were bigwigs at European record companies. Julia had initially been hired by the wives of these well-chosen, "useful" men, to watch their kids after school and to tutor them in English "in her native tongue," so the document read. Very clever! The native tongue, it would seem, was eventually put to better use on their husbands (one was indeed the fading singer Lady Selena and Guy had mentioned, a Monsieur Sacamerde) and that was that. In all three instances, the affairs ended badly as each of the men tried to break off the liaison. Julia had then taken important personal items—"trophies" was the word employed in the transcripts—from the unsuspecting wives: clothing, jewelry, fur pieces, and prescription pills. Of course! Her favorite things. They all caught on pretty quickly after that.

"Wow." We sat in fascinated silence, passing the translated papers back and forth. "I still don't understand, Jamey." I felt a little nauseous. Or maybe it was just hunger. "Someone really has it in for Julia. Imagine the time, effort, and money it must have taken to pay an investigator to collect all this. But what do you suppose they want me to do about it? Am I supposed to go to the press? No one in LA actually puts anything evil in writing, if they can help it; they just whisper it, or leak an e-mail or memo. Do you think I should maybe call her when she gets back from her spa trip?" God, I was a wimp, even at this late date. I surprised even myself.

Jamey poured a soda. "What do you mean, when she's back from the spa?"

"Oh, she's locked herself in some bare bones starvation cell, designed to help her lose ten percent of her body weight in . . ."

"No, she hasn't," he interrupted. I looked up from the sizzling onions. "I just saw her at the Phoenix airport, all bandaged up, waiting to be wheeled onto the plane."

"Who?"

"The star correspondent, Julia Mallis."

"No way!"

"Way!"

"Did she see you?"

"Yup." His grin widened. "I'm pretty sure she was mortified, but there wasn't much she could do; she couldn't move the wheelchair by herself. She was sedated, I think, but not *too* far gone to tell me she was recovering from yet another car accident. Of course, that would be an accident that left bruising and bandages *only* on and around her midriff, right up to her neck."

"Fascinating."

"Always. More fascinating, I think, is that she dyed her hair back from blond blond to way darker than the original brown. It's almost black."

Hmm. So: Julia was having a Cher moment; serious acting for a serious director required serious surgery . . .

"Well, you know whatever Julia's had done, Charlie's behind it, telling her to 'glam down, *way* down' for his unwritten movie role. I'm seeing Sarah tomorrow to go over some new Coyote Club logos." I jutted my chin at the artwork, set next to a stack of invitations and Deep Throat's new data dump. "I did hear that Charlie's furious. Simon's now demanding an Executive Producer credit for his 'fifty-cent donation.'"

On a cloud of my Opium (which preceded her by at least a minute), Isabel floated in and proceeded to fuss over "the Man," who'd soared meteorically in status since she'd gotten wind that he'd avenged her unfairly disgraced TV priest. She peeked past his shoulder at the new logos thoughtfully. "You know, I think maybe Paco is coyote too . . . we should send T-shirts to all the nuns in *Un Día Grande:* PARE LOS DEPREDADORES!"

"That's a great idea, Isabel." Her eyes shifted to the other two stacks: Julia's Big Stud condom ad was on top of one; the invite to her

Youth Movement luncheon atop the other. "Aha!" she cried bitterly. "*She* is the biggest coyote of all!"

Guy arrived at that moment, swishing grandly through the kitchen door that Jamey had left ajar. He was back—and out of black, fully restored to his former *Brideshead Revisited* glory and well-earned position of office maven, air-kissing all around. Jamey ran upstairs while Isabel, entranced by so much peacock finery and mood elevation on a man, allowed herself to be fawned over, "Look at *you* and your glossy glossy hair—I *hate* you!" I rushed to hide Deep Throat's dossier, lest it spark a setback in Guy's very progressive (and very expensive) four-days-a-week therapy at St. Somebody's. In the commotion, I saw Isabel fold the luncheon invitation into her jacket pocket and slip quietly out the door.

Guy was fired up. "Group was great today! Everyone agrees I'm making excellent progress with my special art project. They say I have real flair." One important element of said treatment, according to the progressively expensive doctors, was art therapy, to revive Guy's depressed spirits and allow him to "express and overcome his deep loss." Jamey had kindly enough complied, giving Guy free rein to update the office décor and reinstall the stolen goods. Guy took his appointment very seriously, overseeing the activity with all the precision of a military exercise. "Out with the old, in with the new!" he singsonged, unloading paint chips, bits of framing, upholstery and carpet swatches on the table, arranging them for me to admire. Suddenly, his yammering stopped cold. I looked up: he was sifting through the coyote artwork thoughtfully. "Are these . . . ferrets? They look like ferrets. You know, Si—*he* used to call me ferret . . ."

"Those are coyote, Guy. Why don't you sit down?"

"Do you wanna know what I know?" he began as usual, but I could tell his heart wasn't in it.

"Of course I do, sweetie; you always know the best stuff." I patted his knee, poor thing.

He sat straighter. "Well, I know all about Si— *their* new movie. *Yoolya* is trying to soften her image: less va va voom aging Ann-Margret temptress, you know, and more 'kind and gentle' to children. Anyhoo, *Yoolya* will play a modern-day Mary Poppins-type nanny." He looked at me, incredulous. "It's so against type, it's almost brilliant!" Against type? Oh, if Guy only knew . . . My mind raced to the dossier stashed in the closet. Well, *somebody* knew something. That was for sure.

CHAPTER 20

¡UN DÍA GRANDE!

While heeding the profit of my counsel, avail yourself
also of any helpful circumstances over and beyond the
ordinary rules. In all fighting, the direct method may
be used for joining battle, but indirect methods will be
needed in order to secure victory.

— Sun Tzu, *The Art of War*

I hung up the phone, un-muted the TV, and turned to Sarah,
seated at my kitchen table. "That was Mallory again, from
Donaccia's boutique. I've told her ten times we're not going to that
ridiculous luncheon. I have no interest in fighting with Julia today."
Since the auction, you'll be pleased to know, I'd been very busy practicing temperance, focus, and restraint, heeding Lady Selena's wise
words of advice. Maintaining this righteous state of grace, however,
had its challenges, and I was wavering a bit this morning. I sipped
from my mug and grimaced. "And I wish Isabel had shown up. I'm so
used to her coffee I can't even drink my own anymore!" It wasn't like
Isabel not to call if there was a problem; we'd become, well, simpa-
tico of late, and I'd hoped it was a permanent achievement.

"Are you guys going to any of these?" Sarah inquired, ignoring my
mood and flipping through the invite pile on the table. As we were in
the midst of Awards Season, events and dinners feting everyone and

everything were stacking up fast and furious, sometimes two or three to an evening. But the disease-of-the-week circuit, the pay-to-play tribute club, persevered regardless.

These mounting obligations triggered only one thought: a desperate need for more suitable clothing. Sarah and I were meant to go shopping today. "What's that pretty purple and silver one for again? Some long, Latin name."

"Ha!" she blurted. "The CGA? I can't pronounce it either, but Charlie likes to call it 'Circumcisions Gone Awry,' for kids who've had unfortunate surgical experiences—a very popular event."

"Ah yes: brought to you by Doctors Without Conscience! Jamey flagged another one—for SAG, which I guess he thought benefited the Screen Actors Guild. But I checked: it's Surgery Against Grotesquerie, the tagline of which should be 'When Bad Plastic Surgery Happens to Good People.'"

Sarah giggled wickedly. "The 'Glamour Don't' Squad! I know it well. It says here, though, the evening will feature an acoustic set by Jon Bon Jovi *and* James Taylor. Not bad for twenty-five grand and an open bar. Hey, speaking of grotesquerie, are you going to Julia's barbeque?"

I made a face. "Jamey says we have to, but it'll be the last appearance we'll need to make all together, as part of the deal he worked out after Simon ransomed the office furniture: Jamey's stuff for a month's peace and a party." I paused. "How sick is that—it actually made sense when he explained it?"

But Sarah was already gazing past me at the TV. "Turn it up, Stace. Something's going on in Beverly Hills. Another car chase?"

I pressed the volume and we both moved closer to the screen: *Live Breaking News.* "It looks like Rodeo Drive's blocked off. There's a protest or something." And then the phone rang: Mallory, again. "Mal, I told you—"

"Stacey," she broke in. "You better get down here. Your housekeeper's gone berserk! She's corralled a bunch of other cleaning women and youth group girls. They're all wearing your T-shirts and shouting angry stuff in Spanish. They've even called the press! They're blocking the entrance to Donaccia's boutique; Julia and a bunch of girls are trapped inside. The cops are just getting here now."

Sure enough, front and center on the screen was Isabel, with a bullhorn, in command and mightily pissed off. She and the rest of her keyed-up posse sported PARE LOS DEPREDADORES! T-shirts featuring Julia's silk-screened face, slashed red through (from Simon and Julia's Christmas card!) in place of our usual coyote image. Damn, but she's clever! My heart swelled with pride as I grabbed the car keys. My Isabel! Such spirit! Such solidarity! "Come on Sarah. We're going to the luncheon after all."

As Rodeo was blockaded by flashing police vehicles and press vans, we parked a few blocks away and made our way on foot through the crowd of amused onlookers and bewildered tourists, as close as we could get to the entrance of Donaccia Scroccone's techno disco fashion rave. The cops were trying to clear the storefront, attempting to placate the mass of belligerent maids as well as the high-strung socialites for whom they worked. I spied the newly raven-haired Julia, chosen symbol of this class war, just inside the window, Lurex-for-day and scowling at the errant housekeepers. Some *Shinier* girls (Libbet included) cowered alongside her, squinched up next to Donnacia's emaciated mannequins (attired in a manner that would make the most hardened Vegas showgirl blush). I began my quest for Isabel, straining to find her among the thirty or so angry, chanting, Julia-T-shirted protestors. So many bodies and signs! Useless. Light bulb: I stared at their shoes, and . . . Aha! I'd know those silver YSL strappies anywhere!

Isabel was motioning menacingly with her sign, berating a female officer, dark eyes flashing, hoochie finger wagging. I poured apologies on the policewoman and tugged Isabel away to calm her down. Tears welled behind my eyes—and hers, too, if I'm not mistaken. We were both overcome. "Isabel, this is amazing!" I swept my arm around the scene she had so spectacularly orchestrated. "I'm so impressed! I just don't want you to get hurt . . ." I glanced over at the officer who was hastily scribbling a ticket, glowering back at us.

Isabel puffed with pride and waved my concern away. "See there?" She indicated a young, frightened woman in a starched uniform wringing her hands on the sidelines. "That's Esmeralda. She works for the bad one," Isabel pointed to Julia's image on her T-shirt and made a disgusted face. "She reminds Esme she signed a confidentiality agreement and must not say anything to anyone, or else. I don't want my daughter to end up like that. I knew we had to do something . . . *big*, to make people listen, to make this terrible program stop. I watch all you've done and I get inspired." She pumped her fist in the air, triumphant. A thought occurred to me: Isabel's rally today *truly* illustrated the spirit and mission of the allegorical Coyote Club. Isabel and her friends—and their daughters—were another group of disenfranchised women, not so very different from the charter Kabbalah Circle members. Both groups had banded together to take control, fending off the bullies who preyed on them with seeming impunity. This subset hadn't had any voice in the past, but Isabel had managed to change all that today.

I grabbed Isabel and led her over to the news vans. Crews were setting up, testing their equipment, getting the lay of the land. I offered us up for interviews; an impromptu press conference—right up my alley. Isabel laid out her side of the story as the talking heads thrust their mics and jockeyed for position. I listened, admiring her eloquence and ardor.

Then it was my turn, and another Big Idea crystallized as I formulated my statement—Lady Selena and the Kabbalah girls would love this! "As one of the founders of the Coyote Club, I've been inspired by all the support we've received from the community. Interest and membership have grown tremendously, and with that have come pledges of financial support. With these monies, I'd like to announce the formation of the Coyote Club Youth Scholarship Fund, providing college and trade education programs to those in need. More details will be forthcoming in the next few weeks." Isabel and I grinned at each other and, points made, headed back into the crowd to tell the others and help restore order.

Isabel gathered her victorious circle and I went off in search of Sarah, whom I'd lost somewhere near the front of the boutique. There was a couples-counseling-on-acid surreality to the street scene. Some, like Isabel and me, were emotional and talking sincerely; others were at each other's throats, threatening and jabbing. The cameras caught it all.

A few very strange things occurred in rapid succession: Barb hurried by (still admirably spa trim, for her, though her choice of shiny striped cigarette pants and matching disco wife-beater flattered very little in comparison to her sleek security-tape catsuit). She tapped my shoulder in a familiar manner, gave a quick half-hug, and smiled almost . . . genuinely? Odd; new meds, perhaps? I stared at her striped back, confused, and ran smack into an even more suspiciously over-friendly (but spectacularly turned out, as always) Ritzy, in canary-yellow Cavalli, hobbled by two equally weighted shopping bags filled with shoe boxes. Wow. Regardless of circumstance, these girls could shop! I instinctively looked past her for signs of Inga . . . "Stacey," Ritzy cried, unable to motion, "I told Sarah I wanted to make a lunch date to, y'know, get to know each other better. Maybe you'll come to the house? We really *should* talk. . . . Call me!" She raised what she could of her staple-gunned eyebrows, beaming boundless friendship and love my way. Hmm. I quickly attributed this unheard-of attempt at normalcy to a stiletto-induced endorphin rush and brushed quickly past. Just then, my arm was grabbed like a life vest by a dejected and tearful Mallory, slumped quite alone to the side of the activity.

"Stacey," she sniffled, eyes pleading, "this has been the very worst day! Julia ignored me completely. She didn't acknowledge me as co-chair, and wouldn't even stand next to me in the *Shinier Sheet* committee photograph. And *then*, I thought I'd misplaced my opening remarks, but it turns out she stole them from my bag, performed *my* speech herself, and took all the credit! I don't think she even likes me at all."

"Mallory," I began quietly, "how you can stand here in the middle of this street—in the middle of this *issue*, and whine about *Julia* is beyond me. Reporters will be here any minute, looking for statements from Julia *and* from you about your so-called youth group. Get your priorities straight and figure out what, if anything, you stand for. Here's a suggestion: shut down your program and donate whatever you've raised to the Scholarship Fund I'm starting."

Her shrewd eyes lit up. "Will it get me into the Coyote Club?"

Jeez! A one-track mind if ever there was one. "Well, it certainly couldn't hurt . . . but you have bigger issues at the moment, I should think." I glanced around again: reporters were indeed on the hunt, inching closer. "You know, Mal, I just cannot comprehend why you continue to grovel for Julia's approval. She's incapable of . . ." My jaw dropped, mid-sentence, to the asphalt. I was bowled over, and any residual interest in Mallory evaporated. My wandering eyes had found Sarah, wedged very unfortunately in a most unpleasant Julia/Barb/Donaccia three-way, a camera crew approaching stealthily. Julia, for something new, was mid-imperious diatribe, gesturing snootily at Sarah: Charlie-related, I assumed, or more likely his complete lack of relating to her. It couldn't possibly be the volatile issues at hand. And then it hit me: I saw what she'd been up to in Arizona. But it couldn't be, could it? Naww . . . well, now. I supposed it could: Julia had had her boobs taken out! She was flat as a boy now—bone thin, as always, and dressed in the height of Donaccia's Britney Spears-influenced disco designs but . . . flat as a boy! What would become of her Web site now?

Sarah (never fear) was getting her licks in, but I couldn't hear her words, stunned as I was by Julia's entirely renovated midsection. I moved closer, not even under my own power; simple curiosity seemed to carry me. Julia erupted yet again, haughtily pouring scorn:

"... *need* to discuss my *role*! ... input is *critical! You* tell him from *me* ... another deal—a *big* one! ... may not have *time* for him ... my *rider* ... no roses, only shell-pink calla lilies in my trailer, *and* a private area for my B–12 injections!" Sarah let Julia's edicts hurtle by and made goofy, amazed faces at me, not so surreptitiously pointing to Julia's chest in case I hadn't noticed. Julia met my gaze and held it. She opened her mouth to speak, hesitated, and closed it again as Sarah hurried out of frame to my side. And not a moment too soon: the gaggle of reporters descended on the momentarily off-balance, oddly silent Julia for a statement, the highly questionable founder of the highly questionable youth movement. An eruption of glee and the reporters broke away shaking their heads, clearly having captured on tape some ingeniously brazen manifesto, a modern-day version of "Let them eat cake!" as a sound byte for the News at Four.

Left alone with only Barb standing loyally by, Julia turned and released an avalanche of pent-up arrogance and fury. With each hurtful, targeted syllable, I could see Barb's stoic face twitch and sag with the unbearable weight of Julia's relentless, condescending derision. Hmm. Maybe there was some trouble in paradise after all ...

CHAPTER 21

CALIFORNICATION

How victory may be produced for them out of the enemy's own tactics—that is what the multitude cannot comprehend. All men can see the tactics by which I conquer, but what none can see is the strategy out of which victory is evolved.

—Sun Tzu, *The Art of War*

fter Isabel's brilliant protest and the ensuing media coverage, Lady Selena and I were deluged with phone calls, inquiries, and donations. With her help, and a raft of her lawyers, we got down to business, setting up bank accounts, consulting psychologists and other trained professionals, creating guidelines and bylaws. We also set up a foundation office staffed by Bettina, Amy, and the Winking Wife. Isabel's daughter and the two girls from Mallory's house worked as paid interns. The phone requests had turned more serious, and we were soon assessing the broader value of our initiative: "My daughter/son/sister/brother is being bullied at school/on the bus/in the neighborhood, and I'm wondering if we can start a 'junior' club; something like, 'Coyote Club Takes Back the Playground'?" "If we held a meeting, would someone from the organization come and speak?" Well of *course* we'd sanction a junior committee! Of *course* we'd speak! We *had* struck a nerve! We had *won*!

*   *   *

As if a button had been pushed invisibly from somewhere behind the scenes, time fast-forwarded in that sneaky way it has, freezing frame just before Oscar Weekend and what promised to be the mother of all informal barbeques.

The day of Julia's party, Sarah insisted we confab on her patio instead of meeting at the Polo Lounge, site of (now) so many triumphs and victories. I was annoyed, in that Sarah's house was twenty minutes in the opposite direction from Dante's salon, my next stop. It also didn't help that, rather than pass our time not-eating together amiably, Sarah kept glancing at her watch and checking her phone, as if to ensure a working dial tone. It was driving me crazy. I put down my fork. "Sarah, what's up? Why are you so anxious?"

"Oh—it's nothing. Just stuff with the kids," she mumbled distractedly.

She paced toward the rosebushes, restlessly tapping the elaborately embellished invite on her wrist. I continued to pick at my salad, uneasy. "So," she finally spoke, "what do we think? An 'informal' barbeque. Dress: 'casual.' I wonder what the translation for that is, exactly, on planet Mallis?"

I mustered some enthusiasm. "Well, since I now consider myself fluent in all that is Mallisious . . . let's see. Here's what we know: the party's called for six p.m., and the run-of-show consists of a blessing from Jamey, a blessing from a rabbi, and a screening of Julia's *Mary Poppins* moment. I'd have to say—and I'm speaking strictly from personal experience—there's absolutely nothing about this that's informal. I'm thinking 'floor-length beaded gown' as appropriate attire. Now, having said that, since Jamey's speaking, do I throw him in black tie and tails or send him in as Farmer John?"

She grinned, raising her eyebrows in delight. "Hmm: a dilemma. I know, why don't I call Ritzy?"

I made a face. "Tonto? Are you nuts? Like she'd tell the truth."

Sarah hesitated. "She's not so bad, Stacey."

Jamey's famous words of warning blared like a siren in my head, about agendas crossing and uncrossing, alliances changing in the blink of an eye. Sarah had been spending more and more time with Ritzy while I'd been occupied with Coyote Club business; her name had come up an awful lot in our conversations of late. I'd wondered what it all meant—but then again, I reasoned, Sarah hadn't deceived me yet, and that had to count for something. Didn't it? Anyway, she had known Ritzy for years. I relented. Slightly. "Maybe you're right. Come to think of it, she was actually even sort of . . . *nice* to me at Isabel's rally. I haven't seen her since, though. Has she had a total lobotomy *and* a personality overhaul?" I smiled sweetly.

Sarah smiled back, just as sweetly. Oh, something very definitely was up. "She's taken up Buddhism, y'know. . . . I'll just go inside to give her a call and ask what she's wearing. She plans her wardrobe months in advance and is usually on target. Give me a minute."

"Your phone's right here."

"Oh, right. Well, I need to get her number. It's inside."

I sighed, annoyed again. Always so many games afoot in this town, and I've always hated poker. I pulled out my cell, using the time to call the salon yet again to reconfirm my blowout. You never could tell with Dante. He racked up more *affaires de coeur* in a month than I had throughout my twenties. His emotional gamut of "besotted with lust" and "heartbreaking catatonia" was exhausting to listen to but, I had to admit, the man was a genius with a brush, a blow dryer, and a bottle of hairspray. Worth the drama and inconsistency, at any price.

Tonight's affair marked the last corporately mandated event we'd have to attend under false pretenses, and the promise of that eased my mind. A bit. Regardless of Ritzy's forthcoming advice, I decided, I'd wear a vintage knockoff Courrèges mini-dress a la Mrs. Peel—a favored weapon from my New York arsenal of little black dresses. Just like the old days, for comfort and luck. Maybe I'd dress Jamey as Steed . . .

"Cocktail."

I looked up from my Blackberry. "What?"

"Ritzy says cocktail attire will be fine."

"Oh. Good. I've gotta go—Dante's actually on schedule." Sarah seemed disappointed. "What's wrong? I'll see you tonight."

"Listen, can you meet for breakfast tomorrow? I want to talk to you about something."

I knew it. "I've been here for over an hour, talk to me now. Is it about tonight?"

"No," she shook her head. "We'll talk tomorrow." She checked her watch, again. "It's all good, I promise. Nine o'clock? Polo Lounge?"

"Sure," I said, truly uncomfortable.

She brightened. "Great! So I'll see you later at Julia's." She waved from the door, ducking back inside as her phone finally rang.

Jamey and I rolled up to the House of Mallis an hour before the called-for time. In their heavily negotiated moment of truce, Jamey and Simon had agreed to go over the program one last time, on site. Simon, in his suspicion, wanted every last opportunity to script and approve all of Jamey's "unscripted, ad-libbed" farewell remarks. Jamey, of course, wanted to ensure that the public torch of Pacificus would be passed appropriately as well. The two mistrustful cats would circle each other, hair on end, each daring the other to blink first.

After all, as Julia would (and did) say, "anyone and everyone BIG" would be attending. Plus press. Simon always did like to walk on the wild side. If we played our cards right, the thought prevailed, we could all tiptoe through tonight's minefield of (not so) hidden agendas, each winning some semblance of victory and peace of mind. That was the objective, anyway: superb playacting on a beautifully designed and spotlighted stage (subsidized by Commerz), to the benefit of all agendas involved.

We ambled in under the Gothic front arch, over which an enormous banner proclaimed WHY TO HONOR SIMON MALLIS—if only I'd had a magic marker, how I'd love to have added a question mark! We passed through the marble vestibule (slash erstwhile disco room) and followed the trail of catering noises out to the garden where I'd first met Sarah. I nudged Jamey as we passed the infamous staircase cam, its red blinking eye winking hello. We waved back. Cater-waiters hauled bags of ice, stacked glassware and plates, and tended the rows of stainless steel grills for the barbequed feast. Over the clatter, Simon could be heard bleating directions through an upstairs window. He spotted us stranded amid the activity and called that he'd be right down.

Jamey, an excited glint in his eye, whispered, "Stace, quick! Show me where you guys were sitting. I wanna check the bushes and see if there really are cameras and mics." He followed me to a cluster of hydrangea and pretended to tie his shoelaces, resting one foot on the bench as he pushed apart some branches. Oh yeah. "*Tie*" your Gucci loafers. Good one, hot stuff!

Simon approached from behind, his keen eyes registering the scene and more than likely our intent. He cleared his throat and extended his hand. "James, my boy!" Jamey jumped, composing himself as he did. "Stacey." A dazzling malevolent smile, as always, plastered on his slick face. He pecked my cheek. That faint but persistent meatloaf-y scent arose again. Gamey. Did he never bathe? "Barb and Julia are somewhere in the house. We have top hair and makeup teams here, you know, from our film crew." His eyes danced and he cocked his head, mock-assessing me. "Maybe you could do with a touchup. Hmm, Stacey?"

"No thanks, Simon, I'll live."

"I understand," he cooed. "It's just that, well, I wouldn't want you to be sweaty. Or so tired-looking. For the cameras, I mean."

God, I despised him, the controlling misogynist freak. He deserved Julia and all her fury. He smiled again, sharpened teeth gleaming in the twilight. "Why don't you go on inside and see what the girls are up to. I'm sure you and Julia would *adore* spending some quiet time together."

I looked to Jamey, piqued, who glared evenly back at Simon. "Go on ahead, Stace. Simon and I have a few things to go over. I'll come find you in a bit."

"Yes, Stacey. I want to wrap this up before Rabbi Slivovitz arrives." I smiled to myself: Slivovitz, like the vodka? Reading my mind, Simon said, tiredly, "Yes, Stacey, like the vodka."

Without a word (what would be the point?), I turned on my heel and chased down a harried waiter for a drink. Anything would do. Strangely, I was not poured kosher wine. The house was quiet, save for expected catering-related sounds. I roamed the few rooms I'd been in during Julia's Shiny-girl dance party. Coffee service was halfway set on the zinc bar, next to an oversized glass-topped humidor stocked with Cuban cigars. For after the screening, I mused, when the would-be investors would be lining up to hand over their checks. I heard some crashing noises followed by a woman cursing to the side of the bar. Curious, I moved closer and stuck my head in the doorway: Barb. Standing in the middle of an elegant, brightly lit screening room, which looked almost exactly like the one at Pacificus Tower.

"Stacey!" she called out. Videotapes and film reels overflowed in her arms. She fumbled over herself, knocking a pile of printed brochures to the floor, also presumably for review by financiers. "Come on in," she called happily. "I'm just setting up."

"Hey Barb." I paused. Oh, why not. "Can I help you? I see you have your hands full."

"Everything's under control, but thanks for offering." She smiled winningly and put her stash down on one of the burgundy velvet seats. "Y'know, I have to say I think *you*, of all people, will be very pleasantly surprised at the piece we're going to screen tonight. I have a really good feeling about it."

A conversation. Okay, I'd bite. "Well, I'm looking forward to it. I know you've been busy shooting."

She bent to pick up the fallen handouts, smiling and humming still. "So, what do you think?" She swept her arm back gracefully, displaying the décor like a designer show-house.

"It's spectacular. Just like the one in the Tower."

"Yes," she nodded warmly. "Simon and I designed them both, from a stunning home-theater we had once at a villa in Cannes. Now those were days . . ." she sighed wistfully. Just as quickly, she brightened again. "But things are definitely looking up; it's just the beginning of very good things to come!" She resumed her humming and carefully doled out brochures on seats, along with take-home cassettes affixed with the Crossfire Features logo.

"I'm so glad for you, Barb. You deserve every happiness and success for the future." As long as you're not in mine, I silently added. "By the way, can you tell me where I might find Julia?"

Without looking up, she answered, "Oh, she's probably upstairs, being endlessly groomed. You know how she is . . ." She broke off, rethinking. She stood straight. "*OR* . . ."—she drew out the word—"you know, a better bet might be to look in the pool house. In fact, you really *should* have a look in there and see our new offices. The view is really quite something at this time of day."

I turned to go. "The pool house—don't forget," she called after me. As I shut the door and walked away I could have sworn I heard her humming turn to laughter.

To the pool house, then. I went back outside and checked on Jamey and Simon: both were bent over papers, each debating and "correcting" the other's speech. I made my way down the slate steps and turned toward the far left corner of the property, where a kidney-shaped mosaic pool shimmered and twinkled with floating candles and flower petals. Barb was right; the view from here really was fabulous. City lights were just beginning to illuminate, as if by magic, grid by grid to the ocean.

From a distance the bungalow appeared to be empty, but as I approached I could see there were in fact some dim lights within. As I neared, I detected some curious scuffling noises, of a sort. I stopped to listen: these were very specific, very distinct scuffling noises, I was too well aware. Some seriously acrobatic hair and makeup artists, perhaps? Hmm. Not unless they were renegade escapees from Cirque du Soleil. Increasingly emphatic moaning and grunting, too . . .

I made my way around the side of the house (very Mrs. Peel and stealth-like, by the way, even without the leather catsuit), carefully, so as not to tear the thirty-eight-dollar Wolford fishnets I'd bought specially, and peeked in a small window. Now here *was* a view! My hand flew reflexively to cover my mouth to make sure I wouldn't scream (or laugh) out loud . . . Well! My *my*, Julia: very blond again! And such stamina! *And* with her Man of the Year not a hundred yards away! Balls o' steel, our Julia had! But who was the limber, energetic stallion on top of her on the wet bar? One of the cater-waiters? I guessed it had to be—they were all actors and models, right? Who else was here? And he did have Harlequin Romance hair and muscles for miles . . .

The situation, I appraised delightedly, warranted much closer inspection—for simple clarity, of course. I skulked around to the far side of the bungalow for better viewing. Well, good for her, I thought, an image of her pink, detestable husband flashing in my mind. A second later, I thought, well, good for Barb!

I turned the corner, tiptoed through some low brush and was rewarded with a much better angle. Oh my! My heart dropped to my stomach, or did my stomach leap to my mouth? Both, I think, and at the same time. The stud was sweating profusely . . . a dead giveaway! The mysterious and beautiful stranger was, most unfortunately—and yet very definitively—Ritzy's much prized and wholly adored teenage son, Luke. How could I ever forget that vacant, cherubic face gazing out from Ritzy's diamond chunk of a locket? My, how he'd grown! I would have never thought to see him come so alive, and most especially not in these circumstances!

I backed away as silently as possible. The wheels in my head were spinning out of control, piecing together disjointed fragments of information. Disoriented, I stumbled back toward the house. Other guests had arrived; Simon was greeting the rabbi and his posse, introducing them to Jamey. I stole up the steps unnoticed and searched out a restroom, to clean up and think for a while.

When I emerged ten minutes later, the crowd had multiplied. I found Jamey waiting for me by the stage, double-fisted, not far from Simon and the rabbi. Without a word I took a wineglass from him and drank it down quickly. Jamey barely noticed, watching the now-steady stream of guests flowing out to the lawn. I took the scotch from his other hand and drank that down as well. Before I could begin to relay my discovery, I noticed Phil and his date du jour heading our way. A few yards back, a refreshed and radiant Julia (in a Sinfonia Folata peacock beaded strapless gown) was on her way to Simon's side.

Playacting her part in the evening's script to a perfect tee, Julia stopped and welcomed us graciously. We air-kissed and embraced, smiling extravagantly as photographers from the trades snapped away. Simon and Barb joined in and again, we glad-handed animatedly for the cameras, staging quite a convincing "farewell show" if I do say so—a Herculean effort not unnoticed by the gathering crowd of Industry leaders and financiers. The very point, naturally.

Simon and Julia stepped aside and continued the photo op, now featuring the WHY rabbi from Houston and a very large check. "I want food," Jamey muttered, to no one in particular. "And a double scotch too, if I'm to carry on with this."

Julia wheeled around, ever the ready, willing hostess, speaking both to Jamey and the rabbi. Here was her opening: "Rabbi, in honor of your and Simon's shared heritage, I've planned a very special treat for supper." She snapped her fingers and the nearest cater-waiters hastened over, bearing colorful trays bursting with Julia's guest-of-honor fare. She Brite-smiled widely in an attempt to charm the rabbi, and pronounced the foreign words with gusto. "Here we have mini Texan cheeseburgers, on *challah* bread, of course, and some grilled lobster, on potato *latkes*. Hand-made marshmallows are for dessert. And this young man has brought a strawberry milkshake, just for you!" She was triumphant, beaming with pride at her menu-planning expertise and execution.

No one moved a muscle; it was too uncomfortable a moment even to look at each other. Rabbi Slivovitz tilted his head and stared at Julia uncomprehendingly, at first, then narrowed his eyelids in obvious contempt. After too many painful beats, he finally spoke. "Is this a joke?" Cameras flashed again and Julia, flustered, looked wildly from Simon to Jamey for assistance. Simon opened his mouth to run interference, but the rabbi cut him off, raising his voice and becoming more incensed with each word. "I can't eat any of this! I am strictly kosher, at least while I am working! You should know this—it is disrespectful and detestable, to say the least! Dairy with meat, and on the same plate! Shellfish too!" He made a face and mumbled something exceedingly derisive, I'm sure, in Hebrew. "You Hollywood people, with all your temptations and shortcuts—there are no words! Bring me a cup of tea, please, in an unused paper cup," he growled, "and let's get this farce over with!" Disgusted, he stalked off to his entourage of lost boys (presumably the wayward youths themselves, as they sported black robes over baggy, drooping Sean John jeans, skull-and-cross-bone earrings and were smoking something that smelled suspiciously like burning carpet), who were waiting for him behind the small stage.

Julia, mortified, burst into tears and Simon, though enraged, tried to console her. "Don't cry, honey! You don't want to ruin your face."

She turned on him, reeling dangerously. "How *dare* you let that rude, hooded man talk to me like that! And what an unattractive outfit to wear to my party! After all the trouble I've gone to—you didn't even stick up for me!" She stared witheringly at Simon, eyes dark and defiant. "I *refuse* to be talked to that way, by *anyone*—let alone in my own home!" She was indignant, pushing that moral offensive as far as she could take it. Anything, to be absolved and the extreme faux pas forgotten. Barb rolled her eyes theatrically, I smiled (oh so much fun!), and Simon ran a hand through what was left of his hair. Oh yeah—just the beginning of a very long night. For all of us. For his part, Jamey grabbed the heaping plate and milkshake (using his scotch as a chaser) intended for the rabbi, and began eating with gusto.

"Hey, Julia!" he cried out between gigantic mouthfuls of cheeseburger, "the food's terrific. Don't listen to what anyone says!" Jamey grinned as Simon glared at him. Julia threw her shoulders back and ran off after a waiter carrying a tray of champagne flutes. She took two, drank them down like shots, turned back toward us, and gave us the finger.

Very nice. I laughed hard, spilling wine on myself as I did. Julia continued to torment Simon, strutting across the lawn and forcefully mouth-kissing male arrivals. Her vamping continued even as the check presentation and toasting of her husband unfolded on the stage, from which she knew Simon would have an even better view of her antics. As Jamey began his almost-earnest "Goodbye Simon from Pacificus" speech, Julia grabbed a strangely unwilling Scott Sturm in a determined lip-lock, gripping the sides of his head tightly even as he squealed to break away.

Sarah and Charlie had come up from behind while the circus played on; Ritzy, Max, and Luke Snippington were with them. Ritzy tapped me on the shoulder. "Great dress, Stace, even if it is black!" she whispered, giving a thumbs-up sign. With one hand she grabbed the diamond chunk at her neck, with the other she pulled her son proudly forward. "This is my baby, Luke." Oh, Ritzy. He was no baby, that was for sure.

I pantomimed my hello, trying to erase the steamy image of him from my mind. Both Simon and Rabbi Slivovitz scowled from the stage, displeased with our inattention. The trepidation I'd experienced my first night in this house returned; I had a sense that anything could happen, at any moment.

The program ended, and we headed toward the screening room. Julia was nowhere to be found. I was bursting to tell Sarah what I'd seen in the pool house, but Ritzy simply would not go away. She was wound tightly tonight, overly excitable and animated, even for her, chattering small talk incessantly. She held on to her "baby" who, eyes glazed and true to his seventeen years, clearly didn't have much to add to a conversation with fully clothed, adult women.

The lights dimmed, happily, and the Crossfire Features logo appeared on the screen. Simon swaggered proudly in front of it and asked everyone to take their seats. The murmuring died away, and all eyes focused politely on him.

"Friends, colleagues . . . thank you for joining us this very special evening." With a sweeping motion he indicated Julia and Barb, who stood slightly off to his side. "Not only does this mark the official launch of my and Barb Spurndoff's new production company, Crossfire, but we are truly excited to share with you a rough few minutes of our very first project, *Lolly Popps' Adventures*, currently in preproduction. This film, the first in a planned series of three, stars a very beautiful and talented actress—who also happens to be my very beautiful and talented wife: Julia Mallis." Julia basked and preened along with the applause. Simon continued, "We were very lucky to get Julia, actually. She's been roped into Charlie Truehart's next feature"—he rolled his eyes and drawled dramatically—"and we all know how difficult it is to say no to Charlie when he wants something." Indistinct, confused chuckling emanated from the insider-heavy crowd; a low groan of pain emanated from Charlie, and Sarah elbowed me, hard. Jamey played with his Blackberry Game Boy, and down the row Ritzy gripped Luke's leg even tighter next to an already-napping Max.

"In any event, we are thrilled to present you with this exciting 'first look,' which showcases Julia's innumerable talents. Some might say this casting is entirely against type for my glamorous wife, but after this viewing, I'm sure you'll agree that her unique, surprising abilities deserve all of your financial and marketing support."

He went on to give a storyline overview of *Lolly Popps' Adventures*: a young woman, Lolly Popps (Julia), the daughter of a wealthy but distracted industrialist in modern-day England. Lolly's mother died in childbirth. Grieving and unable to care for young Lolly on his own, Mr. Popps sent her to be raised in a convent. Although the nuns were kind, Lolly understands there is a void in her life that only her father's love can fill. She resolves, upon entering the larger world, that her mission will be that no young child go without love and attention; she has untold amounts of each to give. She begins her career as a nanny, selecting families with as much care as they employ to select her. "Barb and I have put together a few minutes of film, for your review and your hopeful investment. So, ladies and gentlemen, without further ado . . . I am pleased to present Julia Mallis, in *Lolly Popps' Adventures.*

Another round of light applause, and the houselights dissolved. Simon, Barb, and Julia took their seats as up on the screen the Crossfire graphic morphed elaborately into title and above-the-line credits, saccharine orchestration swelling. Max Snippington (he of the Bank of California Film Fund) snorted loudly once, then settled back into peaceful slumber. Curiously, Ritzy didn't rouse him as she usually did. She didn't seem to notice him at all, staring intently ahead at the screen, biting her lip, squeezing her baby for dear life. Surely, I mused, Max's underwriting and approval was all but depended upon by Simon . . . Uneasy now, I followed Ritzy's mesmerized gaze back to the screen.

The camera followed Julia (dressed more conservatively than I'd have thought possible: long black braid, Laura Ashley schoolmarm florals) as she strode purposefully down a cobblestoned street, heading for the one row house (in a row of row houses) with a bright red door. No one answers her knock, so she (Lolly Popps, that is) tries the doorknob, discovers it's open, and enters the foyer. She calls out—no response. Cautiously, she walks to the staircase and calls upstairs. Still no answer. She climbs slowly, uncertain, and puts her ear to a door that appears to lead to a child's nursery. She hears excited whispering within, and smiles to herself. Her little charges, perhaps, are hiding, playing a game! Her hand rests on the doorknob; she takes a deep breath and pushes open the door. The camera cuts to an angle behind her, so we see what she sees. And what is it that we all see? Well! Simon had never spoken truer words than in his introduction . . .

Grainy black and white film replaced the Technicolor images of a few moments earlier. Art house intention? I think not. It was a bedroom, all right, but not one belonging to a child. This interior was opulent and richly appointed, with furs and satin throws on the bed. It was somehow familiar, but I couldn't place it, exactly. Richly textured covers began to undulate and strains of moaning were heard; sporadic and muffled, at first, they soon increased in tone and velocity. At last, a woman's dark form emerged from underneath, throwing her arms and hair back in ecstasy: Julia! Surprised gasps and guffaws escaped from the crowd. After half a second, I realized where I'd seen a still from this film: Deep Throat's second delivery! No sooner did this occur than the film jumped abruptly: Julia and two toreadors, in—where was it? A dressing room, maybe, after a bullfight? "Blood" was smeared everywhere, and believe me, these hombres were quite the *toros machos*. Julia could have won a bronco-busting contest in Vegas! *Olé!* And . . . *cut!* A subtitle announced SPRING BREAK! in English. The low-budget scene featured Julia as a (not so) young coed frolicking nude on a yacht, entertaining the strapping male crew with pitchers of frozen drinks and whipped cream. . . . She licked something, but it most certainly was no lollypop. The next few interludes, I gathered from the enormous Dux bed and shag carpeting, took place right here on property, in the bungalow d'amour, interspliced with mug shots and news clippings. I recognized a young waiter from Spago as well as a pool boy from the Beverly Hills Hotel.

Moaning and grunting, it was soon apparent, sounded the same in any language. The filmed montage continued—and was very well edited, I must say, jumping every five or ten seconds to yet another lowlight of Julia's now well exposed and illustrious body of work, as a full-piece orchestra played on—fittingly, the theme from *Lolly Popps' Adventures*. While the piece lacked art or storyline, the producer certainly held fast to the theme: there sure was a lot of licking going on! It seemed that, for all the questionable back-story and incessant bravado, Julia did indeed have quite an extensive performance career behind her.

Stunned guffaws and titters of bewilderment spackled the crowded theater. Looking around, I saw only one expression: mouths open, jaws to the floor. Shock and Awe! Within seconds of comprehending the extent of the manipulation and meddling, Simon had made a mad dash for the projection room, only to find the door locked tight. Mortified, cursing, and furious, he grabbed the fire axe from its case and began hacking away at the lock, incandescent with rage. He tried desperately, heroically, and ultimately unsuccessfully to break the door down and put an end to the excruciating humiliation. Julia had stood and shrieked just once, face covered by her hands, then faded dramatically (but very lyrically) away into Barb's outstretched, waiting arms. There was nothing to be done until the psychically disturbing tape played itself out, which it finally did. "To be continued . . . with your indulgence!" were the words left on the dark screen. Silence.

Guests fidgeted uncomfortably; most had already edged single file toward the door, wanting only to get away from the embarrassment, and quickly. Aside from clothing rustles and investment brochures crumpling, the only sounds were Barb's motherly murmurs to Julia and Simon's uneven hyperventilating breaths, encompassing a rage and humiliation so severe his wheezing resounded like an iron lung. Any veneer of respectability had been stripped away; exposed in its stead was a nefarious legacy of hubris, fiercely guarded deception, and hypocrisy. His ambitions, his sham of a marriage, his dominion of fear and control: collapsed by a five-minute film. His disgrace would be rapid and complete. He stood impotent, raw, unhinged; fire axe still clutched tightly in hand. A few simple ticks of the clock, and he was reduced, diminished, before the very masses over which he once so mightily ruled.

The first rows dispersed and our aisle stood to file out, as if from a plane. Ritzy giggled nervously, hissing into Luke's ear. Sarah, as always finding humor, poked me playfully as we shuffled toward the door. As I turned I caught Barb's eye. She was glowing, triumphant, rocking Julia's sobbing head back and forth in her arms. I do believe she even *winked* at me. Emotional vindication for her, I understood in a flash, and in a very big way. So *that's* what she'd been planning earlier . . . literally humming with anticipation. I acknowledged her and smiled sadly, then shook my head. I understood her desire to destroy Julia, believe me—but at what price? At the risk of her and Simon's future? A fine example, I realized, of the depths of damage that years of humiliation and neglect can inflict upon a woman spurned. She had seen her opportunity and seized it—maybe it was just as simple as that. In any event, as she'd earlier predicted, things would surely change, now, indeed. She most definitely had, with that five-minute film, changed the balance of power forever, for better or worse. Proving Julia wrong yet again, Barb's gut, even after endless and hopeless surgery, had been right on target.

We joined the lineup for the valet, queuing under the still-waving banner, WHY TO HONOR SIMON MALLIS. Hmm. I looked over at Jamey, talking quietly in a corner to a reporter from *Variety*, no doubt trying to learn the extent of the next day's printed fallout. In his mind, of course, the evening's purpose had been about properly excising Simon and Barb from Pacificus and sending them off into the sunset. *Not* about underwriting a scandalous melee. Flipping through the evening's sorry events, I debated whether this reality was actually the most satisfying of all possible outcomes. Aware it would take a long while to unwind before achieving actual sleep, I thought I'd detail the account as soon as possible, and replay it within a few different scenarios to see if in fact it was true—that truth *is* actually stranger to believe in, and live with, than fiction.

In the midst of this sniggering, murmuring crowd, Sarah alone was in unusually high spirits. As Charlie claimed their car, she invited us to join them for a glass of champagne. One glance at Jamey's grim face (that look meant only one thing—hours of damage control to downplay the imminent pandemonium, and it was, after all, morning in Munich) and I begged off, a brain bath of Ambien, herbal tea, and the computer more suited to my mood. As she slid into the passenger seat, Sarah called out to remind me of our breakfast date. I watched their taillights inch slowly into the backed-up departures lane.

"*Secrets and Lies*," Jamey said quietly as our car pulled up. "That's the headline *Variety's* going with." Oy. He punched at his cell, dialing for dollars, hunting any unlucky Commerz attorney who might just be awake at this hour. No music, then. Well, that was okay. I sighed and pulled down the sun visor, sliding open the makeup mirror and angling it for the best rear view. I gazed at the slowly receding House of Mallis for what I hoped would be the last time. There was no need to worry about them, I knew implicitly, as the sum total of my experiences flooded my mind. Simon, Barb, Julia—they were survivors. They would endure, outlast, and overcome a plague, let alone a little bad press. In fact, I'd bet that in a month or two, Julia would hire a new publicist and be in high demand on the *Extra/Entertainment Tonight/Access Hollywood* circuit—the "Mea Culpa" tour, publicly atoning for her past to win back her husband's support and jump-start some sort of new life out of the ashes. There had to be a hidden angle or "victim" card somewhere in her misspent youth, to be played out for all it was worth. Barb had probably inadvertently done her a favor. Oh, yeah. They'd be back, never you fear, after only some minor regrouping and yet another revisionist rewrite. And with a vengeance, of that I was sure. They'd be more intense and ruthless than ever and, as always, playing hard, for keeps. I, for one, would most certainly be staying tuned.

I leaned back against the headrest, hypnotized by the street lamps whirring by at staccato, entrancing intervals. I closed my eyes, listening to a barely awake German lawyer drone heavily on speakerphone as Jamey sped down Sunset Boulevard. Free at last, free at last. . . . Could it really be true?

CHAPTER 22

BREAKFAST OF CHAMPIONS

He who can modify his tactics in relation to his opponent and thereby succeed in winning, may be called a heaven-born captain.

–Sun-Tzu, *The Art of War*

The next morning I awoke, disoriented, to the vibration of the garage door rumbling underneath the bed. Jamey. I glanced at the clock just as the radio alarm popped on: seven a.m. I couldn't even remember him coming to bed, having last spotted him on the office phone. And now he'd gone off already, so early.

I sighed, bringing myself into the present by focusing on a gently swaying bower of magenta bougainvillea, hummingbirds buzzing by. Peace. Yet another day of mellow, eucalyptus-scented air and intolerably electric blue sky. Would it never rain again? I buried my face in the pillow and groaned. Today should be gloomy and overcast—a groggy, hangover day, useful for brooding over pots of coffee, pondering the meaning of life and last evening's sorry tale of woe. But why did *I* feel so uneasy? So . . . lost? I found myself wondering what this serene morning looked like over at the Mallis homestead and shuddered myself up and out of bed. We were finally released from their haughty, oppressive grip, but after so many months of imprisonment, mind-control, and obsession, I wasn't actually sure how to feel about it all. I tried to wash my face clean of this worry: let them be someone else's heartbreak, for a change—not mine. Nope. I was resolved.

I downed some Advil and padded to the office, just in time to appreciate the German shepherd's morning constitutional of hysteria. Through the screened window, I yelled, "All right, already, I'm up! You can stop it now." The barking and whining ceased. Atten-SHUN! I could just make out the animal's form, ears up, through a giant oleander bush not fifteen feet from the window. I had recently come to suspect that the dog was, in fact, far more shrewd than I'd at first believed. But without irrefutable evidence, as is always the case, I would not be able to confront him. I narrowed my eyes and waited a beat: no more noise came forth.

I focused my contempt on the New York-skyline screensaver and debated whether to open the document I'd composed the night before. Actually, it was more that I'd ranted in the file, throwing up details and commentary in one giant spasm—to be mulled over and refined at a later date. The last missive in my Letter from LA compilation, destined for . . . whom? Not my friends, obviously.

I gazed longingly at the phone, yearning to dial 212. To *connect*. With my hard-learned distrust of phone lines, I'd taken to calling back east much less frequently, understanding that it was virtually impossible even to try to describe the insanely complex social machinations in terms any thinking person could (or would want to) comprehend. I could tell that my friends had begun to feel as uncomfortable listening as I did trying to explain; at the end of the day, all they could really see was a charmed and glamorous life unfolding on another coast. We defaulted then to much simpler, less emotional top-line question/answer sessions: "What/who was she wearing/doing/ saying?" or, "Is he tall/straight/sexy in person?," foregoing the larger, more frangible issue of my sanity. It all made perfect sense to me, though. A sick sort of sense, yet sense nonetheless. But after last night's hyperreal pyrotechnics—yeesh! I rubbed my eyes. The phone was clearly not an option.

It was official, then, I took note, at seven twenty-six a.m. on a warm and sunny February morning in the West. Confirmed now beyond a shadow of a doubt; I was a woman without a country. Misunderstood, lonely, and alone on both coasts. I glared at the outlined form of the dog, still sitting quietly in place as if awaiting further instruction. His mewling, victimized presence now annoyed me. I'd eat him too, I thought.

I was astonished by this predatory urge. What was wrong with me? "Woof!" I barked. Nothing. And then it dawned: the *immediacy* of mission was gone. That was it. I was disengaged; a heaven-born captain with zero motivation. I'd have to move on, now. But on to what? I drew a blank and shook away the fog of self-pity and confusion.

Seven-thirty now: time for coffee, a quick shower, and then the requisite forty-five-minute ritual of hair, makeup, and wardrobe dissection necessary even to enter the hallowed patio of the Polo Lounge. Cocktail dress in the morning—ugh! With endless practice, I'd managed to hone my complicated prep time down to a personal best of twenty-four minutes, start to finish, but hey, to achieve that mean feat I'd need all my faculties as well as razor-sharp concentration. I didn't dare attempt that crazy pace this morning.

My eyes settled on a notepad covered with Jamey's scrawled handwriting. Airline flight numbers and dates, with both our names. To New York. My blood quickened, even without caffeine. What could it mean? I pulled my old Filofax from a desk drawer and leafed through its pages: someone else's life, not mine. Sure enough, today's date was circled in red: it was our six-month anniversary. Six months of living under siege in LA. I vaguely remembered marking the page, secretly believing I'd have figured out a way to get us home by this late date, happily resuming our once-merry lives . . .

All right, here we go: Coffee. Shower. Shave. Shine! I'd reached the car door as the telephone rang inside: Guy. Breathless. Thrilled. Crazed. Concerned. And desperate for minutely detailed information. Dramatic pleading; begging, even—to call back ASAP. Always one to give before he got, he dutifully revealed (crowed) that it was he who'd so graciously advised Julia on the McMenu as retribution for barring his presence from her event. Oh yes: a tiny bit of non-kosher revenge, served up on cold potato pancakes.

I rolled down the hill to the hotel, pulling up to the valet right on time. What was the big mystery, I wondered, that warranted a call time so early in the day? Most unusual for Sarah, who usually came alive midday at the earliest. I strolled through the Polo Lounge to the back patio and paused, scanning the tables. Business breakfasters in groups of two and three were scooping up fifteen-dollar bowls of raisin bran, engaged in conversation. No Sarah. But I did spy Jack Nicholson in our shared naughty banquette. I overheard a familiar voice from behind a large tree, and tiptoed around to inspect: Ritzy, holding forth on a headset (with her yogi, no doubt) at an empty table set for five, a magnum of champagne icing in its bucket. I noted wryly that Buddhism (the aesthetic, non-ascetic kind) certainly agreed with her: she looked fabulous in head-to-toe white Dior with Loree Rodkin *prana*-symbols flashing "om" at her neck, ears, and wrists. I snuck back to the maitre d' stand, internally debating the plural of jeroboam, and waited.

A few minutes passed. Nothing. And then: Ritzy's celestially enhanced form embraced a man behind the tree. Lots of laughter and happy voices: a celebration? Drawn by curiosity, I inched closer. Sarah and Charlie had appeared, having most likely entered from the side street. I stood frozen, confounded; suddenly exhausted and cranky. All three turned my way, smiling widely. Sarah ran to embrace me and guided me back to the table, her arm tight for support. I felt drugged.

"I don't understand. You got me dressed and down the hill for . . . what? And why is *she* here?" I sulked, indicating Ritzy. All three laughed.

Sarah patted the seat next to her. "It's okay, I promise. We'll tell you everything." I sat, irritated, as Charlie passed me a glass of champagne and then filled the remaining flutes. Bollinger Special Cuvée Brut, I noticed, nerves working overtime: Mrs. Peel's favorite.

"Stacey," Ritzy's voice broke my dull reverie, "this is a victory breakfast!"

I looked at Sarah. "What on earth is she talking about?"

Ritzy continued breezily. "I was sure you'd have guessed by now. Haven't you been getting my 'special deliveries'?" She was all mock-innocence and mystery at once, trying to keep from giggling at what I'm sure was a bewildered expression on my face.

I turned back to Sarah. "I mean it. What's she talking about?"

Sarah spoke slowly, as if to a child, "Stace. Ritzy's your Deep Throat. Get it?"

My heart pounded. "But why?"

Ritzy couldn't contain herself. "Once I discovered that that . . . *C-word* had been sullying my angelic little boy . . ." I shot a cauterizing look. She began again. "Well, okay—so maybe he's not exactly a little boy, but he's still *my* boy, and she's been his 'Auntie Julia' since he was twelve, so . . . Anyway, once I figured out he was climbing through the garden to be with *her*—he told me she said it would be excellent 'training'—ugh!" She made a revolted face and grabbed at her stomach—*verklempt*, poor thing. She held up a hand, clearly needing a minute, took a deep, cleansing yoga breath and continued. "Well, I just snapped, you know? And really—after everything Max and I have done for them, over the years. You wouldn't believe . . . Well, you probably would. Anyway, I felt really badly about the way I'd treated you, in the beginning and all—I mean, because of *her*. I thought I'd hire a detective and kill two birds with one stone, sort-of-thing: get the skinny, once and for all, on the evil Julefest Queen to get her to leave Luke alone. Then I photocopied everything and slipped it to you, thinking you might be able to use the information, somehow. Oh—I forgot. I also sent copies to Barb and Phil." She tipped her glass at me and took a sip, relishing her Ellery Queen-like moment of unveiling.

"What did you expect me to do?" I asked, bewildered still,

although at the same time respectfully amazed that Ritzy was capable of retaining an actual thought, let alone pulling off the caper at hand. And then it dawned: *The enemy of my enemy is . . . a friend.* Our agendas had crossed!

"Well, *someone* had to stop her. And I knew it would either have to be you or Barb. Phil's too boring, and you're so, well, detached and cool. I guess Barb had more on the line. And yes, Sarah told me what y'all have been doing. I thought I might give you some food for thought. I was supposed to go to Sarah's yesterday and tell you this—Sarah said it was only fair—but my Auric healing session ran awful late. I just hate that, don't you?" she prattled on, refilling her glass. "I mean, I *kinda* had an itty-bitty inkling that Barb would pull *something*, but wow! I so admire her! What a hoot!" She took another dainty sip, ever the southern belle, seat-dancing to her own private beat. And just as abruptly she stopped and intently studied her nail color. Ah, Ritzy. Detached and cool—was she kidding? I guess I'd take that. How was it that no one could see the gooey, marshmallow mess underneath? I sighed. Sarah and Charlie watched me closely.

"Well!" There were no other words. Ritzy was Deep Throat. I would never have guessed. I pulled a Julia, shooting the gold liquid back in one quick gulp. I held out my glass to Charlie to refill. He grinned back madly.

I averted my eyes. "Well, thanks for the inside dirt, but I'm sorry to say it doesn't mean anything to me anymore. I'm out. My game-playing days are over. I need to refocus now and figure out what I'm going to do with my life." Oddly, no one's mood dampened in the least. "And you two? What else is going on?" I glared at them both, suspicious anew. Their smiles widened even further. From behind me appeared a huge bouquet of multicolored California poppies tied with a red satin ribbon, airline tickets dangling from the bow.

"Happy Anniversary, honey!" Jamey. "Can you believe it's been six months already?"

Why did everyone always seem to know everything but me? In the same sweet tone, I replied, "Doesn't it just feel like forever?"

Jamey leaned down and kissed me. "We'll leave after the Oscars and stay in New York as long as you'd like."

I was so overcome with emotion that I could hardly speak. Sarah and Charlie embraced as well; Ritzy busied herself refilling glasses and snapped her fingers, alerting the waiter to bring another bottle.

"Well!" I tried to compose myself, dabbing my eyes with a pink napkin as we settled back down. "So—what do we do now?" I asked. "Order food?" I looked around the table inquisitively. "No more earth-shattering surprises, I take it? After last night, I don't think I could handle anything else."

Covert, knowing glances were exchanged. Finally, Charlie spoke. "Well, then. I guess you won't want to look inside these." He pushed two large envelopes toward me. Now what? "You may not be able to handle it, but if I were you I'd take a peek."

Gingerly, I picked up the first package. A *Gloss* logo was embossed on the upper left corner, and inside were mocked-up tear sheets. The Coyote Club had received double-page coverage, set to run in the very next issue: THE HILLS ARE ALIVE (AND SO ARE THE WIVES) IN HOLLYWOOD! "How did you get this? How do you know Nancy?" I looked back and forth between Charlie and Jamey in amazement.

"I met her over the phone, right after the auction," Charlie smiled mischievously. "Don't you want to see what's inside the other envelope?"

I recognized the name of an impressive Century City law firm. "This is the best part! Open it!" Ritzy bobbed up and down with barely contained excitement. I hesitated, then picked up a knife and slit open the seal. I pulled out what looked like a contract.

My hands were trembling. "Charlie, what's going on?" Ritzy looked like she might actually propel from her chair, her high-pitched squeals almost comical. "Just hit me. I'm too shell-shocked to absorb printed words." Ritzy thrust a gem laden knuckle in her mouth.

"It's an offer, Stacey," Charlie said. "I want to buy your story, and I want you to develop it with me into a film. Your—and Sun Tzu's—adventures in Hollywood will be our next picture"—he nodded toward Jamey—"distributed by Pacificus, of course. *The Art of Social War.* And talk about brilliant casting: Julia Mallis is contractually signed, sealed, and set to play, as her ultimate penance . . . drum roll, please: Julia Mallis!" The cork was popped on a new magnum and glasses were refilled all around. "*This*, my friend and, hopefully, new colleague," he paused dramatically, "was the long-term karmic plan!" Jamey and he clinked glasses, jubilant.

"See, Stace," said Sarah gently, raising her glass to the table, "it doesn't happen very often, but sometimes the good guys *do* win, even out here."

"To Stacey!" cried Charlie.

I rejoined silently, "To Sun Tzu!'" and thanked him: *If you know the enemy and know yourself, your victory will not stand in doubt; if you know Heaven and you know Earth, you may make your victory complete.*

My ears rang, overwhelmed, as I tried to absorb the size of this windfall. But somehow I still managed to hear Ritzy begin mounting a new campaign, having pulled a detailed list of casting suggestions from her coordinating Dior tote: actresses she deemed worthy enough, thin enough, and, most important, spiritual enough to play her in the movie. I hugged Jamey, joyful tears welling again. *Anger may in time turn to gladness; vexation may be succeeded by content.* I bit his earlobe lightly. "I'm just gonna run to the Ladies' and fix my face. Then we'll plan our New York trip. We need a *rest*!"

CODA: ENEMIES, A LOVE STORY

*H*umming "Belladonna," I fished powder and lipstick from my bag, nudged aside the emergency Benadryl, and laughed: thank God those days are over! As I attempted to un-smudge my eyeliner, my cell rang. "Give a girl some privacy. I'll be right—"

"I can't talk long, and I can't say how I know, but you need to listen!"

Rain on my parade! I checked the screen, PRIVATE CALL appeared. "Who is this? I'm in the middle of someth—"

"Stacey!" the unknown voice commanded, hissing impatiently. "Listen to me! You're on the *radar*. You need to be *careful!* Simon's gunning for—"

"Wait a sec—*Barb* exposed their ugly lies, or should I say ugly 'truths'?"

"Doesn't matter. They look foolish, and your movie'll only make it worse. They blame you for everything. You're the 'horse's head': the one thing Jamey loves that's exposed. Check your brakes! Better—hire a car and driver! Buy only bottles of wine, and have them opened at the table! Don't open any packages! Get out of . . ."

My movie? But how could they possibly know? "You listen to me: the war game's over. It's finished. *They're* finished. By their own hand. I—"

The voice spat bitterly. "Stacey! This is *real;* not amateur hour! Don't you understand? You're a *player,* now. You've 'engaged.' Once you start *playing,* the game never ends!"

"Nice gaslight, mystery caller." I stabbed the OFF button like it might burn me and checked my startled reflection, blood quickening hot. It was a joke. Right? But . . . the caller sounded so insistent, so certain . . . Jeez! I chuckled nervously and splashed water on my face, trying to wash away this unwelcome tarnish from my otherwise glittering, perfect Hollywood Ending.

As the cool wet hit, however, Bam! I caught my breath. My mind stumbled on a sudden, sharp boulder of clarity: How, at this late stage, could I possibly be so reluctant to believe that the perverse, perfidious cowboy was *not* hot on our trail, stirring up professional-grade trouble in a confused bid for revenge, or even for sheer sport? Had I learned nothing? I pressed a face towel to my eyes, following through the logic: rather than accept responsibility for his own morally ambiguous lies and activities, he'd insist instead that Jamey and I somehow pay personally for exposing them. But of course! Sixteen whole hours had passed since the final nail of career disembowelment had been hammered. Surely he'd be mining his Sun Tzu for an inkling of inspiration, seething in his overheated exiled dementia, his depraved down-time of disgrace.

I pondered the ultimate life lesson learned: there *is* no such thing as a Hollywood Ending. There is no swell of a string section. There is no fade to black. But somehow, if you look hard enough, there *is* always an opportunity for a new beginning . . .

Fortified by this epiphany, I checked my reflection again. This time, curiously, I felt a surge of energy. A familiar voice enlightened, *"The clever combatant imposes his will on the enemy but does not allow the enemy's will to be imposed on him."* I fingered the contract lightly—my hard-won, hard-earned future, nestled safely in my lush and bountiful green tote. Smiling sardonically, I understood at once: *this* was my new beginning! And now *I* was the one with something to protect.

I giggled at the Hitchcockian overtones—and, duh, inspected the (empty) stalls for good measure, shaking off the weirdness (but *still*) and hurried to rejoin the celebratory table. Sarah rolled her eyes as Ritzy pitched away; Charlie talked timeline with Jamey. Jack sauntered out, Warren Beatty sauntered in. And I floated in a fugue state above it all, senses heightened. I studied the crowd, surveyed the exits. Colors, scents, and sounds were vividly hyperreal. I sniffed the honeysuckled air, surveilling the bodies and agendas around me as if through an infra-red lens. I downed a Benadryl (mental note: Buy more. No—buy stock!) and gripped the contract tightly. Oh, the game was very much on, indeed. I grinned at my friends and rubbed Jamey's neck. Bring it on!